THE BUTTERFLY HOUSE

THE BUTTERFLY HOUSE

KATRINE ENGBERG

Translated by Tara Chace

THORNDIKE PRESS
A part of Gale, a Cengage Company

GALE
A Cengage Company

**LIBRARY OF CONGRESS CIP DATA ON FILE.
CATALOGUING IN PUBLICATION FOR THIS BOOK
IS AVAILABLE FROM THE LIBRARY OF CONGRESS.**

ISBN-13: 978-1-4328-9520-4 (hardcover alk. paper)

Published in 2022 by arrangement with Scout Press/Gallery Books, a Division of Simon & Schuster.

Printed in Mexico
Print Number: 01   Print Year: 2022

To Sysse Engberg, heroine and mother

■ ■ ■ ■

SATURDAY, OCTOBER 14

■ ■ ■ ■

PROLOGUE

The clear glass ampoules sat in the locked cabinet alongside disposable syringes and sharps containers — morphine and Oxy-Contin for strong pain, Propafenone for atrial fibrillation, and the blood thinner Pradaxa, safely sealed in little boxes and wrapped in clear plastic: standard medications in the cardiology department at Copenhagen's National Hospital, paths to relief and a better quality of life, sometimes even a cure.

The nurse cast a quick glance over the medications and did the calculations in her head. How heavy could he be? The patient's weight was on the whiteboard at the head of his bed, but she was too exhausted to go check.

The night had dragged on forever. Just before her shift ended the day before, someone had called in sick and she had ended up pulling a double shift. Instead of spending an evening home with her family, she had worked for almost sixteen hours. Her brain was echoing with beeping alarms, requests, and questions from anxious patients. Her feet ached in the ergonomic shoes, and her neck felt stiff.

She yawned, rubbed her eyes, and caught her reflection in the shiny metal door of the medication cabinet. No thirty-two-year-old should have chronic bags under their eyes. This job was wearing her out. Just one hour left, then her shift would end, and she could go home and sleep while the kids got up and ate Coco Pops in front of the TV.

She selected three ampoules, put them in the pocket of her scrubs, and locked the cabinet behind her. Three 10 ml ampoules of 50 mg/ml ajmaline, that would be plenty. The patient couldn't weigh more than 150 pounds or so, which meant that 30 ml of the anti-arrhythmia drug would be twice the recommended maximum dose. Enough to cause immediate cardiac arrest and release him from his suffering. *And all the rest of us,* she thought, setting off down the empty morning hallway toward room eight. The old man was demanding. He was foul-mouthed and rude, and complained about most things, from the weak hospital coffee to the doctors' arrogance. The whole ward was tired of his cranky personality.

She had always been one to speak up and do something about a situation, not a role that makes one popular, but what else could she do? Stand idly by and complain about poor staffing ratios and the shortage of beds like her colleagues? No way! She had not become a nurse just to fetch coffee and bandage abrasions. She wanted to make a difference.

A cleaning lady, sporting a head scarf and a downcast expression, pushed her mopping cart down the hall without looking up from the linoleum floor. The nurse strode past her with the ampoules hidden in her pocket. Her heart rate sped up. Soon she would perform, live up to her full potential, and try to save a life. The anticipation started throbbing through her, as if it had a pulse of its own, a life to counterbalance the emptiness that normally filled her. In this moment, she would be indispensable. The stakes were high, so much rested on her shoulders. In this moment, she would be God.

She locked the door to the staff bathroom, quickly cleaned her hands and the countertop by the sink with alcohol, and laid out the ajmaline ampoules neatly side by side. With experienced fingers, she removed the disposable syringe from its packaging and drew the medicine up, flicking it per instinct to make sure it held no air bubbles. She crumpled the packaging up into a little ball and stuffed it down to the bottom of the trash can, then, with the syringe hidden in the pocket of her scrubs, she opened the door.

In front of room eight she cast a discreet glance down the hallway; no sign of colleagues or patients headed for the restroom. She pushed the door open and stepped into the darkness. A quiet snore from the bed told her the patient was asleep. She could work in peace.

She approached the bed, looking at the old man, who was lying on his back with his mouth open slightly. Gray, bony, and dried up with a little bubble of saliva at the corner of his mouth, his eyelids twitching ever so slightly. *Is there anything,* she thought, *more superfluous in this world than grumpy old men?*

She opened the cap of the venous catheter that adorned the thin-skinned back of his hand, and drew the syringe from her pocket. Direct access to the blood that flows to the heart, an open gateway for God's outstretched fingertip.

The good thing about ajmaline is that it is

fast acting; the cardiac arrest would occur almost instantaneously. She connected the syringe to the catheter, knowing she would just have time to hide the syringe before the monitor alarm was activated.

The patient moved a little in his sleep. She gently stroked his hand. Then she pushed the plunger all the way down.

■ ■ ■ ■

MONDAY,
OCTOBER 9

FIVE DAYS EARLIER

■ ■ ■ ■

CHAPTER 1

"Ugh, this sucks!"

Frederik wiped the water off his forehead and put the cap back on his head. He pulled up the hood of his rain poncho, made sure his under-seat bag was closed, and set off on his bike. Getting out of bed was always tough when the alarm went off at five fifteen, but some mornings were worse than others. This morning the driving rain made it hard to remember why he had ever said yes to this newspaper route. Six days a week, fifteen buildings in downtown Copenhagen, 620 flights of stairs up and down. Unfortunately it was the only way to make the money for his sophomore-class trip. And he wasn't going to miss out on that.

The distribution point vanished into the dimness behind him as he rode along over the cobblestones. The phone in his pocket pumped music into his ears and reenergized him: "I got my black shirt on, I got my black

17

gloves on." Even in the rain there was something cool about having the city's busiest pedestrian shopping street to himself. He stood up on the pedals and rode along Strøget until the old market square, Gammeltorv, and the new market square, Nytorv, opened up on either side of him. The neighborhood was full of neat stucco apartment buildings with muntin windows and copper gutters currently overflowing with autumn rain, grafted trees, and iconic Copenhagen benches with trash stuffed between their dark-green slats. The city's municipal court's sand-colored columns seemed to glow in the early-morning darkness, a moral juxtaposition to the age-old basement pubs across the square. During the daytime the two squares served as a hub for bicycle messengers, tourists, and people selling cheap nickel-alloy jewelry. At this hour it was completely deserted.

Frederik hopped off his bike and leaned it against the fountain in the middle of the square. He pulled out his earbuds and felt his jacket pocket to make sure he had enough coins for a warm cinnamon roll. Passing the fountain, he cast a quick glance at the surface of the water, which was rippling from the raindrops in the dark.

There was something in the water.

There was often something in the water. Every day city workers fished out beer cans, plastic bags, and curiously solitary shoes.

But this was no shoe.

Frederik reeled. Three yards away from him, in Copenhagen's oldest fountain, a person floated facedown with their arms out to the side. The raindrops hit the person's naked back with innocent plops, splashing up into the air like hundreds of tiny, individual fountains.

For a second, Frederik couldn't move. He was paralyzed, like in those nightmares he sometimes woke up from, sad that he had grown too big to be comforted by his mother.

"Help! Hello?" he yelled hoarsely and incoherently. "There's someone in the water."

He knew he should jump into the fountain and turn the body, administer first aid, do something, but the warm urine running down his leg emphasized how unable he was to help anyone at all. Frederik looked back at the body in the water. This time really understanding what he was looking at. He had never seen a dead person before.

His legs trembling, he ran over to the twenty-four-hour convenience store. The automatic doors opened, the scent of cinnamon and butter hitting him just as he spotted the humming, blond checker. Water dripped into Frederik's eyes from the visor of his cap, and he wiped it off, fresh water and salt.

"Help, damn it! Call the police!"

The checker stared at him wide-eyed. Then she dropped her tray of cinnamon rolls and reached for the phone.

Rain poured down on Copenhagen, blurring the contours of tile roofs and plastered facades. The sky sent cascades of unseasonably warm water straight onto the umbrellas and cobblestones of Old Market Square.

Investigator Jeppe Kørner squinted his eyes shut and decided to risk an upward glance. Not a single reassuring patch of clear sky on the horizon. Maybe the world really was dissolving, the oceans claiming back the last remaining landmasses. He wiped his face with a wet hand, stifled a yawn, and ducked under the crime scene tape. Water seeped into his sneakers at the seams, making them squelch with every step.

Through sheets of rain he saw miserable plastic-draped silhouettes busy erecting pavilion canopies around the fountain, the kind people rent for garden parties hoping they won't need them. Jeppe ran to the closest pavilion for shelter and looked at his watch. It was a little after seven, and the sun was just rising somewhere behind the rain clouds, not that it made much difference. Today daylight would be no more than varying shades of gray.

A naked body floated in the fountain in front of him, reflecting the light from the crime scene work lamps. Jeppe took in the scene as he pulled a protective suit over his wet clothes. The body was lying facedown, like a snorkeler in the Red Sea. A woman's body, as far as he could tell from the shoulder width and the arch of the back. Naked, middle-aged, dark hair with some gray, the scalp just visible between wet locks of hair.

"The name of the fountain is Caritas, did you know that?"

Jeppe turned around and found himself eye to eye with crime scene technician J. H. Clausen. The hood of his blue protective suit outlined a wrinkled face, making him look like a wet garden gnome in an oversize space suit.

"You'll be pleased to hear that the answer is no, Clausen. I did not know that."

"*Caritas* means 'charity' in Latin," Clausen explained, wiping his bushy eyebrows and then shaking water off his hands. "That's why the figure on top is a pregnant woman. The symbol of altruism, you know."

"I'm more interested in why there's a body in the basin." Jeppe nodded toward the fountain. "What have we got?"

Clausen looked around and found an umbrella leaning against one of the legs of the pavilion. He opened it and tentatively took a step out under the open sky.

"Damned weather, impossible working conditions," he muttered. "Come on!"

Tall Jeppe had to walk in a stoop to fit under Clausen's umbrella. At the stone rim of the basin they stopped to look at the body. Droplets ran down the white skin, making it look like a marble statue. A police photographer was trying to find workable angles all while shielding his camera from the rain.

"The medical examiner will obviously need to get her up out of the basin for a postmortem before we can say too much about her," Clausen began. "But she's female, Caucasian, average height. I would guess about fifty years old."

A gust of wind gently nudged the body, so it floated past them to the other side of the basin.

"She was found by a paperboy at five forty

a.m.," Clausen continued. "The call came in to emergency services from the convenience store on the corner two minutes later. The first responders pulled her to the edge of the fountain and tried to resuscitate her, per protocol. I don't know why the body hasn't been taken out of the water yet. The paperboy and shop clerk are sitting in the store with an officer, waiting to be interviewed. The shop clerk arrived at five a.m. and is positive that there wasn't anything in the fountain at that point, so the crime must have occurred sometime between five and five forty this morning."

"You're saying *this* is the crime scene?" Jeppe pulled his hood back to get a better view of the large public square. "She was killed in the middle of Strøget?"

Clausen turned to Jeppe, which caused the umbrella he was holding high above their heads to tilt. Rain gushed down on the both of them. Jeppe's hair was instantly soaked.

"Oh, sorry, Kørner, for crying out loud! Did you get wet? Well, I'm being inaccurate. She could hardly have been killed here, for a number of reasons."

"I guess it would be too risky . . ." Jeppe tried to ignore the raindrops sneaking down the back of his neck and inside his raincoat.

"Yes, the risk of someone coming by would be too big. The mere fact that someone has dared to dump a body in the fountain at Old Market Square is . . . well, that's beyond my comprehension." Clausen shook his head, dumbfounded. "But that's not the only reason. Can you see those small incisions in the skin on the front of her arms? They're facing down toward the water, so they're hard to see."

Jeppe squinted to get a better look through the rain. Bobbing in the surface of the water, a symmetrical pattern of small, parallel cuts was visible on the wrists, gaping gashes of whitish flesh. An image of a whale rotting on the beach flashed through Jeppe's brain, and he swallowed his discomfort.

"There's no blood in the water?"

"Exactly!" Clausen nodded in affirmation. "She must have bled profusely, and yet there's no sign of blood, not in the fountain and not around it. We would have found some if she had been killed here, despite the rain. She died somewhere else."

"There's plenty of surveillance cameras we could retrieve recordings from." Jeppe looked around at the old house facades. "If the killer dumped the body, there must be footage of that."

"If?" Clausen sounded indignant. "She

didn't cut herself and then jump naked into the fountain, I can promise you that."

"What were they made with, the cuts?"

"I can't say yet. Nyboe needs to get her up onto the table first," Clausen said, referring to Professor Nyboe, the forensic pathologist, who usually conducted autopsies for major murder cases. "But no matter what, the murder weapon isn't here in the square. The dogs have been looking for half an hour and haven't found anything. Also there's no sign of her clothes."

Something buzzed in Jeppe's pocket. He wiped his hand on the seat of his pants and carefully took out his phone. Seeing *Mom* on the screen, he declined the call. What did she want now?

"In other words," he said, "someone brought a naked body to the middle of Strøget and tossed it in the fountain early this morning?"

"Looks like it, yes," Clausen said, his face apologetic, as if he were partly responsible for the absurd scenario.

"Who the hell does that?" Jeppe rubbed his burning eyes. He was short on sleep, and in the few hours he had slept, he had tossed and turned. Dealing with a dead woman in a fountain wasn't exactly how he had imagined spending his day.

Disconnected lyrics from Supertramp's annoying rain song ran through his head: *"Oh no it's raining again. Too bad I'm losing a friend."* If only Jeppe could at least pick the music his tired brain had to torment him with. Usually snippets of ultra-commercial pop music ran on a continual loop underneath his thoughts when he was stressed out. *"It's raining again. Oh no, my love's at an end."* Jeppe pulled his hood back up and strode over to the convenience store, where the paperboy was waiting.

The cry was unbearable. A persistent, helpless wail on the same frequency as screams of terror or a dentist's drill. The worst sound in the world.

Detective Anette Werner rolled over and closed her eyes tight. Svend was with the baby; this was her chance to catch up on a little of the sleep she hadn't gotten the night before. She put a pillow over her head to block out the noise. Tried to think of something she wouldn't give up for a night of uninterrupted sleep but couldn't come up with a single thing.

The crying mixed with Svend's soothing voice in the next room. If only he would shut the door; maybe she should get up and do it herself? Actually, she needed to pee anyway. Before August 1, she would have ignored a full bladder and slept on, but now she could no longer rely on her bombed-to-hell forty-four-year-old body to do its part.

Anette pushed herself laboriously into a sitting position and swung her legs over the edge of the bed. When would this permanent hungover, jet-lagged state be over?

She got up slowly, every single joint in her body gradually resigning itself to the weight of those bones, which were no longer supported by strong muscles. Her breasts ached. She looked down and noted that she had once again forgotten to take off her shoes last night. Then she dragged herself like a zombie across the carpeted floor, past the baby's room, out to the bathroom. How could Svend be so calm and optimistic? She locked the door and looked at herself in the mirror.

I look like the living dead, she thought, and sat down on the toilet. *I wish I were dead.*

That was more or less what she had thought a year ago when she found out she was pregnant. They weren't going to have kids, had agreed on that ages ago. It just wasn't for them. Instead, they would focus on being the world's most adoring dog parents. Sometime around her fortieth birthday they had stopped discussing kids

27

altogether. Ironically, that might have been why they had grown careless about birth control; the idea that sex could lead to parenthood had somehow slipped their minds. For a long time, Anette had just thought she was sick, that she had inherited her father's bad heart and that her pulse was racing toward a bypass operation or a pacemaker. The doctor's results from the blood tests had been a relief. And a shock.

I wish I were dead.

Apart from that, things had gone fine from there. Unexpectedly enough Svend had been overjoyed about the news and had never questioned the prospect of parenthood. The pregnancy had passed without a hitch. The first-trimester screening had looked great, the birth itself was quick and uncomplicated. She had defied the bad odds and beaten every conceivable record for first-time pregnancies for the over-forty set. But when her little baby girl was placed in her arms, neat and clean, and immediately started sucking, Anette hadn't felt a thing. The bond, which was supposed to occur instinctively, had to be forced along, and the love was somehow hard to feel. For her, anyway.

For Svend it was different.

In the last two and a half months, his love

for the new, tiny human being had only grown stronger and stronger. The look on his face when he held her! His eyes beaming with pride. Svend swam like a fish into family life and was already more a father than anything else. Anette was trying; she really was. If only she wasn't so exhausted all the time.

She rested her elbows on her thighs, leaned forward, and put her forehead on her hands.

"Honey, are you asleep?"

Anette lifted her head with a jerk, her neck so tight she instantly felt a headache looming. Svend's voice came from the hallway. He must be standing right outside.

"I'm peeing," she said. "Can't it wait, like, two minutes?"

She heard the irritation in her own voice; the same resentment she had often witnessed in other women, but rarely displayed herself. Now it was like she couldn't get rid of it. She stood up, washed her hands, and opened the door.

"She's hungry. That's why she won't settle. See, she's rooting!" Svend gently lifted their daughter up and kissed her on the forehead before holding her out to Anette.

She reached out her arms and felt the

29

already familiar spasm of fear that she would drop the delicate life on the floor. People who compare having dogs to having children don't know anything, she thought, even though she had been exactly one of those until two and a half months ago. She looked at the crying baby in her arms.

"I miss the boys," she said. "When are we picking them up?"

"The dogs will be fine at my mom's for another couple of weeks," Svend said, eyeing her with concern. "They go for walks in the forest three times a day. We need to focus on little Gudrun right now."

"Stop calling her that! We haven't agreed on a name yet." Anette squeezed past her husband with a brusqueness that forced him up against the wall of the narrow hallway outside their bathroom.

"I thought you wanted her name to be Gudrun?"

"I'm going to go sit in the car and breast-feed her," Anette said, heading for the front door. "And please don't say anything. I just prefer it out there." She slammed the door behind her, as hard as she could with the baby in her arms, jogged through the rain to the car, and eased the door open. The baby stopped crying, maybe because of the unexpected sensation of rainwater hitting her face.

The car smelled familiar and safe, of work and dogs. Anette made herself comfortable, pulled up her blouse, and put her daughter to a swollen breast. The baby latched on and started sucking right away, settling down. Anette exhaled heavily and tried to shake the persistent feeling of stress in her body. She gently wiped a raindrop off the baby's forehead and stroked her soft scalp. When she lay like this, quiet and peaceful, parenthood felt good. It was the crying and the nighttime battles that were hard to cope with. And maternity leave. Anette missed her job.

She looked out at the house. Svend was probably vacuuming or tidying up. With a quick push she opened the glove compartment and pulled out her police radio. It was actually supposed to be sitting in its charging station at police headquarters, but Anette had not gotten around to dropping it off. It was only a matter of time before someone noticed the radio was missing and deactivated it, but she would enjoy listening to it until then. She checked to make sure the volume was low, so as not to scare the baby, and switched it on. The familiar static sound caused a rush of emotion in the pit of her stomach.

And we need an escort for the deceased at Old Market Square in Copenhagen. We're going to transport the victim from where she was found to the trauma center for the autopsy. We'll maintain barriers on Frederiksberggade, and around Old Market Square until the crime scene technicians from NKC East are done gathering evidence and effects. . . .

A murder at Old Market Square? Her colleagues from police headquarters would be investigating that. Anette winced, feeling sore. Why did something as natural as breastfeeding have to hurt so darned much?

We need to obtain surveillance footage from all the cameras in the area. An investigative team led by Investigator Kørner will be in charge of this. . . .

Investigator Jeppe Kørner, who worked in the police's crimes against persons unit, section 1, better known as Homicide. Her partner.

Kørner and Werner, now without Werner. Werner, now without her job. Anette switched off the radio.

"Does anyone know what's keeping Saidani?" Jeppe asked casually, tinkering with the computer cables, his back to his colleagues. In principle he was the most likely to know where Detective Sara Saidani was since he had spent most of the night in her bed, but — they had agreed — for the time being this detail didn't concern the rest of the Homicide crew.

"Maybe she has a sick kid, like usual?" Detective Thomas Larsen guessed. "Rubella? Plague? Those kids are constantly coming down with something that keeps her from coming to work." He tossed the paper cup he'd just drained of expensive takeout coffee into the trash in a neat arc. Larsen had neither children nor any desire to acquire them — a view he did not hesitate to share with his colleagues.

Jeppe looked at the clock over the door. It was 10:05.

"We'll have to start without her," he said.

He made sure the computer was connected and adjusted the brightness of the image that flickered before him on the meeting room's flat screen. Then he turned and nodded to his twelve colleagues who were waiting, notebooks on their laps and eyes alert. A mutilated woman found in a fountain on Strøget was no everyday occurrence.

"All right!" Jeppe began. "The call came in to Dispatch at five forty-two a.m. and we had the first patrol car on the scene six minutes later. The physician who rode along with the first responders declared the victim dead at six fifteen a.m." He folded his arms over his chest. "Lima Eleven immediately decided the death was suspicious and called us."

The door to the meeting room quietly opened and Sara Saidani slipped in and found a chair. Her dark curls glistened with rainwater, and her eyes beamed. Jeppe experienced the familiar surge of feeling wide awake when she was nearby. Sara Saidani, colleague in the Investigations Unit, mother of two, divorced, ethnically Tunisian, with hazel eyes and skin like honey.

"Welcome, Saidani." Jeppe glanced down at the notepad in front of him even though he knew quite well what it said.

"The deceased has been preliminarily identified as health-care aide Bettina Holte, fifty-four years old, resides in Husum. She was reported missing yesterday, so her picture is in POLSAS, but the identification hasn't been confirmed yet."

POLSAS was the police's internal reporting system, where all information about open and closed cases was stored. It sounded fancy and efficient. It wasn't.

"Her family has been summoned to an identification, so we'll hear back soon. The body was naked, lying facedown, as you can

34

see in this photo."

Jeppe pointed to the grainy image, pushed a button, and moved to a close-up of a white body in black water.

"According to a witness statement," Jeppe said, "the body was not in the fountain at five a.m., so we're operating on the assumption that she was brought there between five and five forty a.m. We're working on securing footage from all the surveillance cameras. . . ."

"Kørner?"

"Yes, Saidani?"

"I took the liberty of gathering the footage from the city's cameras in that area and looking through them. That's why I was late." Sara Saidani held up a USB flash drive pinched between two fingers. "The footage from the camera above the convenience store is good. Fast-forward to five seventeen a.m."

Jeppe accepted the flash drive with an appreciative nod, opened the recording, and fast-forwarded. The screen showed a sped-up version of a dark, empty public square without any movement other than a bicycle tipping over in the wind. At 5:16 a.m., Jeppe slowed the playback to normal speed, and after a minute a shadow appeared at the top of the frame.

"He's coming from Studiestræde, heading toward the fountain," Larsen said enthusiastically. "What's he riding on?"

"He or she is riding a cargo bike. Just watch!" Sara snapped her fingers in irritation and pointed to the screen.

The dark figure approached the fountain and the streetlamps over Frederiksberggade. Sure enough, the person rode in on a cargo bike and was covered by a dark-colored rain poncho with the hood on. It was impossible to tell if it was a man or a woman, or even a human. The bike stopped by the fountain, and the rider dismounted easily, as if the move was familiar.

"He gets off like a man, swinging his leg around behind the seat," Larsen said. He stood up and demonstrated what he meant.

Sara quickly pointed out, "That's how I get off my bike, too. That doesn't mean anything. Now watch the cargo. . . ."

The figure in the rain poncho pulled a dark cloth or plastic cover off the long flatbed of what looked like a cargo bike. The bright skin of a dead body lit up in the dark. The figure quickly and effortlessly lifted it over the edge of the basin. Once the body was in the water, the figure continued to stand there.

Jeppe counted two seconds, five.

"What's he doing?" he asked.

"Staring," Larsen suggested. "Saying goodbye."

After seven long seconds, the dark figure climbed onto the cargo bike and rode away from the fountain, back in the same direction it had come from.

Jeppe waited for a second to make sure there was nothing more to see, then stopped the playback. A murderer on a cargo bike, *only in Denmark*! He sighed.

"Saidani, would you please send the footage to our forensic friends at NKC and ask them to look for other surveillance cameras in the area so we can track where the bike rider came from? We ought to be able to follow his or her route through most of the city."

Sara's eyes settled on him from the second row of chairs. She looked happy, her face bright with enthusiasm. Love, perhaps? Jeppe hurriedly averted his gaze before he broke into an inappropriate smile.

"As always, we're working with how, why, and who," he said. "Falck and I will be partners; Saidani, you're stuck with Larsen."

Larsen raised both arms in a victory pose, and Jeppe felt a stab of irritation that the fool got to hang out with Sara. But there was no way around it. They couldn't risk people gossiping.

"Falck and I will take the autopsy and then talk to Bettina Holte's immediate family, assuming of course that it *is* her. Saidani checks mail, phone, and social media as usual."

Sara nodded and then asked, "Are all of her things missing — her wallet, phone, the clothes she was wearing?"

"Nothing has turned up yet."

"Ask her family members to hand over her computer and get her phone number so I can pull her call history. Maybe she communicated with the killer," Sara said.

"Will do," Jeppe said. "Larsen handles witnesses and talks to her colleagues, neighbors, and whoever else there might be to question."

Jeppe looked around the room at the team. His own investigation team plus reinforcements, ready for the first twenty-four-hour, labor-intensive push to gather evidence.

"We need to do a door-to-door around Old Market Square and question any potential witnesses we find in connection with that. Maybe there was a sleepless neighbor who looked out a window at quarter past five this morning."

One of the officers raised a gigantic paw

in the air and nodded, the light bouncing off his bald head. Jeppe recognized him as either Morten or Martin, one of the young, recent hires.

"I'll take the door-to-door," he volunteered.

"Excellent," Jeppe said. "You'll report directly to Detective Larsen. Thank you."

The bald Morten or Martin nodded again.

"We need to examine the bike from the surveillance footage. Can we identify the make? Who sells them? Was a bike like that stolen in the last couple of months? And so on."

Larsen volunteered, brash and ambitious as always. Jeppe nodded to him and then looked at the superintendent in the front row.

"Supe, I'm assuming that you'll brief the press?"

Her somber eyes met his. Supe, as she was called, had been threatening to retire for a long time, but as far as Jeppe could tell, she was perkier and sharper than ever. And he predicted that she would keep it up for a few more years. Now she gave him a youthful thumbs-up. She found press conferences only mildly disruptive, whereas to Jeppe they were almost insurmountable obstacles.

He smiled at her gratefully.

"Any questions?" he asked, looking around the room. His eyes rested on Detective Falck, who stared down at the table in front of him, as if something was expected of him that he wasn't able to do. He had just returned from a relatively long disability leave due to stress and did not seem entirely back in fighting form. Falck was an old-timer, whose mustache competed with his eyebrows for the prize for bushiest and grayest. His potbelly was usually kept in check by a pair of colorful suspenders, and his general work tempo varied between moderate and snail's pace.

Jeppe slapped his hand on the table and declared, "Let's get to it!"

Everyone got up and moved toward the door, holding notepads and empty coffee cups, while they milled around chatting and arranging details. Sara Saidani and Thomas Larsen left the room together, Larsen with his hand casually on her shoulder. Jeppe ran his tongue over a blister he had on the inside of his cheek and bit down on it. A minute later only he and the superintendent were left in the meeting room.

She regarded him soberly and said, "Kørner, I need you to tell me that you can run this investigation, that you're up to it."

"What do you mean? You're the one who

picked me."

"I'm not questioning your competence," the superintendent said, raising her eyebrows and with them her heavy eyelids.

"So why are you asking?"

"Calm down! I just have a bad feeling about this case. It's not going to be an easy one to handle or solve, and you don't have your partner. . . ."

So that was her concern! That he wasn't up to leading a big investigation without Anette Werner at his side. Jeppe smiled at her reassuringly.

"I wonder if this case won't be solved faster now that I don't have Werner slowing me down."

The superintendent patted him on the shoulder and left the room. She did not look convinced.

CHAPTER 2

"Who are you talking to, Isak?"

The young patient raised a pale face from his book and stared in surprise.

"No one," Isak answered. "Was I talking out loud?"

"Yes, you were." Social worker Simon Hartvig smiled reassuringly but without seeking eye contact.

It was a matter of spotting the psychotic symptoms in time so they didn't have a chance to develop. Isak seemed calm right now.

"It's fine," Simon said. "Just keep reading."

The common room walls were painted orange and decorated with movie posters — *Grease, Pretty Woman, Dumb and Dumber.* Two other patients were playing foosball, and a group in the corner was making friendship-bracelet key chains, kept busy by his enthusiastic colleague Ursula. The rain drummed softly on the roof, a scent of freshly baked bread hung in the air, and soon there would be phone time until lunch. This place was actually really nice. The enhanced Inpatient Ward U8 housed some of the country's most severely mentally ill pediatric patients, children and teenagers with conditions like paranoid schizophrenia. But on a calm Monday morning like the present, one might easily believe that this was just a regular, old boarding school. A boarding school with guitar lessons and a twenty-four-hour staff, crafts, home cooking, and locks on the windows.

Simon sat back in his chair and peered out the window at the hospital grounds. The copper beech just outside dripped discouragingly, making the yard outside the Bispcbjerg Hospital's pediatric psychiatry center look more like a cemetery than a place for children to play. It angered him that the kids didn't have a more inspiring outdoor space, a natural area that could be utilized and serve as a backdrop for edifying experiences. He had been lobbying to set up a kitchen garden on the grounds for a long time. All modern research showed a clear correlation between outdoor activity, a healthy diet, and mental well-being, so nothing could be more appropriate than a kitchen garden at a psychiatric hospital, could it?

The bureaucracy was unbearably slow, though, and his previous proposals to get the cafeteria to go organic and to convert a shuttered section of the hospital into a rec center had both failed. But this time things looked more hopeful.

Along with his colleague Gorm, he had set up a committee six months earlier that wrote letters to the city council and collected signatures from employees and family members. So far they had managed to raise 150,000 kroner for the kitchen-garden project. Unfortunately the plans were on hold with the city's Technical and Environmental Administration, which believed that the current hospital grounds should be preserved, possibly even protected as a conservation area. But the committee wasn't planning on giving up. Simon would see to that.

He scanned the common room to make sure everyone was calm and engaged. The key-chain group had abandoned their embroidery floss and were now playing air hockey instead. Isak was still reading with his legs pulled up underneath him.

Sometimes working in health care felt like renovating a fixer-upper with modeling clay.

Often he went home from his shift feeling like his work as a social worker didn't make any difference, that he wasn't doing enough. Even though he was young and newly qualified, he already felt the impotence crawling under his skin. The system didn't encourage individuals to take initiative or foster a can-do attitude. But it was impossible for him to accept that conditions weren't better for the patients and that the beautiful old hospital's space wasn't being put to good enough use. More so because he loved the place and appreciated the old buildings that had been built to outlive those who had built them. They reminded him of a bygone era, where solutions lasted and were more than just stopgap measures.

Society had moved on. Now washing machines broke two months after their warranties ended, buildings were made of drywall instead of plaster, and disorders were something managed with painkillers without considering what had caused the pain to begin with.

It was all just symptomatic treatment. Idleness had won; the system was broken.

He got up to go do his rounds.

"Hey, who's winning?" he asked. "You're not cheating, are you, Isolde? I'm keeping an eye on you!"

He tweaked Isolde's arm and walked on with a laugh. One of the upsides of being young was that the patients could relate to him better than to many of his older colleagues. He cleaned up the embroidery floss, even though they were supposed to do it themselves, and found himself next to Isak's chair again.

"Did you have breakfast?"

Isak nodded absentmindedly.

Simon's question seemed innocent, but as a matter of fact it was essential. Isak sometimes forgot to eat, and when he did, his antipsychotics caused nausea. The last time he threw up his Seroquel he disappeared on the hospital grounds and was missing for several hours. Later they found four ducks by the pond with their heads ripped off.

Simon had been working with Isak for nearly six months and was getting to know his history. The schizophrenia had emerged in his early teenage years, but because he already had an Asperger's diagnosis, his family had long thought this was another disorder on the autism specrum. It had taken way too much time for him to get the right treatment. Simon had seen the last of the remaining hope fade slowly but surely from the family's eyes as Isak's condition deteriorated and his diagnoses piled up.

Now his father mostly came to visit on his own, sometimes with a magazine or a book for Isak, always with a sad smile that broke Simon's heart. His own father had never shown him that kind of devotion. Isak's parents were loving people forced to watch helplessly as their son grew sicker and sicker and gradually moved further and further away from the dream of ever living a *normal* life.

"Do you want to go to the quiet room while the others have their phone time?"

"Yes, please," Isak said, standing up abruptly.

He knew that Isak liked the little room decorated with floral wallpaper, scented oils, and soothing music, partly because it was a quiet place to read, but also because he didn't have to see everyone else having fun online. Isak wasn't allowed to access the internet.

"Do you have your book?"

Isak held up his worn copy of *Papillon*. He was over six feet tall, skinny as a Masai warrior, and had a wobbly, arrhythmic gait as if the floor sent shocks up through the soles of his feet with every step he took. In the quiet room he sank down into a beanbag chair, pulled his feet up under himself, and went back to reading.

Simon checked that the alarm was in his pocket. Isak was almost eighteen and would soon be transferred in the adult OPUS system, which provided integrated outreach treatment for young adults with psychotic symptoms, a transition that Isak wasn't ready for at all. The idea was completely untenable. Where was he going to live? In a residential home for mentally ill students with a ratio of one dayshift social worker to ten youths? Or if there wasn't room, then in a group home or a shelter? Or on the street even? If so he would clock in and out of hospitals and get worse and worse, until . . . How long would it last until things ended badly?

Simon closed the door with anger bubbling in his blood. It was clear to him that he needed to take drastic measures if he was going to change things.

Knives hung from hooks along the tiled wall next to electric oscillating saws and handsaws, heavy and robust work tools made to open rib cages and split skulls, a world of steel and disinfectable surfaces, clinical and precise, to handle the deceased's waste, decomposition, and chaos. There were spray hoses, nonskid flooring, magnetic bulletin boards, and work lights, and every surface and corner had discreet holes to guide the messy bodily fluids and the final remnants of life away.

Jeppe Kørner snapped up his protective suit and glanced at the oversize grabbing claw that hung from the ceiling. He regretted the chorizo sandwich he had eaten for an early lunch, because the sausage turned out to be a gift that kept on giving. The autopsy hallway in the pathology department was not the place to be reminded of the taste of dead meat.

Next to Jeppe Detective Falck pulled a white scrub cap over his gray hair, which made him look more than ever like a cartoon teddy bear, Paddington perhaps, trapped in a cold world of stainless steel and bodies waiting to be cut open.

"I think they've already started." Jeppe pointed toward the farthest autopsy bay and started walking. Paddington followed.

Professor Nyboe was standing next to a forensic tech and a police photographer by the stainless steel table in the middle of the room. Under the bright lights, they cast shadows over the lifeless body on the examination table, making its skin shine like patches of sunlit snow on a faded gray hill.

"Who do we have there?" Nyboe looked up, his long wrinkly neck evocative of an aristocratic tortoise. "Kørner and Falck, come on over. We're just finishing up the external examination."

Jeppe came closer and looked at the dead woman. She lay faceup, her chin raised slightly and the palms of her hands open, still naked with a waxy pallor, her jaw broad and her chin prominent. Her legs were muscular with varicose veins; the hair on both her head and genitals was graying and curly. In this, the very last bodily surrender, she was defenseless, every defect and flaw clearly visible. Still, there was a strange, frail beauty to the dead person lying on the table.

"Has she been definitively identified?"

"As suspected, this is Bettina Holte, fifty-four-year-old health-care aide. She lives in Husum with her husband and is the mother of two grown children. The family positively ID'ed her."

Jeppe nodded to Falck and said, "Will you just make sure that the search has been completely called off?"

Falck took a couple of steps away and fumbled around with his protective suit, trying to get to his phone.

"And what did she die of?" Jeppe asked.

With concentration, Nyboe rubbed a cotton swab over one of her nipples and then deposited the swab into a sterile bag before replying, "She died of cardiac arrest, Kørner, like everyone else. You want to know more *before* I've done the autopsy?"

"Just tell me what you know now." Jeppe suppressed a sigh. "If you would be so kind."

"Kind is my middle name," Nyboe replied.

Nyboe took a metal stick from the worktable behind him, one of those telescoping pointers that schoolteachers used to use in the old days when they had to point out Djibouti on the world map. Nyboe directed the tip of the pointer to the body's wrist.

"Do you see those cuts? There, there, and there." He moved the pointer from arm to arm and then to the hip.

Jeppe leaned forward. Across each wrist and on the top of her left hip, the skin gaped open in centimeter-wide slits, carved completely symmetrically over each other in two parallel lines. Twelve little cuts in total, meticulously made over three of the body's major arteries.

"Bettina Holte bled out. I haven't found any other external injuries apart from those cuts. So I can tell you this with a reasonably high probability."

"Bled out?" Jeppe actively shut out the sound of Falck's phone conversation in the background. "Isn't it usually suicide when someone cuts their wrists and bleeds out?"

"Not in this case. I can assure you that this was not a suicide." Nyboe moved the pointer back to the pale arm. "Can you see those red marks on her forearms? The woman was restrained with some kind of wide straps, also around the ankles, and maybe around the actual hand as well. The skin is red there at any rate." He pointed again.

"Why around the hand?"

"So the victim couldn't do this," Nyboe said, raising his gloved hand, making a fist, and bending it forward. "That would stop the bleeding. Or slow it down at least."

Nyboe put the pointer away and adopted a pensive posture, one finger on his chin.

"Rigor mortis indicates that the death occurred sometime between midnight and three a.m. last night — the cooling from two hours in the fountain unfortunately makes the calculations a little iffy — and furthermore that the woman was lying completely flat on her back when she died. The killer probably strapped her down, cut her arteries, and then waited for her to bleed out."

Jeppe noticed that Falck had joined them again and was taking notes. He was humming to himself unknowingly while he wrote, an unwelcome distraction from the music in Jeppe's own head.

"The killer must have gagged her or used some kind of anesthetic, no? Otherwise surely she would have called for help."

"Yes, and screamed from the pain," Nyboe said. He started clipping the body's fingernails, which were painted with red nail polish, collecting the clippings in a little bag. "Bleeding out is painful. Maybe not for the first ten to fifteen minutes, but once the heart and the vital organs start shutting down, it hurts quite badly. With those cuts it must have taken about a half hour before she died. It would have gone faster if her carotid arteries had been cut."

"So this was meant to take some time?"

Nyboe nodded thoughtfully and closed the bag of fingernail clippings.

"That was probably the intention, yes."

"Man!" Jeppe shook off his discomfort. "Then surely the killer didn't anesthetize her."

"The toxicology report will obviously confirm that, but my guess is that, no, he didn't." Nyboe flipped his headlamp down and forced the body's mouth open so he could shine the light into it. "No obvious injuries to the teeth, but she could easily have been gagged, maybe with a wadded-up plastic bag or a soft ball. It's not hard to keep people from screaming."

Jeppe closed his eyes for a long moment and tried to picture it, the woman undressed and strapped down, bleeding, unable to scream out in pain, while the life slowly and painfully left her.

"Are there signs of anything sexual?" Jeppe asked.

Nyboe stuck a very long cotton swab down into the woman's throat and then handed it to the forensic tech before responding.

"Nothing obvious," he said. "Since she was found naked it would be probable, but there are no signs of penetration, resistance, or semen in her orifices."

"Okay," Jeppe said, leaning over the table and looking at the woman's wrist. "Why all these cuts? Why didn't the killer just cut right across the arteries?"

"Aha! Kørner, a relevant question for once." Nyboe turned and searched his workbench, picking up a scalpel. "I don't know. To start, I'd like to know what the cuts were made with."

The forensic tech lifted the body's head from the table, Nyboe made an incision across her neck, set the scalpel down, and then peeled the face off the cranium all the way to the chest. Jeppe knew that the next step was to saw the cranium open, so the brain could be removed and weighed, sliced and examined. After it would be placed in her abdomen along with her other organs, and the skin stitched closed. The skull would be filled with cellulose and absorbent paper. If you put the brain back into the cranium there was a risk that fluid would seep out during the funeral.

"Here, give me your hand!" Nyboe instructed.

Jeppe held out his arm so it hovered over the faceless body on the autopsy table.

"Uh, what are you going to do?" Jeppe asked.

"I don't think I could make cuts as symmetrical as these, no matter how hard I tried." Nyboe pulled up Jeppe's sleeve, rotating his palm so it faced up, and rested the edge of a new scalpel on the thin skin covering Jeppe's wrist. "Not even with my smallest scalpel."

"In other words, we're looking for a special murder weapon?" Jeppe said, pulling his arm back and tugging his sleeve back down.

"Yes, Kørner, in other words." Nyboe tipped the scalpel back and forth so it flashed under the bright lights. "We're looking for a special murder weapon."

■ ■ ■ ■

"Suicidal thoughts?" Esther de Laurenti repeated, pausing to consider the question.

The psychiatrist regarded her with a learned wrinkle over his frameless lenses, and she wondered yet again whether she, a sixty-nine-year-old woman, could take such a young doctor seriously. How old was he anyway, his early thirties? Esther glanced around the office, skillfully avoiding his questioning gaze. The wall behind him was covered with glass-front cabinets made of polished walnut, filled with professional books about psychiatry and medicine; the other walls were covered with modern art and preserved butterflies in glass display cases.

"Have you had suicidal thoughts?"

Apparently Esther had considered the question for too long. She noticed that this time around he spoke louder, in case she simply hadn't heard him, and decided on the spot that she didn't like him. Seeking his help had been a long shot in the first place. Some of her old friends from academia recommended him warmly, others couldn't distance themselves enough from his methods. Young Peter Demant was a psychiatrist his patients either loved or hated.

"No . . . ," Esther said. "Uh, that is, no, not for a long time."

"But you *have* had them?" He pointed at her with his Montblanc pen like some lawyer in a courtroom movie.

"As I said, I went through something really devastating a year ago. I lost two people who were close to me. In the wake of that episode . . . well, after that . . ." Esther reached for her glass of water, drank a sip, and put the glass back. "I moved out of my childhood home, and that was hard for me as well. I did go through some very dark spells, but it is a long time ago now. So, to answer your current question, no, I'm not having suicidal thoughts."

He wrote something on his notepad and regarded her over the top of his eyeglasses.

"And yet you've come to see me," he said. "Why?"

Yes, why had she?

Esther wasn't depressed per se. Her life was pleasant enough without being stellar. She had retired from her job as associate professor of comparative literature at the University of Copenhagen and lived with her old friend and tenant, Gregers, and her two pugs, Dóxa and Epistéme, in a beautiful, centrally located apartment on Peblinge Dossering, overlooking the Lakes, less than a mile from Rosenborg Castle. She had been able to buy the place outright after selling her building on Klosterstræde, in the heart of Copenhagen's old medieval core. She had money, was in relatively good shape physically, and had tons of time to pursue her writing ambitions.

She just didn't get any writing done. The murder mystery she had dreamed of writing up until a year ago, she had now abandoned for good, and she couldn't seem to start on anything else. Inspiration had long faded, and every time she sat down to the keyboard, she was overcome by fatigue and complete apathy. Instead, the days were spent on basic maintenance and mundane tasks like grocery shopping, walks, reading the paper, dinner parties, and so on. She didn't accomplish anything. The days just passed.

"It's like I'm sort of numb on the inside, like I'm stuck," she said. "I'm not doing badly. I'm just not really doing well, either. Does that make sense?"

"That absolutely makes sense, and you're far from the only one who feels that way." The psychiatrist thoughtfully tilted his round, clean-shaven face to one side and smiled fleetingly. "Depression is a wide-spread disease."

"Oh, but I'm not depressed," Esther said, shaking her head in surprise so her earrings jingled against her neck. "I'm just . . . stuck."

"Stuck in what sense?"

She weighed her words carefully before responding. He really wasn't getting it.

"Like I said, my life sort of fell apart the summer before last, and it's been hard to pick up the pieces. It's not that I feel depressed the whole time, just . . ."

"How about insomnia? How have you been sleeping at night?"

"Well, I do wake up around three or four most nights."

"And how's your appetite?"

Esther shrugged. She had actually lost nearly ten pounds in the last couple of months; she just didn't really feel like eating.

The psychiatrist took off his glasses in a rehearsed motion, which was meant to radiate authority, and regarded her seriously. Esther saw through his agenda but also noted with irritation that it was working.

"You've experienced an upheaval in your life, from retiring and then from the two deaths. You're having a hard time eating and sleeping, and you walk around with a general sense of despondency. Have I understood that correctly?"

"Yes, I suppose that's it."

"To me it sounds as if you're traumatized. Maybe the situation doesn't feel urgent to you and you are not actually feeling depressed. My guess is that your coping strategy is to clench your teeth and struggle through the day. At the same time, you are what I would call emotionally immature. The type who doesn't dwell on the difficult and the unhappy, and who refuses to be a victim. A survivor, someone who bounces back up."

Esther felt a warm discomfort sneaking up her throat and spreading over her face. She turned away from his piercing eyes and studied the decorations on the wall. Who the hell collects maimed butterflies, anyway?

"But now the trauma is catching up with you. Unprocessed emotions have a way of doing that," Peter Demant said, putting his glasses back on. "Let's plan a course of treatment for this fall. You'll come in every two weeks, and we can get to the bottom of what's holding you back."

"Couldn't a pill help me?" Esther held up a hand defensively. "A happy pill?"

"You mean an antidepressant?" He smiled

wryly, setting his notepad down on the highly polished desk in front of the window. "Those don't make people happy, only relieve the acute crisis for those suffering from depression. It's not something I prescribe until I've had a chance to become familiar with a patient's condition."

"It's not that I don't want therapy. I just have . . ."

"No one is forcing you into anything. If you're asking for my advice, therapy is the way forward, to begin with at any rate." He stood up. "If you wish to continue treatment, then make an appointment in a couple of weeks, but please hurry, my appointments fill up quickly."

Peter walked around his desk and opened the door to the waiting room. In the doorway he shook her hand.

"Thank you for coming," he said.

Esther was relegated to the smiling receptionist who sat ready, manning the credit card terminal. Esther found her wallet and entered her PIN, took her receipt, and hurried out to the gilded curlicues in the imposing stairwell.

She had been in there for forty-five minutes and ought to be furious at the sum on the receipt. Normally she would have been furious, too. Normally she would have protested to this kind of rip-off. She clenched the railing and quickly descended, eager to get out into the fresh air. Maybe this *was* the way forward, even though it would be a difficult, expensive endeavor. Was it just childish vanity that made her feel so exposed, almost humiliated? Because the psychiatrist was so certain of his observations, that he could pin her personality down in an instant. Because she apparently radiated gloomy self-denial.

Sankt Annæ Square greeted her with heavy clouds and puddles on its wide sidewalks. She stepped out into the wind and let the door bang shut behind her, closed her eyes for a moment, and inhaled deeply before she began walking. There was a juice bar across the square. She cut over to it and walked into the shop's warm pink-and-black interior with its pumping bass. People sat on barstools, chatting over the loud music, as if everything was just fine. Esther got in line and watched the young men behind the bar juggling apples and winking flirtatiously at the female patrons. It looked a bit forced. Still, there was something oddly soothing about the display.

She ordered a smoothie and received a flirtatious smile back from a young man who couldn't be more than a third of her age. His blue eyes shone with a zest for life and faith in the world. His enthusiasm was contagious. When Esther reached to get her wallet out of her purse, she realized that she was still holding the receipt from Demant's office in her hand. Without thinking, she crumpled it up and tossed it in the cup intended for tips and cute girls' phone numbers. Then she returned his smile.

CHAPTER 3

The Holte family's whitewashed brick home stood in a peaceful residential neighborhood a couple of miles west of Copenhagen, amid bungalows and prewar houses with sandboxes and swing sets in their yards. Jeppe looked out the car window with a brief memory of his own former suburban Copenhagen home, which he and his ex-wife had finally sold. The lilacs, the garden shed, and the half-finished patio now belonged to new owners. He didn't miss any of it.

At the end of a long driveway a well-built carport made of high-quality wood welcomed visitors along with pots of lavender plants and a freshly painted fence. This family clearly loved their home and spent time and energy on it. Jeppe and Detective Falck followed a stone pathway, with no moss between the stones, lined by neatly tended planting beds up to a white front door.

Under the doorbell a brassy sign read

BETTINA & MICHAEL, both with the last name Holte. Jeppe rang the bell and stepped back so that he and Falck stood shoulder to shoulder when the door opened. A woman peered out at them from under a set of very long bangs, which seemed to force her red-rimmed gaze even farther down. When she saw them, she spontaneously shook her head and started crying. As if their presence made an unreal situation more real and thus more painful.

"How are you?" Jeppe began. "We're from the Copenhagen Police, Homicide Department. We need to speak to Michael. . . ."

The woman turned and started walking away from the open door but only made it a few steps before it seemed to occur to her that it might be interpreted as rude. She turned around again.

"I'm sorry. Please come in. I'm Michael's sister, Rikke. Normally visitors are asked to take their shoes off in this house, but . . . just wipe them off so you don't leave tracks. Bettina . . ." She stopped, looked defeatedly down at the whitewashed wooden floor and then continued into a kitchen/multipurpose room that took up most of the first floor of the house. The walls were painted white with practically no adornment, the window-sills free of knickknacks, and everything looked extremely clean. This home, thought Jeppe, gave a functional but not particularly warm first impression.

The man who sat hunched over at the kitchen island in the middle of the room seemed like a direct extension of his house, graying brown hair worn combed back in a neat haircut, clean-shaven cheeks, and a discreetly woven car logo on the chest of his white shirt.

"Michael, the police are here."

Michael Holte looked up and immediately lost some of his well-coifed sleekness. His eyes were deep-set with heavy lids and dark circles underneath, but it was hard to tell whether that was due to lack of sleep and despair or if he always looked this way. He stood up, revealing an athletic build. Michael Holte was, despite his sad eyes, a handsome man in his midfifties, more attractive, Jeppe thought cruelly, than his newly deceased wife.

"I'm Lead Investigator Jeppe Kørner and this is Detective Falck. We're very sorry about your wife. Please know that we fully understand if this is the last thing you have the energy for right now. We just need to ask you a few questions."

Michael Holte nodded briefly and gestured toward a white sofa set.

"Let's sit in the living area," Michael said. "Rikke, could you bring us something to drink?" He looked at Jeppe questioningly.

"Water is fine, thanks."

Michael Holte fastidiously pulled up his pressed trouser legs before bending his knees and taking a seat on the sofa, stiffly upright, as if it truly wasn't to his liking to sit on something soft. Rikke entered with a pitcher of water and glasses and sat down right next to her brother. He instinctively pulled away from her slightly. Not enough that she noticed it, but enough that Jeppe did.

"Bettina disappeared yesterday. Tell us where, when, and by whom she was last seen."

Michael Holte took a deep breath before responding.

"Bettina goes dancing every Sunday at four p.m. at Pejsegaarden School of Dance up by Husum Square. It's, um, jazz dance. She loves it. Yesterday she left at three thirty, on foot as usual, with an umbrella and her workout clothes. She normally gets a cup of coffee with the others afterward. I talked to the dance instructor, who said she was in a good mood when she waved goodbye to walk home in the rain. No one has seen her since then. Until . . ."

He looked down at the floor. Jeppe waited for a moment before continuing.

"What time did she said goodbye?"

"A few minutes before six, I think. When she wasn't home by supper, I started to worry. She didn't answer her phone, and none of the other students from her dance class knew anything. At nine o'clock I called the police. You know, one always thinks the worst . . ."

Jeppe watched as Michael Holte remembered that the worst was exactly what had happened.

"Your wife worked at Herlev Hospital, is that right?" Jeppe asked.

"Yes, in the maternity ward. She was the training supervisor for the student health-care aides. Bettina has always worked with children in one capacity or another."

"And did she like her job?"

Michael Holte tilted his head slightly from side to side in a gesture that meant neither yes nor no.

"It was not the most exciting job that Bettina's had," he said. "She's worked at lots of different places, but she needed something that wasn't too demanding. Her previous job sort of worked her half to death."

"Did she get along with her coworkers,

with her boss?"

"Absolutely, no problems there," Michael said, and then took a sip of water. "My wife is not afraid to speak her mind, but she's quite competent and professional. And people know where they stand with her."

Not always a quality that makes a person popular, Jeppe thought.

"So did she have any enemies to speak of?" he asked. "Anyone she might have had a falling-out with? A former girlfriend or an ex-boyfriend?"

"Bettina and I have been together since high school." Michael eyed him sharply. "There aren't any ex-boyfriends."

Jeppe nodded. "I ask because the crime has . . . elements that might suggest a perpetrator with some emotional involvement."

Michael's sister put her hands over her face and started sobbing. Her brother sent her a look of annoyance.

"Why don't you go up to the study and get ahold of an undertaker, like we talked about?" he asked. "Please."

She blinked indecisively beneath the heavy bangs and then got up and quickly left the living room in her stocking feet.

"It's never good to be alone in a situation like this," Jeppe said with an understanding smile, "even though it can be trying to have company. . . ."

Michael stopped him with a tired look.

Jeppe cleared his throat and continued, "What else did Bettina like to do in her free time, besides dancing?"

"You mean like hobbies?" Michael asked, seeming perplexed. "She liked gardening. . . ."

He paused.

"How long have you two been a couple?"

Michael's phone vibrated on the glass table, and he glanced at the screen before declining the call.

"Bettina and I have been married for twenty-seven years. We've raised two children together and have been empty nesters for a while now." He lowered his voice as if to confide something to the detectives. "The honeymoon phase was well and truly over, and we've had our challenges like anyone else, but we've chosen to face them together. We're a good team."

"In other words, you have no idea who would have had a motive to hurt your wife?"

"My wife . . . ," Michael began, and then swallowed. "In my wildest imagination, I can't imagine it being anything other than a crazy person, a psychopath, who should be locked up."

Jeppe decided not to comment. Victims' families generally tipped the killer to be *an unknown psychopath,* even though it often turned out to be someone in the family itself.

"Where were you yesterday afternoon at four p.m.?" Jeppe asked.

There was a pause, just a brief one, before he answered, "Here. I did a little work, made dinner, waited for Bettina."

"Can anyone confirm that?" Jeppe asked. "We need to ask, I hope you understand."

"Unfortunately, no," Michael said, shaking his head.

"Okay. In a case as serious as this one, we'll need to examine some of Bettina's belongings. We'd like to send a team out here to collect evidence and take some samples."

Michael nodded reluctantly. What Jeppe didn't tell him was that the forensic investigators would primarily be searching for traces of blood. He glanced at his old Omega watch, handed down from his father and now worn on his right wrist, which reliably lost a minute every day. It was 2:30 p.m.

"We would also like to borrow your wife's computer, if that's all right, and get her phone number, email address, and all the passwords you know. And then I'll ask you to write a list of your wife's friends, coworkers, boss, and family, including contact information. Falck here will give you an email address to send it to, preferably as soon as possible."

Falck dug around in his pockets looking for a pen, and it struck Jeppe that what he was beginning to miss about Anette was all the things about her he usually found the most annoying. Right now he wouldn't mind a partner with some energy and initiative, even if it was of the obnoxious kind.

"I'll get her laptop for you." Michael got on his feet. "It's upstairs."

He left the kitchen. Jeppe could hear him exchange a few words with his sister irritably. A moment later, he was back in the living room holding a silver-colored computer.

"Thank you. We'll leave you in peace for now. I'm sure you have quite a few things to sort out. We'll be in touch as soon as there are any developments in the case. Make sure to call us if you happen to think of anything that might be relevant."

When he reached the front door, Jeppe realized that Falck had not kept up. He took a step back and saw the older detective still sitting calmly on the sofa, fiddling with the cap of his pen.

"Falck, are you coming?" Jeppe prompted.

"Yeah, sure, I'm on my way."

Falck got up from the sofa with some difficulty, as if his round belly was pulling him down into the cushions. An investigator didn't need to resemble a triathlete, but it's a plus to be able to get up from the furniture while interviewing witnesses and next of kin.

When they passed Michael Holte at the door, Jeppe could smell sweat lurking beneath the man's overpowering cologne, a pungent, panicky smell that did not match the neatly groomed man. Jeppe walked away from his firm handshake with the thought that the smell might not be the only thing Michael was trying to cover up.

The little break room next to the head nurse's office echoed with clinking cups and hoarse laughter. Jette with the thick upper arms and ginger helmet was celebrating her birthday with cake for the staff to go with the afternoon coffee in the cardiology department's Ward 3144, probably a cinnamon braid, judging by the smell.

Trine Bremen approached with a sense of unease. Even before she made it through the doorway, the laughter stopped, as if the other nurses could tell she was coming. She felt the heat rise up over her jaw, the mark of shame. She had stopped saying hello ages ago and didn't say anything now, just headed straight for the vinyl-covered cupboards to get a glass. With her back to her coworkers, she quickly filled the glass, counting the seconds in her head. The conversation started up again behind her, but forced now, chitchat about weather and traffic. She knew quite well what they said about her when she wasn't there. She also knew who had started the rumors, that it was Jette who was making up stories. Because she envied her skill and youth, more likely than not.

Trine turned off the tap and left the break room with her head held high. They wouldn't get her down, not now, not ever. She hurried down the hallway with the glass in her hand.

What had she expected? That they would suddenly offer her coffee and welcome her smilingly in their midst?

It was no different from how it had been in school, at the rec center, or at the vocational school. Always the same development. It usually started with cheerful, welcoming faces. But gradually the eyes hardened with doubt, distance, and finally scorn. The more she talked and tried to gain allies, the more she pushed people away. As if her eagerness and enthusiasm just made things worse.

Trine found a chair in an empty patient's room. As she sat, her cup of water sloshed, spilling onto her white leather shoes. She looked at the puddle of water between her feet and wiped her eyes with her free hand. Crying didn't help anything. She ran into the same problem again and again and knew perfectly well why.

Her diagnosis: *borderline personality disorder.* What good did it do to be intelligent and skillful when people around you only saw what was different and wrong?

Thank God for Klaus! She had met him one night when she had tagged along with the study group to an Irish pub just to stand by the bar alone feeling foolish. Klaus had been standing next to her. He was a few years older than her, bald and a little fat, but he saw past her awkwardness and liked the sensitive, earnest girl within. He didn't mind her quirks and her talkativeness; it seemed as if he enjoyed not having to say so much himself. And he tolerated her mood swings. They had quickly become a couple, and Trine hadn't waited long before she made it clear to him that she wanted marriage and kids.

A month later they married. Not the big princess wedding of Trine's dreams, but still long before any of her classmates.

"Hey, could I see you in room sixteen?"

Trine looked up into Chief Physician Dyring's kind brown eyes. He was an elderly man but always warm and charming with both patients and coworkers. Kept the mood up, even when they were understaffed and busy. The doctors were generally immune to the nurses' gossip, at least they never seemed to take notice. Professionalism was what counted to them, not whether or not one could be bothered to listen to coworkers' boring vacation stories.

"Of course, I'm coming." Trine set down her glass, got up, and followed the chief physician. "I'm actually not even on break now. I just needed to sit for a minute and rest my feet. It's been a hard shift, it seems like. I don't know if there's something in the water, or what's up, but the patients sure are ornery today. . . ."

Dr. Dyring nodded absentmindedly and led the way into a room, where a female patient had been admitted the day before for observation for an aortic dissection. She was heavyset with short hair and not particularly old, only about sixty-five. And she seemed less than satisfied with having to lie there and wait.

"Vibeke is getting a CT scan later today if the scanner is available. We need to check if the dissection is stable or if it is spreading. I've also ordered an EKG so we can see if her heart is pumping properly," Dr. Dyring said, putting his hand on the patient's shoulder and giving it a friendly pat. "Isn't that right, Vibeke?"

The patient shrugged grumpily. Dr. Dyring didn't take notice of her brusqueness.

"But I've heard something about a lack of feeling in your hands and feet, and chest pain. Is that right?" he asked.

"I'm not used to lying down like this for so long," Vibeke replied. "That's probably why I'm feeling so awful."

"If you weren't feeling awful, you wouldn't be lying here in the first place," Dr. Dyring said with a warm smile. "And you need to rest quietly until we know how big the dissection is and whether there's a risk that your aorta will rupture. We can't have that, can we?"

"If I could just have my own room," Vibeke said, eyeing the patient in the other bed pointedly. "I noticed that there's a room available farther down the hall. I mean, why do we pay taxes our whole life if we can't receive proper treatment when we get sick?"

Trine rolled her eyes. It wasn't true that there were empty beds; quite the opposite. There weren't enough beds in the ward, just like they were short on staff, amenities, and enough employees to cover when someone called in sick or went on vacation.

"Well, we'll have you on your feet and home again soon," the doctor continued unaffected. "Now, for starters, I'm going to ask Trine here to temporarily pause your blood thinner until we know whether you're going to have an operation." He turned to Trine. "We'll have her back on the seventy-five milligrams of aspirin again right away if she gets a stent. Let's start with twenty milligrams of morphine as needed for pain. Remember to record the precise quantities, so we can transition to fixed doses as soon as possible."

Dr. Dyring patted Trine's upper arm and left the room. Trine set to work routinely checking the patient's case notes and IV bags, so there was no risk of an overdose. Not that it wasn't tempting to turn up this specific patient's metoprolol so she could really experience what it meant to feel awful.

Trine noted the doses on the medication chart and examined the IV with practiced motions. She hung the drip bag and checked the patient's telemetry, pulse, and blood pressure. Efficient, professional, essential.

"Can I ask for something to drink, or do I have to get that myself, too?"

Trine stopped to look at the patient, who met her eyes with a defiant stare. She felt it again. Something falling apart inside her, triggering a feeling of insignificance, like some pissant who gets squashed under a rain boot.

There was a linden tree on either side of the stone staircase leading up to the front door of Elijah's Church. Under their branches one could take shelter and sit and watch the people on Vesterbro Square, above the traffic and hidden from the world.

Marie Birch often sat here. She liked to watch the fearless bikers zipping across red lights, and schoolkids on field trips wearing yellow traffic safety vests and holding one another's hands. On these steps she could sit in peace and decide how much she wanted to engage with the world.

Today, not so much.

She found a cracker in her pocket and wrapped the jacket more tightly around her. It was a little big on her and too thin for the season, the fabric worn on the elbows. But she wasn't particular. In elementary school she had worn flip-flops so late into the year, well into winter, that the bigger kids had started calling her Flip-Flop. Her mother had tried to get her to wear boots, but Marie refused. In the end she got sent home with a note. Still, she pretty much never felt cold. Not even when she slept in King's Garden on chilly summer nights, or when she went dumpster diving behind the big Salvation Army store on Vesterbrogade, and certainly not now on these stairs under the linden trees.

The cracker tasted dry and of some nondescript vegetable, but she didn't care about the taste as long as what she ate was relatively healthy. When she was little she had loved fatty foods and sweets. Her mother had to hide their cookies in a cupboard behind the cleaning supplies so Marie wouldn't eat them all up. Mom had pinched those chubby cheeks and mocked her appetite every time she slathered Nutella on yet another piece of toast.

They had been a normal family. Aside from not having a father, but Mom had always gone to great lengths to normalize that fact.

Sperm donor.

Marie had told the other kids in the preschool that her dad was some sort of robot that had an important job in a distant galaxy and that's why he couldn't be home. He had never really been missed, not until later when she realized that his absence had played a part after all. She and Mother had gone on vacations, spent Easter with Grandma and Grandpa; she had been a Cub Scout. Marie remembered those times with a warm fuzzy feeling in her chest.

When had it changed?

Marie thought of the Christmas when Mother had forgotten to buy groceries and they ate leftovers on Christmas Eve. Mother had alternated between trying to save the mood with jokes and laughter and scolding Marie for sitting around pouting. She couldn't change it now, could she? Marie felt the lump in her throat that made it hard to swallow. She still got it now, even after all this time.

She spit out a mouthful of dry cracker over the railing and wiped her mouth on her jacket sleeve. One day they had returned home, from grocery shopping maybe or from school, and Mother had lain down on the floor just inside the front door without taking off her coat. Marie still remembered the sensation of her hoodie's fabric against her neck, where sweat gathered as she watched her mom lying there. Had she been fired from yet another job, or was it some-thing with a boyfriend? Marie didn't know.

After that Christmas Marie had begun tearing the toilet paper meticulously along the perforated line, so the paper didn't rip, and something bad happened to Mother. *It's sick,* Mother had said. *Stop it!* But what was she supposed to do with the thoughts in her head and the tension in her body? When Mother lay under a blanket in the living room, paralyzed with grief, colorless-ness spreading around her? When Mother couldn't comfort her?

Marie was nine when Mother had her first psychological examination. The same year her mother was committed to the psychiat-ric emergency department for the first time and Marie started sleeping at her grand-mother's more often. Everyday life had slowly fallen apart, day by day. Her play-mates stopped wanting to come over; they thought her mother was weird. With time she stopped spending time at home herself and found older friends to hang out with on the streets instead, staying out late most nights. When she did come home, she would spread the comforter over her mother on the sofa before she went to bed. Until the night her mother wasn't lying on the sofa anymore.

At the age of eleven she packed all her things into one moving box and one suitcase, while the social services lady watched. Her guinea pig couldn't come. There was no room for him at the residential institution.

An ambulance raced past on Vesterbrogade, and the wailing sirens vibrated in Marie's diaphragm long after the sound was gone.

She had told her story so many times — to caseworkers and other grown-ups with wide eyes and damp palms — that she no longer knew how much of it was true. Not that she was lying, there was just so much she could no longer remember. The details were lost in the common repression that everybody seemed to agree was preferable. The fact of it was that she had become a nomad. She had met many adults who had tried to help from nine to five, but had never let them in.

Darkness was already settling over the square. When you live on the streets, you learn to value summer's soft light and hate fall's long, chilly nights. Tonight, though, she had a place to sleep, a bed and a roof. That wasn't worrying her.

The woman in the fountain was.

■ ■ ■ ■

When five o'clock came around, Jeppe hit the wall. He had made it through the day in relatively good shape, but by late afternoon it became almost impossible not to fall asleep. *The other way around, dear body,* he thought, *sleep at night instead.* He wished for something stronger than coffee, but he was done with that kind of thing. Instead, he went to the bathroom and held his head under the cold tap water, letting it run over his hair, until his ears went numb. He dried himself on the rough paper towels without looking at himself in the mirror and went down the hall to the meeting room. Falck was sitting at the table with a cup of coffee and his notepad, looking like someone who wasn't working.

Jeppe printed out a picture of Bettina Holte and stuck it on the whiteboard with a magnet. A metallic crunching sound filled the room, and the board fell down on Jeppe's foot. He tried to pick it up and re-attach it to the stand but realized that a nut was missing. As if the building wasn't falling apart enough on its own. Since the majority of staffers in the Homicide Unit had moved into the department's new building on Teglholmen, the old police headquarters had seriously started to crumble around those detectives who remained. The plaster fell off in chunks, and the linoleum floors bulged under damp patches blooming like daffodils in the spring. To work here was starting to feel like keeping the *Titanic* afloat with balloons and a stick of chewing gum. Besides, Anette was always the one who dealt with this kind of thing.

Falck sat comfortably with his coffee and watched Jeppe struggle with the whiteboard without making a move to get up. No two partners are the same, truly.

When the whiteboard was more or less balanced, Jeppe grabbed a marker and wrote the most important facts about the victim and the death next to the picture.

"The forensic techs didn't find anything in the home. No blood, nothing that looked like a murder weapon. If the husband killed her, he did it somewhere else." Jeppe pointed to Falck, who mumbled his assent vaguely. "He could easily have hog-tied his wife, put her in the trunk of his car, and driven her to another location. Maybe he has a garage or a slip at some yacht club?"

"Yeah, I suppose that is a possibility." Falck took a sip of his coffee and discreetly wiped his mustache on his sleeve.

"Maybe that's something you could look into?" Jeppe suggested.

He wrote *GARAGE?* on the whiteboard.

"We have a spouse without an alibi," Jeppe stated. "According to Larsen the neighbors claim the couple fought a lot and that it has escalated over the last couple of years."

"Who doesn't fight after twenty-seven years of marriage?" Falck asked, scribbling in his notepad without looking up. "That doesn't necessarily mean anything."

Jeppe turned back to the board again and studied the picture of Bettina Holte. *Competent and professional,* her husband had called her.

"She worked in the maternity ward at Herlev Hospital. Can you make enemies working there?"

Falck cleared his throat and then said, "Did you know that when the sand tiger shark is pregnant, the embryos eat each other inside the womb until there are only two left?" He kept scribbling meticulously, as if he were writing his memoirs and had the rest of his life to complete them.

Jeppe left the meeting room without succumbing to his urge to slam the door.

In his own uncharacteristically clean office, the double desk was blessedly free of Anette's potato chip bags and old coffee cups. For once a quiet place to work and get a grip on things. Jeppe plopped down on his chair and called Clausen at NKC.

"Kørner!" Clausen exclaimed. "I was just about to call you."

"Have you identified the make of the cargo bike?"

"Not yet, but I might have an idea about our murder weapon."

"Let's hear it!" Jeppe sat up straighter.

"It's not that I would go blabbing about our cases to my family . . . ," Clausen began tentatively, as if he was looking over his shoulder before explaining.

"Of course not."

"Right. Well, anyway, today I happened to meet my eldest daughter for breakfast — she's an orthopedic surgeon, as you may recall — and I may have run the peculiar cuts on the victim's wrists by her, hypothetically speaking, of course."

"Of course." Jeppe leaned back in his chair.

"My daughter thought there was something familiar about the pattern, although she couldn't quite place it, and suggested that we call her friend Monica Kirkskov who works at Medical Museion. She's an expert in antique medical equipment."

"Okay . . . ?"

"I'll send you her number, okay? We'll talk later."

Clausen hung up, and Jeppe sat there holding his phone, looking at its dark display. Back when he was still married to Therese, he, too, had sat at the dining table and bounced investigations off her even though it wasn't allowed. Now she bounced life's challenges off her new husband instead, and a young couple had moved into their former house and painted the facade yellow. Jeppe's belongings were packed up in boxes waiting for him to move into a new apartment in Nyhavn in two weeks. Life moved on. Until it came to an end.

Jeppe's thoughts were interrupted by the phone lighting up with the promised contact information from Clausen.

Monica Kirkskov.

No time to dwell on the past. Life moved on. Jeppe gave her a call.

The microwave signaled with an insisting beep that dinner was ready. Chicken tikka masala for one, delivered to the door by an online grocery delivery, heated up, and ready to be served on psychiatrist Peter Demant's rustic handmade Bornholm ceramics. The meal was perhaps on the fatty side, but today of all days, he needed the kind of comfort food that can be eaten from a bowl while lounging on the sofa.

He poured himself a big glass of milk and carried his food to the coffee table and its view over Holmen's black water. A high-end sound system played Chopin, and his professional books in the built-in shelves sent the sound back with a soothing ring of experience and wisdom. His bare toes sank down into the carpet's deep pile, and the combination of the ice-cold milk and the seasoned chicken took care of the rest. Bite by bite he slowly relaxed and felt the calm suffusing his body.

Peter was exhausted. For the last three weeks, in addition to the many hours he devoted to his own practice and consulting positions, he had poured his energy into a lecture that he had been invited to give in Amsterdam the following week. The world's leading psychiatric convention and he had been invited as keynote speaker. It was a one-time opportunity to further his own theories on new drug treatment options to address self-harming behaviors. He needed valid, documented research outcomes, and that kind of research cost money. The convention was a chance to be seen and heard by just the right people, an entry ticket into the big league of global research. On top of that his paper had been accepted for publication by the prestigious *British Journal of Psychiatry,* yet another feather in his cap. But then he had worked damn hard on that presentation.

The truth was that he had worked damn hard his whole life.

To some people things came easily, good things falling into their laps, and new opportunities unfolding before them daily. For Peter it wasn't so. At school he hadn't been the brightest, the tallest, or the best-looking, nor had he excelled at sports or the performing arts. The girls had quickly grown taller than him and had never bothered to look down. Yet Peter had one quality that had successfully gotten him through school. He was a hard worker, impossible to knock out of the game. Adversity was like a fuel that made him try even harder. And now his hard work was starting to pay off.

He scraped his bowl with a teeth-grinding sound, and he regretted not having bought chocolate. Today he needed the consolation only sweets could provide. From his earliest childhood, Peter had divided the days into three categories depending on his mood, and he still hadn't given up the habit, not even after eight years of studying medicine, his internship, his psychiatry residency, and earning a PhD.

Today had definitely been a three: full of gray skies and bad thoughts, which refused to obey when he ordered them to leave.

The online newspapers described in detail how she had been found naked and mutilated — that was the word they all used: *mutilated* — in the fountain at Old Market Square. There weren't any pictures of her yet, but Peter didn't need them to remember her broad cheeks, the loose skin on her underarms, her greedy, wet mouth. The thought turned his stomach. He didn't have the slightest desire to recall those images.

He carried his dishes into the kitchen, where stainless-steel appliances and black glass windowpanes reflected his prematurely receding hairline and sweaty forehead. He had eaten early and could still fit in a couple of hours of work. Maybe a bath first?

In the walk-in closet his suitcase already lay open, waiting for him to finish packing for Amsterdam. He took off his clothes and tossed them into the laundry hampers — one for darks, one for lights — before stepping onto the heated stone tiles in the bathroom. The warm water ran down his body, soap forming a lather. Peter raised his face to the soft beads of water and forced himself to relax.

CHAPTER 4

There's something about Copenhagen in the fall, an absence of light, a lack of air. Sometimes the city simply seems to ignore the changes in the weather, as if it is too painful to accept that summer is over. In between spells of low-pressure troughs and despondency, a nice day will sometimes turn up with clear skies and jewel-toned autumn leaves. But not today.

Jeppe looked out over the Citadel's dark trees and pulled his collar closed at the neck so the rain wouldn't get in. Door-to-door canvassing around Old Market Square had produced zero results and a defective camera on Teglgårdstræde ruined their chances of tracing where the killer had come from and disappeared to. On the plus side, the crime scene investigators were positive that his cargo bike had to be newer, possibly of the brand Winther, Bullitt, or Acrobat. It was hard to determine from the blurry, rainy recordings, but so far those were the three brands his colleagues were looking into the sales from the last three years running. The bike could easily be older than that, so Jeppe was not optimistic. On the other hand, it placed the likely scene of the crime within a radius of a few kilometers from where the body was found. No one rides a cargo bike very far, especially not when hauling a dead body.

His phone vibrated in his pocket just as Jeppe took his first step down Bredgade. He glanced at the display, took cover under a hotel awning, and took the call, surprised.

"Werner, what the heck? I thought you were happily buried in a diaper pail. Isn't that what happens when you have a baby?"

She pretended to laugh.

"You'll have to ask someone else," she answered. "I'm so tired I can't tell the difference between the diaper pail and Svend." Some lip smacking and grunting could be heard over the phone. "She's nursing right now. I'm nothing more than a freaking milk dispenser these days."

"Well, that sounds kind of nice."

"Yeah, I guess so. Are you in the middle of something?"

Jeppe looked at his watch. It was quarter past eight. The museum had closed ages ago, but Clausen's researcher friend, Monica Kirkskov, was working late and had promised to stay and wait for him. She had an exhibit anyway that she needed to finish.

"It's fine. Is something wrong?" he asked. It got quiet on the other end of the line. "Hello, Anette, is everything okay?"

"Yeah, yeah." She cleared her throat. "I'm a little bored. That's all."

"Uh, okay. How about turning on the TV or doing a crossword puzzle?"

"The body in the fountain," she said, perking up. "Tell me about it!"

"Are you joking?" Jeppe laughed. "You're on maternity leave! Read the newspaper if you want an update. Take care of . . . your daughter. When are you going to name her anyway?"

"We just want to get to know her first," Anette said, and then moaned. "Ah, she's biting. So tell me! Who was the woman in the fountain? What did she die from?"

"Why would you want to know that?"

"Come on!" Her tone grew serious. "Come on, Jeppe!"

"Anette Werner, I'm never going to figure you out, am I?" Jeppe started walking down the sidewalk, shielding his phone from the rain with his free hand. "The victim's name is Bettina Holte. She was a health-care aide.

The killer cut her arteries in several locations on the body and then let her bleed out."

"Ooh, sadistic! Are there any suspects?"

"No, not yet. And now I have to go talk to a grown-up, so you're going to have to focus on breastfeeding!"

"Bettina Holte, you say?"

"Tell Svend I say hello, would you? Talk to you soon!"

Jeppe hung up and picked up the pace. Down the street from the golden onion domes of the Alexander Nevsky Church and next to a bus stop, he could just make out the unassuming sand-colored facade that housed the Medical Museion. Neoclassical columns by the door were the only flashy aspect of an otherwise simple, almost humble front. Jeppe walked up the six steps to the front door, located the doorbell, and was buzzed in right away.

Inside it was dark and deserted between the cool, marbled walls. To the left and right white-painted stairs disappeared up into the darkness, and straight ahead, wide stone steps led up to a large foyer. Jeppe hesitantly walked up the stone steps. His footsteps sounded small in the massive silence that seemed as unwavering as the walls and columns surrounding it. In the middle of the foyer he checked his phone. His mother had called again. Twice. The light from his phone flashed in a glass cabinet next to him. He went closer and shone the light into it. Yellowish skin, dead mouths with the tongues out, empty eye sockets.

Jeppe gasped and took a step back. What was he looking at?

He shone the light from his phone around the room. He was surrounded by glass cabinets full of dead human fetuses. Mutated baby bodies with two heads and their bellies open, floating in formalin, the heads pressed against the glass, as if trying to reach out to him.

"Have you seen the mermaid?"

Jeppe jumped. The voice had come from somewhere in the dark behind the display cases. He shone his light that way and saw a figure approaching in the reflection in the glossy marble.

"She's my favorite, the pearl of our teratology collection."

The figure came over to stand beside Jeppe, took his hand, and guided his cell phone up so the light pointed at a smaller display case in the corner. Inside the glass there was a fetus whose lower body tapered down to a point instead of legs.

"Teratology is the study of congenital

abnormalities. The museum's collection of fetuses and children with malformations and birth defects is one of the best in the world."

The woman's voice was soft and so were the fingers holding Jeppe's hand.

"Uh, could we turn on a light?" Jeppe pulled his hand away. He could tell from her voice that she was moving away from him, and then a bright light filled the foyer.

"Don't worry, most people are afraid of the children."

The woman walked back to him. She was wearing a white shirt and wore her dark brown hair down, the kind of lustrous hair that seemed to glow all on its own. Her legs were long and she had a slight gap between her front teeth. She was, Jeppe thought, one of those rare people who was so beautiful that she made everyone else look ugly.

"You must be Jeppe Kørner. Sorry for taunting you a little with the fetuses. We academics rarely get out and have so few pleasures."

Jeppe returned Monica Kirkskov's smile and reflected briefly on the unfairness of the world: because she looked the way she did, her behavior became beguiling as if by magic, even though one minute ago he had found it disconcerting.

"Thanks for meeting at such short notice. Clausen says you're the leading expert in antique medical devices."

"Clausen is too kind. Come, let's go upstairs to the auditorium."

She led the way up a smaller staircase, and Jeppe followed her through a narrow hallway, to a room with a high ceiling.

"The building is from 1785 and once housed the original Royal Academy of Surgery. This auditorium was used for autopsies."

Jeppe looked around a small lecture hall with wooden benches rising steeply toward the ceiling in a half circle. Bright bulbs shone from a round light fixture in the middle of the vaulted, coffered ceiling.

"This looks kind of like a theater," he said, sitting down on the edge of the speaker's rostrum.

"Exactly." Monica Kirkskov nodded approvingly. "A couple of hundred years ago, autopsies were little theatrical events. The ceiling is modeled after the Pantheon in Rome."

She sat down next to him, and he picked up the scent of lilacs and wrinkled bedsheets.

"You work here?" he asked, instantly regretting his redundant, stupid question.

"I'm an associate professor of scientific history and historical philosophy, meaning that I teach, research, and curate exhibits here at the museum."

"And you can enlighten me about our murder weapon?" Jeppe leaned back to pull his phone out of his pocket.

"Well, that all depends on how bright you are to begin with." She smiled a teasing smile. "But, yes, I do specialize in historical medical devices."

Jeppe found a photo on his phone.

"This is the victim's wrist with incisions from the murder weapon. It's not a pleasant picture. . . ."

"I'm not squeamish."

She leaned forward and studied the image of Bettina Holte's arm briefly, then got up and left the room. Jeppe could hear her opening drawers in the adjoining room. A minute later she returned carrying an object in her hands. She presented it on her flat hand, as if it were a crown jewel.

"And that is?" Jeppe asked, his brow furrowed.

Monica Kirkskov was holding a brass box the size of a Rubik's cube.

"A scarificator. This specific one was given to the museum by me, and I inherited it from my grandmother, who grew up in

Vendsyssel and had inherited it from her grandmother. That takes us back to the middle of the nineteenth century." She set the little metal box on the table. "Before it became part of the collection, I used to use it as a paperweight."

"And what did your grandmother's grandmother use it for?" Jeppe asked, reaching for it.

"Stop! Ah, sorry, but you might trigger it if you press in the wrong place."

"Trigger it?" Jeppe pulled his hand back. "Tell me, what is that thing?"

"Allow me to demonstrate." Monica Kirkskov carefully lifted the box and pushed a little button on its side.

Zing.

The sound was crystalline clear and unmistakable. The music of a switchblade unsheathing, or in this case several switchblades. Twelve little knife blades jutted out of the box. They gleamed, shiny and sharp, in the harsh lights of the auditorium.

"Do you mean to say that *this* is our murder weapon? Those little knives could barely scratch the paint on a car."

"Obviously that's up to you to decide, but a perforated artery is a perforated artery." She turned a little handle on the top of the box that withdrew the knife blades back into the box. "As you know, it's not the size that matters —"

Jeppe cut her short. "What would you use this for?"

She sat back down and carefully put the brass box on the rostrum next to him.

"It's an old medical device. The scarificator was used for bloodletting, back when medical science viewed disease as an imbalance that could be drained from the body. All the way up until the twentieth century, people were bled, not just with scarificators, but also with cups placed on the skin or devices like a lancet or fleam. You let the barber do some bloodletting when you went to get a shave and a haircut anyway."

She leaned back, supporting herself on her hands, breasts pushing against the fabric of her shirt. Jeppe scooted away ever so slightly.

"So, originally the purpose wasn't to hurt or kill?"

"Certainly not. Murdering someone with a scarificator is like playing Beethoven on panpipes." She smiled, baring the charming gap between her front teeth. "It was used to purify the body."

"How exactly?"

"By bleeding small quantities of blood at a time," she said, tossing her hair back over her shoulders. "A deciliter, a half a cup perhaps, which was thought to bring the body into balance. Bloodletting was viewed as a way of getting rid of so-called bad humors. In the event of a serious illness, larger quantities of blood would be drained. Sometimes the bleeding was allowed to continue until the patient fainted."

She crossed her legs slowly without taking her eyes from him. The air between them grew thick. Suddenly Jeppe didn't know where to look. The ringtone from his pocket cut through the charged atmosphere.

"Excuse me," he said, "but I have to answer this one. Call me if you happen to think of anything else that might be important." He got up and handed her a business card. "Thank you for your time. I'll let myself out."

"My pleasure," she replied with a grin. "Good luck with the investigation."

Jeppe jogged down the stairs, feeling her eyes on the back of his neck, and hearing the ringtone in his ears. At the door, he declined the call and let himself out onto Bredgade.

It was his mother. Again.

Esther de Laurenti cleaned up after her half-eaten dinner, so moved by the magical web Maria Callas wove around her that at first she didn't notice the doorbell.

Mi chiamano Mimì, il perché non so. Sola, mi fo, il pranzo da me stessa.

So beautiful, so unbelievably sad with all the illness and death that was coming. The doorbell rang again. She raised the record player's needle arm and went to the front door, where the dogs were already barking. Before opening it she smoothed her short, henna-dyed hair with her hands.

A man Esther had never seen stood on the landing, his back half to her. When he heard the door open, he turned and looked at her in surprise, as if he had been expecting somebody else. He was tall, and his beaming green eyes competed with a pair of deep dimples; his chin was strong and his shoulders wide. She laughed in spontaneous enthusiasm before getting control of herself.

"Yes? How can I help you?"

The man didn't respond, just stood there smiling at her.

She noted that he had short gray curls and was barefoot on the stairwell linoleum floor. Dóxa and Epistéme growled, and she herded them back inside and pulled the door closed behind her.

"I'm forgetting my manners." His voice was deep and clear with a faint accent. "I'm your new downstairs neighbor. Alain. Spelled the French way." He held out his hand and grasped hers in a strong grip. "Yes, well, pardon me for coming up and bothering you like this, but I was unpacking and then I heard the music from . . ."

"Oh, I'm sorry. Was I playing it too loud? I do sometimes."

"Is it even possible to play *La Bohème* too loudly? I don't think so. Certainly not when Rodolfo asks Mimi to tell him about herself and declares his love for her."

He liked opera. Esther smiled.

"I agree. You just can't have too much Puccini. But really, just let me know if my music bothers you in the future. And welcome to the building. It's a lovely place to live."

"I'm starting to sense that." He winked at her and smiled, much too broadly. It embarrassed her. "Well, you'll have to put up with my cooking smells in return. I'm a concert pianist by profession, but I love to cook when I'm off. I'm a bit of a chef, if I do say so myself, always cooking up a *pot-au-feu* or a *boeuf onglet.*"

A concert pianist who could cook. Esther

felt something shift deep down, between her belly and her pelvis, that same flutter you feel on a good roller coaster. She reined herself in. Surely he was married.

"I just got divorced," he admitted. "Completely undramatic, but still it's daunting to move and change neighborhoods when you're our age."

He flattered her, and they both knew it. How old could he be? Maybe fifty-five? Ten to fifteen years younger than her. There was no chance he was flirting with her. Just that French charm surely.

"True! It's hard to move to a new neighborhood when you've been living somewhere for a long time. But it has potential. We've been living here for about nine months, and I keep discovering new places all the time. . . ."

A shadow seemed to fall over his face. He was still smiling, but his eyes shone less brightly.

"You're married?" he asked.

At that moment, the door opened and Gregers stood behind her, wearing a topcoat and his old checked sixpence cap. He stared at them in astonishment.

"Do we have guests?" he asked. He leaned in and lowered his voice ever so slightly. "Who is this buffoon?"

Gregers was eighty-four but frequently acted like a four-year-old. Esther was quite fond of him and normally overlooked his indiscretions, but right this moment she could really have done without them.

"Gregers, this is Alain, our new downstairs neighbor. Alain, this is my tenant, well, my roommate, Gregers Hermansen."

"Alain Jacolbe," Alain said, extending his hand. "A pleasure."

Gregers squinted his eyes and stood in the doorway without moving. An awkward silence overcame them. Finally he nodded slowly.

"We haven't by any chance met before, have we?" Gregers asked. "I never forget a face."

Esther knew that was a downright lie. Gregers forgot pretty much everyone he met, apart from that cute girl at the local bakery, who seemed to have made an indelible impression on him just by handing him his bread and taking his money.

Alain smiled awkwardly and withdrew his hand.

"I don't believe so," he answered. "I'm sure I would remember."

Gregers mumbled something to Esther, of which she could only make out the word *jackass.* Then he edged around them out onto the stairs.

Alain watched him leave, surprised.

"Gregers was born a curmudgeon. Don't take it personally."

"Well, I really ought to be getting back downstairs to my unpacking." Alain shrugged lightly. "But thanks for the chat. . . . I'm sure I'll see you around." He kept standing there with those dimples.

Esther didn't know what to say. Damn, if those eyes didn't turn her into a schoolgirl! It was wholly unsuitable for a woman of almost seventy.

He clasped her hand before she had a chance to react. With a mixture of shock and delight, she watched him raise it up to his lips and kiss the back of her hand with excessive intimacy. She jerked her arm back and hurried into the apartment with a breathless goodbye. On the other side of the door she heard him go back down the stairs at a leisurely pace, contrasting sharply to her own racing pulse.

Until a few minutes ago, the world had been cumbersome and the day insurmountable. Everything had seemed stuck. Now she felt reinvigorated, effervescent.

Alain . . .

How silly! Simply absurd.

Esther walked back to her record player,

taking small, cautious steps, and moved the needle back to the groove. Music filled the room once more, and she closed her eyes, listening.

¡Sí! Mi chiamano Mimì, ma il mio nome è Lucia. La storia mia è breve. A tela o a seta ricamo in casa e fuori . . .

It felt amazing. It felt dangerous.

CHAPTER 5

One could hardly blame the two new parents for not having prepared for one of life's two most important events: having a baby and dying. Being no fools, they had foreseen that it would be a particularly difficult adjustment given their age. Anette Werner, midlife and mother for the first time, had read up on parenting as if she were taking her college entrance exams again. Sleep rhythms, breastfeeding routines, and diaper liners made of paper fleece versus cotton pads had been deliberated and discussed ad absurdum. To her own surprise, Anette was the one who took charge, maybe because it felt most real to her — the baby had grown in her body, after all — maybe because she was the one who was most afraid of the change. When you have had a great marriage for twenty-odd years, you prepare for the tornado looming on the horizon so it doesn't rip everything up by the roots.

But as she was walking along the dark residential streets pushing her award-winning, all-terrain, infant-bassinet-mounted stroller system, she admitted to herself that all her preparations had been in vain.

The baby had come, seen, and conquered. She had screamed and screamed, until they gave up all ambitions of sleeping, eating, or even sitting down, had terrorized them with endless urgent needs, and robbed them of all free time. Anette was so tired, the kind of tired she never could have believed possible, too tired to care about the rain beating down on her face. She just put one leg in front of the other, determined to keep wheeling along until her daughter stopped crying. Which did not seem likely to be any time soon, if ever.

Svend had offered to take the afternoon shift, and Anette knew he wasn't keeping score about who did the most. But she was, and she was way behind. Thus she had prepared the baby carriage with dogged persistence and had set off, her body filled with contradictory emotions: unconditional love for the baby hand in hand with a growing rage at being caught in a seemingly endless cycle of identity loss and drudgery.

For Anette was excruciatingly bored. She

harbored an instinctive urge to protect her baby, so strong that it frightened her, but being on maternity leave was driving her crazy. Anyone who thinks that doing their taxes or recaulking the tub is boring has obviously never been on maternity leave.

Twinkle, twinkle, little star, how I tra-la-la-la-laa! Up above the blah-blah-blah, tra-la diamond in the blah . . .

She struggled to remember the words, put a comforting hand on the baby's belly, and pushed the stroller along angrily. Her daughter reciprocated with a furious wail, which would have fitted a devil banshee perfectly.

Anette shook her head resignedly. Lights were glowing warmly and pleasantly from the houses on her street, and here she was walking like a zombie, singing to her over-tired baby in the dark.

Who are you, if you don't perform and fill out your designated role?

Is having a baby and being a mother enough?

A task that blindsides you, because you face it totally unprepared, having spent your entire life honing your skills for something else, and yet you're expected to just be able to do it instinctively. All the while, the baby senses your general ineptitude and your fear of messing up and feels justifiably fretful. It's not easy.

Anette hummed on and tried to breathe calmly. Little by little her daughter stopped crying and lay there watching with her big, dark blue eyes. Oh, tiny human!

While Anette trudged past the houses on the streets of Greve Strand, her thoughts circled back to what she hadn't had time to think about all day: the case. Between changing diapers, breastfeeding, cuddling, changing diapers again, and doing laundry, Anette had desperately tried to remember where she had heard the victim's name before.

Bettina Holte.

When Jeppe mentioned the name, Anette had recognized it right away, but the memory had stayed hidden somewhere in the sleepy, porridgey mush that was now her brain. Over dinner she had briefly told Svend about the body in the fountain in the silent hope that the name would mean something to him, but in vain.

Anette slowed the pace and then halted. Of course! The maternity ward at the hospital in Herlev. Bettina had been the healthcare aide there.

No way! She knew the fountain victim! She had spoken to her, asked her for advice. The name was so special, it had to be her! Gray-haired and stocky, sturdy and straightforward, she spoke with an authority that did wonders for the nervous women giving birth. An oracle of common sense. But also a little strict, Anette remembered with a flash of irritation. She was the one who had chewed Anette out because she wasn't willing to have an epidural. Why would a health-care aide even care how much anesthesia one of the patients wanted?

Why in the world had she ended up in a fountain with the blood drained out of her?

Anette realized that the baby finally slept. She smiled in relief at her daughter, who now looked like a neatly wrapped angel, turned the stroller around, and trudged back to the house. With a little luck, she could have an hour at the computer and learn more about Bettina Holte before it was time to breastfeed again.

Winded, Jeppe rolled over onto his back and closed his eyes. Let his breathing find its normal balance, as dopamine was released and a sense of well-being raced through his body. His pulse was beating somewhere near his temple, his brain devoid of all thought. Airy head, heavy body. There had to be a way to use good sex in drug rehabilitation. No high could be better than this.

In the borderland between euphoria and sleep, he snuck a peek at his watch. He was going to have to leave soon. Jeppe turned his head and looked at the woman beside him. Beautiful as only the female body could be, she lay there with her back to him, naked and taut, like a string instrument.

He gently traced his finger along her spine from the nape of her neck to her tailbone, and felt his heart contract. She was asleep, always so tired, even more so than him. *That's what having kids will do to you,* she said, whenever he complained.

They had found their way to each other cautiously, the way only two previously burned people could. Or to be precise, two divorced adults. Had approached each other slowly and politely, ever anxious of being too pushy, both petrified of being hurt again. That made their surprise at the passion that had sprung up between them all the greater. When they finally succumbed, their desire gushed like a swollen spring stream, quickly pulling their emotions along with it. As Jeppe regained his faith in love, his back pain had lifted on its own, and the epic identity crisis he had been suffering thanks to his divorce the previous year had faded, like a sun-bleached photo stuck on the wall.

He had better sneak out, before he fell asleep himself.

They had agreed to wait introducing him as Mom's boyfriend to the kids until they felt sure that that was what he actually was. Especially since the kids already knew him as her boss. That of course being the other problem: they worked together, and he was her superior. Although their closest colleagues had gradually found out about them, they had kept things discreet at work. That meant stolen glances across the meeting room table and dates after bedtime, followed by nightly schleps across town to get home.

Jeppe had decided to enjoy the romantic aspects of their semisecret affair instead of letting it bother him. It worked most of the time.

When he had washed up and gotten dressed, he returned to the bedroom and kissed the still sleeping Sara before cautiously letting himself out of her apartment on Burmeistersgade. The old harbor district of Christianshavn was quiet in the wet evening darkness — as quiet as the neighborhood ever got — and Jeppe unlocked his bike feeling alive and peaceful at the same time.

The chain on his bike rattled rhythmically the whole way through town, over Queen Louise's Bridge to Sankt Hans Square. Jeppe's fingers were freezing, but inside his jacket he was sweating. By Sankt Johannes Church, he parked the bike in a rack and checked his phone. There was an email from Nyboe: The victim did not have any alcohol or other drugs in her system. It had been hard to determine due to the lack of blood in her body, but now he was certain. Bettina Holte had been conscious while she was slowly and painfully drained of blood.

Jeppe crossed Nørre Allé and looked up at the third floor. There was a light on.

She hadn't gone to bed yet.

The stairs seemed endless, and yet he seemed to climb them too quickly. His key rattled loudly in the lock; Jeppe closed the front door behind him and held his breath. For a brief moment he thought maybe she had left the light in the hall on for him, but then he heard slow footsteps approaching. Damn.

"You're home late!" Her tone was accusatory. She adjusted the robe around her with a look of despair. "Where have you been at this hour?!"

Jeppe unzipped his rain jacket and hung it on a hook. He crouched down to untie his shoes and take them off. This wasn't tenable any longer.

"You shouldn't have waited up. I didn't ask you to." He tried to sound amiable, but the irritation in his voice was ingrained and familiar. "You know that I often work late. There's no reason for you to wait up. I'm not a child."

Her head drooped, like a puppy that had just been scolded. Jeppe walked over and hugged her.

"Mom, you've got to stop!" He held on tight to her skinny shoulders. She looked so frail, suddenly an old woman. "Everything's fine. I just don't like having to report to you because I happen to be staying at your place for a few months. I'm not mad, just tired. Okay?"

"I was just worried about you," she said with a brave smile. "You know how my mind races. Did anything happen to you? Are you okay? You don't answer when I call —"

"Mom, I'm a policeman. I can't always answer your calls. You know that. . . . You look tired."

"I guess I am." She stifled a yawn. "I'm going to bed. Sleep well, Snuggles." She kissed him on the cheek, went into her bedroom, and shut the door behind her.

Jeppe sat down on one of the hard wooden chairs at the round dining table and rested his head in his hands. On November 1, he would get the keys to his new apartment and be able to put this humiliating chapter behind him. Moving in with your mother after a divorce was no party, no matter how practical it might serve as a temporary solution. The conflicts and grievances of his teen years still lay strikingly close to the surface, even so many years after he had moved away from home. Little things like the way his mom would ask him to wring the dishcloth out *just so,* sent him straight back to the timid boy he had been twenty-five years ago.

But, he reminded himself, it was a tremendous help that she let him stay here between the house sale in the spring and moving into his new apartment in a couple of weeks. It would be over soon. And it had saved him plenty of hassle and money. His only fixed expense right now was the monthly rent on the storage unit for his furniture.

Jeppe opened the fridge and took out a beer. The sound of the can opening blew away the last of his irritation. He was just a spoiled asshole.

He found a pack of cigarettes at the bottom of his bag. He had recently resumed his former bad habit with great pleasure. As long as he only smoked occasionally, it was no less healthy than breathing the city air on his daily bike rides through Copenhagen. He opened the kitchen window and let in the chilly air and the bass rhythms from the nearby dance club, Rust, then perched on the kitchen table with his beer and lit himself a cigarette.

The church bell struck midnight, one solitary serenely clear chime that cut through the damp night air. Jeppe pictured Bettina Holte, restrained with strong straps around her wrists and ankles, a ball in her mouth, her body in convulsions, her eyes open in panic. Bleeding to death was messy. Was she on a bed? Was there plastic underneath? And where did all the blood go, down a drain?

A bed, a floor drain, a private location, where someone could carry a body out to a cargo bike without being seen, somewhere within biking distance of Old Market Square.

Jeppe brushed the thoughts aside, drank his beer, and reread an email from his old friend Johannes. He was writing from South America, where he was trying to save his marriage to his Chilean partner after a —

to put it mildly — turbulent time. *Everything is still fragile,* he wrote. *You never know what tomorrow will bring.*

No, Jeppe thought, flicking his cigarette butt out into the yard. *You never know what tomorrow will bring.*

■ ■ ■ ■

TUESDAY,
OCTOBER 10

■ ■ ■ ■

CHAPTER 6

The sculpture at Bispebjerg Hospital of the Norse goddess Gefion, swinging her bronze whip over her bulls, was just a replica of the original at Langelinie, and only a sixth of the size. The pool around it was accordingly modest, more cute than impressive. But today the cuteness went unnoticed.

In the fountain, beneath the bronze bulls, the body of a naked man floated quietly. Tall, by the looks of it, and doughy, with dark hair, a beard, and colorful tattoos on both arms. He was lying faceup, which meant the cuts on both wrists and in his left groin were freely visible. Twelve small symmetrical cuts. His open mouth revealed a pierced tongue, and his dead brown eyes reflected the sky, like little pools of mercury.

"At least it's not raining today," Clausen muttered.

He didn't sound as if he seriously thought it made a difference. Two bestial murders in two days. Not the kind of situation that could be improved by a pause in the autumn rains.

"Someone is sending us a message," Jeppe said. "And I am afraid it isn't over yet."

His eyes felt grainy. He shouldn't have stayed up smoking and speculating till three thirty.

"What a fucking mess!"

The two men leaned in over the dead body to study the incisions up close. The flesh had lost its color in the water, and the wounds gaped like unnatural little gateways into a soul, which had long since departed. The dead man looked like a Hieronymus Bosch figure, a warning from hell.

"Did you get ahold of Monica Kirkskov?" Clausen asked with a faint smile.

"Yeah, thanks. She had some interesting information about a possible murder weapon, a scarificator. Nyboe is on it."

Jeppe took pictures of the body's face and tattoos with his cell phone and emailed them to Sara. *New victim, same MO. See if you can identify.* They were professional in their emails; the private stuff was exchanged by text. Well, and in bed. Jeppe put away his phone and scanned the scene around the fountain.

Behind the white pavilions crime scene

investigators were currently setting up, were redbrick hospital buildings, colored brown by the overnight rain. Muntin windows, blue wooden doors, and trees whose brown leaves were struggling to hold on for just a little longer. It looked quite serene.

"Who discovered him?"

Clausen pointed to an elderly man, slumped on a stoop, his head in his hands and an anxious dachshund on a leash. The hood of his dark blue rain poncho was sticking to the top of his head. An officer was squatting beside him, talking soothingly to man and dog alike.

"He was out walking his dog and took a shortcut through the hospital grounds. He doesn't usually go that way, he says, and didn't have a phone with him, so he had to go into the ER to sound the alarm. He's pretty shaken up."

"What time?" Jeppe asked, pulling a stick of chewing gum out of his pocket. The cigarette taste wasn't so easy to get rid of.

"The call came in to the main switchboard at six oh-eight a.m. Private security guards patrol the hospital grounds at night, one of them walked past the fountain at about five twenty. Everything was normal then."

"So again, a relatively narrow time slot for when the body could have been dumped in the fountain," Jeppe established, looking up at the eaves of the surrounding buildings.

Clausen lifted his chin to see what he was looking at.

"Yes, it'll be exciting to see what we have in the way of surveillance," he said.

"I'll get Falck started on finding footage from whatever cameras there might be. I wouldn't be surprised if there was something we could use."

A drop fell into the water in front of them. Both men watched the ripple spread on the smooth surface and reach the dead body, pulled up their hoods simultaneously, and let the rain start drumming on the fabric.

"Why does he throw the bodies in fountains?" Jeppe asked.

Clausen hesitated. "Maybe this sounds silly, but in a number of religions, you wash the deceased to remove their sins before their journey to the realm of the dead. Maybe the water is part of a ritual . . . ?"

"A ritual. Or a message." Jeppe pulled the gum out of his mouth, rolled it contemplatively between his thumb and index finger. "Yesterday the body was dumped in a fountain downtown. Why did he come out here to Bispebjerg today?"

"Maybe the risk of being seen with the body in the city was too high now that the media has started writing about a killer with a cargo bike?"

A crime scene investigator called to Clausen from the bushes by one of the hospital buildings.

"Well, Kørner, I have to get back to the evidence. We found bicycle tire prints, and we are trying to cast before the rain ruins them." Clausen hurried off in a bouncy gait, which made his small body in the rain poncho look like a hopping tent.

Jeppe stayed by the fountain, watching the dead man with his vacant skyward stare. The dead have a secret that the living will never know. What was the connection between Bettina Holte, a fifty-four-year-old health-care aide from Husum, and this younger man with a pierced tongue?

The forensics had gotten set up and were about to start the first on-site examinations of the victim. Jeppe took a few steps back to make room. Just as Professor Nyboe pulled a mask up over his mouth and leaned down over the body, Jeppe's cell phone rang.

It was Sara.

"Yes?"

"Hi." Sara's voice was thick with excitement. "I think I have something on the victim. I ran the images of his tattoos through that new American identification program and got a match. The pinup on his left bicep matched a profile. I found him in POLSAS."

"In POLSAS? Does he have a criminal record?"

"No. Apparently he filled out one of those background-check forms to work with children. That includes uploading a picture to the system, you know. It's a few years old now, if it is him at all. Right now all we have to go by is the tattoo, but if it is him, his name is Nicola Ambrosio, born in Naples, Italy, in 1983. Lives at number forty-two Amagerbrogade, fifth floor on the right."

"Nicola?" Denmark probably wasn't the funnest country to live in if you were a man named Nicola. "Do you have time to go out to Amagerbrogade and check?"

"I'm on my way," Sara said.

"Good. Call me when you know more." Jeppe wanted to say something to her, just a small private word that could bridge over the smooth work-related sentences they had just exchanged. "Sara . . . ?"

She didn't answer. It took a couple of seconds for him to realize that she had already hung up.

"And what does that reaction tell you?"

Peter Demant looked his first patient of

the day right in the eyes with a look he knew was perceived as attentive. He had practiced that look. To tell the truth, it was hard for him to focus on what the girl in front of him was saying. Not that she wasn't exciting to work with, quite the contrary. She had started therapy with him three months earlier, when her family had gotten sick of waiting for the help available through public-health resources. She had just turned seventeen and was showing signs of a personality disorder, which had not been definitively diagnosed. It is hard to correctly diagnose young people who are generally struggling to get to know themselves and figure out where they fit in the world. What's normal behavior for a teenager? At what point does it become aberrant?

In this young woman's case, it was her escalating OCD that had alarmed her family. When she was washing her hands more than fifty times a day her mother had finally contacted the school psychologist. That was three years ago, and the young woman in front of him had only deteriorated since.

To begin with, her mother had come with her to therapy, which had put a real damper on his ability to build trust. Now that she was coming on her own, things were slowly beginning to improve.

"That I'm . . ." The young woman breathed high up in her chest. "That I'm angry with my mother."

Mother, it was always the mother who was to blame for people's imbalances. Sometimes with an absent father to top it off, but always the poor, inadequate mother.

Peter took a sip from his water glass on the little marquetry table next to his armchair and realized that his fingers were trembling. Reflecting on the three categories he used to categorize his mood on any given day, today was yet another three, a bristly, restless day. It was the thought of death that tormented him. He risked losing everything — the clinic, his research, the profitable business-world consulting fees, his status as staff specialist in the psychiatric wards at both Glostrup and Bispebjerg Hospitals.

The prestige, the money, the respect.

"Is it my fault?" the girl asked, eyeing him expectantly.

"I'm sorry, could you please repeat that last thing you said?" Peter smiled. "I was just making a note."

"Maybe I should really move out? Get my own place? Don't people say that change is the best medicine?" She shook her head despondently.

"Medicine is the best medicine." Peter

reached for the yellow prescription pad but then hesitated. He couldn't allow his own inner turmoil to get in the way of the professional empathy his patients required. He had to pull himself together. "Why are you talking about moving? Ask yourself if it is about a desire for change and improvement or if you're running away."

She bowed her head with a sniffle.

"You've come so far in terms of looking your challenges in the eye and taking charge of your own life," he said, imbuing his voice with warmth. "You've worked so hard and accomplished so much. You have nothing to run away from."

"Thanks," she said. "You're right."

He got up and walked around the table, squatted down, and warily stroked her cheek. "Are you okay?"

She nodded and wiped her nose on her sleeve. Like a cute little puppy, innocent and adorable. Peter wanted to pick her up onto his lap.

"Our session is just about over for today, but we'll see each other again in two weeks, right?" He walked her out past the receptionist's empty desk with his arm around her shoulders.

"Louise will be in late today, so call tomorrow to make your next appointment.

Take care of yourself."

He put his arm around her shoulders and held her for a full half minute. Then he released her, let her out in the hallway, and lingered in the front office, quietly, hardly breathing. The patient's confidence and body heat had given him a brief moment of peace that already threatened to vanish in a flash. His body returned to feeling like a block of concrete, stiff and heavy. He forced himself to take deep breaths, down into his belly, until he felt the blood flowing and heart beating. No good losing his composure.

He realized that he was biting his cuticles. Spat irritably and went to the bathroom, splashed cold water on his face and dried himself thoroughly. The face in the mirror was round like a child's and just as uncertain. Sometimes he hated that reflection. He found the light switch without taking his eyes off the mirror and relished being able to turn off himself.

He had half an hour until his next patient, which meant that he could fit in a little work on his presentation. He fetched himself a glass of milk from the kitchenette and returned to his office, opened the door, and stepped inside. The office was dark; he must have bumped the switch on his way out. The scant daylight from the window facing the posh Sankt Annæ Square shone over his desk and landed on the wall, where his butterfly collection was mounted. Here in the dark they looked alive behind the glass; like they might fly away at any moment. The blue morpho's electric wings, the golden leopard spots of the silver-washed fritillary, the impressive Atlas moth, and especially the bashful little glasswing, frail and ephemeral, almost transparent, but only seemingly. Glasswing larvae store toxins from jessamine plants in their bodies, so they become lethal to their enemies.

The butterfly that draws the least attention to itself is the most dangerous.

Amagerbrogade rumbled with aggressive midmorning traffic. Jeppe stopped at number 42 and peered up at a modern residential building. The street level of the facade was painted a mustardy yellow and housed one of those jewelry shops that sold jangly nine-karat-gold bangle bracelets. On the street behind him, an irritable van driver honked at a crossing woman with a stroller, who was apparently too slow, and she responded with a string of four-letter words shouted over her child's head.

Nicola Ambrosio's girlfriend, Malene

135

Pedersen, had shown Sara Saidani pictures that confirmed that it was indeed his dead body that had been found in the Lille Gefion Fountain. Without going into detail, Sara had warned the girlfriend that Nicola might have been involved in an accident, and promised Jeppe that she would stay until he arrived so they could inform and question her together.

"Kørner! Over here."

He heard Sara's voice from the sidewalk behind him. From behind a group of elderly men, who were engrossed in a heated soccer debate in the middle of the sidewalk, Sara emerged next to a tall, black-haired woman in heels. The woman wore a bright mint-green down jacket and had a cigarette hanging on her lower lip and a very small dog on a leash.

"The dog needed to go out," Sara explained. "I thought we'd have time before you arrived."

She sounded tired in the way she often did when impatient. The downside to being quicker on the uptake than most people was that you often had to wait for them. That slightly stingy trait in a person who was otherwise as copious as Sara was one of the things Jeppe secretly loved the most.

"This is Malene Pedersen, Nicola's girlfriend," Sara said. "And Jeppe Kørner, detective with the Copenhagen Police."

Malene Pedersen held out her free hand to greet him. It was the left, and the handshake as a result not quite successful. She then tossed what was left of her cigarette onto the bike lane and pulled her keys out from the deep parka pockets.

She was pretty in that neighbor's daughter way, but with artificially long eyelashes and breasts that defied gravity, practically levitating up near her chin. The embellishments detracted a bit from her natural charm but of course added in another regard, though not in a way Jeppe knew how to fully appreciate.

They walked up to the fifth-floor apartment and sat down on a turquoise-colored velvet sofa. The dog settled down in its owners lap with its itty-bitty tail between its legs.

Jeppe informed her of the death, as gently as he could. With each word, a fresh tear trickled down Malene Pedersen's cheeks. After a few minutes she gave up wiping them away.

"The autopsy is underway right now, and we need to ask you to come in to officially identify Nicola, not that there's any doubt it's him. Does he have other immediate family?"

"His family lives in Italy . . . Oh, God, his mother." She fiddled nervously with the hair at the back of her head, where a hairpiece looked to be braided in.

"Where was he supposed to be last night?"

"At work. He left after dinner, the way he always does on Mondays. Nicola works part-time in a day care during the day and drives a taxi at night to earn a little extra money."

"Was he behaving normally?"

"Absolutely."

The dog whined and she rubbed its belly without looking.

"We're treating Nicola's death as a murder. Do you know of anyone who might have had reason to harm him or get even for something? Someone who was jealous, had money at stake, an old family dispute, anything you can think of." Jeppe nodded soothingly as he spoke.

"Nicola is a big, strong guy with tats and piercings, but nevertheless he's the nicest guy you'll ever meet, the kind of guy who plays with the kids at parties. My nephews love him." Malene grabbed a tissue and blew her nose. "Was it a fare in his cab who killed him?"

After a moment's hesitation, Jeppe asked, "Have you ever heard of a Bettina Holte?"

"The body in the fountain?" She suddenly looked confused. "Nicola mentioned that! He knew her, was totally shocked about it. What does she have to do with Nicola's death?"

"There are some similarities between the two deaths," Jeppe said cautiously. "For the time being we are investigating them as the work of the same person. How did Nicola know Bettina Holte?"

Malene Pedersen sat with her mouth open, staring into space for a moment and then said, "They used to work together. About two or three years ago, I think."

"Worked together in what sense?"

She stood up so abruptly that her dog fell onto the sofa with an anxious yelp, then crossed the room to an old leather suitcase in the corner, which she opened and started digging around in. Photographs and letters were piled onto the floor in stacks. After a few minutes she came back to the sofa with a brochure in her hand.

"Nicola used to work as a social worker in a residential care facility. He isn't certified, but like I said, he is really great with kids. He knew her from that place, the woman in the fountain. It was before we met, so I don't know much about it, but he showed me the brochure yesterday when we were talking about the murder."

She handed Jeppe the color brochure, about six-by-eight inches with twenty or so pages, well-worn on the edges and faded. The cover showed a blue stucco half-timbered building surrounded by tall trees under the headline *The Butterfly House — Residential Psychiatric Treatment for Children and Teens.*

Jeppe quickly flipped through it. Near the end there was a group photo of the staff, arranged like a grinning soccer team on the lawn under a flagpole. Bettina Holte stood far right on the front row, with a closed-lip smile. Nicola Ambrosio towered in the back with broad shoulders and white teeth.

"Can I take this with me?"

Malene Pedersen shrugged.

"Thank you." Jeppe looked at Sara. "Have you called someone?"

"Malene's mother is on her way. She lives in Dragør, so she should be here soon."

"Good." Jeppe gently patted Malene Pedersen's hand. "My colleague will stay with you until your mother arrives. You can give her the names of Nicola's relatives and friends, okay?"

She put her face in her hands and sobbed. Jeppe knew all too well what was in store for her, was familiar with the stages of shock, realization, anger, and depression. He knew that he couldn't help, and he let himself out of the apartment with a not unfamiliar twang of inadequacy.

On the stairs, his phone rang. The name on the display cheered him up a bit.

"Werner! You just can't live without me, can you?"

"Nope, Kørner. Obviously I'm the boil on your butt that you just can't get rid of."

Jeppe laughed grudgingly.

"What can I do for you, Anette?"

"I just wanted to hear a status report on the second death. Are we talking the same MO?

He could hear the baby whining in the background.

"Status report? What do you need that for? Tell me, do I need to ask Svend to lash you to the armchair so you can relax and enjoy your maternity leave?" Jeppe had reached the front door and let himself out into Amagerbrogade's engine noise and squeaking brakes.

"*Relax?* That's probably the last word I would describe maternity leave with. Fuck, it's hard!" He could hear her adjusting both phone and baby again. "Come on, Jeppe. Give me something! My life's pretty bland right now. I could use a bit of diversion."

Jeppe walked toward Norgesgade and his parked car.

"Well, all right, what do you want to know?"

She didn't skip a beat. "Are the two killings in some way connected?"

"Ha, Anette, I know you!" Jeppe dodged a group of teenagers with their noses in their cell phones. "If you get involved, you're not going to be able to quit."

"Oh, come on! What do you think I'm going to do? Go out investigating with my sleeping baby around in a stroller?"

"You would!" Jeppe stopped, hesitating for a second. "Well . . . I'll give you one word. One! If you want more diversion than that, you're going to have to subscribe to Netflix. Got it?"

"Yes, fine. Well, out with it, already!"

Jeppe glanced down at the brochure in his hand.

"The one word you're getting from me — and you *promise* not to use it for anything — is: *Butterfly. Butterfly House.* There, you see? You tricked me into giving you two words after all. And now I have an autopsy I need to get to. Will you tell Svend and the baby I say hi?"

"Jeppe? Know what I think?"

"No, what do you think?"

"I think you miss me!"

CHAPTER 7

Anette Werner hung up the phone and looked down at her little girl, who had fallen asleep at her breast. The morning nap was one of the more reliable stretches of sleep for the day, if you could talk about a stretch of sleep. The baby mostly slept for an hour or two before lunch, and Anette usually lay down herself to catch up on some of the sleep she had lost overnight. She'd better do that now.

Carefully she pried a tender nipple out of her daughter's mouth and carried her over to the sofa, which they had blocked in with pillows, and which she for some reason seemed to prefer over her expensive designer crib.

The breathless transition from arms to sofa went smoothly. Anette closed her nursing bra, pulled her top back into place, and sat down at the computer on the dining table between unread newspapers and breast pump parts. She would just do a quick search before she lay down.

The Butterfly House. A Google search revealed it to be a residential home for kids with psychiatric disorders, owned and run by a Rita Wilkins, at an address near the village Gundsømagle. Privately owned then, not run by the national health service, offering board to a handful of mentally ill kids, with a particular focus on schizophrenia and personality disorders. The home's web page had been taken down, and further searches revealed that the Butterfly House had closed two years ago, but Google's image archives showed cozy teenage rooms, a firepit, and a rural setting with woods and a pond in the backyard.

Jeppe must be hinting that the victims had a connection to this same program. Bettina Holte was a health-care aide, so without knowing what the new victim's profession was, it was reasonable to assume that she and the second victim had both worked there.

Not that she cared, of course. Anette closed the computer and lay down on the sofa next to her infant daughter, grabbed a pillow and a blanket, and snuggled into that position on her side, where her chronically tender breasts hurt the least. She closed her eyes and tried to relax, listened to the baby's quiet breathing, and let the thoughts flicker tiredly through her head.

Bettina Holte had kept Anette company during one of her first, nervous breastfeeding sessions, had spoken to her soothingly and distracted her from the nipple pain. She had talked about the challenge of being a parent and about being present in the moment. Anette had quickly zoned out and stopped paying attention.

She rolled onto her back, took a deep breath, and let her feet fall out to the sides. Lifted her head and looked at the movement in the baby's eyelids. What did she dream about when she slept? The same things she thought about when she was awake?

Speaking of being awake, Anette really ought to be resting. Damn it if she was going to use her scant sleep time lying there speculating about a case she wasn't even expected to be working on. You would think Jeppe had infected her with all his talk about intuition and gut feeling. His nonsense about her connection to a sixth sense possibly opening up when she gave birth, cosmic awakening.

Anette sat up. These kinds of thoughts gave her heartburn. Investigative work was

90 percent elbow grease and 10 percent luck. Nothing else.

Irritably she flung the blanket aside and got up from the sofa. If she couldn't sleep, she might as well be working. She reopened the computer and had just jotted down the address of the now closed residential facility on an old envelope when Svend came in from his home office.

"I thought you were going to sleep when Cutykins was napping? Aren't you exhausted?"

Nicknames were one of Svend's specialties. One of many qualities she normally loved about her husband, but that had now started to annoy her.

"Can we just call her *the baby* until we give her a name?" Anette closed the computer with a hard click.

"Hey, can't I decide what to call my own daughter?" He eyed the computer skeptically. "What are you up to?"

"Nothing," Anette said, thrusting the envelope into the pocket of her sweatpants and standing up, causing the chair to rattle and skitter across the floor.

The baby started fussing.

Svend cocked his head to the side. Accusatorily.

"Oh, whatever, I guess she's just not that

tired after all. I'll take her."

Anette hurried over to her daughter and gently picked her up. Her little cheek was warm, she was probably overdressed. It was so hard to decide how to dress her, Anette thought; too cold, too hot, never just right.

Never just right.

"You want me to make us some lunch?"

Lunch? Anette was so removed from being in touch with her normal, physical needs that she might as well be dead.

"Yeah, please. Lunch would be great. Then I'll try to get the baby to settle down again."

"Shouldn't we just name her Gudrun after your mom?" Svend paused in the kitchen doorway. "Gudrun is a good Nordic name. And we would be paying homage to Grandma."

They had discussed this before, many times. Anette knew it came from a place of love, when he suggested naming their daughter after her late mother. Even so, the suggestion ticked her off.

"My mother hated that name. Why do you think we all called her Didder? No one likes the name Gudrun!" Anette saw the look in Svend's eyes and stopped. She had hurt his feelings. It seemed like she was doing that several times a day lately. He tried to be understanding, not let things get to him, give her space. That just made things worse.

"Is an omelet okay? We don't have much in the fridge."

She nodded and turned her back to him. Svend went into the kitchen, and Anette started rocking and swaying impatiently to calm the baby. It didn't matter how, as long as there was motion.

The baby quickly settled. Anette kept swaying and bouncing, while she looked out the window at the little yard's sad-looking snowberry branches, butterfly bushes, and dark shady patches underneath.

The Butterfly House, a residential program for troubled kids. The envelope with the address burned in her pocket

There was no telling what made Esther decide to cook ravioli from scratch for a completely average Tuesday lunch. She had not made homemade pasta for many years and was not expecting guests. Even so, she began the day — after having taken a long bath, putting on her favorite, lavender sweater, and walking the dogs — by looking up recipes in cookbooks, composing a shopping list, and taking a detour to the good cheese shop to buy proper ricotta. She was hungry. For the first time in a long, long time, she was excited about food: she wanted Italian home cooking, companionship, and wine.

Maria Callas provided the soundtrack as she poured a heap of flour onto the table, cracked the eggs, added oil, and started kneading. Every once in a while she would get carried away by the music and chime in with her tenuous soprano as she worked at the kitchen table, causing Dóxa and Epistéme to howl from their basket. She didn't care. She felt like singing again, like laughing, like living. While working the dough, she poured herself a glass of wine and sipped it in good conscience. There had been phases when her drinking had been decidedly unhealthy, but over the last six months she had managed to get her consumption under control.

The ravioli ended up looking a little clumsy, but they were still tasty. And once she had tossed them in a sage-infused butter sauce and seasoned them well with salt, pepper, and Parmesan, they tasted as life asserting as only homemade pasta can.

Esther drizzled the warm platter of ravioli with chopped parsley, grabbed the wine bottle, and was on her way downstairs before it occurred to her that this was what she had been planning to do the whole time.

When she rang the doorbell, her heart was racing like an enamored teenage girl's, and she felt like she could die a hundred times over before the door opened and she knew her answer.

Alain looked even better today than he had the day before, relaxed and sexy, like a chameleon in the sun. Stubble, heavy eyelids, tousled hair — had she woken him up? He eyed her, slightly disoriented, but then he stepped out onto the landing, pulling the door almost shut behind him.

"*Chérie!* This must be my lucky day."

If men only knew how much mileage they got out of calling a woman *chérie.*

"I was just making lunch and thought that I would welcome my new neighbor to the building."

Alain hesitated for a long moment, leaving Esther with ample time to regret her decision several times over and decide to turn around and go back upstairs. When he finally spoke, his voice was husky.

"That might be the sweetest thing that's ever happened to me in Denmark. Of course *you* cook, of course *you* come down to welcome me. You're" — he put his hand on his chest — "you're *magnifique.* Thank you!"

Alain took the platter from her, and suddenly she was unsure if he was going to take the food and eat it in his apartment without her. There was an awkward silence, as they stood with the platter between them, and she was unsure if she should just turn around and go.

"We'll eat it together! And you brought wine, wonderful! But we can't sit here . . . the apartment is a disaster, boxes every-where, and . . . no, it's just no good. Do you think we could go up to your place, *ché-rie*?"

"Sure." Esther took the platter back from him with a smile. "Good idea."

"I'll just put on a shirt. Set the table, and I'll be there in two minutes."

He opened the door to his apartment, darted in, and closed it behind him before she had a chance to peek in. Of course he didn't want guests in his unfinished apart-ment! He was French, a perfectionist.

She went back up to her place and set the pasta in the oven on low to keep it warm. It really should have been eaten right when it was done, but there was no helping that now. Quickly she cleaned the table and then set it with her best Royal Copenhagen blue-and-white plates, checked her reflection in the cupboard glass, and cursed the blushing that always gave her away when she was excited. Would it be over the top to light candles?

A motion just behind her gave her a shock. Had she forgotten to close the door?

"What in the world are you doing?"

Gregers!

"Lunch. The new downstairs neighbor is coming for lunch. We won't bother you . . ."

"Pshaw!" Gregers walked over and looked in the oven. "Um, I don't feel like pasta. What else have you got?"

"There isn't anything else, and I also only . . ."

There was a knock on the door, restrained and polite. When Alain had said two minutes, he meant it.

"I'll be right there! See you later, okay, Gregers?"

Esther hurried out to the door, hoping that her dancing pulse wasn't showing. Alain had changed into a wrinkled and slightly too short shirt, combed his gray hair, and put on an overwhelming amount of cologne. In his hand he held a stick with a clump of crumpled aluminum foil at the top. He handed it to her like a flower, and it occurred to her that that was exactly what it was meant to be.

"I, uh, didn't have a chance to get to the florist. But a woman like you deserves flowers every day."

Esther accepted the aluminum rose with slight embarrassment. She couldn't quite decide what was more awkward: the hopeless flower or the words that accompanied it.

"Well, come in. I think we'd better sit down and eat right away. Then I can give you a tour afterward."

Alain smiled sweetly and winked. It dawned on Esther that she might have said something flirtatious even though she hadn't actually meant to. Boy, was she rusty!

She led the way to the kitchen, suddenly painfully aware of all the cracks in the varnish of her life: the wrinkles on her face, the dusty surfaces, and the dogs, who were growling at the stranger. Is a person even allowed to think romantic thoughts when she's so old and worn-out?

Gregers sat at the dining table, by one of the two place settings Esther had laid out. Alain hurried over and greeted him politely, but Gregers merely turned to her, looking offended, as if the presence of their new downstairs neighbor was somehow inappropriate.

"Is he going to eat with us?"

Esther could have strangled him.

"Gregers, my friend, did you forget that I mentioned I was having lunch with Alain?"

The silence that followed was as thick as cold oatmeal, and every bit as uncomfortable. Gregers's milky eyes darted back and forth between them. Then he looked down, nodded a couple of times, and grabbed the edge of the table to stand up. He pushed his chair back and stood with difficulty. Esther didn't dare look at either him or Alain. Therefore the noise was her first indication that something was wrong. A moan, but deep and hoarse: like the muted howl of a dying wolf.

She looked at Gregers. He was pressing both hands to his chest, his face ash gray, his eyes glazed over and vacant-looking.

"Gregers, are you okay?"

He didn't respond, didn't react at all.

"Gregers, answer me!"

Esther was already by her friend's side, shaking his arm, yelling at him, probably squeezing way too tight. Still he didn't respond. Alain lightly touched her shoulder.

"He's having a heart attack. We need to call an ambulance."

The twelve panic-filled minutes that elapsed from the 112 call until Gregers was being carried out of the apartment, strapped to a gurney with an oxygen mask, both sped by and seemingly dragged on forever. Esther had experienced this sort of unreality before, had been close enough to death to know its smell. Even so, she wasn't prepared for the fear that filled her and the overwhelming urge to flee. It wasn't until the door closed behind the EMTs that she was able to breathe again, hear sounds, sense the world.

Alain pulled her gently into a warm hug, comforted and calmed her.

"I'd better go to the hospital. Gregers doesn't have anyone but me. I really want to be there for him, if he . . . if he needs me." She reluctantly pried herself out of his arms.

"You're a good person, Esther." Alain nodded understandingly and wiped a tear from her cheek.

She grabbed her purse, her waterproof rain jacket, cell phone, and her comfortable shoes.

Alain watched her get ready, but showed no sign of leaving himself. As she stood in the doorway, his dimples were back.

"It's almost a shame for that lovely food to go to waste, Esther. Should I maybe just eat it?"

A hooded shape wheeled slowly around the corner from narrow Østre Længdevej onto Lindringsvej. Under a tarp a bundle was strapped to the bicycle's cargo rack. The front wheel splashed up water, as it cut through a puddle. Then it was gone.

"So far, this is the only footage we've found of the suspect. The hospital's private security contractors aren't really as on top of the whole video-surveillance thing as they would like their clients to believe. This is from five forty-three a.m. They can't find any other clips from the area that night. Once again he seems to have appeared out of thin air."

Jeppe swallowed some bitter coffee and promised himself to make a fresh pot when he went back for the next cup.

"They've started questioning the hospital staff, but one of us better go help the officers once we're done here."

Jeppe emptied his cup, crumpled it up, and tossed it in the trash can under his desk. The team was seated in his office, all eyes on his computer.

"This is a different situation now. Two killings in two days, same MO. Nyboe confirms that the murder weapon in both cases in all likelihood is a scarificator. Everything currently indicates that the killer is the same. That means that we need to focus on connections between the victims. I'll come back to them. . . ."

Jeppe looked up from his three colleagues to the wall behind them. He still thought of the picture that hung there as new, even though it had been more than a year since he hung it up. A suspect who had been brought in for questioning had smashed the old one, Monet water lilies in a prefab frame. Now it was a Gustav Klimt poster of naked people and skeletons floating around in the clouds, one of the ceiling paintings from Vienna. Jeppe tried to remember what it was called, maybe *Medicine*?

"Falck and I just came back from Nicola Ambrosio's autopsy, and, to put it succinctly, he died exactly the same way as Bettina Holte. Cut with a scarificator on both wrists and the one side of the groin, marks on the skin after having been strapped down and gagged, organ failure, and cardiac arrest due to exsanguination. Time of death sometime between midnight and three a.m. last night. Am I forgetting anything, Falck?"

Falck shook his head slightly, stingy with his bodily motions, right down to the tips of his fingers. Thomas Larsen leaned closer to Sara and said something the others weren't meant to hear.

She smiled in response.

Jeppe cleared his throat and said, "Saidani and I interviewed the victim's girlfriend,

Malene Pedersen, this morning. He was an Italian citizen living in Denmark, thirty-four years old, worked in a day care and drove a taxi at night. She thought he was working. Has his cab turned up?"

"It was found in a parking lot on Tagensvej, not far from where the body was found," Larsen replied. "Parked at the curb and locked. The forensic team is on its way."

"Good," Jeppe said, "but I don't think they'll find anything in the car. The victims don't show signs of having resisted; no scratches, no apparent struggle, no DNA under their fingernails. My guess is that they knew the killer and met him or her willingly."

Jeppe had only his gut instinct to base this on and didn't usually make such sweeping statements. That was Anette Werner's domain. But someone had to do it while she was away.

"His family in Naples has been informed, and the parents are on their way to Copenhagen. According to his girlfriend, Nicola was easygoing with no enemies or old scores to be settled. No substance abuse as far as she knew. But the victims both used to work for the same residential treatment home for mentally ill teens." Jeppe glanced down at his notes. "A place called the Butterfly

House in Gundsømagle outside Roskilde. The place closed two years ago."

"What was a taxi driver doing at a psychiatric facility?"

"That's the million-kroner question, Larsen. Apparently you don't need any kind of certification to work with mentally ill kids."

"Are you kidding me?"

"I'm not kidding, Larsen. That's how it is. Nicola Ambrosio worked temporarily as a caregiver at several institutions and homes, including Butterfly House. For obvious reasons we don't know anything about the home's patients yet, but we know the names of the employees. Sara, were you able to look into the staff?"

Too late, Jeppe remembered that they usually addressed each other by last name only when at work.

Sara held the home's brochure up and pointed to the faces one by one.

"Bettina Holte, our first victim, worked as a health-care aide at Butterfly House, from when the place opened five years ago until it closed two years ago. Nicola Ambrosio, as was already mentioned, worked there part-time as a temporary care worker for a year and a half. The director — and owner — of the place, Rita Wilkins, has been helpful

about providing information about the staff
—"

Jeppe held his hand up to stop Sara and asked, "Where does she live?"

"Up north in Virum, well, the village of Brede to be precise. She has a new facility called Forest-something-or-other. I have it here somewhere."

"Let's interview her first. Who's coming with me?"

Larsen wiggled his index finger.

"Okay, Larsen. We'll head up there as soon as we're done here. Continue, Saidani!"

"Other employees were" — she pointed to a bald man in a soccer outfit — "Kim Sejersen, full-time social worker, and next to him . . ." Sara moved her finger to a tall blond woman. "Nurse Tanja Kruse and the affiliated psychiatrist Peter Demant." She pointed to a man with round cheeks and dark curly hair.

"You'll find them and set up appointments?" Jeppe said. "Then Falck, Larsen, and I will interview them."

She nodded.

"Rita Wilkins says that there were another couple of nurses associated with the place but only part-time. She couldn't remember their names but promised to look in the archives and find them. There was also a chef working there, but he's not in this group photo."

"A chef?"

"Yes, a guy who cooked all the meals. The kids called him Dinner Daddy. His first name is Alex, but she couldn't remember his last name. Said the bad news had rattled her." Sara put the brochure back down on top of a stack of papers. "I've looked at both of the victims' computers — Nicola Ambrosio's just cursorily so far — but haven't found anything suspicious in their emails or social media accounts. On the other hand, their phone histories show that they both received calls from a prepaid cell phone the day they were killed, and those calls lasted for eleven and seven minutes respectively."

"I think that reinforces the idea that the victims knew the killer," Jeppe said, shutting his laptop. "We'll keep all channels open. That residential home definitely seems to be the link, but it's too soon to draw any definite conclusions. The victims' families are still in the picture. We're keeping an eye on Michael Holte and doing a background check on Nicola Ambrosio to see if he had any skeletons in his closet."

"Where would one even buy a scarificator?" Sara asked, tapping a ballpoint pen absentmindedly against her chin. "Do any of you know?"

"Specialized online stores are my guess. They could be located anywhere in the world, so the chance of finding where the murderer bought it is probably pretty small."

"I'll look into it anyway." Sara puckered up her lips and creased her brow the way she always did, when she focused on something. "If that's okay with you?"

"Of course, Saidani." Jeppe turned back to Falck. "Will you go to Bispebjerg Hospital and talk to witnesses? We have a team of people out there already, but I'd like someone from Homicide to supervise."

Falck seemed to consider whether that was of interest to him and then nodded slowly. Jeppe got up and walked over to the window. It was still raining.

"Let's all consider how a psychiatric treatment home could potentially lead to such nasty murders. And keep your eyes and ears open! Two murders in two days — there's definitely a risk that he'll strike again. Let's make sure we manage to stop him. Or her."

Jeppe's phone rang on his desktop. Larsen leaned over and looked indiscreetly at the screen.

"It's your mom," he announced. "You want me to answer?"

"I can handle that on my own, thanks." Jeppe swallowed his annoyance. "We'll leave in ten minutes."

While his colleagues filed out of the office, Jeppe declined the call and chucked his phone back on the desk. Anette would have known how to give Larsen a funny, biting comeback and put him in his place. *Maybe it's* your *mom, Larsen, calling to thank Jeppe for last night.* Something like that.

Jeppe shook his head. He was going to have to up his game.

CHAPTER 8

"If we just lift our arms, then I can —"

Nurse Trine Bremen tried to get the elderly patient to cooperate, but he wasn't listening, just looking around the room, confusion in his watery, aged eyes. He had just been admitted with chest pain and ventricular tachycardia and had obviously received some kind of sedative from one of her colleagues. Either that or he had dementia.

She looked in his chart at the end of the bed. He hadn't been given anything other than aspirin yet.

"Hi, Gregers! Are you awake?" Trine patted his hand and tried to establish eye contact. "Listen, there's no indication that you've had a heart attack. You can relax. We're going to keep you here for a couple of days and run some tests on your coronary arteries so we can find out what's causing your chest pain."

The patient slowly focused on her.

"Hi there," she said. "I'm Trine. Would you like a drink of water?"

He nodded and carefully drank from the plastic cup she handed him. Then he pointed to his heart and cleared his throat.

"I had angioplasty . . . uh, I can't remember when."

"A year ago. It says so in your chart. Don't worry, we know all about it. Everything's under control. How are you feeling now? Still in pain?"

With difficulty, he propped himself up on his elbows.

"Maybe it's a little better now . . . ?" he said. "I'm still thirsty."

Trine poured some more water into his plastic cup and watched as he drank again. He moved as if in slow motion and still seemed confused.

"I need to ask you some questions, Gregers. Are you ready for that?"

He nodded reluctantly.

"The feeling came on all of a sudden, is that right? Can you describe what happened? Dizziness, chest pain?"

He nodded again, looking insecure.

"My chest felt tight. And then I was gone."

"You were gone?" Trine asked, as she wrote *angina pectoris.*

He waved his hand irritably, as if he himself didn't quite know what he meant.

"Have you felt that way before?"

"Not many times," he said, shrugging his shoulders evasively. "Maybe once or twice."

That, Trine knew, probably meant he had been having trouble for a long time. Many patients, especially men, refuse to accept that they're sick.

"Do you smoke?"

Again he made an irritated hand gesture.

"Gave it up years ago," Gregers said. "Say, can a guy get a cup of coffee in here?"

"You need to fast, Gregers. No coffee today." She patted his hand. "And now, could you please help me out. I need to put this IV in your hand."

"Uh," he said, eyeing her skeptically. "Says who?"

Trine counted to ten in her head. She and Klaus had fought again yesterday, yelling at each other until the kids woke up and started crying. It had started with a stupid misunderstanding and then escalated from there, the way it usually did. Something about who did the most housework, about the kids' field trip, and how disappointed they both were in each other. Sometimes maintaining a normal, bearable everyday life for their little family seemed like an insurmountable task. Now she felt worn out, her feet swelling in her support hose, and her ability to deal with cranky old men gone.

"We're going to inject contrast fluid into your arteries so we can do something called a myocardial scintigraphy, just as soon as we can get you in. So you need to be fasting. That's why you need this IV."

"I want to talk to a doctor! Someone in charge." He stared straight ahead, as if she weren't worthy of his attention.

Trine felt a knot of pent-up frustration building in her belly. That old familiar wall in front of her, holding her back every time she dared to feel good enough, pretty enough, popular, and successful. The unlucky cards she had obviously drawn at birth. With a resolute motion, she took her patient's hand and started swabbing it with alcohol.

"What the hell are you doing?" he asked, pulling his hand back. "I want to talk to one of your supervisors!"

"They'll tell you the same thing I just have: You need an IV so that we can give you medicine and painkillers." She grabbed his frail fingers in a firm grip and brought the needle close to the thin skin on the back of his hand.

He howled in affected pain.

"What the hell kind of way is that to treat people? I'm going to complain!"

"I haven't even touched you yet." Trine saw the needle shaking between her fingers and gulped, suddenly on the verge of tears. "It's your own fault if I hurt you with this needle. You need to lie still."

"I don't take orders from you!"

Right as he slapped her hand away, the alarm went off. Not the nurse call button, which normally just meant a full bed pan, but the actual code alarm. That alarm always meant an emergency.

Trine dropped the IV and ran toward the sound. The alarm set off a stress response in her and surely in her coworkers as well. That's what it was designed to do: trigger immediate action. She felt an irrational spark of elation. After all, her expertise could mean the difference between life and death.

She ran as fast as she could down the white and gray hallway, past open doors, chairs, and beds. By the time she reached room seventeen, breathing hard, the endorphins were coursing through her body, making her feel high.

A small group was already gathered around the bed closest to the door, in which a frail woman suffering from a postoperative infection was lying. She'd had a pacemaker replaced, if Trine remembered correctly. Dr. Buch was resuscitating the patient along with an attendant and two of her nursing coworkers: Pia doing the external ventilation and Rebekka preparing the defibrillator paddles. A volley of orders flew back and forth.

"What's the rhythm?"

"No pulse, V-fib!"

"Stand clear. Check breathing and pulse!"

"Continue CPR!"

They worked together as one, a well-oiled machine, a coveted little club. Trine stepped up to the bed.

"Should I get the adrenaline ready?" she asked.

The doctor glanced fleetingly at her. She was young, not much older than Trine.

"Thanks, Trine, but we've got it."

The rejection stung. But only half as much as the very brief look Pia and Rebekka exchanged over the bed. She wasn't welcome.

Trine turned around and left the room without saying a word, put the voices and the hectic energy behind her and returned to the calm of the hallway. She wouldn't give them the pleasure of seeing her cry.

"It can't be here, can it?"

Jeppe pulled over to the side, peering out the windshield. An idyllic pond lay glassy and dark between weeping willows and beech trees, whose branches stretched up into the low-hanging clouds. Their leaves had only just started to turn, fluctuating from a bottle green to bright yellow and then dark red.

Out Thomas Larsen's passenger-side window, the old buildings of Brede Works, the cradle of Danish industry, were glowing white, and under them chuckled the water of the Mølleåen. Once upon a time the millstream had supplied energy for both copper production and clothing factories. Nowadays it was all just a museum and there was no one around, no traffic, no noise from stamping presses or assembly lines.

Jeppe remembered his mother dragging him out here to a special exhibit on China back when his cultural upbringing was at the top of her priority list. Back when they spent every weekend at the Louisiana Museum or the National Museum or attending plays, reading or watching art films in the original language. Poor Mom, his becoming a policeman must be the biggest disappointment of her life.

"The GPS says farther out, toward the Open Air Museum. Go straight ahead and then up the hill to the right." Larsen pointed through the fogged-up windshield. "Over there somewhere."

They crossed the creek toward the tall trees. As the road brought them up the hill, it started raining again.

"It should be on the right."

Jeppe stopped the car in front of a white stucco house with a glossy black tile roof behind a beech hedge and an electronic wrought iron gate. A discreet sign under the doorbell next to the gate confirmed that they had arrived at the Forest's Edge Youth Center. They got out and let the sound of the slamming car doors echo in the silence among the trees. Apart from the melancholy dripping from the branches, there wasn't a sound. It was both soothing and eerie.

The door opened before they had a chance to ring the bell, revealing a woman in her sixties standing in the doorway. She had short hair and glasses, was average height, and wore practical casual wear in faded summery colors. In one hand she held a lit cigarette.

"Come in! The gate closes automatically." Her voice and the gray skin on her face indicated that the cigarette in her hand was far from her first. Rita Wilkins looked like a woman who had worked hard and lived hard.

"We're celebrating a birthday today, so there's leftover coffee and cake in the kitchen. Let's go sit in there."

Rita Wilkins took a final, greedy puff on her cigarette and then put it out against the sole of her shoe in a practiced motion, before holding her hand out to them, her distracted eyes not making eye contact. She guided them through a front hall, so full of raincoats, backpacks, and shoes they almost couldn't see the walls and into a big open kitchen with a flowered tablecloth on the table, children's drawings on the cabinets, and stacks of dirty plates in the sink from the birthday breakfast. The kitchen looked like a normal family kitchen, just on a larger scale.

"The coffee is still hot, I bet. Just help yourselves!"

She pointed to an insulated carafe surrounded by multicolor mugs on the long table, then went to the sink and started rinsing plates and putting them in the dishwasher. She was in constant motion, almost gruff, not worrying about making noise or chipping the dishes.

They sat down, and Larsen poured them both coffee while Jeppe took out his notepad.

"As Detective Larsen explained on the phone, we're here to talk about the two murders that have taken place in Copenhagen in the last two days. One commonality between the victims is that they both worked in your old Butterfly House treatment facility . . ." Jeppe paused to give her an opportunity to respond, but she just nodded and returned to washing the dishes. "Could you tell us a little about that place?"

"Well, basically Butterfly House was a residential program," she explained without turning around, "that offered specialized rehab for children and teenagers suffering from psychiatric disorders or social challenges: schizophrenia, anxiety, eating disorders, and so on. Serious cases, but ones that still didn't qualify for full institutional care. My husband at the time, Robert, and I opened the home five years ago with a small, dynamic group of employees. We had room for up to six patients."

"But the facility closed two years ago. Why was that?"

She turned off the water and dug around

in the cupboard under the sink, took out a scouring pad, and straightened back up.

"There's a time and a place for everything. The kids were growing up. When they turn eighteen, they enter the adult system. . . ."

"But couldn't you have taken in new residents?" Jeppe put his pen to the paper but didn't write anything.

She shrugged her shoulders and turned the tap on again.

"Were there problems among the staff?" Jeppe asked.

"No, none of that. The staff was a great team, a real community. The core group of us worked together closely, and it was a prerequisite that we could cooperate smoothly."

And yet the facility had closed after only three years.

"So, the home functioned well?"

She hesitated for a moment with her back turned.

"When you're dealing with mental illness, there are always challenges. It can be tough work. But, yes, Butterfly House was a good place."

A hint of sadness had crept into her voice, which Jeppe couldn't quite decode.

"You had a number of nurses working. . . ."

"We had three, one full-time and two temps. Tanja Kruse worked full-time, and . . ." She shook her head tiredly. "I haven't been able to think of the names of the other two yet, or Alex's last name. The old contracts are up in one of the boxes in the attic; I just haven't had time to go through them."

"What about the young patients? Where did they go when Butterfly closed?"

"They were scattered to the winds and dispersed in the system." She had frozen at the sink, her voice distant. "We all were."

"Is it possible that one of the kids" — Jeppe searched for the right words — "could have a reason to take revenge against former staff members?"

She didn't respond to that.

Jeppe exchanged a glance with Larsen and was just about to ask again when Rita Wilkins dumped cutlery off a plate, straight into the sink, and then seemed to freeze again, her hands under the running water. To his surprise, Jeppe noticed that she was crying.

"I'm sorry that we need to be so blunt. . . ."

"I understand," she said, holding her hand up to stop him. "Of course you do. It's all just a little . . . much, all of this."

She turned off the water, dried her hands on her pants, and came over to the table, for the first time looking Jeppe in the eye.

"You're asking what happened to our patients." She took a deep breath and then exhaled heavily, sat down on the edge of a chair, and put her hands on the table, palms down, as if she didn't trust them to stay still if she didn't watch them. "Have you heard about Pernille?"

"No."

"Pernille Ramsgaard was one of the four kids who lived at Butterfly House. She had a serious eating disorder and was in really bad shape at times." Rita Wilkins broke off the eye contact and turned her hands palms up so she could inspect them while she talked.

"A little over two years ago, Pernille committed suicide. She was only seventeen. It's so sad when they lose hope that things can get better." Rita Wilkins grabbed a mug and passed it to Larsen, who immediately got up from his chair and poured her some coffee. When the mug was half full, she yanked it toward herself so that he had to jerk the carafe back upright to avoid spilling on the tablecloth.

"But unfortunately it happens. We had done everything we could for Pernille, but in the end she didn't want to keep going. Tragic, really tragic . . ."

"Is that why you closed Butterfly House?"

"Her parents blamed us for her death," she said, looking up.

"Us?" Jeppe held his pen at the ready, over the still blank page of his notepad.

"Robert and me, the whole staff." She drank a little coffee, set down the cup, and placed her hands flat on the table again. "They thought we had failed, that we were responsible for Pernille's death. Their grief and anger were understandable. . . ."

"Do you believe they were justified in feeling that way?"

She shrugged and said, "They sued us. That didn't get them anywhere. But it cost us the place. The committee dropped our grant, just like that. The cost per patient is one hundred and fifty thousand kroner a month for round-the-clock care. I mean, there was nowhere else for us to get that money."

Her chin crumpled.

Jeppe hesitated. The woman before him was clearly upset. Why, then, did he still get the sense that she was carefully picking and choosing what she did and didn't tell them?

"Did Bettina Holte and Nicola Ambrosio have a special connection with Pernille, more so than the others?"

"No, not really." Rita got up abruptly, walked back to the sink, and continued tossing the cutlery into the dishwasher with the rest of the dirty dishes.

"The only person Pernille was more attached to than the rest of us was her caseworker."

Jeppe flipped back through his notes and asked, "Kim Sejersen, the social worker?"

"Yes, but really we all participated in the treatment as one big family." She closed the door of the dishwasher and turned the knob until it started humming.

"Ramsgaard, you said? Pernille Ramsgaard?"

"Her father's name is Bo, her mother, Lisbeth. They still contact me regularly. I have their address and phone numbers if you want to talk to them."

Rita walked over to a chest of drawers, opened one, and pulled out an address book. Jeppe watched her write on a slip of paper and gestured to Larsen that he should take it.

"Call them and ask if we can stop by!"

While Larsen called, Jeppe checked his own phone. Monica Kirkskov, the scientist at the Medical Museion, had texted that she had more information and would like to meet. And his mother had called twice. What was with all this sudden attention? Jeppe put the phone back in his pocket and stood up.

"Thank you for your time. Call us when you find the names of the old employees or if you happen to think of anything else we should know. And please look after yourself. There's a killer on the loose, so don't go around on your own for the next few days."

Rita was already on her feet. They followed her to the open front door, where she immediately lit another cigarette. Smoke billowed out into the moist forest air between the beech trees. A few yards from the door, Jeppe turned around.

"How did she kill herself, Pernille?"

Rita's lined face seemed to contract around the cigarette in a hungry hiss.

"She stole a knife while she was on kitchen duty and lay down in the bathtub at night. Cut her own wrists. We didn't find her until the next morning. In the water."

CHAPTER 9

The one policeman was in uniform and tall, like a catalog model, the other somewhat shorter, an older guy in civilian clothes with brightly colored suspenders. They introduced themselves as Officer Truelsen and Detective Falck respectively. Although their demeanor was subdued and discreet, they stood out on the ward, gleaming like a lighthouse in the sea, making the patients nervous. Simon Hartvig shook their hands with sweaty palms. Uniforms had no place in a psychiatric ward. The body found in the hospital's fountain that morning had already created plenty of alarm as it was. Simon fumbled to unlock the U8 staff room and hurriedly shepherded the policemen inside. The room smelled slightly from the lunch plates, still stacked in the sink, that he had promised to wash but not yet gotten around to. Now, in the company of these two pillars of authority, the scent of cured meats and liverwurst made him feel strangely awkward. The ward was used to police presence because officers would often bring new patients in. But this was different.

"We assume you're aware that a body was discovered on the hospital grounds this morning?" the catalog model asked.

Simon nodded.

"We're talking to staff members in all the wards of the hospital to find out if any of you saw anything. Could we have a seat?"

"Of course, I'm sorry." He pulled out a chair and sat down.

The policemen followed suit. It grew quiet, and it occurred to him that they were waiting for him to say something.

"Of course," he said again. "I heard about the body earlier, but unfortunately I don't know anything about it at all and haven't seen or heard anything relevant."

"When did your shift start?"

"Ten last night. I'm on the night shift most of this week."

"Long shift, huh?" the catalog model said, looking at his watch.

Simon's pulse accelerated. What was it with the police that made it seem like they could read your mind?

"Actually I've been off since noon, but I

had a meeting with one of my colleagues about a garden project. I was just on my way home. . . ."

"And you haven't seen anything suspicious, here on the ward or outside?"

"Nothing." He cleared his throat. "It's been really quiet. A coworker and I chatted and played cards most of the night."

"Have you by any chance seen a cargo bike on hospital grounds . . . ?"

"Uh, no . . . ?" Simon shook his head.

The two policemen exchanged a glance and then slowly stood. The older one tutted cryptically and looked at Simon. "Where can we find the charge nurse?"

"She's in her office," Simon said, quickly getting to his feet. "I'll get her for you."

He strode down the hall and found his colleague at her desk. She stood up smiling nervously.

"My turn?" she asked.

"Yes, they'd like to see you. I'm going home — just have to grab my coat."

"That's right, you're on duty again tonight."

They walked back to the staff room and the charge nurse greeted the two policemen. Simon took his coat and backpack from the row of hooks but didn't get any further before he heard her voice behind him.

"Simon, did you tell the police about Isak?"

"About Isak?" He turned around, trying to sound casual. "What do you mean?"

She hesitated and then said, "Well, how he must know both of the victims from his time at Butterfly House."

Simon froze with his raincoat halfway on and his backpack in his hand. The older of the two policemen eyed him suspiciously with a vertical wrinkle between his eyebrows.

"You wouldn't have time to stick around for a minute, would you?" the detective asked.

His expression strongly suggested that answering no was not an option. Simon took off his coat again and sat down. His shoulders felt heavy, like kettlebells.

Detective Falck cleared his throat and said, "Do I understand this correctly that you have a patient in this ward who used to live at Butterfly House?"

The charge nurse cast a sidelong glance at him, but he avoided her gaze. Then she nodded.

"Yes, we do. Isak Brügger, age seventeen. He'll be eighteen soon. He was admitted this spring after having lived in a treatment home in Næstved, where he moved when

Butterfly House closed. Simon is his case manager." She turned to him. "I suppose you're the one who knows him best. . . ."

Simon nodded reluctantly. The policemen seemed to be studying him but with no indication of what they were thinking.

"If you would be so kind as to tell us a little about Isak. . . ."

"I've only been assigned to him for about six months," he said with a shrug.

"What's wrong with him?"

The charge nurse interrupted. "We can't go into details about the individual patients. But most of our teenagers have schizophrenia combined with other diagnoses, personality disorders, for example."

"Is Isak dangerous?"

Simon looked down at the table, anger suddenly churning in his stomach. Every person can be pushed into violence if the circumstances are right, diagnosis or not. He had felt that on his own body.

"Isak sometimes displays externalizing behaviors when he's feeling stressed," the nurse said, her voice revealing that the question had bothered her as well. "But he's in treatment and we staff members are always here with him."

"*Displays externalizing behaviors* . . . is that a nice way of saying he's dangerous?" the

185

older detective asked, looking around at the impersonal staff room as if hoping to find better answers lurking in the corners.

The charge nurse looked over at Simon, seeking support. When he didn't respond, she sighed.

"Isak can be violent," she said, "but only when he is under a lot of pressure."

The two policemen sat for half a minute, looking at them. Then the catalog model leaned forward on his elbows and squinted his eyes.

"Does he think he's two different people?"

"Schizophrenia is an overall designation for mental illnesses that interfere with thoughts and feelings, not with personality." The charge nurse could not keep the sarcasm out of her voice. "Isak is a sweet, gifted boy. He just has some challenges."

"Can he go out? Is he allowed to leave the hospital when he wants to?" asked the older detective, his eyes on Simon.

"Isak has been committed," Simon answered, addressing the colorful suspenders instead of his face. "Certainly he's allowed to leave the ward, but only for a home visit and only by agreement."

"Is he on red or yellow papers?"

When patients are committed in Denmark, a yellow form means the admission is for the patient's own possibility of recovery, a red form that the patient is a danger to himself and others.

"I don't understand why you're asking so many questions about Isak. He hasn't left the hospital in weeks. Everyone can confirm that. How could his connections to an old treatment center be important to the murder?" Simon heard the irritation build in his own voice, even though he was trying to quash it.

"Two former employees of the treatment center have been murdered. One of them was found a few hundred yards from here. That makes it important for us to find out as much about Isak as we can. So, red or yellow?" The older detective's voice sounded a little sharp around the edges.

"Red. And, of course, that means he's *crazy,* right?" Simon straightened up. "Being schizophrenic doesn't automatically make you a murderer."

The police officers exchanged yet another glance and then stood up.

"Should we see if Isak is willing to talk to us?"

"Yes." The charge nurse smiled anxiously. "Uh, why don't we see if he is in the mood to chat? But I have to second what Simon said. Isak has been on short, accompanied trips on the hospital grounds this week, and as we said our patients aren't allowed to leave the ward without our knowledge."

Simon got up, opened the door, and led the way to Isak's room. He knocked and then peeked in. The charge nurse and the two policemen waited behind him.

"I'm afraid he's resting." Simon turned back around toward them. "Sometimes Isak sleeps fitfully in the night; it's not unusual for him to be tired during the day."

"Can't we wake him up?" the older detective asked.

"Oh, there's no waking Isak up once he finally falls asleep."

"Then I suppose we'll have to come back," the detective said, and turned to the nurse. "We would like to review the ward's security systems with you before we interview the rest of the staff. Could we do that now?"

"Of course."

Both officers gave Simon firm handshakes before the nurse led them back to her office. He watched them disappear around the corner and felt relief spread through his body. When they were gone from view, he carefully opened the door and went into the room. Isak lay heavy and motionless, his back to the world. The skin on his cheeks was diaphanous, taut over his angular bones, and his body quivered with the excess energy that constantly trembled through him, even in his sleep.

Simon sat down on the edge of the bed and looked at the sleeping boy. Was Isak aware, he wondered, of what he had to do for his sake?

Grief permeates all living things and drains out their color. Grief is a nothingness that runs through blood vessels, stalks, and bricks, until only the shell of what has been remains. Jeppe regarded the Ramsgaard family's house with a tingling sense of unease. The terraced house showed no clear signs of neglect. And yet a sadness hung so heavily over the place that it was palpable, even from out in the car. Maybe it was the swing set, swaying in the wind, green with moss and outgrown by the family's kids, maybe the name sign, where Pernille Ramsgaard was still listed two years after her death.

Even the doorbell sounded sad, a frail, uncertain tone that could hardly be heard from the front step.

Jeppe pulled back the hood of his raincoat and pricked up his ears to listen for motion inside. Thomas Larsen came up beside him just as the door was opened a crack. A small face at belly button height peeked timidly out at them without saying anything.

"Hi, is your mom or dad home?"

The child vanished into the house but left the door ajar. Jeppe cautiously pushed it open and stepped into a dark hallway. There were stacks of flattened moving boxes along the wall, and the bulb in the overhead light had burned out. They hesitantly followed her, passing the boxes and ending up in a living room, where newspapers and little piles of clothes were strewn on the furniture and a gray membrane of dust lay over every horizontal surface. On a shelf stood a family portrait with a young girl, who must be Pernille, smiling a close-lipped smile between her mother, father, and two other children. It looked to have been taken many years ago. On the faded sofa next to the shelf a man wearing earbuds was lying with his eyes closed. His hair was tinged with gray and hung in thin curls over his forehead, an unruly beard on his chin. He had to be nearing sixty and looked like someone who had given up on his appearance a long time ago.

"Dad's napping," whispered the child, who on closer inspection turned out to be a girl. She looked like she was ten or eleven, but small for her age and skinny. "Mom's not home."

She didn't provide any more details, just looked at them anxiously with her big eyes.

"We need to talk to your dad." Jeppe tried a reassuring smile. "Would you wake him up?"

The girl responded by running out of the room.

Jeppe stepped over the piles on the floor and gently put a hand on the man's shoulder. Bo Ramsgaard opened his eyes and looked at him, disoriented. He removed his earbuds, sat up, and pushed the curls off his forehead.

"You must be from the police?" he mumbled.

"Are you Bo Ramsgaard?"

The man nodded sluggishly.

"For good measure, we need to inform you that you may eventually be under investigation in this case, and that you're therefore not obligated to speak to us."

"Yeah, yeah!" He reached back behind the sofa and turned off his sound system. "Lisbeth's not home."

Jeppe looked around for somewhere to sit but quickly gave up the idea. "Are you moving?"

"Maybe," he said, and then stretched noisily and leaned back on the sofa.

"Like my colleague, Detective Larsen here, explained on the phone, we're here because of the murders that took place in Copenhagen today and yesterday. The two victims both worked at the Butterfly House while your daughter Pernille lived there. . . ."

"Hallelujah!" Bo exclaimed, and then waved both hands in the air next to his face.

"I'm sorry . . . ?" Jeppe said, puzzled.

"Forget about it. That was inappropriate. You had questions?"

Jeppe searched for an explanation for the father's outburst but didn't find it in his eyes, which were looking calmly back at him from under those gray curls.

"I am very sorry to learn of your daughter's death. Can I ask to begin with why she lived at Butterfly House?"

"Because she was too sick to live at home."

"What was wrong with her? Is it okay to ask about that?"

"I'm only happy to talk about Pernille," Bo said with a pained smile. "It's much worse not to talk about her. . . . Pernille suffered from bulimia. She was an elite gymnast and very focused on being as thin as possible. Got something like a high from throwing up a meal, and then she hated herself afterward. She started cutting herself

192

when she was thirteen."

The father picked up a pillow off the floor and put it in his lap. He talked routinely about his daughter's illness, but Jeppe sensed a deep pain still streaming under his words. The pain unique to parents who can't help their children.

"We tried everything. Pernille's teenage years were one succession of hospital stays, interventions, and treatment. She moved into Butterfly House after a month at Bispebjerg Hospital. The psychiatrist at the hospital, Peter Demant, was the one who advised the move. He was also affiliated with Butterfly House."

The father ran his hands through the thin curls and sighed heavily. His lips were tightly pursed, as if they were holding back a well of emotions.

"Pernille was a delicate girl, a sensitive soul. Gifted and goal-oriented, as I mentioned she was a dedicated gymnast. Her chances of getting onto the national team and participating in the Olympics were good, until . . . My wife and I supported her. She was in treatment, and even though there were relapses, things were gradually getting better." He smoothed the pillow in his lap as he spoke, running his hand over the same spot again and again. "At first living at the Butterfly House was okay, but then . . . she started losing weight again and had a hard time sleeping at night. We didn't realize how bad it was until it was too late."

"What went wrong?"

Bo didn't seem to hear the question.

"We should have moved her," he said. "We discussed it, but . . . it wasn't that easy to just do. Plus we were having some difficulties at home at the time." He looked up. "It can be hard to decide from a distance whether it's the situation around your child that is wrong or if she's just going through a bad phase. Pernille was loyal to that place and its methods, didn't tell us anything."

"Then what happened?"

"In July 2015 she was home for vacation. She was doing all right then, skinny but eating, and participating in family life. When she went back to that place after summer, it only took a week. Then she couldn't cope anymore."

"She slit her wrists?"

"Yes."

A pained look shot through the father's face. But there was more to the expression than pain. He was angry.

"What exactly couldn't she endure anymore?"

"I don't know. She didn't leave a goodbye

note, and the employees had no explanation for what happened."

"I understand from Rita Wilkins that you later sued Butterfly House. . . ."

"We felt this tremendous need to talk about Pernille's death and to understand what had happened, but they refused. They were nice enough in the days immediately following her death, while we were packing up her things and trying to accept the fact that she was gone. But the second we started asking questions, they all referred us to Rita, and Rita refused to talk to us." A haze clouded over his eyes, making them distant. "You always ask yourself if there was anything you could have done. But we also started asking ourselves if maybe there was something *they* could have done, something they *didn't* do. Why else would they refuse to talk to us like that? What were they trying to hide?"

Jeppe pushed one of the stacks aside on the dining table and perched on the edge. His legs relaxed, but his brain was teeming with information.

"What role did Bettina Holte and Nicola Ambrosio play in all of this? Was Pernille closely connected to them?"

"Not particularly." Bo shrugged. "Pernille got along well with everyone. She didn't have high standards for other people, only for herself."

"I'm assuming that you and your wife knew them? Could you tell us anything about them? What they were like?"

Bo raised his eyebrows so far, they disappeared up under his gray curls.

"What's there to say? They were friendly enough, just not particularly good at their jobs."

Jeppe tried to figure out what was going on inside the man on the sofa. Bo seemed tormented but also oddly reluctant. Was he hiding something?

"I can certainly understand how it must be difficult to talk about Pernille, but we have two murders to solve, two very nasty murders, and your daughter knew the victims. . . ."

Bo shook his head angrily and looked away.

"I need to understand this," Jeppe said after a moment's hesitation. "Do you mean that Rita Wilkins and her employees were partly responsible for Pernille's death?"

The father's face crumpled up, as if someone had just run a piece of chalk down a clean blackboard.

"Rita apparently had the all right connections, and managed to convince the local authorities to give her grant money to start a residential program in her private home. Several of the social workers weren't certified. They didn't have the necessary credentials. The staff was either incompetent or too lax to do anything." Bo's hand dropped back down onto the pillow.

"Where were you Sunday night and Monday night?"

"Here. Both nights." Bo looked Jeppe straight in the eye, completely calm. "With my daughter and my wife. We were asleep, or trying, at least. Sleep has been pretty challenging since Pernille's death."

"And your wife can confirm that you were here?"

He flung up his hands as if to say, *Duh.* Jeppe took that as a yes.

"Where is she, Lisbeth?" Jeppe asked.

"At a retreat, near Växjö in Sweden. She'll be home Thursday."

"We need to ask for her cell phone number so we can contact her."

"Phones aren't allowed at the retreat, but there is a landline in the office in case of emergencies."

"Daddy?" The skinny girl had snuck in and was standing by the end of the sofa. "We're supposed to answer that thing for school."

"Yes, honey. I'm coming." Bo smiled tiredly at his daughter and looked pointedly at his watch. "Well, you'll have to excuse me, but I need to take care of my daughter and get started on dinner."

"We're almost done. . . ." Jeppe held up a finger to show that they only needed a minute. "Do you know anything about the other three teenagers who lived at the home?"

"Marie, Kenny, and Isak. We tried to get them to talk, too, after Pernille killed herself, but . . . not a peep. Watertight bulkheads. I have no idea where they are today." He got up and tossed the pillow onto the sofa. "Dinner calls. Do you guys need anything else?"

"If you could give us the number for your wife's retreat." Jeppe stood up and handed his notepad to the father, who found a number on his phone and wrote it down. "Oh, you don't happen to own a cargo bike, do you?"

"A cargo bike? No, the front yard is full of bikes of all sizes, but no cargo bike. Why, do you need to haul something heavy?"

Jeppe ignored this, and they walked back past the moving boxes to the front door. He stopped there for a moment to do up his jacket, then turned around as an afterthought.

"Who do you think is killing the staff from Butterfly House?"

"No idea," Bo said, his eyes dark, "but when you find out who it is, I'll be the first to thank him."

CHAPTER 10

There are two kinds of people: those who eat to live and those who live to eat. Over the twenty-odd years of their marriage, Anette and Svend had frequently said so to each other, both knowing that he fell in the latter category. When he opened his eyes in the morning, the first thing Svend thought of was what he would make for dinner. He often started preparing bread or a casserole right after breakfast. It was one of the many qualities that made her love him.

Anette pushed what was left of the factory-breaded chicken breast around on her plate. You truly don't know what you've got until it's gone.

"Are you done?" Svend reached for her plate, their daughter in the crook of his arm.

She nodded and let him clear the table as she emptied her glass of tap water. *When breastfeeding it is important to drink plenty of water, preferably two liters a day.* Well, fine!

If that's what it took. . . . "Not the most exciting meal, I know, but there's really not much time for real cooking with the princess here." Svend kissed the baby's chubby cheeks and made a goofy face at her.

"It's fine. I wouldn't mind being able to fit into my jeans again soon." Anette looked down at her spare tire, resting unattractively in her lap. Childbearing machine, milk cow. When would her body start feeling like her own again?

"Did you buy diapers?"

Diapers! The one thing she was supposed to remember today.

"Ugh, damn it. I forgot. Sorry! Are we totally out?"

"Hm, well, we might make it. . . ."

"I can run over to BabySam now, before they close," Anette said, jumping up. "Then I can pick up wipes, too." She hurried out to the front hall and yanked her raincoat down from the hook. "There's breast milk in the freezer, you can feed her a bottle."

Svend followed her with the baby, who was beginning to fuss.

"You don't need to drive anywhere. We still have a few. . . ."

"I'm going! There's nothing worse than running out of diapers. It's fine. I kind of need some air." Anette kissed her daughter on the forehead and ran out to the car. It wasn't until she let the clutch out that she realized she had forgotten to kiss Svend goodbye.

Gundsømagle. If she drove fast, she could be there in twenty minutes, about the same amount of time it would take her to drive to the baby supply store in Køge. Then she could get the diapers on the way home afterward.

Anette pulled the envelope with the home's address out of her pocket and entered it into the car's GPS, her eyes sort of half on the road. If the bigwigs knew she was heading out by herself to do some investigating in the middle of her maternity leave, she would be suspended on the spot. Luckily they did not.

In a few minutes she was on the highway and could speed up. The wipers whipped back and forth across the windshield, and she turned on the radio, not caring what they were playing. Enjoyed the simple pleasure of being on the move and by herself for once.

Anette had never speculated much about love. Either it was there, like with Svend and the dogs, or it wasn't. In reality, love between parents and children was probably a modern phenomenon. She would bet that her great-grandparents had a more practical approach to parenting; something about having extra manpower and someone to take care of you when you got old. An exchange of goods and services like so many other relationships whose ultimate goal was to ensure the survival of the species.

She drove through Østrup and then sped up again. Love could be a burden as much as a gift, especially when it was expected and demanded.

On the outskirts of the village Gundsømagle, a dirt road called Dybendalsvej ran like a furrow through the muddy autumn fields. The disused home was easy to find, for there was only one house on the street, a For Sale sign out front marking the spot. Set back a little from the road and hidden behind an overgrown hedgerow at the end of a bumpy driveway sat Butterfly House, a main house with two wings, blue plaster walls, red tile roof, and a flagpole out front. Boarded-up windows and bushes that had started to take over the courtyard in front were the first signs that the place was no longer inhabited. If the place had closed two years ago, why hadn't the house been sold yet?

The rain beat down on her face. She wasn't going to get anything out of standing there in the fading light getting wet. Quickly, she walked up to the main house and tried the door.

It creaked but was locked and didn't push open. She wouldn't be surprised if an abandoned building like this was used by the homeless or teenagers looking for a place to party. There must be a way to get in.

Around back, Anette found a set of crumbling stairs, which, sure enough, led down to a door with a lock that had been broken. She cautiously opened it and stepped into a cellar with a low ceiling, turned on her phone's flashlight, and moved down a dusty gray hallway, past a large room with tiles on the walls and a series of metal shelves that no one had bothered to take with them.

She edged her way around a chest freezer, which sat with the lid open, leaning against the wall, and wound up in front of a metal door just next to the stairs that led up to the ground floor. Anette tried the handle. The metal door was locked. Hm, maybe something of value had been left in the cellar after all.

Anette continued up the stairs, moving cautiously on the mildew-covered steps while holding on tightly to the handrail. Her foot hit a bottle, and it rolled down, hitting the concrete floor with a clink that sent a little chill up her spine. Suddenly she was acutely aware of the slackness of her pelvic floor and her nonexistent abdominal muscles. Good thing she knew the house was abandoned!

The first floor had high ceilings and was more pleasant, despite the same damp smell and stacks of junk as in the basement. She shone her light around and saw a mostly gutted kitchen. The appliances had obviously been too valuable to leave behind. Her footsteps echoed between the bare walls and empty rooms. What had happened here that had ended up costing two people their lives in the most gruesome way?

After the kitchen she came to a long hallway with doors on both sides. She opened the first one: a bathroom. After that, a room with a closet and an outline on the wallpaper where the bed had once been. She stepped in and walked around the room, looking closely, trying to read the space, the way Jeppe always did, but didn't detect anything other than her own increasingly full breasts. She really needed to head back home soon.

The next room looked exactly the same. Anette shone her light around at the empty walls; on one of them someone had written a few words down by the floor, where the bed appeared to have been. She walked closer. Two words in felt tip marker, the handwriting childish and bold: *INVISIBLE MARIE.*

Marie? Anette turned on her flash and took a picture. On impulse, she checked outside the door. Well, I'll be, an old name sign. This room had once been inhabited by a Marie Birch.

She checked the other doors along the hallway but didn't find any other name signs. Who was Marie Birch, and why was she invisible?

Anette heard the sound of something scraping against the floor in the dark and jumped, knocking her breast against the doorframe. The pain made her curl over, her chest throbbing. She ought to be too mature for unexpected noises in an abandoned house to frighten the wits out of her. Anette cursed out loud. Here she was traipsing around in a deserted house for a murder investigation she wasn't even part of while her baby was missing her back home. It was just wrong.

She fumbled her way through the darkness, toward the front door, too anxious to get out to bother using the phone's flashlight. By the time her hand finally hit the door handle, her palms were so sweaty she almost couldn't turn the dead bolt.

The car engine broke the silence with a roar. Anette raced back down the country road, taking no notice of either potholes in the gravel or possible crossing animals. When she reached the highway, the car clock showed that she had been at the home for more than half an hour. BabySam was closed. Now she had to hurry back much faster than the permitted fifty miles per hour speed limit and either lie or fess up when she returned home without diapers. Both seemed equally unappealing.

Marie Birch closed her eyes and inhaled the sea breeze until her head felt light. It was a salty smell, fresh and good with hints of diesel oil, seaweed, wood, and glue, a scent that painted adventures and distant horizons on her retinas. Just like the Japanese garden she had once built on the windowsill of her room after she read a book about Japanese dolls. She had collected rocks and twigs, found scraps of fabric, and clipped cardboard for months, gluing and folding by the window in her room. As soon as she came home from school, she would vanish into her garden. Homey yet at the same time full of longing. Her mother had cried when she first saw it. A couple of months later, she had thrown it out without even asking Marie.

She got up from the bench in the camper, filled a pot, and fired up the little camp stove. Marie had gathered herbs at Refshaleøen all summer, sweet chervil and yarrow, and hung them to dry from the ceiling. Now she drank them as tea.

Pernille was the one who had taught her to drink tea. She had drunk it to smother her hunger, bucketsful of calorie-free, hot tea between all those meals she didn't eat. Tea to make it cozy, tea for hunger, tea to wash down the pills.

Marie poured boiling water over the herbs and watched as it turned brown. The steam billowed up from her cup to settle under the low ceiling, like Mother's long baths that used to fill the bathroom with thick steam for hours. One time the door was closed for so long that Marie ended up going in. She found Mother on a footstool with her terry-cloth bathrobe open and her hand full of pills, bottom lip trembling unsettlingly. When Mother noticed her, she threw the pills in the trash can and went to bed.

The next morning her mother hugged her tight. *I'm doing my best with you, sweetie. I'm really doing my best, so much so that some-times there's no room for myself.*

Marie fished the sweet chervil out of her cup, burning her fingers on the hot tea. She sat down on the bench and looked out at the city's reflection in the dark water. Two were dead. Still, she was calm.

When you've suffered from panic attacks most of your life, calm is never something you take for granted. The panic attacks sit in your body until you die. Marie remembered each and every one of them. One morning at Butterfly House she had woken up with blood on her thighs; her first menstruation and no mother to discuss it with. She wasn't prepared and didn't know what to do about the stained sheet. Bettina had taken care of the situation in her usual no-nonsense manner, finding pads and changing the sheets without commenting. But in the kitchen over breakfast Bettina had shared the news with everyone. Nicola had congratulated her and played a celebratory song. Marie had cringed.

Was it the experience, the unwanted reveal, or her own insecurity that had triggered the attack?

Or was it the antianxiety medicine she took after breakfast that felt invasive and wrong? Like a foreign body that was trying

209

to destroy her from inside, planting compulsive suicidal thoughts and claustrophobia in her head and body?

Whatever the trigger, the attack came on, forcing her to lie flat on her stomach to dull the nausea and the cold sweats. She threw up her breakfast and her mouth went dry from trying to explain what was wrong.

He had come and sat with her. Too close, uncomfortable, she pulled away from his touch. What had he said? Gently, as he stroked her forehead, his hands lingering on her skin: *Don't be afraid, Marie. I'll help you. Everything will be all right again.*

She drank the tea in little gulps. It tasted bitter and healthy.

The anxiety that had crippled her for years seemed far away now. It was almost as if the deaths alleviated her agony, erased Bettina's rough hands, and reduced Nicola's clumsy guitar playing to faint ripples on her past. But then she was the lucky one. She had escaped the system and was able to live on her own. Things were different now.

She had to go see him, even though the thought of stepping into a hospital and having to talk to nurses and social workers turned her stomach.

There was no way around it.

■ ■ ■ ■

"Is there anything else you need?"

Esther de Laurenti kept her tone more accommodating than she felt. There was something about Gregers that occasionally made it hard — no, impossible — to practice normal courtesy and consideration.

"Is a little peace and quiet too much to ask?" Gregers scowled at the poor other patient, who had the misfortune to be sharing the hospital room.

Esther lifted the tray with its dirty plates off the bed and set it on a table by the wall. She had brought a portion of the homemade pasta for Gregers and let Alain have the rest.

"Why don't you just be happy the tests are over with and you're finally allowed to eat again?"

"Those spaghetti things were cold." Gregers pulled the blanket up to his chin like a spoiled child. "And I'm *not* a big fan of macaroni!"

"Well, I'm sorry I couldn't warm them up right here by your bed. Although obviously you *could* have eaten the hospital chicken breast for dinner if my homemade ravioli weren't good enough for you." She drew the curtain between the two beds, smiling

211

apologetically at the other patient. Listening to other people's bellyaching is about as much fun as getting a root canal.

"Just tell me if you want me to leave, Gregers. I am not here for my own personal amusement."

Gregers lay there fuming, looking at the dark windows and then grumbled, "You can stay for a bit." Then he pointed to an armchair in the corner of the room.

"Oh, how kind of you," Esther said sarcastically.

He cleared his throat.

"Wouldn't you please stay for a bit, Esther? I'm having such stupid thoughts."

Knowing that was as close to an apology as she would ever get from Gregers, she sat down and smiled at him encouragingly.

"Would you like to tell me about them, your thoughts?"

"Just, you know," he said, looking down, "am I going to get out of here alive? That kind of thing. There's no point in talking about it."

She hesitated, suspecting that her next question would not be welcome. "Gregers, have you considered that we should maybe contact your kids? If maybe now . . ."

"No way!"

Gregers had lost touch with his three adult

children when he and his wife divorced twenty-one years earlier, and whatever the reason for the falling-out, the wound was so deep that it didn't seem like anything could heal it. Esther, who had given up a child for adoption at birth herself and hadn't had any opportunity to make contact, had a really hard time understanding his stance. Not a day went by when she didn't regret giving up her baby and wished she could go back and change it.

"I guess I could just sit here and read the paper. How's that?"

Gregers nodded gratefully. He looked tired.

She found the iPad in her purse and started reading *Politiken* online. Browsed the newspaper and found the most recent article about the murders in the city's fountains. She always read the culture and crime sections first; something might miraculously inspire her to start writing again.

The police confirmed that both cases were likely the work of a single killer and were searching for people who had seen a cargo bike that apparently had something to do with the murders. They were also asking people with knowledge of the identity of two unnamed nurses and a cook named Alex who had worked at a now closed

213

residential facility to come forward. The journalist had found one of their former coworkers and obtained a statement from him. Esther was puzzled by the name, Peter Demant. The psychiatrist she had seen just yesterday had worked with the two murder victims? The hairs on the back of her neck rose just thinking about it: a mixture of thrill and curiosity.

She found Jeppe Kørner's number in her contacts and called. Since their paths had crossed the previous year in connection with a murder case, they had stayed in touch, more than that even. They had become friends.

"Kørner speaking." He sounded busy. He usually did.

"Hi, Jeppe. I'm sorry. Of course you're busy with the case."

"Hi, Esther. Yeah, you can say that again. I'm still stuck at the station. Everything all right?"

Suddenly it occurred to her how long it had been since they had last spoken. Over the last year, their growing friendship had surprised them both. Usually they talked on the phone once a week and routinely met for dinner or to see a play. To her great surprise, Jeppe had turned out to enjoy the theater as much as she did, and she liked to skim through the season's schedules to find performances that would interest them both. Despite their age difference and their completely different lives, they had become confidants. But she hadn't gotten around to telling Jeppe about her depression or the fact that she had begun seeing a psychiatrist, and now it seemed silly to start explaining that she was feeling better again. Why waste his time with longwinded coincidences when he was busy solving a double homicide? Just because she was curious.

"Gregers is having heart trouble." Esther decided to stick to the essentials. "He's lying here next to me at National Hospital."

"Oh no," Jeppe sighed. "I'm sorry to hear that. Is he okay?"

"Yes, or hopefully he will be. They're going to run some tests and then make a decision on whether to operate."

"Do you want me to come?"

"Thank you, Jeppe," Esther said, her heart overflowing at his compassion. "That means so much to me. I know how busy you are. How about this: I'll keep you posted by text for the time being? Then we'll see if things start to improve for him."

She said goodbye to Jeppe and put her phone away, then looked over at Gregers and realized he had fallen asleep, the little stinker. Hopefully the doctors could offer him yet another balloon dilation so his blocked arteries could be of use for a little longer. Age might be against him, but other than that he was as healthy as a busker. It would be a shame if he wasn't able to make the most of the rest of his life.

She packed up her things, put on her waterproof trench coat, and practically crashed into a nurse entering the room with a pill tray.

"Hi, I was just on my way out. Gregers is asleep," she whispered with a smile, trying to edge around the nurse.

"Are you his wife?"

"No, I'm a good friend. I just came by with some dinner."

"Well, that was sweet of you. Hopefully he'll get a good rest. I can give him a little something to help him sleep if he wakes up." The nurse moved past her into the room.

Esther turned around hesitantly in the doorway to watch her. *Trine,* her name tag read. Trine started checking the blood pressure of the patient by the door, smiling and efficient. Half a minute later she looked back up at Esther, who hadn't yet left.

"Can I help you?"

"Oh, no. I just wanted to . . . Gregers doesn't need sleeping pills. He always sleeps like a rock."

"We'll take good care of your friend," the nurse said, and smiled.

Esther nodded and closed the door behind her with a nagging feeling that she ought to stay at the hospital.

"Man, that roast was tough! It was like gnawing on Queen Elizabeth's labia."

"Whoa, Larsen, just because Anette Werner isn't here, you don't need to talk like her." Sara thwacked Thomas Larsen on the shoulder. Even so, Jeppe noted that she was smiling at the crude joke.

The smell of roast pork hung heavily over Homicide's small break room. Jeppe cracked the window open, gathered up the remnants of the team's dinner, and tossed them in the trash. No need to expose anyone to that meal a second time.

Falck yawned loudly without covering his mouth, while Larsen balanced paper cups of coffee, offering them around. Even Sara had one, and she usually never drank coffee. Jeppe poured milk into his and yawned as well.

"Okay, folks." Jeppe noted on his Omega watch that it was close to 9:00 p.m. "Let's do a summary and divvy up tasks for tomorrow, so we can go home to bed. Falck, how did it go at Bispebjerg Hospital, any witnesses to our fountain murder?"

Falck straightened up with unexpected zippiness and said, "No usable testimony unfortunately. We were there most of the day. But it turns out that one of the patients in their pediatric psych ward used to live at Butterfly House and knew both victims."

He paused for dramatic effect, letting the statement sink in.

"Isak Brügger?" Jeppe volunteered.

Falck, looking slightly deflated at having his big reveal spoiled, said, "Unfortunately he was asleep, and it didn't seem right to wake him up. So we haven't talked to him yet. The staff says he hasn't left the hospital all week. It's a closed ward, doors are kept locked and it's staffed around the clock. We'll interview him in the next couple of days."

"It *might* be a coincidence?" Jeppe squeezed his eyes shut.

"Yeah, or it might not. We'll see." Falck raised one bushy eyebrow and hooked his thumbs under his suspender straps.

"By the way I've located psychiatrist Peter Demant," Sara broke in, looking every bit as tired as she felt, "and nurse Tanja Kruse. They both live and work in Copenhagen. . . ."

"We'll interview them tomorrow." Jeppe nodded at Falck to indicate that he should set it up.

"But I haven't yet found the cook from Butterfly House. It's kind of hard since we only have the name Alex to go on. The same is true of the two part-time nurses, whose names the owner couldn't remember at all." Sara sounded defensive, as if it bugged her to not yet have completed her assignment.

"Rita Wilkins did promise to locate those names. Let's call her so we can proceed. Remind me, were there any other staff members?"

"One more, a man named Kim Sejersen. He was a social worker, so we've asked their union for help locating him."

Jeppe got up and walked over to close the window. The sentimental scent of rain on asphalt hit him, and he stood there for a second breathing it in before latching the window shut and turning back to the others.

"Larsen and I interviewed Bo Ramsgaard, the father of Pernille, one of Butterfly House's other residents. His daughter committed suicide when she was only seventeen, even though she was in treatment. He claims that the staff neglected their work and let the kids down. He thinks they didn't intervene soon enough in his daughter's case. He and his wife, Lisbeth, sued Rita Wilkins and got the home shut down, but the case ended there. They tried to get the police to bring charges against the director but lacked evidence of the alleged neglect. Apparently none of the other employees was willing to testify." Jeppe returned to his chair and sat down. "But the Ramsgaard family does have a clear-cut motive of revenge."

"Do they have alibis?" Sara was leaning forward on her elbows like an eager teenager.

"Hard to say. The mother is at a meditation retreat in Sweden, where the attendees are not allowed to bring their phones, one of those disconnect sorts of retreats. The father claims they were both home on Sunday night, but we don't have her confirmation of that yet. And he seems . . . I don't know . . . what do you think, Larsen?"

"I think he seems pretty fucked-up," Larsen said, flipping the hair out of his eyes with a slight toss of his head.

"Agreed." Jeppe let out a sigh. "So, based on the golden rule of motive plus opportunity, I think we ought to keep an eye on Bo Ramsgaard. I've asked for a surveillance team to be stationed outside their house overnight." He checked his watch again. "We need to get some sleep. Falck and I will interview Tanja Kruse and Peter Demant from Butterfly House tomorrow. Larsen, will you call Rita Wilkins for the last few pieces of information?"

"I'm on it," Larsen confirmed. "I might look into her ex-husband, Robert Wilkins, too. He was apparently a co-owner of the place."

"Good plan," Jeppe said, catching Sara's eye. "And, Saidani . . ."

"I'm trying to locate the former residents — the kids." Sara smiled and looked down at her notes. "Isak Brügger lives at Bispebjerg Hospital; Marie Birch, who's apparently living on the streets; and Kenny Ewald, who moved to Asia somewhere. I think I might also look into Pernille's —".

Sara was interrupted by a knock on the door. It opened before any of them had a chance to respond to reveal a rain-soaked Monica Kirkskov. When she spotted Jeppe, she broke into a big grin.

"There you are!"

"Monica, what are you doing here?"

Jeppe could sense the other detectives sending him curious looks. Out of the corner of his eye he saw Thomas Larsen sit up in his chair with an interested smile. She was uncommonly pretty, Jeppe could certainly see that. Dark, rain-moistened curls outlined her face, and her curves were emphasized by her raincoat's belt.

"Yes, well, you said I should call if I thought of anything. I did actually try earlier today, but . . . anyway, police headquarters is right on my way home from the museum. . . ."

She was looking only at him.

Jeppe, feeling slightly embarrassed, turned to his colleagues and said, "This is Monica Kirkskov, an expert on antique medical devices, including the scarificator."

"Am I interrupting something?"

"Oh, it's fine. We were actually just wrapping things up here." Jeppe clasped his hands. "Let's call it a day."

He sought out Sara's eyes to signal that she should wait for him, but she deftly avoided his gaze and exited the break room without saying goodbye.

Larsen edged past Jeppe, giving him a rather unsubtle look, which left Jeppe feeling like a cad who had been caught red-handed.

"Well, what are you selling?" Jeppe held out his hand in invitation. "I mean, what information do you have?"

"Let me just slip out of my coat, if that's okay?" Monica asked coyly.

"I'm sorry. It's been a long day." Jeppe pulled out a chair for her but remained standing himself.

"The reason I stopped by is that I heard on the news that Peter Demant is connected to your murder case."

"And you know him?"

She nodded vigorously.

"We studied medicine together ten to twelve years ago, until I dropped out. I haven't been in touch with him since and didn't know him well, but . . ." She furrowed her brow and smiled to herself, as if she wasn't quite sure how to proceed. "How much do you know about humoral pathology?"

"Uh, yeah. I wouldn't say that's my forte," Jeppe conceded.

"In antiquity, people believed in humorism, which is to say that the body was a system comprising four liquids. For the body to be healthy it was essential for these liquids, or humors, to be in balance. The liquids were blood, phlegm, black bile, and yellow bile."

"Yummy."

She chuckled and said, "Not only that. The treatments were all liquid-related and had to do with bringing balance to the body, for example by giving people emetics. Or by bleeding them, sometimes with a scarificator."

Jeppe pricked up his ears.

"The body's four liquids were linked to the four seasons and the four fundamental elements — it was all really very holistic — and people were said to have four different temperaments, depending on which bodily liquid they had the most of. The thoughtful melancholic had too much black bile, for example. And the friendly, but somewhat passive, phlegmatic had too much mucous, and so on."

She eyed him expectantly. Jeppe smiled. Her mellow voice hit him right in the abdomen.

"That's very interesting," he conceded, "but I don't really see —"

"This might be totally ridiculous. I know how it must sound, but . . ." She leaned forward, giving him an unobstructed view of her cleavage. "Cholerics, who had too much yellow bile and were associated with the blood circulation, were aggressive and extroverted, considered quick thinkers, very independent and decisive. In antiquity most murderers would probably have been seen as having a choleric temperament."

"We have a rather different way of classifying criminals today, I suppose," Jeppe said, wondering if she had really come here to tell him about the antiquity's view of human nature.

"I'm aware of that. But bleeding someone to death with a scarificator isn't exactly a modern way of killing. It might make sense to consider a historical view of things. Or maybe not, that's for you to decide." She held up her hand to indicate that she was getting to the point. "The study of the four bodily liquids and how they relate to disease and temperament dates all the way back to Hippocrates, but over time it has developed into a regular typology of anthroposophical temperaments, among others by Rudolf Steiner, the founder of the Waldorf philosophy of education. According to that typology, the choleric looks a specific way. He is short and stocky, upright, with sharp features and dark eyes. He walks decisively and quickly and usually has red or dark hair."

Jeppe cleared his throat. She waved her hand again to show that she wasn't done.

"Perhaps it sounds silly, but back in medical school we actually used to call Peter Demant 'the choleric' behind his back, because that is exactly how he looks and acts."

Jeppe looked at her without responding.

"Okay," she said, shaking her head with a laugh, "perhaps it's not exactly a smoking gun, but maybe it could be useful to you anyway?"

Monica Kirkskov smiled, and Jeppe suddenly wasn't sure what exactly she thought could be useful to him. He held out his hand to her.

"At any rate, thank you so much for stopping by."

She rose, took her coat, and put it on slowly without losing that subtle, Mona Lisa smile. Only after her coat was tied did she accept his hand with a handshake that lasted slightly too long, and then they walked to the elevator.

"Thanks for the visit," he said. "It was . . . interesting."

For a long moment they stood maintaining charged eye contact until the elevator doors opened and she got in. The last he saw of her before the doors closed was her smile.

Sara's office was empty, and her things were gone. That wasn't unexpected. She had to get home to relieve her mother, who had been babysitting. Jeppe checked his cell phone. She hadn't called or written, and when he called her, she didn't pick up. He waited a bit and then tried again, but still in vain. Apparently they would not be sleeping together tonight.

All right, then! Jeppe threw his backpack on, pulled up his hood, and walked down to his bike and the steady rain.

Home to Mom.

■ ■ ■ ■

WEDNESDAY,
OCTOBER 11

■ ■ ■ ■

Chapter 11

Whines from the rusty brakes of an early-morning garbage truck cut through the tower room, as his mother referred to the guest bedroom, and woke Jeppe from his sporadic sleep. The first thing he did was reach for his phone to see if more bodies had been found in any of Copenhagen's fountains this morning. Phew! None. There was, however, a text message from Monica Kirkskov, saying that he was welcome to call if he had questions. Absolutely any time, she said.

Sara on the other hand had not been in touch, and as Jeppe lay there waking up, he contemplated where that left them. Not for the first time in their frail relationship he was thrown back to the trembling uncertainty that had been the basic emotion of his early teenage love endeavors. What did she want from him? What did he want from her, for that matter? Start a family or just have fun for as long as it lasted? Settle down or let love flare up and then die down on its own?

Jeppe looked up at the portrait of a woman his mother had over the guest bed. A strong face with a heavy brow and judging eyes that followed you everywhere. *How difficult and complicated everything is, when you're a grown-up,* he thought, swinging his legs over the side of the bed.

Under the cool water of the shower he tried to clear his head. Poor sleep, along with back pain and unnecessary worry, was yet another one of the gifts life bestowed upon you when you grew up. His mother had left early, probably to her yoga class, but had left a little breakfast of bread and boiled eggs for him. She had also set out an expired can of mackerel and a package of rice. Sometimes she was confused just after waking up. The gesture was touching, though, and Jeppe appreciated it. He also appreciated that his mother wasn't there. In the mornings he preferred to be alone. Sometimes that went for the rest of the day, too.

At eight forty-five, Detective Falck pulled up to the curb at the corner of Nørre Allé and Sankt Hans Square to pick Jeppe up in one of the police's black Opel Vectras.

Falck's big belly was pushing against the steering wheel and made the car seem undersize compared to its driver.

"Maybe I should drive?" Jeppe asked, eyeing him skeptically.

"No, no, it's fine. Hop in."

Jeppe climbed into the passenger seat and buckled his seat belt. Only when he was completely settled did Falck flip on the turn signal and gently pull out onto the road. He rolled up to the intersection at about fifteen miles per hour, just in time for the light to turn red. He slammed on the brakes sending Jeppe's forehead dangerously close to the windshield.

"Whoa, red light!"

Jeppe sat back in his seat, ignoring Falck's playful Groucho Marx eyebrow wiggle.

"Do you know why dinosaurs can't clap?" Falck asked cheerfully.

"No I don't, Falck," Jeppe said with a sigh. "Because their arms are too short?"

"Because they're extinct!" Falck's teddy bear laugh filled the car.

Jeppe leaned his cheek against his side window, watching his breath fog up the glass.

When they reached Copenhagen's Latin quarter, Falck turned onto Sankt Peders Stræde and started looking for a parking spot. The neighborhood's four- to five-story apartment buildings from the 1800s housed bars, vegetarian restaurants, and bizarre secondhand shops, and the narrow streets varied confusingly between picturesque idylls and punk. The residents lovingly referred to their neighborhood as the "Pissoir," not because of its many pubs, but because back in the day people here used to let their livestock piss in the streets.

Falck turned off the engine and pointed to a pastel green town house with a fetish shop on the street level.

"She has a workshop up on the second floor," Falck explained. "I told her we'd be there at nine."

He maneuvered himself free of the steering wheel and out onto the sidewalk. Jeppe watched him ring the doorbell by the name *Reborn Dolls / Tanja Kruse.* A moment later they were buzzed in the building's narrow door and climbed the old, crooked staircase to the second floor.

A tall, ample woman wearing a gaudy poncho over pink leggings stood in the rust-red-trimmed doorway, waiting for them with a coffee mug in her hand. She was about thirty-five, her face void of makeup and her hair still wet from her morning shower. When she saw them, she broke into a big smile that pressed her eyes into narrow slits.

"Good morning, welcome! There's coffee."

She herded them affably into a low-ceilinged single-story apartment with crooked wood floors and drafty windows. They could have stepped right into nineteenth-century Copenhagen, if it weren't for the retrofitted electricity and the digital devices around the place.

The apartment's walls were covered with shelves and cabinets overflowing with colored fabric, steel containers, paint, and unidentifiable objects. On an old-fashioned workbench in the middle of the room a French press was steaming alongside a sleeping baby.

"Let me just move Amalie out of the way, so we can sit here."

Tanja gently picked up the little one in her arms and moved her to a cot in the corner of the room. It wasn't until she set the bundle down that Jeppe realized the baby wasn't real. Tanja saw him looking and flashed another big smile.

"Although they're just dolls, they come alive for those of us who have them. I know it's hard to understand, but there it is."

"May I?" Jeppe asked.

She nodded.

Jeppe approached the doll and leaned closer. It had round cheeks, puckered lips, and plump arms, soft baby hair, and teeny tiny fingers. Jeppe had to force himself to understand that it was indeed a doll — it seemed so real.

"Some people collect model airplanes, others dolls," Tanja said, meeting his questioning gaze. "They're an enormous comfort to those of us who can't have children."

"You make them yourself?"

"Yes. Amalie is my own, but I make and send dolls to collectors all over the world, custom orders. There's a big market for them."

She pulled a barstool up to the workbench and started pouring coffee. Jeppe sat down and discovered another doll lying in a basket under the workbench. It lacked both hair and skin color and clearly wasn't finished yet. A photo of a real baby was taped to its belly.

"That's for a customer in North Carolina whose baby was stillborn. We're re-creating little Micah in vinyl to help lessen the grief."

Jeppe suppressed a shudder and set his notepad on the workbench. He looked for a pen, using the brief pause to clear his mind. Dolls had never really been his thing. And dolls modeled after dead babies definitely gave him the creeps.

"Does this mean that you're not working as a nurse anymore?"

"Yes." She smiled again, eyes disappearing behind fleshy cheeks. "After Butterfly House, I decided to take the doll business seriously and start my own company."

Jeppe nodded.

"Well, you know why we're here. . . ."

Her smile instantly transformed into an expression of concern. "Yes, it's terrible to think about. . . . Completely inconceivable that they've been killed."

"Could you please tell us a little about Butterfly House?"

"What do you want to know?"

"Was it a nice place to work?" Jeppe asked, intently ignoring the doll's insistent stare from the basket below. "What were your coworkers like, and the young people who lived in the home?"

"It's been a couple of years, but one does get close to each other, of course." She rolled her lips absentmindedly, as if they were dry. It looked like a bad habit. "Nicola was such a nice guy, and that psychiatrist, Peter Demant, well, he was good, there's no denying that. Rita, the director, had a firm hand, but then again that was necessary."

"What do you mean by a 'firm hand'?" Jeppe scooted his chair a bit so the doll in the basket wasn't staring directly at him.

"You need to be strong when you're working with kids like that. Boy, they were hard work! Each in their own way. Just kids of course, sweet and lovely, but also . . . challenged. And challenging."

"Are you by any chance talking specifically about Isak Brügger?"

She avoided his gaze.

"You won't get me to say anything negative about any of my patients."

"I am by no means asking you to share confidential information or bad-mouth anyone," Jeppe said, holding both hands up in front of him. "But our two murder cases seem somehow connected to Butterfly House. Two of your former coworkers are dead . . ." He left the rest of that thought for her to finish.

"Isak," she began, then made a face that seemed to denote both discomfort and make it look like she was trying to remember. "He was such an unbelievably sweet, lovely boy, but when he was in a bad phase, he could definitely act out. We weren't that many grown-ups, so sometimes we had to restrain him until he calmed down on his own."

"You strapped him down?" Jeppe heard a touch of indignation in his question, but too late to correct it.

"It's easy to have opinions about psychiatry when you're not personally dealing with the mentally ill. You guys all sit up there on your high horse and expect the rest of us to keep the *deviants* under control." She sneered the word. "How are we supposed to provide quality care when we're constantly understaffed?"

"It wasn't meant as a criticism."

Tanja sighed heavily. "Sometimes it was necessary for Isak to relax and calm his body. Strapping him down was the way to do it so he didn't take it out on the others."

"Can you tell us a little about the other three residents?"

"They didn't act out in the same way. Marie was a sweet girl, just extremely introverted and crippled by severe anxiety attacks. She mostly kept to herself; I don't think she ever felt comfortable with us grown-ups. Her mother had committed suicide when she was eleven, maybe that was why. She would always pull away and not answer when you asked her something. Kenny was totally different. He came from a loving extended family on a farm near Lemvig in northwestern Jutland. He had

ADHD and was quite a handful, but he actually got along well most of the time. He was just a misfit and had a really hard time concentrating." Tanja seemed to have calmed down again, even broke into one of her unexpected, big smiles.

"And then there was Pernille, who later committed suicide," Jeppe prompted. "What can you tell us about her?"

Tanja stood up and walked over to the little kitchenette, poured herself a glass of water, and returned to the workbench.

"Pernille had an eating disorder. She was a lovely girl, just extremely sensitive, had no filter. Could go from singing and dancing for us all to the depths of despair in a couple of minutes."

Tanja glanced across the room at her doll, as if it gave her the affirmation she needed.

"Why do you think she killed herself?" Jeppe asked.

She opened her mouth to speak, but the ringtone from Falck's phone interrupted her answer. He checked the screen, stood up with difficulty, and walked to the front door to take the call. Tanja watched him go and then responded thoughtfully.

"I've been asked that many times. I don't know, I don't suppose anyone really does. But Kim's death was important." She poured more coffee and wiped the edge of her cup with her thumb.

"Kim?"

"Kim Sejersen, her caseworker. He died suddenly three years ago. Pernille killed herself less than a year after his death. She was very close to him. So tragic, she was a sweet girl; I was very fond of her."

So that's why they hadn't been able to find him. Yet another one of the home's employees who wasn't around any longer. Why hadn't Rita Wilkins mentioned that he was dead?

"Who has asked you?"

She looked at him in confusion.

"You said that you have been asked about Pernille's death many times. Who asked you?"

"Well, the family, right? Pernille's father has called so many times, not just me, but the whole staff. It's tiring, but he is grieving, of course. . . ."

Jeppe wrote *Bo Ramsgaard* on his notepad and underlined the name.

"And where were you the last two nights?"

"I returned home yesterday from a long weekend in Ystad, Sweden. A romantic getaway. It's cheaper if you go Sunday to Tuesday . . . a spa hotel, really nice place . . ."

"And your partner can confirm that, I presume?"

"I can give you her number, so you can call her and ask. Her name is Ursula Wichmann."

"Thank you for the coffee," Jeppe said, standing up. "You may hear from us again. And be careful. Not to frighten you, but there seems to be . . ."

She nodded anxiously. "I'll make sure I'm not alone."

Tanja lifted the doll up in her arms and walked Jeppe to the front door to say goodbye. Jeppe wondered if the doll had gone with her on the spa vacation or if it had had to stay home all by itself.

Falck was standing on the street below, still talking on his phone. When he saw Jeppe, he wrapped up the conversation and unlocked the car. They got in, Falck squeezing into his seat behind the wheel and Jeppe reluctantly next to him in the passenger seat.

"Larsen and Saidani have been in touch with Kenny Ewald's parents, who say that he's living in Manila," Falck muttered as he felt around for the seat belt. "He's working at a nightclub and hasn't been back to Denmark for almost a year."

"So he's out of the picture. What about Marie Birch?"

"It's as if she vanished into thin air. She doesn't have any family and apparently hasn't had contact with the public-health service since she turned eighteen. The trail goes cold after Butterfly House closed. Saidani has heard rumors that she might hang out around the Central Station downtown, but the police there don't know her." Falck started driving. "Peculiar lady, that Tanja."

Jeppe smiled in surprise. Falck so rarely shared what he was thinking.

"Yeah, definitely one of a kind."

"I'm not a big fan of dolls," Falck admitted.

"I'm with you on that one, Falck. Me neither."

"Oh, damn it!"

Simon Hartvig cursed to himself as he dug around in his coat pockets. Aside from bike lights and an old rubber band, they were empty. He gave the white wall of the staff room a quick punch and started again. It wasn't until he had searched them all again to no avail that he remembered having left the blister pack in the front pocket of his backpack. He unzipped the bag, pushed out a pill, and swallowed it dry right there by the coat hooks.

"Hey, were you the one who baked bread

this morning?"

He whirled around and saw Gorm standing in the doorway, his eyebrows raised.

"Ha-ha, yes," Simon said. "You gotta have something to do when you're on the night shift."

Gorm shut the door behind him and took a roll from the bread basket on the breakfast table.

"Kind of above and beyond the call of duty, all this baking. Is it spelt flour?" Gorm buttered it and took a bite.

"It's a blend of øland and emmer wheats," Simon replied. "Milled in my own flour mill and made with sourdough."

"Tastes good."

"I figured they wouldn't go to waste," Simon said, still lingering by the coat hooks.

Gorm sat down and watched him with a strange look in his eyes. Gorm was weird. Friendly and professional, but one you couldn't really figure out. A once-burned child, he often thought, when Gorm walked through the ward with his bike helmet pushed way down over his forehead and his piercing eyes, always shifting uneasily here and there.

But his eyes weren't shifty now. Right now, Gorm was looking straight at him, scrutinizing him.

Simon tore himself away from the coat hooks, walked over to the sink, and started washing the baking dishes.

"This kind of dough sure is hard to wash off if you let it dry. . . ."

He glanced over his shoulder at Gorm, who was still watching him, bread in hand. The room fell quiet.

The charge nurse opened the door and interrupted the awkward moment.

"Wow, smells great in here," she said. "Have you guys seen Isak this morning?"

"No, I think he's in his room." Simon turned off the water.

"He has a visitor! A young girl who says she knows him. She's waiting out by the front desk." The charge nurse smiled nervously. "It would really be a shame if he missed her. Would you go see if he's awake?"

"Of course!" Simon set the dough bowl down and dried his hands on his pants, only too happy to have an excuse to leave. "I'll go get him."

When he entered the room, Isak was lying in bed looking at the ceiling.

"Hey, champ, you have a visitor," Simon said, patting him gently.

Isak slowly turned his head and looked at him.

"It's a girl. She says you know each other."

"A girl?"

Isak was dressed in under a minute. On his way out the door he instinctively stopped by the bookshelf and pulled out a book.

A young girl was waiting in the quiet room on one of the pink beanbag chairs. She looked small and skinny under her many layers of wool and leather, and her wispy dreadlocks stuck out from under a knit hat. Her highwater pants revealed dirty ankles and a pair of worn slip-on shoes. Simon thought she seemed familiar, but couldn't place her.

"Hi, Isak."

Isak stood still, staring at her.

"Always a book in your hand, that's the way I remember you, too."

"Hi, I'm Simon," he said, holding out his hand to her. "Nice to meet you."

She didn't take his hand, just eyed him warily. He was struck by her big gray eyes under the edge of her hat. That look! Still just as sharp and dangerous, just as unpredictable. It had been a long time. Back then her hair was short and her body heavier. He couldn't think of her name, but in that instant he knew exactly who she was.

Simon gave Isak a wave and left the quiet room, grabbed his coat, and hurried out into the rain. Feeling the heavy drops on his forehead, he took a deep breath, as if something heavy had been sitting on his chest for the last ten minutes. Had she recognized him, too?

He biked home to Hans Egedes Gade in Nørrebro in the highest gear. By the time he let himself into his apartment on the third floor, he was drenched with both rain and sweat, and the pulse in his temple was throbbing unpleasantly. His dad had called and left a message again. Simon deleted it without listening. He peeled off his clothes and tossed them into the laundry, got out a dry T-shirt, and pulled the blinds so the dim daylight disappeared. Lay down on the twin bed in the bedroom, pulled the comforter up, and closed his eyes.

This was it. The worst time of day, the time when sleep was supposed to come but never did. He could lie here for hours with the Ritalin throbbing in his blood, listening to the pulse in his ear.

This was going to have to end soon. He couldn't take it much longer.

Chapter 12

The unique currents in Sortedam Lake — one of the string of manmade lakes in Copenhagen that dated back to the Renaissance — were the reason no one discovered her until nine thirty. A moderate easterly wind had blown her across the lake to the little island, paradoxically named Fish Island, an overgrown spot in the middle of the waters, where birds could hide and breed in peace. There she lay in the lee by the stones, until a park service crew boat bumped into her, and the boat's operator, Frank Thomas, who was already under a great deal of stress, had to put his head between his knees to keep from passing out.

Once the police cordoned off the area, and the medical examiner and his team arrived, they determined that the lake's ducks and rats had started eating the body. The eyes especially and then the places on the body where the skin had been sliced up with twelve little symmetrical cuts.

Her colleagues at Forest's Edge had not thought twice about her absence. Wednesday was her usual riding day, so they just assumed she was with her horse. The staff believed she had gone home after dinner yesterday. At any rate, they hadn't seen her since then.

Jeppe and Falck stood at the edge of the lake with the old municipal hospital building behind them watching as Rita Wilkins's body was removed from the water by the crime scene technicians from NKC East. She was naked, the cuts on her wrists gaping like the gills of a dead fish.

Three murders in three days. Jeppe had rejoiced too soon, thinking they had steered clear of one today.

"Falck, we have to notify the next of kin. Ask Larsen to go by her ex-husband Robert Wilkins's place and talk to him. And then we need to put the remaining employees from Butterfly House under surveillance. Peter Demant and Tanja Kruse must be monitored day and night until we've found the killer. Get that going!"

This case was turning into a regular disaster, and they hadn't come even one step closer to solving it. The superintendent was talking about calling in reinforcements, whatever the hell that meant, and the media was hounding both her and him. He had better get ahold of Mosbæk and ask him to meet.

Mosbæk was one of the police psychologists and, in Jeppe's opinion, the best. Unfortunately he was also the psychologist Jeppe had personally consulted when his wife left him and life came crashing down on him a year and a half ago. Now Jeppe felt slightly embarrassed around him, the way you do when you've allowed yourself to be vulnerable with someone, but he would just have to suck it up. He needed to understand what could possibly be motivating the killer, and Mosbæk was the right person to consult.

The surveillance team that had watched Bo Ramsgaard last night confirmed that he had not left his house on the outskirts of Østerbro from the time he came home from work on Tuesday afternoon until he had driven off in his car this morning. The car had been out in front of the dark house all night. Could he have snuck out the back door and climbed over the wooden fence between the small backyards of the terraced houses? Had he left by bike, maybe a cargo bike?

Jeppe rubbed a hand over his face. The

phone in his pocket rang and rang. He let it ring.

Motive plus opportunity. Who, aside from Pernille's father, had both?

Isak Brügger was in a locked ward at Bispebjerg Hospital, so no *opportunity.* Sara had reached Kenny Ewald by phone early this morning and he was definitely in Manila, so no *opportunity.* There was still no sign of Marie Birch. He had asked Falck to put together a routine search for her.

Heavy clouds gave the day a dark hue, but there was still a sharpness to the light over the lakes, forcing him to squint.

Jeppe walked down the bank a little way. His mother had taught him that you think better when walking. And as long as you keep moving, you don't sink, he thought laconically, kicking a pebble into the water and looking up at the clouds that might burst any minute. The wind was mild, unnaturally warm given the season.

His phone buzzed again. This time he answered it.

"Anette?! What do you want now?"

"Is it true that a third body has been found in the Lakes? Oh, and hello to you, too."

"Tell me," Jeppe said, kicking another pebble into the water. "Is there really nothing better for you to do than listen to police radio? But, yes. They found another body, so I'm a tad busy, as I'm sure you can imagine. . . ."

"Who is it? Someone else from Butterfly House?"

"Anette, I'm going to hang up in three, two, . . ."

"Does the name Marie Birch mean anything to you?"

Jeppe looked out over the lake with increasing impatience. "She's one of the kids from the residential home. Why do you want to know?"

"Have you talked to her?"

"No, she's disappeared, possibly living at the Central Station. Anette, what do you need her for?"

"I'll tell you someday when you're not busy. Tell Uncle Suspenders that I said hello!" She hung up.

Jeppe stuffed the phone into his pocket, shaking his head, and walked back to the scene. He scanned the police group on the bank and found Falck by the car, busy scratching his ear.

"Falck, we're leaving! Where does Bo Ramsgaard work again? We need to talk to him."

"At the airport. You want to go there now?

252

It's rush hour."

"We have to muscle him a bit about this alibi. Let's go!" Jeppe got into the car.

Falck calmly fastened the suspenders to the waistline of his trousers and squeezed in behind the wheel.

Jeppe let out a deep-felt sigh. Having Uncle Suspenders as a partner didn't make investigating three brutal murders any easier. Maybe that was what the superintendent should be thinking of *reinforcing.*

"Drive, Falck! Step on it, if you would be so kind!"

Falck floored it, not realizing the car was still in neutral. Disoriented, he looked down the right side of his paunch toward the shift and in doing so the car veered left into the oncoming lane. Then it stalled.

"Whoops. Give me two seconds."

Jeppe leaned back in his seat and closed his eyes. If he counted slowly to a million, maybe they would make it by then.

Falck swore at the car, got it going, and drove on at a speed that Jeppe, even with his eyes closed, identified as agonizingly tortoise-like. The phone buzzed in his pocket, probably his mother again. He really was going to have to explain to her that she couldn't keep bothering him at work unless it was serious. He let it ring.

After what felt as never-ending as a physics midterm, the car stopped.

"I think we can park here. He works at the conveyer belt."

"You mean security?"

"Yeah, the conveyer belt."

They got out of the car and walked into Terminal 3, where travelers circled around each other's luggage carts, their eyes darting, confused, from sign to sign. At the security, Jeppe found an agent who lead them around the massive lines to checkpoint number six, where Bo Ramsgaard stood in a white uniform shirt and a dark blue tie, instructing people on what to put in which bin and how their toiletries should be in their own separate plastic bag. His tired curls and beard looked even more unruly in contrast to his streamlined uniform. He was not happy to see them.

"We're sorry to have to bother you here at work, but we need to speak to you. It can't wait."

He didn't respond, just flagged someone to take over the position he was manning, and walked off with a brief nod to his coworkers. Jeppe and Falck followed him into a small windowless staff room, its walls lined with artificial wood paneling, making the place look like a sauna.

"What is it?" he asked. "I am only allowed a ten-minute break."

He sat down on top of the table that occupied most of the floor space in the room, thus making it impossible for Jeppe and Falck to do anything but stand uncomfortably just inside the door.

An empathetic guy, Jeppe thought, would have let them sit, too.

"Where were you last night?" he asked.

"Home with Nathalie, our youngest. Why?"

"Can your daughter confirm that?"

"Of course." He stroked his beard with thumb and forefinger. "What's happened?"

Jeppe saw no reason to tell him about Rita. Maybe they could trick him into saying too much in the event that he had something to hide.

"That's beside the point. You said that your wife was home in the evening and overnight both Sunday and Monday?"

"No," Bo Ramsgaard replied without hesitation. "You misunderstood. Lisbeth left for her retreat on Monday, but I was still home with my daughter every night this week. And last week, for that matter."

Jeppe hesitated. As long as the man maintained that he had been at home, there wasn't much to be done about it. They had to get ahold of Lisbeth Ramsgaard's meditation center in Sweden somehow. So far no one answered the landline, so they might have to send someone there in person. She could be complicit.

"We've learned that Pernille's caseworker, Kim Sejersen, died three years ago." Jeppe crossed his arms over his chest. "What can you tell us about him?"

"Kim was a talented social worker," Bo Ramsgaard said, one of his eyes twitching a little. "We were grateful that he was supportive of our daughter and helped her so much. In the beginning at Butterfly House, with his help, she improved, gained weight, and was happier than she had been for a long time."

"And then?"

"Yeah, then she had a panic attack and started losing weight again. . . ."

Jeppe heard the catch in the father's voice and wondered if all parents wouldn't feel a compulsion to blame someone for their child's suicide, anything but carry the weight of it themselves.

"How did Kim die?" he asked gently.

The father looked at them, like they ought to know. Maybe they should have.

"An accident, apparently he drowned."

Jeppe felt a tingle travel down his spine, as

if a daddy longlegs had just run down his back.

"That must have been hard for Pernille?" he asked.

"Hard? These kids find it hard if something they didn't expect is served for lunch. A death is a disaster."

"Do you think it's possible that Kim's death helped trigger Pernille's suicide?"

"Ugh, enough already!" Out of the blue, Bo slammed his fist down onto the table. "The problem wasn't that Kim died, although it was a tough blow of course."

"What was the problem then?" Jeppe could tell that the father was growing seriously angry.

"Just because we weren't able to prove it at the time doesn't mean that Rita and the rest of the staff didn't share responsibility for Pernille's death. They neglected their jobs. Maybe even worse than that! We just found out about it too late . . ."

He buried his face in his hands, spoke into them.

"When they autopsied Pernille the pathologists found fresh cuts in her arms. My daughter had cut in the past but had totally stopped. She was home on vacation until a week before her suicide and then there were no marks on her arms at all. She must have started cutting again after she went back to Butterfly House."

"And what does that mean?"

The father shook his head resignedly, as if explaining was costing him all his energy, and he assumed that energy to be wasted.

"It means that she started doing noticeably worse once she returned to Butterfly House. It means the staff didn't tell us that she had started cutting again. Maybe because they weren't aware that she was doing it or maybe they didn't think it worth mentioning to us, but either is equally horrible. My daughter only held out for a week and then killed herself."

It was hot and stuffy in the little room. The smell of yesterday's drinking mixed with the father's gloom made it hard to breathe. Jeppe and Falck exchanged glances.

"If you hear from your wife, ask her to contact us right away. We'll let you get back to work. Thanks for your time."

Bo pointed his finger at them and hissed, "Ask Peter Demant what went on at that place! He has never been willing to talk to us about Pernille's death. Why would he deny us that? Ask for access to my daughter's medical records. I'll give you permission."

"Okay . . ." Jeppe hesitated, wondering

how to interpret that statement. A concrete tip or just the expression of a grieving parent's desire for revenge?

"A couple of kroner for something to eat?"

The man asking was surprisingly well dressed and no more than thirty, but his brown teeth and the smell of decay revealed that he was probably down on his luck.

"Panhandling is illegal in Denmark, as I'm sure you know," Anette Werner said, waving the man away as she tried to scan the chaotic bustle of life in Copenhagen's main train station. "And what the heck are you going to buy for a couple of kroner anyway? That won't even get you condiments at the hot dog stand." She hadn't been somewhere so crowded in a while and was out of practice with the noise and constant, unwanted bodily contact. "Hey, you, actually, wait! Come back! I have a question."

The man scowled at her and asked, "Are you a cop? How did I not guess that. . . ."

"Do you know Marie Birch, a young girl, hangs out here sometimes?"

He started to walk away again.

"Hey, wait. This is for you!" She pulled a crumpled two-hundred kroner bill out of her pocket and held it out. The man snatched the bill so quickly, Anette didn't even see it disappear.

"I don't know her. But if she seriously hangs out here, then you should check down in the arches."

"R-Chest, what's that?"

"Arches, *A-R-C-H-E-S*, down along the tracks by Vesterport Station, below the Palads movie theater. Check the arches! You'll find everything under the sun down there. Walk down along track one and then toward Vesterport."

The man turned around and vanished neatly into the crowd of commuters. Ten seconds later he was gone.

Anette walked toward the tracks. At a hot dog cart she bought a chili dog, which she gulped down on the escalator leading to the platform. It felt like old times. It felt good. She was supposed to have gone to infant swim class today, but Svend had given her a pass so that she could nap. Instead, here she was, for a moment feeling like her old self again. It was as good as sleeping, perhaps even better.

Down on the platform she quickly checked for guards, then hurried into the tunnel under the actual station building. She had to cross the tracks and climb over an unambiguous NO ADMITTANCE sign, the platform tapering to a narrow walkway along the tracks, darkness closing in around her. Now and then a locked door appeared in the wall, covered with uninspired graffiti and lit by powerful outdoor lights. The sky became visible above her as she reached the open area by the station square, but then disappeared again as she continued underneath the Liberty Column and Hotel Royal.

Anette walked with purpose, as fast as the narrow passage permitted. No one noticed her, no one yelled at her, though her being here was definitely off-limits.

At Vesterport Station, the tracks once again ran out under the open sky. Anette walked alongside them, passing the arches in the concrete foundation that the panhandler had described. They appeared to have been modeled after those Roman aqueducts she had seen in school books ages ago.

There were a lot of arches, close to twenty of them. In front of each arch was an illuminated advertising panel, although the ads had recently been taken down. Anette peered into the first arch and saw a space about a yard deep, which was completely empty. No sign of life. She continued, peeking into the next arch with the same result. An S-train pulled into the station. Anette kicked the illuminated panel, hoping she looked like someone who had a reason to be there. When the train drove on, she moved on to the next arch and then the next. Nothing hiding there other than dry leaves and empty beer cans.

It wasn't until the last arch before the bridge at Kampmannsgade that she found something. Two half-moon shaped openings in the wall with bars over them. Both were about thirty inches wide, but different heights: the first was five feet high, the second only about eighteen inches.

She grabbed the bars in front of the tall opening, but they didn't budge. The ones in front of the smaller opening, on the other hand, were on the verge of falling off. She pulled out her phone and shone a light into the darkness. A shaft ran ten or fifteen feet into the foundation, where it appeared to come to an abrupt end.

Anette cursed. Her only choice was to crawl in and see if the shaft continued downward.

She got on her stomach and wormed her way along, phone in hand. The dust made her nose itch, and her breasts weren't crazy about being squashed into the hard concrete underneath. But the shaft did in fact open down into a little room, where she was just able to stand upright. Here she saw the first signs of life: plastic bags of clothes, a mattress, trash from a meal in the corner. Anette shone her light around and discovered a corridor that continued, parallel to the track bed. What the hell kind of a labyrinth was this?

She made a point of memorizing where she had come in and, crouching over, she continued into the darkness. There was a stench of pee and of something sweet and rotten. The dark corners hissed with rats fleeing her footsteps.

After about fifteen feet she came to a junction, where the corridor crossed both another corridor that ran perpendicular to it and a shaft that led further down. Which way now?

She perked up her ears, but couldn't hear anything but the rats and a distant whine from the train rails. If Jeppe were here, he would have some kind of gut sense, put a crystal on his forehead, and let his intuition guide him. Anette considered if there might be something to his theory, that becoming a mother had really made her more sensitive. She closed her eyes and took a deep breath.

"What the fuck are you doing here?"

Anette jumped. The voice sounded mean, and whoever had spoken was hidden in the shadows.

"Who's asking?" She clenched her fists.

Silence. Then a rustling in the branch of the perpendicular corridor that ran off to the left. Footsteps coming closer slowly, dragging.

A man came into view.

Anette forced herself not to scream. She was not an easy scare, but the sight of him was overwhelming. He was bald and muscular, and walked hunched over like herself, his bulging shoulders completely filling the narrow corridor. And he was blue.

The man's face and scalp, his neck and hands: all of his visible skin was covered with tight, colorful tattoos, transforming him into some kind of fantasy-novel giant. A bunch of piercings glinted in his forehead, his cheeks, and his nose.

"You have ten seconds to tell me what you're doing here!"

"Say, what, am I standing on your lawn or something?" Anette knew better than to let his appearance intimidate her. "I didn't know the whole railway system belonged to you."

"Are you looking for a place to shoot up?" He sounded a little less gruff.

"I'm looking for a young girl, who's missing. Rumor has it she's living here."

The blue giant fell quiet for a moment. Then he turned around and started walking

264

away, his torso almost horizontal under the low ceiling.

"Come!"

Anette stood for a moment, uncertain. Then she followed him. The giant walked a long way, turned to the right, and crawled down one level to a room that was about fifteen feet by ten. Down here the ceiling was higher, and they were both able to stand upright. Along one wall lay a mattress with a sleeping bag, and next to that there was a shelf full of books and clothes. Three computer screens — along with accompanying keyboards, drives, and various flashing boxes — glowed on top of a wobbly particleboard desk. Aside from the lack of windows, it was almost pleasant here, in a squatter kind of way.

The giant turned around to face her, putting his hands together in front of his crotch like a soldier. His eyes shone bright in the dark blue face.

"Are you a copper?"

"I haven't heard that word in a long time," Anette said. She couldn't help but smile. "But yes, I am actually with the police."

"You're not welcome here. You ought to know that! We handle things on our own down here."

Anette crossed her arms in front of her

chest. She vaguely remembered a story, something about a body that had once been found on the tracks by Vesterport that someone said had came from "the Colony." This must be it.

"I'm here on private business, not for work." That wasn't completely a lie. Anette glanced at the multiple computer screens. "Tell me, what kind of place is this?"

"The Colony, you mean?" he said with a smile. "A secret city within the city. Copenhagen is an old city, you know, it has burned down and been rebuilt on top of the ruins so many times that there are all kinds of tunnels and spaces underneath the city. They make room for those of us who can't stand the light."

Anette shrugged, trying to show that she was cool with that. That she wasn't the least bit interested in whatever type of illegal activities people pursued down here, whether it be computer hacking or drug sales.

"I'm looking for a girl named Marie Birch. She's nineteen and used to live in a residential place called Butterfly House in Gundsømagle."

It was impossible to read his facial expression. In fact, she could hardly say that the giant even had a facial expression. At least not one that could be made out down there in the dark.

"Nineteen? That makes her an adult. Why, did she mess up?"

Anette hesitated and then said, "Not that I know of. I'm looking for Marie because someone she knows is dead. Maybe she knows something about why, maybe not."

The giant knew something. She could tell from the way he was standing. Son of a bitch, she could *sense* it! He knew Marie, maybe even cared about her.

"Three people have been murdered in Copenhagen since Monday, and the killer hasn't been found. Marie knows the victims. She might also know the killer. I'd really like to find her before the killer does."

He turned around, walked over to the shelf and dug around among his books. Then he approached her with a folder in his hands.

"*If* we're talking about the same person, she doesn't live here anymore."

"But she *did* live here?" Anette couldn't hide her enthusiasm.

"Again, *if* we're talking about the same person. She lived in a room farther down the corridor last winter. When spring came, she moved outdoors."

"But you know her? Is she doing okay?

267

Has she recovered?"

The giant raised one eyebrow, his piercings clinking.

"You're asking *me*, if she's healthy? Would you look at me!"

That made Anette laugh. He laughed, too. Clearly he had warmed up a little.

"People only come down here to live if they've had a few hard knocks from life. Things aren't easy for Marie, but she's a good girl."

"Do you know where she is now?"

He shifted the folder back and forth a little bit between his huge, blue hands. Then he apparently decided to trust her.

"She lives with the Count, out in Fredens Havn by Christiania."

"Motherfucker!" Anette exclaimed.

"Bless you!" said the giant.

She could see his teeth shining white in the darkness and assumed he was smiling.

"Right, sorry. But I didn't actually think I'd find her —"

"You haven't found her yet. But if you do, and it is the Marie I know, then give her this. It's a project we worked on together. If you don't find her, then just throw it out."

The giant handed the folder to Anette.

"Can you find your way out? I don't like

to show myself on the platform during the day."

"I've got it. Thank you."

Anette shuffled down the corridor she had come from and hoisted herself strenuously back up to street level where she could crawl the last few yards out into the light. She wasn't claustrophobic, but when she was finally standing under the arch again, breathing the fresh air and looking up at the dark clouds in the sky, she felt an overwhelming sense of relief. What made people live underground like that?

What sent a young girl down among the monsters of the dark?

Anette could find one plausible reason only: Marie Birch must be on the run. But what was she fleeing from? Why was she hiding?

Anette glanced down at the folder the giant had given her. It was an ordinary, worn file folder, held shut by a rubber band. She pulled the cover open a tad and saw a thick stack of papers containing what appeared to be medical terms . . . *the current expansion to the subgroups of affective disorders . . . the psychiatric diagnostic categories . . .*

Anette closed the folder again and looked down at herself. If she didn't beat Svend and the baby home, she was going to have a hard time explaining why her clothes were dark gray with soot and dust following a peaceful midday nap on the sofa. The lying was starting to get to her.

Fredens Havn. Now how the hell was she going to make it out there?

CHAPTER 13

Jeppe made his way through the packed restaurant on Store Strandstræde twice before he saw Peter Demant sitting in the covered atrium. He was at a table for two alone, reading next to what was left of the steak he had eaten for lunch. A fire was burning in the open fireplace in the atrium, apparently solely for the lone psychiatrist and his book.

Jeppe was reminded of nineteenth-century artists in Paris. There was something melancholy about the man with the dark curly hair, sitting there alone, something romantic yet at the same time sad.

Falck had stayed at headquarters to ask the Swedish police for help locating Lisbeth Ramsgaard and to arrange the surveillance details for the remaining former staff members from Butterfly House. In all honesty, Jeppe couldn't really face bringing Falck along, even though he wasn't supposed to interview a suspect alone. No one needed to know.

When he was next to the table, the psychiatrist looked up from his book with a finger marking the spot on the page.

"Yes?" Peter Demant said, not unfriendly but not particularly welcoming either.

"Jeppe Kørner, from the Copenhagen Police. Your receptionist said I could find you here."

"I'm eating my lunch." His face was still neutral.

"Bon appétit." Jeppe sat down. "I need to ask you some questions about the murders of your former colleagues from Butterfly House. Since there's a risk that you might be charged in this case, and your statements could later be used in a court of law, you have the right not to answer. Naturally, I would prefer if you cooperated."

Demant folded over the corner of his page in the book and put it down. Then he pushed his plate aside, folded his hands on the table, and nodded.

"Where were you the last three nights?" Jeppe asked.

"At home, in bed. Last night I had a video session at ten p.m. with a client who lives in France."

Jeppe raised an eyebrow. "What's the

272

client's name?"

"You know very well that I can't give you that," the psychiatrist said with a wry smile. "I'm a doctor and bound by doctor-patient confidentiality."

He could soon enough be required to drop that confidentiality obligation, Jeppe thought, but let it slide for now.

"How close was your relationship with the three people who have been killed?"

"It was nonexistent. I haven't had any contact whatsoever with any of the people who worked at Rita's place since it closed. And back when it was open, I pretty much only knew Rita. I was just a consultant and only stopped by every now and then, I didn't work there full-time." He spoke calmly, with a straight face.

"You haven't stayed in touch with a single one of your colleagues from Butterfly House?"

"Why should I?" Peter shrugged. "I'm a busy man. Butterfly House was only one of several places I was affiliated with, and when it closed two years ago, my employment obviously ceased."

"What about back then? What was your relationship like with your colleagues when the home was still open?"

"Listen, in addition to my own private

practice, I work part-time at both Bispebjerg and Glostrup Hospitals and also func-
tion as a consultant with various clinics and
journals, all that on top of my various
international commitments," the psychiatrist said, and smiled again. He looked like
someone who often had to make an effort
not to talk down to people. "I'm sure you
can imagine how many I meet and work
with in one context or another. At the risk
of sounding conceited, I just don't remember the Butterfly House personnel very
well."

"May I ask why such a busy man as
yourself would choose to work for a small,
private residential program like that, way
out in the countryside? It doesn't seem like
an obvious choice."

"Not fancy enough, you mean?" he asked,
raising his eyebrows. "Maybe I'm just passionate about my profession, want to make
a difference in the lives of mentally ill teenagers . . ."

Jeppe couldn't decide whether there was a
touch of sarcasm in his voice.

"What about Rita Wilkins?" Jeppe asked.
"She hired you. You must be able to remember her?"

Demant poured himself some mineral
water from a green bottle and gestured to

see if Jeppe would like some. Jeppe waved his hand to say no.

"Rita is one of luckily many firebrands we have here in Denmark, one of the people who is passionate about improving conditions for vulnerable teens, offering better options than what the national health service can, an opportunity to heal."

"Rita Wilkins was murdered last night," Jeppe said. "We found her this morning."

"I'm really sorry to hear that." Demant bowed his head.

"Do you have any idea who might have had reason to kill her?"

He didn't respond right away, but started chewing on his index finger's cuticles. The motion seemed childish and incongruent with his otherwise professional image.

"No."

"I'm assuming that you're familiar with Pernille Ramsgaard's suicide?" Jeppe asked, searching the psychiatrist's round face for a reaction.

"Of course. She was one of my patients at Butterfly House, a tragic case."

"Do you happen to know why she committed suicide?"

"That's not something I'm at liberty to discuss. Doctor-patient confidentiality does not end when a patient dies."

Jeppe decided there was no reason for him to hide what he knew himself.

"Her father claims that the substandard treatment at the home contributed to her death."

"Yes," Demant said with a sad smile. "That's the same crap he's been spewing for the last two years. I feel terrible for the family, but honestly it's tiring to put up with their continual accusations."

"So Bo Ramsgaard's allegations against Butterfly House aren't true?"

"No!" He shook his head adamantly. "They're categorically false. The professional work environment at the home was constructive, and, in my opinion, the kids there had optimal conditions to thrive and recover. Pernille's father seems compelled to blame someone for her death. Maybe he should look to himself instead. But of course that kind of thing can lead to painful realizations. . . ."

"Coffee?" A young server appeared by the table. Demant smiled warmly at her.

"You're so sweet, Frederikke. Two espressi, thank you, and as you know, milk on the side."

"Of course, Peter."

The server cleared his plate. The psychiatrist followed her with his eyes. Once she

276

was gone, he continued, sounding somewhat lost in thought.

"Unfortunately one often sees —"

"Wait a minute," Jeppe held up a hand. "What did you mean by saying that Bo Ramsgaard should look to himself?"

"Let me say this much: Pernille was a neglected child. She grew up with parents who transferred all of their own failed ambitions onto their children, pushing them ahead like prize-winning cows without seeing them for who they were, especially the father . . . elite gymnastics, private school, and so on."

"Was Pernille's family the source of her illness?"

"They were a contributing, possibly a triggering factor at least." Demant smiled. "It is important to note that she had just been home on vacation when she decided to take her own life. But there's never just one reason. The mind isn't so simplistic."

Demant drank a sip of water, then shook his head resignedly. The fireplace was making Jeppe's right cheek burn. He pulled out his notepad and skimmed a page.

"Three years ago," Jeppe began, "one of the social workers who worked at Butterfly House died, a Kim Sejersen —"

"He drowned in the pond by the home,"

Demant broke in. "There was a summer party."

"A party?"

"That's what I understood, although I wasn't there myself. So, unfortunately, I don't know anything about the accident. I hardly knew the man."

"Pernille was said to have been very close to Kim. He was her" — Jeppe glanced at his notepad — "case manager. Do you know anything about their relationship? Was she very upset that he had died?"

"I've already said more than I should." A shadow fell over the psychiatrist's face. "Like I told you, my confidentiality obligations are sacrosanct."

"Let me in turn remind you what's at stake here. Three of your coworkers have been murdered and the killer is on the loose."

Demant sighed heavily, then said, "What I *can* say is something about how mentally ill teenagers generally interact with the rest of the world."

"Well, let's start there" — Jeppe clicked his ballpoint ready to write — "and see how far we get."

"First and foremost, you have to understand that for many mentally ill teens, it is extremely difficult to distinguish reality from imagination. That is part and parcel of the schizophrenia diagnosis."

"According to her father, Pernille Ramsgaard had an eating disorder," Jeppe interrupted. "She wasn't schizophrenic, was she?"

Demant held up his hand and continued, "*Generally* teens with mental illness find that their perception of reality is quite precarious. If an adult, a caregiver for example, takes a particular interest, a mentally ill teenager can easily develop the delusion that there is a deeper bond, a romantic relationship for example."

The server placed two tiny coffee cups and a small pitcher of warm milk on the table between them. Demant poured milk into his cup and lifted it halfway up to his mouth.

"If the adult rejects the young person, no matter how considerately it's done, the teen may feel betrayed and let down."

"Are you insinuating that Pernille had a crush on Kim Sejersen and that he turned her down?" Jeppe copied Demant's milk ritual and eyed the dark brown brew in his cup skeptically. It looked like it might eat the enamel right off his teeth.

Demant pretended that Jeppe had not spoken.

"When a mentally ill teenager feels betrayed, that has the potential to elicit a desire for revenge. The teen might express this outwardly or through self-harm."

"So, what you're saying is that Pernille Ramsgaard killed herself because she was in love with her case manager and grieved over his death?"

"I never said that." The psychiatrist emptied the espresso cup and wiped his mouth genteelly on a cloth napkin.

"But you are saying that a mentally ill teenager's connection to their caregivers can turn into disappointment and rage, right?" Jeppe took a hesitant sip of the strong coffee.

"I am speaking *only* generally, in theoretical terms."

"Considering that we're dealing with three murdered caregivers, that's an interesting theory." Jeppe set his cup down and pushed it slightly away.

"It's not a theory. It's merely speculation. I'll leave it up to others to connect my statement with the murders."

And yet he had chosen to say it.

"If we just pretend for a moment that the theory applies, which of the young people might have felt that way? Pernille is dead, and Kenny lives in Manila, but Isak and Marie are in Copenhagen. . . . Could one of the two be feeling the kind of desire for revenge that you're describing?"

"I don't discuss my patients." Demant made a hand gesture as if to brush it all aside. "Never!"

He drummed his hands on the table and then leaned forward as if to confide a secret.

"Remember, feelings are never simple. Revenge is inextricably linked to a bad conscience; guilt goes hand in hand with resentment at having felt pressured to do the thing one feels guilty about. A double-edged sword, which makes the bearer both victim and executioner."

He nodded a couple of times as if to validate this statement.

"Okay, thanks," Jeppe said, concluding that he wasn't going to get anything factual out of the psychiatrist, and stood up. "For the time being you would probably be wise not to meet with anyone tied to Butterfly House. Or with people who are mentally unstable."

"Uh, you do remember that I'm a psychiatrist, right?" Demant laughed briefly. "Mentally unstable people would be pretty hard for me to avoid."

"You know what I mean. Also we're going to put you under surveillance for the next little while, two officers. They'll keep a discreet distance, but we can't risk more . . ."

Demant stopped him with a brief nod.

"Also, I'm going to need a confirmation of your alibi from yesterday, the video call with your patient in France. I understand that it might be awkward to have to ask a patient for such a thing, but unfortunately there's no way around that. Oh, and Bo Ramsgaard gave the police permission to review his daughter's medical records from her time at Butterfly House."

Demant blinked a couple of times, and said, "I don't know where her records are. That was a long time ago."

"Two years isn't that long. Surely you keep digital records? Bring them to police headquarters first thing tomorrow. Can we say around eight? Is that enough time for you to locate them?"

He nodded reluctantly, and Jeppe held out his hand in parting. The psychiatrist's hand was small but powerful.

"Oh, by the way, just one last thing," Jeppe said. "There was a cook and two nurses working at Butterfly House whose names Rita Wilkins couldn't remember. Can you?"

"No, unfortunately not."

Peter Demant answered without hesitation. All the same, Jeppe was absolutely certain that he was lying.

The music pressed on her eardrums. Marie Birch raised her face toward the vaulted ceiling of Holmen Church and tried to follow the organist's race up and down the musical scale. The hard, wooden pew yielded beneath her as she lay down. Churches were good places to find shelter when it rained. Mostly they were quiet and empty, but every now and then the chorus would practice, and then it was almost as if they were playing her a private concert.

The organ sounds crashed down over her and left her nerve endings bristling. Sometimes she would get so angry. Even if she knew there was no point to the anger, that it was only taking a toll on herself. With time she had learned to talk sense into herself, but it didn't always work.

The thought of all those times she had stood outside a locked office door and waited humbly for a doctor who was too busy with paperwork to see her. The thought of backs turned, testy side looks, and stressed out, understaffed departments with nothing to offer but their exhausted sympathy. And pills.

So sorry.
You know how it is.

We're increasing your dose.

Marie clenched her fists and pressed them to her eyes.

Kim had been different. The only one to take the time for those long talks she so needed; he had helped her toward understanding herself. It was mainly thanks to him that she had found the strength to break free from psychiatry and was now able to stand on her own two feet. The thought of the open wards' weekly doctor rounds where so-called sensible plans for the future were made in just fifteen minutes. Psychiatric hospitals just didn't have the resources to treat people; they were merely parking garages, where the sick were supposed to share the space with other sick, who weren't getting the help they needed, either. Plenty of expertise and goodwill, but no time, no hands.

Marie had lost count of the number of times she had waited in a group of psychotic patients only to learn that there was only one bed left in Copenhagen and that they were going to have to choose among themselves which one of them needed it most.

She hadn't chosen to live on the street; she had been pushed out. Society wasn't spacious enough to accommodate her, especially now that she was an adult. On the contrary, she sensed mistrust and even outspoken aggression from a world that otherwise gloated about how it cared for the sick. It was a lie meant for the healthy to maintain their self-image as being decent and inclusive. But their caring didn't extend to the mentally ill. There was never any real sympathy for diverters, for the crazy ones who hit their heads on the wall. They were dangerous.

When did I become dangerous? she wondered. Quiet, introverted, damaged Marie. Somewhere along the way the anxious child she was had let go of her fear and embraced her fury. She was no longer afraid of the dark, of being alone, of the shadows. Now *she* was the darkness and the shadows. Didn't hesitate to fight back when someone hurt her. When had that happened? When she lay strapped down by the belt screaming at the naked walls? When murky chemistry intoxicated her body? When Kim died?

When you have to bear the unbearable over and over again, you have to make the pain your ally.

"So take me home, a poor sinner, to Your righteousness . . . ," a crisp soprano sang out beautifully somewhere above her.

Marie sat up, gathered her things, and

headed for the exit.

There was still a lot to do.

CHAPTER 14

"The party's over, it's over, the party's over, it's fucking over now. . . ."

Prophets of Rage's nihilistic rock mantra ran on repeat through Jeppe's tired brain, throbbing to the beat of his pulse as he walked down Gothersgade toward Queen Louise's Bridge. Like so many times before, he longed for a pill that could smother his internal soundtrack. That pill did not exist, of this he was quite sure after having tried most of them, but as long as there was money in medical research, maybe there was hope. Until then there was nothing to do but try to reduce the stress that set off the music in his head in the first place. Solve the case, amigo, then you'll be freed from this incessant internal jukebox!

He crossed the busy thoroughfare Farimagsgade and checked his phone without slowing his pace. An email had come in from Nyboe confirming that all three victims had died the same way and within the same time frame on the previous three nights — between midnight and 3:00 a.m.

And the superintendent had called more than once. She would have to wait. Jeppe didn't need to be reminded of the importance of finding the murderer who was tossing his victims in the city's water holes.

The sound of the traffic broke through the soundtrack in his brain just as Gothersgade opened up to reveal the Lakes, Copenhagen's own little piece of Paris. The police psychologist was waiting for him lakeshore, by the bridge.

Mosbæk was one of those people who looked like the embodiment of a child's drawing. A thin wreath of hair highlighted his balding pate, and a permanent smile beamed in the middle of his full beard. Mosbæk radiated positivity, especially right now, holding a leash with a shaggy puppy, trying to stop it from running in circles around him.

"A puppy is really the best cure in the world for a bad mood, Jeppe. No! Settle down, Maslow, heel!" Mosbæk went in for a hug, but luckily the bouncing dog prevented it.

"I hope you don't mind that I brought the dog?" Mosbæk asked, extricating himself from the leash with a grin. "He's just a puppy, so I'm bringing him to work until he learns to be alone. You're my last appointment of the day, so a little end-of-work stroll seemed appropriate."

Jeppe eyed the dog skeptically. It didn't really matter what he thought about its presence since the little bugger was here, whipping around their legs.

"Should we walk?" Jeppe suggested.

"He's an Australian cattle dog, bred for herding. You can pet him."

Jeppe waved aside the offer and began strolling along the lakeshore under the fading fall foliage on the chestnut trees. Mosbæk and the puppy trotted after him. The lakeside path was teeming with joggers in provocatively tight Lycra, and Mosbæk had to zigzag apologetically to avoid tripping them with the leash.

"Well, Jeppe . . . what a mess of a case."

"Three dead in three days." Jeppe waited while Mosbæk caught up with him. "And there still isn't a single witness or piece of concrete evidence. I need your help to understand why someone chooses to kill people this way."

"I assume that we're basing our theory on the victims' ties to each other through the residential program?"

"Exactly. Do you know about the young girl's suicide?"

"Pernille Ramsgaard, yes."

"Her parents have an obvious motive of revenge, but seemingly an alibi for last night when Rita Wilkins was killed. The father, on the other hand, claims that the staff at Butterfly House failed the residents, especially the psychiatrist who was affiliated . . ."

"Peter Demant."

"You know him?"

"Come, Maslow, come!" Mosbæk spun around to unwind the leash from around his legs. "I've met him a few times. Peculiar guy."

"Agreed. But whether or not he failed the residents at Butterfly House, he doesn't have an obvious reason to start murdering his former colleagues, does he?" Jeppe stopped again to wait for Mosbæk and the dog. "And then there are the residents. One, Isak, is an inpatient in the pediatric psych ward, which is locked and monitored twenty-four hours a day, and the other, Marie, is missing and no one's been able to find her. And then to make matters worse, there were also two nurses and a cook who we can't find, plus one social worker who's dead —"

"I'm going to stop you for a minute,

Jeppe." Mosbæk stroked his beard with his free hand. "Sometimes we blind ourselves, staring at all the things we don't know. Let's start somewhere else, like with what we actually do know: the murderer's modus operandi is unusual. Bleeding out is a classic suicide method, but is not traditionally used for murder."

"And, by the way, the method of the young girl, who committed suicide. She slit her wrists," Jeppe interjected.

"Good, so there's a potential connection there, a comment from the murderer. And the murder weapon is unusual, too, I understand. A scarificator, which was historically used to treat people, not to kill them. Heel, Maslow! Good boy!" Mosbæk fed the dog a treat from his pocket and sent it a goofy smile. "What about the locations where the bodies were found?"

"Fountains in the city, the lake here. The bodies apparently have to lie in the water when we find them."

"And what does that tell you, Jeppe?"

"What do you mean?"

"Pernille Ramsgaard was found in a bathtub. . . ." Mosbæk opened his hand, as if to reveal a possible clue he had hidden there.

Suddenly Jeppe remembered why Mosbæk was the one he always called when he got stuck on a case.

"At any rate, I think you should consider it a possibility, that the locations of the bodies is a comment on the suicide. Our killer runs quite a risk of being seen when he dumps bodies in the middle of the city. The third victim was found right around here, right?" Mosbæk stopped and nodded toward a house on Søgade. "Are you familiar with that building?"

Jeppe looked at the big facade of yellow brick with horizontal stripes of red interlaid. It was topped off by a large green copper dome.

"Isn't it part of the university . . . ?"

"It is now, yes. But until the millennium it was the Copenhagen Municipal Hospital. And that building there" — Mosbæk pointed to a facade that faced the lake — "was once the notorious Ward Six for Mental and Neurological Diseases, in other words, the psych ward."

Jeppe turned around to look at Fish Island. Clouds hung low over the rooftops, coloring everything a leaden gray, drawing everything downward into the depths of the water. It was only a hundred meters from the old hospital to the little island.

"The locations where the bodies were found are all associated with psychiatry.

Maslow, leave it!" Mosbæk pulled the eager puppy away from an approaching German shepherd.

"Is this the work of a sick man?"

"What's a sick man, Jeppe?" Mosbæk sighed. "Are you healthy yourself?"

"Healthy enough not to murder people, yeah."

"There is no health; physicians say that we, at best, enjoy but a neutrality." Mosbæk eyed Jeppe expectantly. "Are you familiar with John Donne, the English baroque poet?"

"I don't think he's made it onto my reading list, no."

"That's a mistake. *An Anatomy of the World* is a classic. Among other things, Donne says, 'We are born ruinous.'

"The point is . . ." Mosbæk was searching for the right words. "Who is sick and who is healthy? You could argue that any deviation from societal norms is pathological. You could also argue the opposite."

"You know what I mean. . . ."

"Yes, and I don't mean to quibble. These are just muddy waters, is all I'm saying."

Jeppe eyed him skeptically.

"All right, anyway, there seems to be a water theme to it all, no?" Mosbæk explained. "But that's just it. On the one side the water can symbolize purification and maybe could be interpreted as a mania for cleanliness as part of some broader pathological picture. There is a close connection, for example, between fear of bacteria and OCD."

"A psychopath, then?" Jeppe asked. "I can tell you don't buy that."

"No, not really. The killings are too organized, planned down to the slightest detail and carried out very neatly. It takes vision and courage to leave a body in the middle of Strøget." Mosbæk squatted down to pet his puppy lovingly.

"So what sort of a person is our killer? Can you say anything about that?"

"Cautiously, yes. I don't dare come up with a formal profile just off the cuff, though." Mosbæk stood back up and wiped a bit of puppy drool off on his trouser leg. "We're talking about a person with tremendous motivation. Three murders in just as many days requires a massive incentive, meaning the emotion behind it must be very strong. My guess is that the killer has been saving up, so to speak, planning for a long time and amassing the rage that *must* be behind this."

"Agreed. Anything else?"

"Hm . . . people who progress to violence

generally have the flaw that they feel like rulers of the world and completely insignificant at the same time."

They moved out of the way of a group of young soldiers in sweats who came running along the lakeshore path at high speed wearing fully packed backpacks, their eyes focused ahead.

"Why does the murderer let his victims bleed out like that?"

"I think you already know, Jeppe." Mosbæk gave him an almost apologetic look. "It has to be about making them suffer before they die."

They started walking again, the tip of a headache starting to throb behind Jeppe's eyes. The person with the most obvious motive was Bo Ramsgaard. He had lost his daughter and for that he openly blamed the very people who were now dying one by one. His alibi was even shaky. It was obvious. Even so, there was something off about the theory, which Jeppe couldn't quite put his finger on.

He looked out over the murky lake waters, where the clouds were drawn neatly on the surface and let Mosbæk's words sink in. The puppy barked and happily jumped up his leg, so that he nearly lost his balance.

We are born ruinous. Yes, he thought,

Mosbæk's right. We are all lost.

Esther de Laurenti hammered away at the keyboard at breakneck speed without looking at the words forming on the screen in front of her. She was on a roll and had neither time to think, edit what she had written, nor take a break to pee. She had no idea where it was coming from. All of a sudden she was just full of words, tripping over themselves to get onto the paper.

The doorbell pulled her abruptly out of her flow.

She hurried to the door and yanked it open. Alain stood on the landing, wide-eyed and startled by the sudden movement.

She raised her eyebrows in an impatient unspoken question, but he just stood there as if paralyzed, saying nothing for several seconds. He was holding her pasta bowl in his hands and was wearing a sailor's sweater and worn jeans, his feet still bare. He was unreasonably, annoyingly handsome, she thought, and before she knew it, she had taken the bowl from his hand and pulled him inside.

When the door closed, they were standing close in the narrow vestibule; he a head taller and about fifteen years younger, Esther filled with a fierce energy.

And desire.

She set the pasta bowl on the floor.

He looked at her, his eyes smiling, and once again she was the sixteen-, twenty-three-, thirty-eight-, forty-six-year-old sensual woman she had always been. She was still that woman, not a dried-up, depressive, anxious shadow of her former self.

The back of his head was soft, and he didn't resist as she pulled him down toward her. That first kiss almost wasn't a kiss, but more of a light grazing of cheeks, noses, lips. The next was dizzyingly wet and hot and lasted both forever and only for an instant.

Esther felt her legs give out. She hadn't been kissed like that in many years, maybe ever.

Alain picked her up in his arms and carried her through the apartment. She sheepishly rested her forehead against his shoulder to minimize the risk of eye contact that could break the magical spell.

In the bedroom he carefully put her down on the bed and she felt her first flash of panic. Who was this man, anyway? She hardly knew him, had no idea what he was up to.

Mixed in with her nerves was also a fair amount of vanity. Was she really going to take her clothes off in front of a stranger, a

Frenchman no less, reveal her age spots and varicose veins, her saggy skin and brittle bones?

He started unbuttoning her shirt.

Apparently so. He was slow and focused, a bit clumsy, and it helped with her insecurity that he too seemed nervous.

She kissed him again. He wanted her, too. Why would he pretend?

Alain pushed Esther over onto her back, suddenly violent, and lay down on top of her. She closed her eyes. The swarming thoughts wandered from her brain, down her body, making her quiver.

It was over fast, and after that it was awkward.

That's how it is when you don't know each other, she thought, not daring to reach over and stroke his cheek. At least all her parts still worked.

After they had lain side by side for a bit, he sat up and started putting on his clothes without looking at her. He was regretting it, that much was clear, and Esther desperately searched for a way to smooth over the situation.

Once he was dressed, he turned to her with heavy eyes.

"Sorry! I was much too rough. Maybe I was just nervous. You are . . ." He exhaled with a smile, designed to illustrate how amazing she was. "I've always loved mature women — wise, gorgeous, experienced women. You're . . . out of my league."

Esther was so surprised that she practically fell off the bed. He was insecure?! More than she was?

She laughed.

"I'm at least as nervous as you. You are totally amazing, Alain. Really! And I'm just an old hag who . . ."

"Stop! Don't ever say that about yourself!" He kissed her palms tenderly and continued to her belly. For a second she thought he was going to seduce her again. Then he stopped.

"What time is it? I actually came up to ask you if I could borrow your car. I have to move a dresser that the movers forgot in my old apartment."

"Is this how you normally go about asking a neighbor for a favor?" She smiled and sat up in the bed.

He gestured nonchalantly with his hands.

"Well, you're going to be popular in this building. But unfortunately I don't have a car."

"Okay. Voilà, then I'll have to figure something else out." He leaned over and kissed her on the mouth, languidly sensuous, before releasing her and standing up. "I need to run, *chérie,* but we'll see each other again soon, very soon."

She pulled the covers up around her.

He turned around in the doorway.

"*Chérie,* you don't happen to have any cash I can borrow? Five hundred kroner, a thousand? I have a friend who drives a pirate taxi. Maybe he could help me with the dresser."

Esther got out of bed, dragging the blanket with her.

"It would just be until I can get to an ATM."

She found a thousand-kroner bill in her purse in the hallway and handed it to him. He accepted it and stuck it in his pocket.

"You're a gem, thank you! You'll get it back later." He kissed her gently on the cheek and let himself out.

Esther stood in the echo of the door closing, the heavy blanket around her naked, newly kissed body and felt her heart beating so hard she could hardly breathe.

CHAPTER 15

By the time Svend and the baby came home from the pool, Anette had finished her shower. She took a deep breath and told him about the case. She couldn't keep lying; after all, there was a limit to how many times a person could drive to BabySam without actually bringing home diapers.

Svend was not thrilled.

She certainly couldn't blame him. Still, she tried to explain how it was just an idea she wanted to pursue, that she wasn't seriously investigating the case. She just needed some adult time, and for her adult time meant work. She promised to be back before dinner. When she went to kiss him goodbye, Svend gave her his cheek instead of his lips.

Fredens Havn was one of Copenhagen's lesser known illegal settlements, located right next to the most famous one, namely Christiania. In the shallow waters of

Erdkehlgraven along Refshalevej, small enclaves of old boats, driftwood, trash, and mobile homes floated on the sea, about fifty yards from shore. The haphazard, makeshift assemblage housed a handful of residents, who were on their tenth year of defying the Coastal Authority's orders to vacate the harbor and instead doing their best to make it flourish. Potted plants climbed up colorful sheets of corrugated metal, and pirate flags fluttered over the ramshackle floating "homes."

It wasn't until Anette had parked her car on the grassy shoulder that it dawned on her that she would need a boat to get out there. Or swim. She walked down to the shoreline and peered out over the water. After a few minutes a young man turned up at the shoreline about ten yards away. He was carrying an instrument case on his back containing what to Anette's untrained eye had to be a cello or a contrabass, and an inflatable Spider-Man boat and a paddle in his arms. He tossed the tiny boat into the water, knelt carefully on its wobbling surface, and started paddling.

"Hey, hey, you there!"

The young man with the instrument case looked around.

"Do you have room for one more in your

rubber-ducky thing?"

He spotted her and squinted.

"Who are you looking for?" he asked skeptically.

"Marie."

He hesitated, looking rather ridiculous kneeling in the inflatable kiddy boat.

"Does she know you're coming?"

Anette threw her hands up in the air and said, "I was just supposed to be here on the bank at five p.m." When lying, it was usually best to keep things fairly vague.

"It's going to be tight," he said, turning his Spider-Man boat around and paddling back to shore.

"That's fine." Anette walked down to the water's edge. "How should we do it?"

"Get in on your knees behind me, and hold on to my case. Spread your legs a little, as they say."

Anette managed to install herself behind the young man and his case without capsizing them. As he paddled them out to Fredens Havn, she realized how ludicrous they must look and couldn't help laughing.

He laughed, too.

"Hey, knock it off or we're going end up in the water for crying out loud."

Anette stifled her chuckles against the instrument case and tried to remember when she had last laughed.

"Here we are! Welcome to Donkey Island. Marie lives over there." He pointed to a small graffiti-covered camper and headed off in the opposite direction toward an aging wooden boat. The pontoon-supported dock was covered in artificial turf and in raised wooden beds tidy rows of neatly pruned edible plants sprouted.

Anette walked cautiously across the unstable dock toward the camper. *Murder She Wrote* was written across it in pink paint.

When Anette was a few yards from the camper, the door opened and a skinny girl scowled out at her.

"You have thirty seconds to explain who you are and why you're here, before the Count releases the dogs."

"The Count? Wait, what is this? Sesame Street?" Anette gave her a smile, although the bubbly elation from the boat trip was waning.

"Twenty seconds."

She seemed to be serious in her threat, although she was no more than five foot three and didn't look very strong as far as Anette could tell under the woven blankets she was wrapped up in. Her hair looked like something that had been pulled out of a cat brush.

"My name is Anette Werner. I'm a detective with the Copenhagen Police, but I'm here on private business, no gun." She opened her jacket to show that she wasn't armed. "That being said, the police *are* looking for you. They want to talk to you about the murders of three former employees of the Butterfly House."

"I have nothing to say to the police or to you. Goodbye!" The girl shut her door.

Anette stayed put for a bit, wondering who the Count was and what kind of dogs he had. Then she called to the closed door that looked thin enough that everything must be audible from inside, "Uh, also I have something for you, a folder. From your tattooed friend."

Silence from the camper. Then the door opened ajar and a skinny hand appeared. Anette handed the folder she had received from the blue giant to the girl. The door closed; a minute went by. Then it opened again.

"Come in."

Anette stepped into the diminutive camper, feeling it bobbing under her weight. It was pretty primitive on the inside, but surprisingly tidy and pleasant; someone had put the effort into building a custom bench into the corner and making cushions for it.

"Who did you say gave you this?" the girl asked, standing with the folder in front of her.

"I'm just going to have a seat." Anette slumped onto the bench. "First tell me: *Are* you Marie Birch?"

The girl nodded brusquely.

"You're wanted in a murder investigation. As I said, I'm not here to officially interview you, but I can't withhold my knowledge of where you are. The police will surely come pay you a visit."

"They won't find me here when they do." A shadow slid over Marie's face. "I won't talk to them. Where did you find the folder?"

"I got it from a guy I met down in the Colony by Vesterport. He asked me to give it to you when I found you. What is it?"

Marie smiled fleetingly but didn't respond. Instead, she opened a little cupboard under the table and took out two avocadoes, which she halved, peeled, and started cutting into slices on a plastic cutting board.

"What are you doing?"

"As a gift for your bringing my folder. You're breastfeeding, right?"

"How did you know?"

Marie kept slicing, and said, "You need vitamin D and good fats. That'll stop it feeling so tight and hurting so much."

For once in her life, Anette didn't know what to say. The gesture was bizarre and at the same time, oddly touching.

Marie set a plastic plate of sliced avocado in front of her.

"It means a lot to me, that folder. Thank you for bringing it."

Anette, who wasn't a big fan of avocado, dutifully took a piece. Marie Birch was not what you'd call the conventional type.

"How did you end up living out here?"

"Fredens Havn isn't just a place to spend the night. It's a place where you can really *live*. You can shut out all the noise here." She spoke the words mechanically, almost like a slogan. "Don't forget to eat!"

Anette took another piece and said, "But before this you lived in the Colony under Vesterport. Down there's quite a lot of noise, isn't there?"

Marie again didn't respond to Anette's question. Perhaps better to start with something else. Anette pulled her phone out of her pocket, pressed the Photos app, and showed the screen to the young woman.

"Did you write this?" she asked.

Marie recoiled a little at the sight of the picture from the residential home, clearly uncomfortable.

"Why?" Anette put the phone away.

"*Invisible Marie.* What's there to explain? When no one sees you, you don't exist."

Anette swallowed a slice of avocado with growing discomfort.

"I met a woman named Bettina Holte. She worked at Butterfly House while you lived there."

Marie stared at her blankly. Then she blinked deliberately and sighed as if making a decision.

"I'll talk to you, but *only* to you . . . Bettina made fun of what I wrote: Invincible Marie, ha-ha." The memory did not appear to amuse her.

"And now she's dead, along with Nicola and Rita."

"I thought you said you were here on private business, not as a detective?" Marie's voice grew hostile again.

Anette changed tactics.

"Was Butterfly House a good place to live?"

"No. The owner, Rita, was *old-school,* as she put it. That means hard-nosed and cheap. No expenses spent."

"Can you give me an example of what that meant? Just so I can understand . . ."

Marie explained with a patronizing look, "It meant that she hired people who weren't trained in how to take care of us, people who had no idea how to deescalate a situation with a kid who was acting out. People who were promised sleep when they were on the night shift even if that meant giving large doses of sedatives to the patients. Having staff that's awake at night costs extra. It only got worse when the psychiatrist came, Peter Demant." Marie's cheeks were flushed, glowing red in her otherwise ashen face.

"How did he make things worse?"

"Peter increased the dosage of antipsychotics we were being given . . . radically. Apparently it was a part of his theory, that the health officials' recommendations are way too conservative. I also suspect that he was switching between different types of antipsychotics. Several of us started having panic attacks and horrific hallucinations. When we complained, he always had an explanation and just brushed us off."

Anette looked down at what was left of her avocado. It glistened on the plate.

"He introduced the restraints. Do you know what those are?" Marie held out one arm and grasped her wrist tightly with the other hand. "You are strapped down to a gurney with leather straps so you can't move. And then you lie there until you've calmed down. Or until the social worker has time to come and unstrap you again. Sometimes it takes half an hour. Other times you lie there all night." The words poured out of her, like smooth skipping stones over a stormy sea.

"But . . ." Anette protested, her body tense with a growing sense of high alert, "isn't that legal?"

"Not in private residential programs." Marie smiled sadly. "And definitely not the way it was done to us. We were left unsupervised, without help. Sometimes restraints really are the only way to calm a psychotic patient down. Care has a different face in psychiatry than it has in the rest of the world. But it's supposed to be done by the book, records kept . . ."

"Couldn't you complain to someone? A government official . . ."

"Private treatment facilities get a lot of wiggle room. And besides, who believes a schizophrenic psych patient?"

Her last statement sounded so resigned it left a lump in Anette's throat. Things didn't usually get to her like this.

"But . . . didn't any of the grown-ups say anything, do anything?"

"Most of them didn't know any better. They were up against a smooth-talking director and a big-name psychiatrist. What were they supposed to say? Some of them agreed with the iron-and-brimstone approach — Bettina, for example. Others just didn't want to interfere, like Nicola. The only one who tried to change things was Kim."

Anette didn't know who Kim was but decided to wait and hope the girl would explain in her own words. It paid off.

"Kim was a trained social worker and knew right from wrong. He wasn't afraid of Rita; he confronted her, explained how wrong it was to be so reckless with our lives. I think he even threatened to go to the police. But conveniently enough he drowned before he got that far, so we'll never know."

"And you don't believe that he drowned by accident?"

Marie looked out the camper's little window and said nothing for a full minute. Then she shook her head.

"But I still don't *know*. Ask Tanja, our nurse. I have the sense that she knows something. . . ."

There was a knock on the door, and the young man with the instrument case peeked in, smiling at Anette.

"I'm heading back to shore now. Do you want a ride?"

Marie got up, and Anette took that as a

sign that the meeting was over.

"Yes, thank you. Just give us two minutes to say goodbye."

He shut the door, and Anette sought out Marie's eyes.

"I'm guessing that you know you're in danger, and that's the reason why you're hiding in places like these. But no matter who you're running from, they're going to find you. The only people who can protect you are the police. I understand why you don't have a lot of confidence in the system, but won't you let us help you?"

Marie walked past Anette, out onto the pontoon dock and waited for her to follow. Looked up and took a deep breath.

"There's more rain on the way, don't you think? Wind and thunder and a lot more rain . . ." She nodded to herself. Then she walked back into her camper and shut the door.

Jeppe opened the kitchen window, lit a cigarette, and smoked while he regarded the dining table with its dirty plates and dinner leftovers. He had brought lasagna home for his mother, and she had been so delighted that Jeppe had chewed himself out for not doing so more often now that he was even living at her place.

Still she had hardly eaten a thing. His mother wasn't a big eater, had never been, but it was getting worse. She was thinner than ever. There used to be strength in her long limbs, a toughness, tenacity. Now she was frail, delicate, and brittle like glass.

Jeppe stubbed out his cigarette, tossed it out into the rain with a hypocritical *Pardon me* to the universe and started clearing the table. Everything seemed brittle and crazy right now, particularly these murders, which, according to Mosbæk, might be the work of someone mad at the health-care sector. The superintendent had stepped up surveillance in the city. Police officers were stationed by the city's fountains, along the canals, and around the Lakes. Downtown Copenhagen had been declared a temporary stop-and-frisk zone, and patrols were stopping cargo bikes, vans, and other suspicious vehicles throughout the city.

When the leftover lasagna was in the fridge and the dishes washed by hand, Jeppe sat down at the dining table and lit another cigarette. The last of the day, he promised himself. Across town Sara was tucking the kids in, but in a little while he would drive to her place and hope that she wouldn't smell the smoke on him. He needed to be close, to calm down, and sleep next to her, but knew that it wasn't an option right now. Well, then he would just have to make do with sex. He smiled at the thought and inhaled the smoke fully into his lungs.

"What the fuck, Kørner? Did you start smoking again?"

Jeppe practically fell out the window. Anette Werner was standing in his mother's kitchen, her arms crossed, and his mother by her side. Instinctively he ditched his cigarette without stubbing it out and hoped it didn't land on anyone's head. Apparently you never get too old to try to keep your mother from catching you smoking.

"What are you doing here, and unannounced?"

"I was in the neighborhood. Your mom let me in. Didn't you hear the doorbell?" Anette gave his mother a conspiratorial wink.

"Your sweet coworker stopped by," his mother cooed.

Jeppe hopped down from the table and asked, "Could we have a moment alone?"

"Of course, Snuggles. I'll go and watch the news."

His mother closed the door behind herself, and Jeppe shot Anette a warning glance to ward off any potential jokes about his nickname.

"What brings you to Nørrebro?"

"Don't worry, I'm only staying a minute," she said, glancing at her watch. "I have to get home and breastfeed. But I found Marie. I wanted to tell you right away."

"Marie Birch?"

A key witness, whom they had been urgently searching for, and Anette found her just like that? Jeppe felt annoyance surging through his body, pumping in his bloodstream.

"Can't you just be on maternity leave for five minutes already?"

Anette raised her eyebrows in surprise. "Okay, I didn't realize you would be so angry. If I had, I would have called instead." She walked over and held out her hand. "Let's have a cigarette."

"Uh, are you allowed to smoke when you're nursing?"

"It's when you're pregnant that you can't smoke. Besides, I don't smoke, not really."

Jeppe sighed.

"Knock it off, Jepsen. I just had an idea and pursued it without knowing . . . Yeah, well. Anyway, I found her. I know I should have talked to you about it before, but I'm here now."

Jeppe handed her a cigarette and lit it without setting her eyebrows on fire. All

315

things considered, he thought that showed restraint.

She took a deep puff and held on to the smoke before exhaling.

"Oh, that tastes damn good!"

Jeppe laughed against his will and pulled out a chair for her.

"Anette Werner, you are a pain in the butt. Tell me what you know! How did you find her?"

"It started when I recognized Bettina Holte from the maternity ward at Herlev Hospital. I got curious. So I drove out to Butterfly House, after you mentioned it to me. Marie's name was still on the door to her room. And then at Vesterport I met a . . . no, it's too complicated to explain. But anyway I found Marie Birch out in that place they call Fredens Havn."

"I know of it." Jeppe nodded. "It's that mini settlement on the water, where all the freaks live."

"They don't seem so freaky, actually. Marie lives in a camper, which belongs to someone who calls himself the Count. But she says she won't talk to the police. Believe me, if you go out there, you're just going to scare her away. If she hasn't already hightailed it out of there."

"So then, how did you get her to talk?"

Jeppe walked over to the fridge and peeked in. He could go for a beer.

"I brought her a folder that I got from one of her underground friends at the Colony."

"A folder? Underground?" Jeppe wasn't following.

"Never mind. She was happy to get her folder and served me an avocado as thanks. Hey, are you going to give me a beer, or are you just letting out the cold for fun?"

Jeppe, who felt pretty sure that alcohol was not okay when nursing, closed the fridge.

"There's only milk left. Sorry."

Anette took a greedy puff on her cigarette, got up, and doused the cigarette butt under running water in the sink.

"She claimed that Butterfly House had used heavy-handed methods to control the residents, upped their medication doses and left them restrained and unattended. Illegal methods. According to her, Rita and a psychiatrist by the name of Peter Demant were responsible for the strict treatment. Can I throw the cigarette in the trash? Is that okay?"

Jeppe nodded.

"I heard about it from the other side. Demant describes it differently, of course."

"Alibi?"

"Claims he was at home the last three evenings and nights. Had a video consultation yesterday evening for an hour and a half with a patient who lives abroad. It was hard to get the patient's name out of Demant, but we did and the patient confirmed it. The consultation went until eleven thirty p.m., which would make it hard for him to meet Rita at the crime scene and have time to murder her within the midnight to three a.m. time slot, which is the established window for the time of death."

"But not impossible?" Anette sat back down at the table.

"No."

"Marie mentioned a social worker by the name of Kim, who had died in an accident. She more than insinuated that he was murdered."

"By whom?" Jeppe sat down across from his partner. She looked tired. "You look like shit, by the way."

"You try not sleeping at night."

"Me? I haven't slept for a year. All I do, actually, is to *not* sleep at night."

They smiled at each other. Anette's smile ended in a stifled yawn.

"*If* Kim was murdered, and *if* the motive was to shut him up about what was going on, then that would point to Rita Wilkins and Peter Demant."

"Of whom only one is still alive. Ironically enough, Demant himself voiced a theory that one of the kids is killing the staff. In other words, Isak or Marie. Everyone is pointing fingers at each other." Jeppe cocked his head to the side and cracked his neck. "I'm meeting Demant again tomorrow morning, so I'll try to coax some more out of him."

"Damn exciting. I wish I could go." Anette winked. "But I could look into Demant a little online if that could be of use . . . ?"

"Anette Werner, what am I going to do with you?" Jeppe rolled his eyes. "Hey, did Marie Birch mention a girl named Pernille?"

"No."

"She was one of the other kids living at Butterfly House, committed suicide two years ago, the year after Kim's death. According to Demant, because of Kim's death. Her father sued Rita and Robert Wilkins, and they were ultimately forced to shut Butterfly House. He's still grieving. And he's mad."

"Sounds like a slam dunk."

"Unfortunately he seems to have an alibi for last night."

"Yet another alibi. This is straight out of Sherlock Holmes." She smiled wide, her crooked canines showing. Jeppe hadn't seen those in a long time.

"Well, I'd better go home to my family," she said. "Otherwise my breasts will explode."

"We can't have that," Jeppe said, standing up.

In the doorway Anette stopped and looked at him shyly.

Jeppe slapped her on the shoulder and said, "Say hi to everyone back home. I'll come by and see the baby just as soon as I've caught this violent psychopath who is eradicating Copenhagen's therapy community."

"Or after you've been fired for not catching him." Anette started down the stairs. Just before she disappeared from view, she yelled so that it echoed through the entire stairwell, "Night night, Snuggles!"

CHAPTER 16

"Hi, Gorm. Everything okay?"

He walked by his colleague, to the line of coat hooks on the wall. Gorm was sitting in the staff room with a cup of coffee and a crumpled newspaper. He looked tired.

"Yeah, thanks," Gorm said. "But it'll be good to get home and relax a little. It's been a long day."

"Did something happen?" Simon Hartvig asked, removing his wet rain gear while trying to keep too much water from getting on the floor.

"Well, they're all still worked up about the dead body in the fountain yesterday. They've definitely noticed that the police came by. But things are relatively peaceful. They just ate dinner." Gorm got up and put his cup in the dishwasher. "I'll do my rounds and say good night before I head home. Do you want to come with me and say hello?"

"Sure, I'll just change my shoes."

He pulled a pair of sneakers out of his bag, put them on, and started tying the laces.

Behind him Gorm cleared his throat.

"Hey, I need to ask you something. Yesterday, when I checked the medicine room, there were drugs missing compared to the inventory. Three boxes of ten-milligram Ritalin, the thirty-count boxes. Do you know anything about that?"

"What the hell is that supposed to mean?!"

"Chill out, man. I mean, maybe you just forgot to enter them?"

"Of course not!" Simon tried to force his voice to sound calm. "I don't know where they are, but there's probably a logical explanation for it, right? Maybe one of the other wards borrowed some?"

"I've checked," Gorm said, shaking his head. "I'm afraid someone took them."

"Who would do that?" Simon said, looking at the floor. "Me?"

"That's not what I'm saying." Gorm made a conciliatory gesture with his hands. "But I do need to ask. You know, stealing drugs is a serious matter!"

"Fine, but I don't know anything about it." Simon produced a yawn to mask his anxious breathing, then gestured to the door. "Should we go make the rounds?"

He escaped Gorm's scrutinizing gaze, moving on into the common room, where TV voices buzzed and laughter sounded from the foosball table. One of the girls ran over and hugged him, her vibrant enthusiasm soothing his jumpy nerves.

"Well, what a nice greeting, sweetie!" He scanned the sofas. "Where's Isak?"

"In his room. He wasn't hungry today and wanted to be by himself." The last part was said with teenagery sarcasm, as if it were something the girl had heard many times before.

"I'll just pop in and check on him."

Simon went down to Isak's room, knocked, and opened the door. The room was empty.

"Wasn't Isak supposed to be in his room?" Gorm was walking over, busy buckling his bike helmet.

"Isak's not there," Simon persisted. "Where can he be?"

"I don't know."

Simon walked off with Gorm on his heels, searching the quiet room, bathrooms, shower rooms, the crafts room, the kitchen, the admin hallway. With every room they checked, Simon's footsteps felt heavier and heavier. There was no sign of Isak. Finally they returned to his room. It was still empty.

Gorm even opened the cupboard, which they knew was too small for him to hide in, and looked under the bed, which was too low to the ground for him to fit under. Isak wasn't there.

"Where is he?" Gorm asked, the panic in his voice palpable. "Where the hell can he be? What are we going to do?"

Simon walked over to the window facing the yard and the copper beech tree. The windows all locked with the same key that fit the doors and the cabinets where they kept spare cables so the patients couldn't hang themselves with them. All the employees on the ward had a key. Simon patted the pocket where he kept his. Then he gave the window a push and saw it slide open effortlessly.

In that moment, just as the alarm sounded, he understood, without quite daring to think the thought all the way to the end.

"Did you hear?"

Sara greeted him with a question instead of the kiss he had been looking forward to. She had texted as soon as the kids were asleep.

"Yeah, they called me from headquarters to tell me he was gone. They have canine units all over the whole northwest sector. No sign of him yet." Jeppe pulled her in close and kissed her. Enjoyed the feel of her soft breasts against his body and breathed in the scent of her hair and her skin. "Hello, you. I've missed you."

"But that's totally nuts!" She pulled free from his arms. "I mean, Falck was at the hospital just yesterday trying to get to talk to him."

Jeppe unzipped his raincoat and asked, "Where should I hang this? It's pretty wet."

"Just in the hall . . . But, seriously, think about it: A mentally ill teenager escapes from a locked ward and kills off his old counselors one by one? It's like a movie!"

Sara gathered up the laundry that she had been carrying in her arms when he rang the bell. With those long legs sticking out under a well-worn sweatshirt and her curls pulled up into a ponytail, she was the one who looked like something out of a movie. She had no idea how beautiful she was.

"Just because he has had the opportunity to escape doesn't mean he murdered anyone."

"Of course not. But why wouldn't he hate those people who kept him locked up and drove his friend to suicide?" She went to the bathroom and started loading the dirty laundry into the washing machine. "He's schizophrenic. I don't mean to be prejudiced, but there's definitely a possibility that he could be violent."

"But that *is* prejudiced." Jeppe followed her into the bathroom and kissed her to take the edge off his words. He was exhausted, right down to his soul. So exhausted, he could lie down on the hallway floor and sleep for a hundred years.

"Are you okay?" She snapped her fingers. "Did you just fall asleep standing up?"

"I'm just . . ." He shook himself awake. "Do you have a beer? That might help."

"You already reek, as if you came straight from a bar." She sniffed him and then made a face. "Hello, *ashtray*! You want a glass?"

"In the can is fine." While she went to the kitchen Jeppe collapsed onto the sofa. There was something comforting about her teasing. Ashtray! That was the kind of mocking you would expect from a girlfriend.

Sara returned to the living room with beers for both of them, sat down next to him and put her feet in his lap.

"How was your day?" she asked.

Jeppe opened his beer and drank. Ease spread through his body and made him even sleepier.

"Frustrating," he admitted. "Endless.

How about yours?"

"Pretty good. I'm actually surprised at how competent a detective Larsen is turning out to be. He's sharp."

"Really? You didn't use to think that."

"Maybe I was wrong about him," she said, pondering while she drank from her beer. "He's really good with the financial stuff, too. Maybe he's a little slick, and things move a bit fast sometimes, but he actually is both thorough and surprisingly fun. We kind of jibe."

Jeppe couldn't think of a response that wasn't either childish or inappropriate, so he said nothing. They drank in silence.

If he had ever been good at being in love, then he couldn't remember. For him, the early stage of a relationship before some form of mutual declaration of love — the period romantics in Denmark describe with terms like *butterfly dust* or *shooting stars* — had always been a rocky road full of unexpected potholes. It bugged him, not knowing if he and Sara were a couple. He didn't want to feel jealous when she complimented other men. He wasn't that kind of guy.

Jeppe emptied his beer can and leaned his head back against the sofa cushion with a heartfelt sigh. If he just closed his eyes for a second, he would know what to say.

"Jeppe, Jeppe! You can't sleep here."

He woke up disoriented to see Sara leaning over him. She smiled indulgently.

"You're too tired to do anything but sleep. Go home and go to bed, would you?"

"No, it's fine. I'm not tired."

"You've been snoring for twenty minutes, my dear," she pointed out, and then kissed him on the cheek. "Come on. Let's get you onto your bike. We all have to get up early."

Jeppe let her lead him to the front hall like a zombie. Raincoat on, a quick goodbye kiss, and then he was standing on the street, in the rain, with a nagging sense that he had just been kicked out by his girlfriend, or whatever she was. She hadn't even asked about that pretty museum lady who was so clearly interested in him.

He started riding toward Knippelsbro bridge. The wind had picked up and lightning traced hectic heartbeats across the sky. His tired thoughts skipped between a young, schizophrenic man and a beautiful, Tunisian-Danish policewoman. The one escaped at night from the locked ward at Bispebjerg Hospital, the other kept him at arm's length, alternately loving and tolerating him in an unpredictable current of hot and cold.

None of it made any sense, and both left

him feeling helpless and frustrated.

Jeppe passed one of the many patrol cars that had been extraordinarily deployed throughout Copenhagen to keep an eye out for mentally deranged young men and cargo bikes. Hopefully they would find him tomorrow, and everything would be clearer.

It bothered Jeppe that Sara, too, succumbed to the temptation of automatically suspecting *the sick.* Diagnoses make it easy and comfortable to explain the things we don't want to be universally human.

But there were questions Jeppe couldn't find answers to when he tried to imagine a seventeen-year-old psych patient as the murderer.

Where did he kill them? How did he get them to meet with him? Where did he store the cargo bike that he used to transport the bodies to the fountains?

Jeppe pedaled hard, his pulse pounding in his temples. It was easier pointing fingers than it was finding solutions.

As he crossed the broad street Østervold, it hit him that he was doing exactly the same thing with Sara, pointing fingers. Because it was easier to blame her for their uncertain relationship status than to admit his own doubt. It wasn't her hesitation as much as it was his own. The thought of throwing himself wholeheartedly into family life with two kids he hardly knew frightened him. He had been burned before. And the world also contained Monica Kirkskovs who flipped their hair and batted their eyelids, women who came without baggage or commitment, who were casual and easy. Easiness, wasn't that what he longed for, when you got right down to it?

A gust of wind almost knocked him off his bike, making him wobble dangerously in the thunderstorm. Lightning flashed blue over the Lakes.

Everything would be clearer tomorrow. He hoped.

After Trine Bremen had fed her family, folded the laundry, put the kids to bed, and had a good cry in the bathroom, she excused herself to her husband, saying she had a headache and needed to go for an evening stroll. Klaus was understanding, or maybe he was just relieved to get to watch soccer in peace. Hard to tell. Sometimes he seemed downright indifferent toward her and didn't understand that his indifference was part of the problem.

Trine set out into the rain. He hadn't even asked if she needed an umbrella.

She walked to the harbor. Their little

downtown apartment on Fredericiagade was cramped, but the location, on the other hand, was great. They often talked about moving out of the city, where they could get more for their money — space, apple trees, a yard with a trampoline for the kids — but they had yet to take the plunge.

Truthfully, Trine was the one who feared what the peace and calm of the countryside would do to her. Even now, here by the water, the quiet was a disagreeable void, leaving plenty of room for the unwanted thoughts that pinballed nonstop through her head. Being alone with her thoughts was tough. She regretted not bringing her headphones so she could have listened to music and drowned out the messages from her brain telling her how unsound she was. The benzodiazepine made her fat and gave her acne, and it didn't even have the desired effect anymore. Trine felt a manic anxiety closing in.

She looked out over the water and wiped her eyes — apparently they never ran out of tears — and passed a police car driving slowly through Nyhavn. The officers didn't look at her, didn't even glance at this young woman with her long hair and big, blue eyes. Was she really so unattractive?

Trine crossed the Inner Harbor bike

bridge. She had to do something about the situation at work soon. Things were getting so bad she was getting a stomachache every time she walked through the revolving doors into the hospital. The other nurses had pretty much stopped talking to her and they had even gotten a couple of the porters on board with them. It was regular old workplace bullying and it reminded her of her time at Butterfly House: the backstabbing, the distrust, the silence around her. Back then it had been a woman who had started the harassment, too, undermining her reputation and making the work intolerable. Rita. Trine cringed at the thought of Rita.

She had been too open about her own medical history of borderline personality disorder and the antianxiety drugs she took. Naively she had thought it would have a disarming effect and build trust, but it had had the opposite effect. They had used her weakness against her and attacked her with the very weapon she had put in their hands.

She reached the block of modern luxury apartments on Holmen and looked up at the windows of the topmost unit. The lights were on. A police car was parked right in front of the entrance with two cops in it; they must be keeping an eye on him. Trine smiled to herself and started to make her way around the building across the sodden lawn. As long as she kept her distance, she would be invisible in the dark.

When she reached the far side of the property, she walked down the narrow dock along the water to the back door of the building. It was rarely locked. She tried it and felt it open with a cute little creak, letting her into the dark vestibule where a staircase led up to the roof unimpeded. She walked past the light switches and started climbing in darkness.

Through the glass facade she could see glimpses of light, reflecting on the coal-black water. There was something naughty about sneaking past the police. Unannounced. A wave of excitement washed over her, and for a moment she forgot the dreary mood that had brought her out there to begin with. She squeezed the little box in her pocket between sweaty palms.

She wondered if he could sense her coming. Did he have any idea what was coming?

Peter Demant pricked up his ears. Was someone at the door? That couldn't be. He had been standing in his dark library for the last ten or fifteen minutes looking at the police car in front of his building. No one had gotten out of the car, no one had passed it to go in the front door, no one had buzzed. Of course it could be a neighbor, but in the five years Peter had lived here, he had never yet had a neighbor knock on his door. And it was after 10:00 p.m.

There was another knock, this time there was no mistaking it. Only one person in his life was in the habit of stopping by unannounced, and he had no wish to see her. He took a couple of quiet steps and stopped.

Maybe she would ultimately go away again. Ugh, but then the calls would start, and they would keep coming late into the night and in the morning, too, until she eventually turned up in the clinic.

Peter looked through the peephole and reluctantly unlocked the door. There she was, dripping with rain, wrapped in a long, black trench coat worthy of a movie diva.

"Hi, Trine. How did you get in the front door?"

She smiled secretively and streaked past him into the apartment without taking off her shoes. Peter felt nauseated by the wet footprints she left on his hardwood floor, but didn't say anything.

"It's late. What can I do for you?"

Trine sat down on the ottoman that went with his white leather Eames chair and crossed her legs without taking off her coat. He regarded her with growing loathing. Her doughy, scarred face, which she believed could be made attractive by caking it in powder and rouge, that sly look that exposed her enormous, bloated overestimation of her own intellect, and that plump body in cheap clothes, which was occupying his furniture right now. She reminded him of that night at Butterfly House when Bettina Holte had made a pass at him. Stinking of sour wine, too drunk to know her own limits, she had offered herself up. The memory of that night still revolted him.

Peter looked at Trine and thought — not for the first time — that it would be a relief if she ceased to exist.

■ ■ ■ ■

THURSDAY,
OCTOBER 12

■ ■ ■ ■

CHAPTER 17

If you have trouble sleeping at night for more than four weeks, you might have chronic insomnia, unless a baby or a new lover is keeping you awake, of course. For those who lie awake for no reason, sleeplessness is often related to:

Stress.
Unhealthy lifestyle factors (including smoking).
Poor sleep hygiene (an uncomfortable guest bed in your mother's apartment, for example).
Mental illness.

Thursday morning at eight, when Jeppe sat in his office at police headquarters, he was inclined to check all the boxes on the list, including the last one. If you don't have a mental illness to begin with, not sleeping at night will eventually give you one. That feeling of being chronically drunk, motion sick, and jet-lagged increased for every sleepless night that passed, even if one of the reasons for the fatigue was all his enjoyable nighttime messing around with Sara.

Jeppe felt sick.

Right now his coffee cup swam around in his field of vision on the table in front of him like some kind of malignant perpetual-motion machine. He wasn't sure if he had met his mother last night when he got up to pee. Had she actually been standing in the hallway in the dark, looking confused? And had he walked her back to bed again, or was it just something he had dreamed during one of the night's fleeting bubbles of sleep?

Jeppe knew that the feeling would soon recede for the day. As he consumed coffee and breakfast and interacted with other humans, he would slowly but surely begin to feel normal again. Tired but functional, until tonight when it would start all over. He looked at the Klimt poster's hollow-eyed skeletons and decided to hang up something else instead as soon as he had the energy.

A glance at his watch revealed that Peter Demant was late. He didn't really strike Jeppe as the type to not be punctual. On the contrary, he gave off the almost rigid vibe of someone who was in superhuman control, a man who oozed a professional courtesy that seemed precisely dosed and calculated.

A crackling sound made Jeppe look up.

Falck stood in his doorway, eating a Danish out of a paper bakery bag. Today he was wearing suspenders with red and green cars on them, a piece of icing balancing on his mustache.

"Well . . . ?" Falck said.

Just that, a *well* expressed as a question, followed by vigorous munching. Jeppe felt his latent irritation spring to life, sending snide remarks thronging to his mouth.

"Well, what? What's the question, Falck? *Well, how did you sleep last night?* or maybe *Well, did they find another body this morning?* or what about *Well, how did it go with Peter Demant? Did he leave already?* To which I would respond that I didn't sleep well at all, no new victims have been found, and Demant seems to be blowing me off. Any other questions?"

Falck seemed immune to Jeppe's grumpy mood. He made himself comfortable in Anette's chair across the desk from Jeppe.

"Would you like a Halloween bun? They're shaped like little pumpkins, see?"

No, thought Jeppe. *I want a murderer*

locked up, a good night's sleep, and a girl-friend I don't have to be unsure about.

"Why not."

Jeppe let hunger win over his germopho-bia, and they sat chewing in silence until Falck cleared his throat.

"Do you know where ghosts go when they're on vacation?" Falck asked.

Jeppe swallowed a mouthful of his pastry and thought that wherever it was, he wished Falck would go there with them.

"To the Dead Sea."

"Har," Jeppe grunted.

At nine o'clock, he brushed the crumbs off his fingers and called Peter Demant. It went straight to voice mail. Jeppe already knew that he wasn't going to bring Pernille Ramsgaard's files over. Still, he called De-mant's clinic as well, where a friendly answering machine informed him that the clinic didn't open again till Thursday next week.

"Do you think he's run off?" Falck asked, crumpling up the bakery bag. He still had icing in his mustache.

"Either that or he's lying in a fountain somewhere in town and just hasn't been found yet. There's no telling anymore."

"We do have a patrol car sitting outside his front door." Falck nodded pensively. *"For protection."* He put air quotes around the last part to show it might have more to do with surveillance than protection.

"Will you find out who's on duty and call them?"

Falck got up with a pained grunt and left the office. In the silence of his absence, Jeppe tried to empty his brain of all the jumbled thoughts so that he could focus and let the relevant emerge by itself. A revelation was what he was waiting for.

He closed his eyes and calmed his breathing, relaxed his body, and tried to let go of his irritability. Tried to shake the feeling that he was chasing after a beam of light that was nothing but a flicker.

Gaslights.

A glimpse of something.

Then came the image.

There was no thought process or explanation, but it was unambiguous. The image that popped into Jeppe's head was Pernille Ramsgaard's face from the portrait in her parents' house, standing between her siblings, pale with big eyes and a brave smile.

Jeppe opened his eyes. Falck had returned and was standing next to the desk, looking embarrassed, as if he felt self-conscious in the presence of Jeppe's meditations. Falck coughed into his hand and then mumbled in his teddy bear voice.

"The patrol car has been sitting outside Demant's building all night and no one has been seen coming or going. The light in Demant's flat was turned off at eleven thirty p.m., so they assumed he went to bed. But they actually rang his bell a little while ago because they were wondering why he hadn't gone to work this morning. No response. His car is still parked in front, but there's a rear exit that leads directly out to the water."

"So he sailed away by boat? Is that what you're saying?" Jeppe shook his head. "First Isak Brügger runs off, and now Demant has disappeared? And we still haven't spoken to Marie Birch."

"Yes, that is unfortunate."

Three killed, three disappeared, one murderer still on the loose. *Unfortunate* seemed like a relatively inadequate word for the situation.

Jeppe got up. What good did it do to sit there and send prayers to the universe while waiting for the next disaster, whether it be in the form of another corpse or a scolding from his superiors.

"Come on, Falck. Let's go for a ride."

"Okay. Where to?" Falck picked up his raincoat from the desk chair, where it had hung, dripping.

"Out to Fredens Havn to visit Marie Birch. We may risk scaring her away, but we've got to do something."

The short trip from police headquarters to Erdkehlgraven passed in silence. Falck didn't ask how Jeppe knew where Marie Birch was living. He just sat behind the wheel and concentrated on the roadway. Jeppe looked out the window and let the pace of the hectic morning commuter traffic turn into a pulse of its own. At Refshalevej they parked by the water and got out of the car, looking over at the ramshackle floating squatters' homes hidden behind the trees.

Across the water, the rebuilt boathouses at Holmen were visible and off to the left, the modern condos where Peter Demant lived. A stone's throw from the bank groups of pontoons, boats, and shacks floated in the calm water. Jeppe recognized the camper Anette had described.

They approached the water's edge, where two men were standing by a dinghy, talking in hushed tones. When they spotted Jeppe and Falck, they stopped and glared at them. Jeppe walked over.

"Good morning, we're with the Copenhagen Police. We're looking for a young

345

woman, who apparently lives here, Marie Birch."

The two men exchanged looks.

"She's a suspect in a murder case. Withholding information about her location is a punishable offence."

"You're too late," one of the men drawled. His long hair was gathered in a ponytail and he was wearing a heavy sweater that seemed to greedily suck the moisture right out of the air. "Marie lived in my camper, but she's left."

The Count, presumably.

"When?"

"Yesterday. In the afternoon, right? She had packed her bag and all when she came to say goodbye."

"She didn't happen to mention where she was going?" Jeppe asked. "Do you know her family, friends? Anywhere where she might have gone?"

The Count shook his head. Jeppe had a hunch that he wouldn't tell them anything even if he did know.

"If she turns up again, please have her contact us right away." He handed the man his card.

The Count took it with a slight smile that clearly said *Nope.*

Jeppe and Falck trudged back to the car

346

and got in. The two men remained on the shore, staring at them openly.

Jeppe found his cigarettes in a pocket and shook one out. One raised eyebrow from Falck made him put them away again with a resigned sigh. Another dead end. The car fell quiet and Jeppe sensed his colleague's gaze on his cheek.

"Well, damn it, let's swing by Bispebjerg Hospital then. You know who we need to talk to. If Isak Brügger has in fact run away and gone back to the hospital before, maybe he'll do it again."

On Thursday morning Esther found a totally transformed Gregers at the hospital. Even in the hallway she could hear cheerful voices from inside his room, and when she opened the door it revealed the unexpected sight of a grinning Gregers chatting with the patient next to him. He was sitting up in bed, some color in his cheeks.

"Here she is, my young roommate! Esther, come, you have to meet John!" Gregers cocked a thumb at the patient in the bed next to his, who was smiling, his frameless glasses gleaming. "Imagine, it turns out that John used to be a typesetter at *Berlingske.* Can you believe it?"

Gregers himself had worked as a printer

for the newspaper *Politiken* his whole life.

"And now here we are, two old newsprint typographers, in the same room. Isn't that funny?"

Esther went over to the other bed and introduced herself, slightly embarrassed to be fully dressed in the presence of a man in a hospital gown, his skinny asparagus legs poking out.

John's handshake was firm and warm, and she irrationally thought to herself that he didn't look especially sick, although neither did Gregers, she supposed. She pulled over a chair and took off her coat.

"You look like you slept well, Gregers?"

"Like a kitten!"

She laughed in spite of her own so-so mood. Alain hadn't called since he waltzed out her door with a thousand kroner yesterday, and the uncertainty was starting to bother her. Seeing Gregers happy helped, even if it took some getting used to.

"Did you get the results from your scintigraphy exam?"

"They just did their rounds a little while ago." Gregers winked playfully. "It's an open-and-shut case. Balloon expansions in three arteries and then that ought to do me for another ten years, at least. They'll operate on Monday."

"That's great news!" Esther gave his hand a squeeze. "Congratulations, my friend."

"If everything goes well, I can go home the same day. They don't even need to put me under or anything. They can do the whole thing with a catheter from my groin." Gregers smiled, relieved. "In a week, I'll be fetching us bread in the mornings again. You'll see. Then everything will be back to normal."

Esther smiled warmly to her friend, although she morosely suspected that for her things would not be normal for a long time.

"That's wonderful, Gregers. Maybe you'll feel less tired. I'll come on Monday and keep you company after the operation. And make sure you make it home all right."

"It's not a given that he is going to want to leave, what with all the cute girls we have here in the department," John said with a chuckle. "You never get too old to appreciate —"

The door to the room banged open, effectively breaking the cheerful mood. A nurse with long, pinkish hair came in. Esther recognized her as Trine.

"Breakfast time. Cheese or sausage?" she asked, casting a sideways glance at Esther. "Your lady friend can't have any."

"Oh, that's fine." Esther flashed her a

disarming smile. "I just had breakfast."

"So what is it? Cheese or sausage?"

Gregers lifted a finger and asked, "I would just like to be permitted to graciously inquire if this was made by the same cook who prepared that damned overcooked chicken breast without any salt or pepper that you tried to stuff down our throats for dinner yesterday? Because then I'm just having coffee, thanks."

"Ditto!" John agreed with a snicker.

The nurse eyed them with a perfectly straight face. Disappointment emanated off her, so thick you could have sliced it and served that for breakfast instead. After a very long moment she lifted her chin defiantly and slammed two foil-covered trays down on their bedside tables.

"If you knew how worn-out we are and how much pressure we're under you wouldn't make fun at our expense. Enjoy!"

The nurse left the room without looking back.

"Was I too harsh?" For once, Gregers sounded like he honestly wasn't sure.

"She's just having a bad day, Gregers. Don't worry about it," Esther said, standing up. "Now I'll leave you gentlemen to enjoy your meal. I have to get home and walk the dogs anyway."

"Oh, good, then John and I can talk about guy stuff." Gregers winked at his neighbor. "You know, Esther, I remembered where I've seen that peacock before."

"Um, you'll have to be a little more specific," Esther said as she did up her coat. "Which peacock? I mean, you see them all the time."

"The new downstairs neighbor. The guy who was up begging for food when I got sick."

Alain! She blushed unwillingly.

"He worked in the kitchen at that restaurant, well, it's more of a fast-food place, really. The one on Nørrebrogade." Gregers started peeling the aluminum foil off his food. "Ew, is that salami? It's practically fluorescent."

"What are you talking about?" Esther asked. "Alain's a musician."

"That may well be, but six months ago, he was cooking french fries on Nørrebrogade," Gregers said, taking a tentative bite of the roll. "I never forget a face. John, what the hell are those little hard things? Radishes or something?"

Esther left the room with a faint *Enjoy your meal* and a growing uneasiness in her gut.

Isak had not returned to Ward U8 at Bispebjerg Hospital. His room was still empty, aside from the forensic specialist who was kneeling by the window with powder and brushes.

An anxious mood pervaded the whole ward, as if one patient's escape stirred up the pot of fear and possibilities and frightened all the other patients. Scared of the possibilities, scared to miss them.

Jeppe put a brake on his fanciful thoughts. He had probably just seen too many movies. In reality, most of the anxiety was primarily coming from the pale charge nurse in front of him. She stood in the doorway of the unoccupied room with her lips pursed, looking like someone who hadn't slept. Jeppe knew all too well how that felt.

"So you really still don't have any idea where he could be?" The charge nurse sounded resigned. "Is there really no one who's seen him or been in touch with him?"

"Not yet, unfortunately," Jeppe answered.

Falck cleared his throat and asked, "Could we go somewhere where we could talk in private? Possibly the staff room where we sat last time?"

The charge nurse nodded absentmind-edly.

"I guess Simon is the one you really want to talk to," she said. "I'll get him."

She walked them down the hallway to the staff room, switched on the light, and dis-appeared. Two minutes later the door opened and Simon Hartvig stepped in. If the charge nurse looked tired, the social worker looked more dead than alive. The skin on his face had an unhealthy-looking sheen to it, as if he had been in a sweaty panic more than once during the night.

"Would you like some coffee?" he asked, having neither greeted nor looked at them.

"Yes, please."

The electric kettle gurgled away and they sat down on the room's cool vinyl chairs. Falck discreetly loosened the button at the top of his pants. Jeppe pretended he didn't notice.

"Were you on duty when Isak disappeared yesterday?"

"No, he was already gone by the time I came in." The electric kettle finished, mak-ing a clicking sound, and the social worker rose. "But I was the one who discovered that he was missing."

"The windows are usually locked. Do you know how he managed to get out?"

"With a key." Simon took out three mugs and slammed the cupboard closed. He looked tense. "*My* key, I'm afraid. I don't understand how he got it. I thought it was in my pocket. I was carrying it around all day yesterday, but it turned out to be the key to my bike lock."

"So Isak stole your key yesterday, and you discovered it when?"

"Not until I came in for my shift last night and we realized that he had run away. I'm really not careless, this kind of thing never happens to me. The key is always in my pants pocket. I just don't understand."

Jeppe eyed the social worker. He looked like someone who had already had to defend himself quite a bit. Surely the administrators didn't look favorably on an employee who played fast and loose with safety.

"Now that you've had some time to think: Is there an obvious place for him to go? Anyone who might help him that you know of?"

"Not his parents, that's for sure. I've spoken to them — I'm sure you guys have, too — and they haven't seen or heard from him."

"Who else is he close to?"

"Not really anyone." The social worker flung up his arms.

"Other social workers or nurses here on the ward?"

Simon shook his head. "Isak is a real introvert, and he doesn't warm up to people very easily. He has never been good at relationships."

Simon poured instant coffee into three mugs, filled them with boiling water, and placed the mugs on the table along with a liter of organic milk.

"Thanks. What about the other patients from Butterfly House? Was Isak still in touch with any of them? Marie Birch, for example?"

Simon sat down, a pensive wrinkle in his forehead.

"Marie did actually come by to visit Isak at lunchtime yesterday." He stirred his coffee and then tapped the drips off the spoon on the edge of his mug. "He seemed happy to see her."

"Do you know what they talked about?"

"I only said hello to her briefly," Simon said, shaking his head. "My shift was over, and I went home right after she came." He drank, set his cup down, then drank again, seemingly lost in his own thoughts. "She looked like a homeless person, you know, dreadlocks and dirty clothes."

Jeppe studied Simon. Apparently he didn't

know any more about Marie than they did. On the other hand, he seemed burdened by more than worry about Isak's well-being — a guilty conscience, maybe?

"I get that you don't know how Isak got ahold of your key, but how was he able to jump out of the window in the first place without being seen? I thought he was supervised around the clock. . . ."

"The ward is monitored twenty-four hours a day," Simon said, blushing, "but not the individual patients. We just don't have the staffing for that."

"Why do you suppose he ran away?"

Simon shrugged feebly. Redness was spreading from his face to blotches on the side of his neck. Silence filled the room, only a ticking wall clock calling attention to the passage of time.

"Well," Jeppe said, getting up, "obviously we'll be in touch if anyone sees or hears from Isak."

"I'll see you out." Simon hastily got to his feet.

They walked through the orange common room, where a group of wide-eyed teenagers followed their movements, and into the bright white administrators' hallway that led to the door.

"The secretary at the front desk will let

356

you out." Simon Hartvig nodded goodbye and disappeared back down the hallway.

At the front door, Jeppe checked his phone and saw that his mother had called three times and Thomas Larsen once. Jeppe called Larsen. He picked up after one ring.

"Hi, Kørner. I have the names of those last employees from Butterfly House, the nurses and the cook."

"How did you find them?" Jeppe gestured to Falck that he would finish his conversation before going out into the rain.

"I went up to Rita Wilkins's house in Brede and searched through the boxes in her attic. Pretty straightforward actually."

Straightforward, of course. Larsen is the hero of the day!

"Okay, great. Just give me the names."

"One of the part-time nurses is named Andrea Jørgensen. We've located her. She's employed at Holbæk Hospital now. But at the moment she's walking the Camino de Santiago in Spain. She's been out of the country since September." Jeppe heard Larsen rustling some paper. "The other one's name is Trine Bremen. She works at National Hospital, presumably in the cardiology department."

Jeppe repeated the name and workplace to Falck, who took out his phone.

"I'll call from the car," Falck said.

Jeppe gave a thumbs-up and returned to his conversation.

"Okay," he said. "And the cook?"

"His name is Alex Jacobsen. Unfortunately we haven't tracked him down yet." Larsen sounded miffed. "But Saidani is still looking."

"We'll find him."

Jeppe was about to wrap up the call when Larsen stopped him.

"I found something else. . . . The accounting records from Butterfly House were in the attic, too. I haven't had a chance to go through them in detail yet, but to say the very least, they look inadequate."

"In what sense?" Jeppe looked out at the rain, which was fusing sky and parking lot into a sheet of grayness.

"I don't know. Either their economy was a mess, or someone was downright scamming. Hard to say at this point, but I can tell that Rita's ex-husband is listed as the official owner of the property in many of the documents."

"Okay, good, look into it and let me know what you find."

Jeppe hung up and jogged across the parking lot to the car, where Falck was already wedged in behind the wheel.

"I found her." Falck started the car and put it in gear. "Trine Bremen does work in the cardiology department at National Hospital. She's not answering her phone, but we could go there and see if she's at work."

"Excellent, let's do it!"

Falck steered them calmly through Outer Nørrebro, the windshield wipers going full speed.

"I would go bananas," Falck exclaimed as they reached Åboulevard.

"Bananas?" Jeppe looked at him in surprise. "Why?"

"I'd go bananas if I worked in a place like that. Loony tunes."

"Loony tunes?" The childish expression made Jeppe laugh out loud. "It's an ultra-modern, state-of-the-art hospital with every conceivable intervention available, all the bells and whistles."

"Yeah, but I mean having to deal with people who live in a different world all the time. After a while, you wouldn't know up from down yourself."

Jeppe mulled over that unexpected input. Falck might just have a point.

CHAPTER 18

Trine Bremen stuck her fork into the aluminum foil food tray. She was standing in the walkway behind the staff room, where she could hear her colleagues gossiping over lunch. The chicken *was* dry, but she didn't have it in her to walk all the way to the cafeteria for something better right now, even if she knew Jette would love to report her to the charge nurse for eating a patient meal. Klaus had picked a fight again early this morning, right in front of the kids, who had sat there staring down into their cornflakes. He was fed up with everything having to accommodate her ups and downs, fed up with her *disease* taking up all the space in their lives. Disease.

He had said the word with scorn, as if he didn't believe her, as if she could just choose not to be like this.

"You know, she might be out here . . . ?" Jette opened the staff room door, stuck her red pageboy into the hallway, and tried to sound surprised. "Well, look who's hiding! There you are. The police are here, they want to talk to you."

Trine's heart started to flutter. She dumped the rest of the food into the trash and dashed past her coworker into the staff room, where four nurses, two doctors, and an orderly sat quietly staring back and forth between her and the policemen, as if they were watching a match at Wimbledon.

"Trine Bremen?" the younger, slim detective asked. "We need to ask you a few questions relating to a case we're investigating. Is there somewhere we could talk?"

"Come, we'll go to the patient room at the end of the hallway. There we can have some peace and quiet," she said, sending the detectives a loaded look.

Even if it couldn't be heard, she could sense the chins starting to wag the second the staff room door closed behind them. A visit by the police was not exactly auspicious when your coworkers already suspect you of every little thing. Trine felt a bubble of defiance well up inside her. Walking down the hallway flanked by two policemen was like standing at the edge of the high dive: terrifying and exhilarating at the same time.

They sat down in the windowless patient

room, where the only sign of life, apart from the table and chairs, was a dusty plastic toy pirate ship.

"How can I help you?" Trine asked, feeling fairly on top of things again, strong and professional. Her despair over lunch already seemed far away.

"I'm Jeppe Kørner, and this is my colleague, Detective Falck. We're here in connection with the murders of Bettina Holte, Nicola Ambrosio, and Rita Wilkins." It was still the younger detective who did the talking. Falck, who was quite a bit older, looked like he could have used a midday nap. "Am I correct in understanding that you worked at Butterfly House until it closed two years ago?"

Trine noted that he was attractive in a pale, poetic kind of way. She tossed her hair over her shoulder and nodded gloomily.

"It's hard to believe," she said. "Have you caught the people who did it?"

"The killer is unfortunately still at large. May I ask where you were the last several nights, particularly Sunday through Wednesday?"

His eyes were grayish blue with a serious look under dark eyebrows. Trine sucked in her cheeks a little.

"At home," she said. "With my husband

and kids. I've been working the day shift all week."

"Could you write down your husband's phone number so we can contact him?" Falck passed a notepad across the table, and she meticulously wrote Klaus's name and number in all caps.

"How was Butterfly House as a place to work?" the young, attractive one asked.

"It was okay, I guess. Pretty small, and maybe not the world's best work environment. The owners were quite stingy. I only worked there for a little while."

"Are you still in touch with any of your former colleagues?"

She cocked her head to the side. "No, not since Butterfly House closed. I liked Nicola; he was nice. The women could be a little uptight, especially to someone like me."

"What about the residents?" the detective asked, giving her a penetrating look. "How did you get along with them?"

"They were sweet. Very different, very young." Her mind was racing. What if she said something wrong? "I hadn't had much experience with psych patients before I got to Butterfly House, so it was a bit of a shock to me how hard it can be. . . . It wasn't for me."

That last sentence hung, vibrating in the

air between them. The pause gave her time to start worrying that she had already said too much when the detective spoke again. His eyes shone with interest. It was nice.

"So you haven't been in touch with any of the employees or patients from Butterfly House?"

Trine twisted a strand of her hair between her fingers, hesitating.

"I do see Peter Demant from time to time. He's the one who got me the job back then, and we still speak occasionally."

The detective smiled at her as if she had finally given him what he was looking for.

"When did you last see him?"

Trine's pulse accelerated steeply, roaring uncomfortably in her ears. How much should she tell them?

"Yesterday, last night, at his place."

Both policemen sat unmoving, watching her calmly. Even so, she sensed a change in the energy of the room, a tension.

"Confidentially, Peter is my psychiatrist. I stopped by his place yesterday to renew my prescription."

"At what time?"

"Late."

"We had a patrol car parked in front of Peter Demant's place last night. . . ."

Trine's throat was dry, and she had to

clear it before she could speak.

"Really, I didn't see it?"

"Is it normal to pick up prescriptions late at night from your psychiatrist's private home?"

Her violently beating pulse was making Trine's head spin. A nervous dizziness crept up on her. She felt an impulse to knock over the table onto the two men and hit them hard with one of the heavy chairs until they shut up. The urge was familiar — it sometimes surfaced when she was feeling cornered.

"I don't know what's normal and abnormal in your world, but Peter and I know each other well. He's sweet enough to be flexible in those periods when I'm working during clinic hours."

"Then maybe you can tell us where he is now? I had an appointment with him this morning, but he didn't show up. He's not answering his phone and is nowhere to be found."

Trine put her hands in her lap and pinched her own palm, hard. The pain forced her mind off the situation so she could stand being in it.

"Unfortunately I have no idea. I was only with him for ten or fifteen minutes yesterday, just got my prescription and left again."

"When did you get home?"

"I don't know. I wasn't in a hurry and strolled home. Maybe around eleven."

"Can your husband confirm that?"

"Of course! Look, I'm going to have to get back to my patients, so if there's nothing else . . . ?"

She got up. The two detectives also stood. They looked like Laurel and Hardy, standing there side by side. The younger one still had that curious look in his eyes, which gave Trine the jitters.

"Make sure you keep your phone on, so we can contact you. We'll place two officers in front of the ward, and they will escort you home when you get off and keep guard tonight. Three of your former colleagues have already been killed."

Trine let them exit the patient room first and gave them a brave smile goodbye.

"Then let's hope no more die."

There was fussing from the back seat the whole way into the city. Anette kept her eyes as much on the rearview mirror as she did on the road while singing soothingly as best she could. Judging from her daughter's response, it wasn't particularly good.

By the time they reached Nørrevold, Anette was drenched in sweat and her daughter screamed inconsolably. She parked the car by a yellow curb and ran to the back so she could grab the baby from her car seat and hold her. After only a few seconds in her mother's arms, she stopped crying. Anette, on the other hand, started.

Big, salty tears dripped down onto her daughter's downy head. It's just fussing, her mother would have said. Just tired and fussy, that's all.

Anette hauled the stroller out of the trunk one-handed and unfolded it with some difficulty. Then she carefully settled her daughter amid soft blankets, stuffed animals, and colorful gizmos and started pushing the stroller toward Ørstedsparken. The baby lay, calmly looking up at the trees, as if the world were a peaceful place and she had never felt upset about anything in her little life. When she was like this, she was easy to love.

Tanja Kruse waited for Anette with her own baby carriage on the picturesque bridge over the lake. The former nurse from Butterfly House had agreed to meet but had asked if they could combine it with her daily stroller walk. And though it was unusual to combine detective work with baby care, it suited Anette's own situation quite nicely.

"Hi, you must be Tanja." Anette wheeled

her stroller up next to the tall blond-haired woman in a green-striped rain poncho and shook her hand. "I'm Anette Werner. Thank you for meeting me."

"Hi." Tanja Kruse smiled widely, her gums showing. "I've got two policemen in tow, as I'm sure you already know." She nodded toward two uniformed officers standing on the path about a hundred yards away from them. "But they'll give us our space."

"Yes, we . . . thought that was the safest," Anette lied, hoping the officers didn't happen to know her.

Tanja leaned over Anette's stroller.

"Oh, she's so precious. A girl, right? She must have been a bit of a late addition, eh?"

"Something like that."

"What's her name?"

"We haven't decided yet." Anette shrugged, then dutifully looked into Tanja Kruse's beautiful, retro-style baby carriage, in which a doll wearing a crocheted hat lay tucked in under a pretty blanket. A very realistic doll, but still a doll.

"Her name is Amalie," Tanja said proudly.

Anette was rarely at a loss for words, but this would be one of those times. She stood frozen, leaning over the glossy baby carriage, completely and utterly speechless.

"I know she's a doll, don't worry."

"Okay, ha-ha, well, that's good." Anette looked around, embarrassed. "So, which way should we go?"

"We always walk clockwise around the lake."

"Great."

Anette turned her stroller, and they set off along the path, two women with baby carriages and two policemen in tow. They wheeled along in awkward silence, Anette feeling winded and uncharacteristically shy.

"I know my colleagues have already talked to you about the deaths, but as I said, I would really like to ask a few follow-up questions." Anette fished out a pacifier for her daughter and tried to rise above the absurdity of the situation. "Kim Sejersen, can you tell me a little about him? About the accident?"

"Oh, Kim. Such a sweet guy, and a good social worker. So awful that he had to die that way. . . . He was drunk that night. We had all been drinking, but Kim had had too much. I don't know why Rita had decided to throw a summer party. It was really totally improper. Alcohol has no place at a residential treatment facility like that, but Rita has always made her own rules."

Tanja adjusted the blanket around the doll in the baby carriage as she spoke.

"Kim was critical of Rita's management, wanted her to lower the medication doses and change the patients' diets instead. They argued about it frequently, Kim and the psychiatrist and Rita."

They walked along the gravel path that ran parallel to Farimagsgade, the grassy embankment sloping down to the lake on their right. In the summer the grass was always covered with young people chilling, but now only dead leaves and puddles dotted the green. Anette discovered to her relief that her daughter had fallen asleep.

"The party started out fine. We lit a bonfire in the yard, barbecued, and drank red wine. Of course the patients couldn't sleep now that there was a party, and they kept coming out to us. But Kim got drunk and started arguing with the management again. I went to bed around eleven p.m. The atmosphere just wasn't pleasant."

"So you don't actually know what happened to Kim?"

"No . . ." The tall woman walked with her shoulders lifted up toward her ears and her eyes in a squint, surrounded by a web of premature wrinkles. She looked like someone heading straight for a slipped disc and a pair of reading glasses.

"Some people seem to think Pernille had

a crush on Kim," Anette ventured. "And that she felt rejected by him. Could she and her friends have gotten back at him for that —?"

"That is the worst nonsense I've ever heard!" Tanja cut her off. "Just downright lies. The residents adored Kim, and Pernille loved him like an older brother. They would never have done anything to hurt him, never! Besides, she was completely and utterly harmless, never acted out in the least. Who would even say that?"

"Peter Demant," Anette admitted. She didn't see any reason to keep it secret.

"Ha! Demant." She snorted scornfully so that clouds of steam rose around her in the chilly air. "If anyone had reason to murder Kim, it was him!"

"But he wasn't there that night." Anette started pushing her stroller again, and Tanja followed.

"Is that what he says?" She was gripping the handle of her carriage tight and seemed to debate something to herself. "Well, that's a lie. Kim argued with both Rita and Peter Demant that night; I remember it quite vividly."

"Maybe he just remembers it wrong?"

They passed a statue Anette noticed was called *The Dying Gaul,* and there was something oddly appropriate about that.

"Maybe . . ." Tanja sighed. "As I said, I had already gone to bed when Kim drowned, and I haven't actually ever questioned whether it was an accident. Of course you would want it to be an accident, because the thought that someone you know . . . But Demant . . ."

"What about Demant?"

A gust of wind sent an eddy of dried leaves up into the air, and they drifted down over the two women and their carriages like dead butterflies. The leaves were damp and carried a faint whiff of dirt and decay.

"I don't like to spread rumors, but I've never felt confident about Demant. No doubt he's qualified. It's just that he's a little imperial, kind of a despot, if you know what I mean?"

"He was domineering?"

"Oh, and then some! He wanted people to kowtow to him, wanted to be idolized. You know the type?" Tanja gave a little head shake. "Oh, I don't know. I mean, I can hear how backstabbing that sounds. It's just so crazy and incomprehensible that all these people have been murdered. Something has to be wrong, you know, really wrong!"

They wheeled along Nørrevold, back toward their starting point, gravel crunching under the stroller wheels.

"Maybe you should talk to Kim's girlfriend, Inge. I have her address. She has always had her own opinion about what happened back then."

The bridge appeared in front of them. As if on command, Anette's daughter woke up and started to cry.

Tanja was right. Something was wrong, really wrong.

"Okay, status updates!" Jeppe opened the wrapper, took a bite of his Mars bar, and prayed that the gooey caramel would transform into a quick wave of energy.

"Still no useful witness testimony or any new information about the cargo bike that was used to transport the bodies. On the other hand, we have two incidents in the victims' shared history: social worker Kim Sejersen's accidental drowning at Butterfly House on August 8, 2014" — Jeppe pointed to the staff photo hanging on the board — "and the suicide on August 3, 2015, of one of the patients at the home, Pernille Ramsgaard. She slit her wrists and bled to death in a bathtub."

Jeppe washed his candy bar down with lukewarm coffee and enjoyed the rush of sugar and caffeine.

"Larsen has identified the last of the Butterfly House employees. We still haven't located the cook, Alex Jacobsen, but we have been in touch with the two nurses, Andrea Jørgensen and Trine Bremen. The former is on a prolonged hiking tour in Spain and is out of the picture, but Falck and I interviewed Trine Bremen earlier today. She is on friendly terms with Peter Demant and visited him at his home last night."

"Unfortunately she has an alibi for all the other evenings and nights this week," Falck cut in. "I just talked to her husband, Klaus. She has been home with him and the kids every night. Plus, Monday they had the neighbors over for dinner."

"Did you talk to them?"

"Yes, the neighbors confirm that they were over until one in the morning. Played some game called Davoserjaz." Falck shrugged and continued, "A card game. I don't know it, but Trine Bremen didn't murder Nicola Ambrosio Monday night. Unless both her husband and her neighbors are lying."

"She's still the last person to have seen Peter Demant. He hasn't turned up, anything new on him?"

Larsen, Saidani, and Falck all shook their heads simultaneously.

"Isak Brügger is also still missing. Two out

of three suspects have disappeared from the surface of the earth."

"Demant and Brügger. Who's the third?" Falck asked.

"Bo Ramsgaard," Sara said, holding up her phone. "I just talked to his wife, Lisbeth, who's on her way back to Copenhagen. She thinks she'll make it home by eight tonight."

"Can she confirm her husband's alibi?"

"No."

"No?" Jeppe swallowed the piece of chocolate he had just bitten off before he had a chance to chew it.

"It turns out, they're getting a divorce. Officially they still live together, but they take turns sleeping elsewhere. Lisbeth Ramsgaard spent the night with a girlfriend Sunday night and then left for Sweden. She and Bo had agreed that he would stay home with their daughter while she was away. But when our Swedish colleagues reached her earlier today and she turned on her cell phone, she saw that her daughter had called a bunch of times on Tuesday night. She was home alone feeling scared." Sara spoke with the indignation all parents feel at the thought of an abandoned child.

"But Tuesday we had a surveillance team stationed outside the Ramsgaards' house all evening and overnight. . . ." Even as he spoke Jeppe knew his protest was pointless.

"So he went out the back door or some other way. He wasn't home. Why would the daughter lie about that? The mother told me something else as well. . . ." Sara paused for a moment, looking around. "She revealed to me that Bo Ramsgaard has a massive drinking problem."

"Is he . . . ?"

Sara shook her head.

"Or if he is, she's not prepared to admit that. But he does have a temper. In the wake of Pernille's death, he apparently had a violent conflict with their eldest son, so bad they no longer have any contact with each other. Not so strange that she wants a divorce. I'll question her properly as soon as possible."

The office fell quiet. Each of the four detectives followed their train of thought to the same conclusion.

"I guess we should bring Bo Ramsgaard in for questioning, a more formal one."

"Agreed." Sara nodded. "But I don't think we can narrow it down to three suspects, even if that seems to be the general opinion."

Jeppe gave her a questioning look.

"Marie Birch! Hello, what's wrong with you? She must be hiding for a reason. Yes, she's small and skinny, but maybe someone's helping her. Do I need to remind you of how cold-blooded young female murderers can be? And what about Rita's ex-husband, and Alex Jacobsen, the missing cook . . . ?"

There was a knock on the door and the superintendent's friendly face poked in. At the moment it didn't look particularly friendly, though.

"Kørner, my office. Right away, please."

She shut the door, leaving the room in another uncomfortable silence. The detectives all knew that Jeppe had to *walk the carpet* as a scolding from the boss was generally referred to.

Jeppe stood up with what he hoped was most of his dignity intact.

"Falck," he said, "let's go fetch Bo Ramsgaard. Find out where he is. We'll leave in half an hour."

He took the stairs up to admin and found the superintendent's door, annoyance building inside him like trapped steam. He wasn't a magician after all!

The superintendent sat at her desk and regarded him somberly over the top of her eyeglasses.

"Kørner, have a seat."

"I'll stand, thanks."

She took off her glasses, making her brown eyes suddenly twice as big under the heavy eyelids.

"We're not going to have a conflict about this." She wasn't negotiating with him, just warning him. "I know you're doing what you can, but people are scared, Kørner. Three brutal murders, a psychiatric patient on the loose, and no suspect actually charged."

She looked at him with concern. Jeppe resolved that it was probably better not to start defending himself.

"And we're not just talking about a jealous husband or something like that?" she suggested. "It's not Michael Holte who lost his shit?"

Jeppe shook his head.

She sighed impatiently and asked, "What do you expect from me?"

"Time. To be able to work in peace. For you to keep the press and the bigwigs busy while I solve the case."

The superintendent didn't break eye contact, didn't even wink.

Jeppe stood as calmly as he could in the middle of her office floor between her fly-fishing poles and pictures of her grandkids. She regarded him for a long time, then put her glasses back on.

"You have twenty-four hours. I'm sorry, Kørner, but I need to show my superiors and the media that we're taking this seriously. I'm sick of sounding like some TV crime drama, but if there's no breakthrough by tomorrow afternoon, I'm officially handing the case over to Thomas Larsen. Close the door behind you."

CHAPTER 19

Esther de Laurenti opened the door to her apartment and was struck by the quiet in the front hall. She set down her shopping bags and stood still, unmoving in her woolen coat. After spending an hour home alone, dogs will run out to meet their owners, barking and drooling. But right now there was no activity. The hall was quiet, far too quiet.

"Dóxa! Epistéme! Where are you guys?"

Esther closed the front door. A faint sound, a scratching and whining, came from far away. She followed the sound, not caring that she was leaving a trail of wet footprints behind her on the pale wood floor.

At the back of the apartment, the door to Gregers's room was closed. It usually was. The sounds were coming from his room.

"Dóxa! Epistéme!"

Her call elicited a cacophony of angry

barks behind the door. She ran and opened it, and her dogs darted out, jumping up and almost knocking her over. As she crouched down to pet them and reassure them, the anxiety rose in her body. The dogs had followed her to her front door when she left to go do the shopping. She had told them goodbye and promised a long afternoon walk as she closed the door.

There was only one way they could have been shut into Gregers's room. Someone else had been in the apartment while she was gone.

Esther got up slowly. Who had a key aside from herself and Gregers? Their cleaning lady, but she was in Poland for the whole month of October.

She retraced her wet steps to the front hall. Could someone else be here right now? The place didn't look different. The kitchen was still in its usual state of comfortable untidyness, with dishes in the sink, unopened mail, and a box of vegetables on the table waiting to be put away. Esther spun around holding her breath. It would be easier to tell if someone had messed with her things if she were more organized. She carried the shopping bags into the kitchen, hung her coat on the hook, and got out a cloth to wipe the floor. Where would one search if looking for valuables?

The wallet in her purse.

She always kept cash in her purse in the front hall. Not a lot, just enough in case anything unexpected came up. And next to the coat hooks her spare keys in a tidy bundle on the table, only they weren't there anymore.

Esther picked up newspapers and dug around in bowls, looked on the floor underneath and behind the table. The keys were gone.

With her heart in her throat, she found her purse on the hook. That at least was still there. She had left both it and her wallet behind when she went shopping, just tucking a credit card in her pocket. Her wallet was also still there, thank God.

Tuesday morning she had withdrawn four thousand kroner for her hairdresser, who preferred cash, and for an upcoming flea market at Blågård Square this weekend. In fact, she herself still preferred doing her shopping with cash.

She opened her wallet. In it she found a handful of coins and two crumpled hundred kroner bills. She had been robbed.

Her stomach lurched. Alain.

Esther tossed the wallet on the floor and put her hands over her face. The first feeling to wash over her was shame. He had lied to her, used her. How could she have believed that she was still attractive, a wrinkled old hag like her?

She slapped herself on the cheeks over and over again and let a good cry shake her stupid, old body. The dogs crept up to her, whining.

As she wiped her face, she realized that she needed to both change the locks and establish if he had taken anything else from the apartment. He probably thought that she would be too proud to report him to the police, but he was in for a surprise. She would get him evicted from the building before he had even finished moving in.

Esther did another round through the apartment. The art still hung on the walls; the vases were all where they should be. He had rifled through her drawers, she could see that, but hadn't found anything other than old bills and her notepads. They'll be worth a lot someday; he should have had the foresight to nick them, she thought in a vain attempt to regain her footing. All her securities were kept in a safe-deposit box, along with most of her silver. Apparently he had only gotten away with the cash and her keys.

She sat down to her computer and requested a locksmith as soon as possible. Then she typed *Alain Jacolbe* into her browser's search bar. No apparent matches turned up, certainly no concert pianists.

Esther went to the kitchen, opened a bottle of Shiraz and poured herself a large glass of the red wine. She needed something to numb the effect of this quantum-mechanics-worthy love life, which sent her straight from exhilarated to the doldrums of despair.

She brought the wine back to the computer. How do you find information about a man if you don't know his real name?

She drank, letting the alcohol deaden her frayed nerves. What did she know about him, actually? That he was French?

Not necessarily. She didn't speak French herself and had perhaps allowed herself in a moment of weakness to be duped by an accent and a few French terms of endearment. He knew *La Bohème,* loved food. Gregers claimed to have seen him in that fast food place on Nørrebrogade. And he had just moved into her building.

She drank again. It helped a little.

Dóxa and Epistéme barked impatiently. She would need to walk them soon. But first she needed to force herself to think of something besides Alain. The betrayal stung

384

with the force of shame, and she was afraid her legs wouldn't hold her up. She put on a record, but turned it off again as soon as the music started flowing from the speakers, sent Jeppe Kørner a text that Gregers was improving, and considered a bath but rejected the idea at the prospect of having to look at her own naked reflection. Then she sat down at the computer again and opened a newspaper webpage.

Esther read articles about traffic infrastructure, an injured soccer player who was being flown home from Italy, and backlash against a shoe company for a sexist ad. The sentences swam indiscriminately from the screen into her head, having the same effect as the wine. A pleasant numbness spread through her.

The fountain murders occupied multiple columns talking about K9 units, cargo bikes, and unidentified staff members. The words swam before her teary eyes.

Esther closed her computer and got the dogs' leashes. She had to pull herself together! There were worse problems in the world than hers.

"It said Gym H, didn't it? Must be over here."

Jeppe pointed down the long hallway at

Grøndal MultiCenter, past the squash courts, dance studios, and boxing rings, looking for the signs with gym names. Green plants and trees covered the slightly discouraging concrete walls in an attempt to create a cozy, vibrant atmosphere. It certainly wasn't that the place lacked life. Groups of teenagers with sports bags clustered around cell phones, senior citizens drank coffee in the café, and cheerful kid squeals could be heard from all sides.

The schedule in the lobby said that MG Talent Team practiced on Thursdays from 5:00 to 6:00 p.m. in Gym H, and according to Lisbeth Ramsgaard that was where the police would find Bo: at gymnastics with their youngest daughter. She was on board with their bringing him in and promised to arrange for the daughter to go home with a friend until she herself made it to Copenhagen and was able to pick her up. Still, Jeppe felt uncomfortable about the situation.

As he walked down the hallway toward Gym H with Falck and two uniformed officers, the idea of bringing a man in this way — in front of his ten-year-old daughter, her friends, and their parents — seemed less and less appealing. But Jeppe had to push forward, as he no longer had time for being considerate.

Conversation in the hallways dwindled away and people gawked at the little police processional. They left a wake of curious mumbling behind them.

Gym H was full of beams, gym pads, and large trampolines on which children around ten to twelve years old took turns balancing, stretching, and doing backflips. The space smelled of sweat, cleaner, and breaktime bananas, and a salsa hit from last summer played over the crackling sound system.

On bleachers along one of the walls parents and younger siblings were seated. Jeppe spotted Bo Ramsgaard right away. He sat calmly with a gymnastics bag on his lap and watched his daughter practicing a jump on the trampoline. Her skinny little body could hardly get enough height in the jumps to make it all the way around in the air, but she didn't give up. She jumped again and again with a concentrated expression on her little face and anxious sidelong glances at the stands. Most of the parents were chatting, but Bo Ramsgaard was only watching his daughter.

He looked like any other parent, in a cheap windbreaker with curly hair, a normal parent who took his daughter to gymnastic lessons and thought she was the best of them all. Was he also a parent who was unable to forgive the system for having failed his fragile, older daughter?

Bo turned around and looked right at them. Jeppe could tell he understood that they were here for him and knew he wasn't planning to accompany them voluntarily. He looked back at his daughter as if contemplating whether he could snatch her off the trampoline and run before the police reached him. But she was too far away, the trampoline too high. It was a lost cause. He rose, standing like a wounded animal in the line of fire, and looked back and forth from the trampolines to the police.

"Hi, Mr. Ramsgaard. We'd like to —" Jeppe didn't get any further before he was interrupted.

"I'm not coming with you. I'm here with my daughter, what are you thinking, for fuck's sake?" Bo lowered his voice and hissed, "You could have called!"

"Your wife is taking care of your daughter, so if you would just come with us, quietly, no fuss." Out of the corner of his eye Jeppe could see that all activity on the mats and trampolines had stopped. Bo's daughter stood motionless, looking at her father with big, frightened eyes. The whole room was watching. Jeppe lowered his voice still further.

"There's no reason to make this any worse . . ."

The sports bag sailed right over Jeppe's head. The swing came from so low down that he managed to see it and duck out of the way; the shove to his chest, however, he did not see coming. Rage fueled the father's strength, and Jeppe had the wind completely knocked out of him.

"What the hell are you thinking?"

Jeppe straightened up and met the father's furious gaze. While the officers closed in on him, he saw Bo realize that he had crossed a line.

He ran.

Bo Ramsgaard pushed his way past the crowd of parents and coaches, stumbled, got back up, and ran again for the gym exit. The officers were only two steps away and caught him in a firm shoulder lock just as Jeppe reached them. Bo punched at one of the officers, then tipped backward with a roar that echoed through the gym.

The officers rolled him onto his stomach and put a knee on his back.

"Assaulting an on-duty police officer. Do you know what that gets you?"

"My daughter!" Bo exclaimed. "You can't just take me. What the hell?!"

"You daughter will go home with a friend,

and your wife will pick her up there. Arrangements have been made for her."

The two officers pulled Bo to his feet and started walking him toward the exit.

"Leave me alone, you idiots. Listen, I don't have anything to do with it."

Jeppe glanced over his shoulder and made eye contact with the daughter. She was standing on the trampoline, watching her father being led away, so small and thin that she seemed almost see-through. Sticklike arms hanging helplessly at her sides, eyes glazing over.

Jeppe bowed his head in shame.

"Well, then, I'm going to zip home," Gorm said. "I'll get those attachments copied one of these days."

"One of these days?!" Simon Hartvig rolled his eyes at his colleague. "The new application needs to be sent before the weekend. We need to put some pressure on them now, Gorm, or they'll just reject it like everyone else."

"Yeah, okay." Gorm sighed. "I'll get it done. Have a good night!"

He and Gorm fist-bumped and Simon returned to his dinner. He would have preferred to cancel this meeting with the kitchen garden committee — for many reasons — but hadn't had the heart to do it. What was an hour's worth of awkward discomfort compared to the benefit a garden would bring to the patients?

Fresh air, the joy of growing things, healthier food, maybe even a path to lowering medication dosages. Besides it would look unfortunate to cancel, now that Gorm was asking annoying questions. He had to fix that. But not until tomorrow.

As soon as he had eaten his dinner, he would bike home for his first night off all week. He had been looking forward to spending the night in his own bed. Now that joy was deteriorating.

Simon pushed the potatoes around in the parsley sauce on his plate. Winter potatoes in cream sauce with dried herbs would make you lose your appetite, if it wasn't already gone. How the hell could they defend serving this dog food to the patients, to anyone? He took another bite of potato and immediately regretted it. The sauce tasted like mucus in his mouth and made him feel like throwing up.

He gave up. Discreetly, he spit the potato out into his napkin and carried the plate to the cafeteria's dish rack, poured himself a half cup of coffee to wash down a pill, and headed back to the ward. Rejection ran like a thread through his life; a chain of defeats, urged along by his father, by municipal bureaucrats, by the world. To think that those assholes wouldn't let him modernize the hospital cafeteria when he tried! Politicians should be forced to eat this hospital slop, just for a week. Then maybe they would change their minds.

What had gone wrong?

Simon passed one of the big windows overlooking the grounds, where old trees were dripping sadly on the benches and paths. More rain, his raincoat never dried out these days. Isak was out there somewhere in the rain without his medication, without food, without shelter, without anyone to look after him. Unless . . .

If Isak hadn't run away on his own, he must have had help from someone he knew.

Marie.

Simon left the coffee behind and hurried back to Isak's room. The curtains were drawn and the bed was made, the room neatly done up after having been searched by both police and staff. It was just waiting for its occupant. Simon ran his finger over the book spines on Isak's shelf and stopped at the most worn one, *Papillon.* Hadn't Isak taken that with him yesterday? Simon pulled out the book and leafed through it. Inside

the front cover he found what he was looking for. Three words, sloppily written in
pencil.

Fredens Havn, Holmen.

He let the information sink in, in all its
harsh reality. Her suspicious look, the question of whether they were being watched. If
she had wanted to communicate something
secret, this is precisely how it would have
happened.

Isak must be with her.

Simon put the book back and wondered
what he should do now. Call the police and
tell them what he had found?

Gorm had started asking questions and
looking at him weirdly; surely he was checking up on him. Maybe the charge nurse had
already been alerted and was already investigating where the electronic tracker on his
key fob had been. The single potato he had
managed to eat threatened to come back
up. He couldn't risk involving the police.

Not now, when he and Peter Demant were
finally going to meet again.

Marie Birch watched Isak let the gray light
from the streetlamp fall on his face and felt
a familiar pang in her heart. She should
have gone to see him before, shouldn't have
waited so long. Fear had controlled her, the

fear of what *he* might do if she got involved. She knew what he was capable of, had experienced it on her own body.

Now here they were. Set up and hiding in one of the Count's friend's little yellow houses in the area called the Blue Caramel behind Refshalevej, only a hundred yards from Fredens Havn. In the back room, she had made them a temporary home with roll-up mattresses and blankets, flashlights, a camp stove, and a few books. Isak had slept, pretty much since he got out of the taxi last night.

Marie was working up the courage to ask him what had happened that night at Butterfly House — the night Kim died — but the right moment hadn't come yet. She dreaded his reaction, and what he would say. But she couldn't let fear control her anymore. She knew Isak cared about her, and that would have to be safety enough for now.

"I should get started on dinner. You must be hungry, too. Will you help me peel the vegetables?"

"Let me just sit for a little longer, just another minute. This is the first time in forever that I'm not under supervision."

Marie drew damp air down into her lungs and closed her eyes. What would become of them? She had learned to beg, steal, and lie. She was used to life on the streets. Knew which people she could trust and who she should just leave be. Down in the Colony she had gone cold turkey, and now she was off meds, clear in the head, independent.

But Isak . . . Isak didn't have any skills. He had lived his whole life in a bubble, and although the bubble had been filled with pain, it had also protected him. Marie couldn't take care of them both very long, a few days at the most, assuming Isak could even manage off his meds. He might start to react, hallucinate, and have panic attacks, and she had no idea if she would be able to handle that. But she didn't let her uncertainty show, and Isak seemed blissfully unaware.

"Do you remember when we hid in the bushes behind the lake and pretended we had run away, like in the book?" Isak spoke, his eyes still closed up against the light from the streetlamp.

"I do," Marie said with a smile. "We talked about all the things we would do if we could do whatever we wanted."

"I wanted to go to school, a *proper* school, take over my dad's business, make him proud."

"And I wanted to take riding lessons, have

my own horse. Or share one, at least."

"That was the happiest time of my life."

She got a lump in her throat. Why is feeling someone else's pain so much easier than bearing your own? Probably because your own pain can kill you. You store it away in blast-proof boxes and dump them on the bottom of your consciousness, so that the memories only stir when there's a storm.

"Come on, Isak! Let's get going on dinner."

"I'm not feeling well," Isak said, opening his eyes. "I'm cold."

Marie noticed the beads of sweat on his temples and his chest, which was pumping like the hi-hat at a techno party.

It was starting already. And she had nothing but root vegetables and good intentions with which to tackle the symptoms.

"Find a book, Isak. Wrap yourself in the blanket and try and see if you can read a little."

Isak's hands flapped around his head for no reason.

"I'm not scared, Marie. I can handle it."

"Sit, Isak. I'll make dinner. Let's see if we can relax together, okay?"

Marie squatted down and lit the camp stove, poured water into the pot, and took out a bag of parsley roots. Her question would have to wait a little longer. But not too long. She could hear Isak flipping through pages and mumbling breathlessly to himself.

Almost imperceptibly she opened her little hunting knife and dropped it discreetly into her pocket.

CHAPTER 20

Peter Demant is a quack!

Demant's overmedication leads to suicide.

Take away Demant's authorization!

Anette yawned and browsed on through hate-filled Facebook updates with one hand while rocking her daughter's cradle with the other. Apart from the elephant lamp and the blue light from the computer the bedroom was dark.

Fatigue was creeping over Anette like a lazy wave, inescapable and warm. From the kitchen, she could hear Svend clanking dishes and felt a stab of longing for the days when evenings were spent together — dishes, an evening coffee, a kiss, and real conversation. Now they put the baby to bed and cleaned the kitchen in shifts, swapped a tired high five when they passed each other in the hallway, and divvied the tasks up between them instead of doing them together. It was a different life. Was it so taboo to say that she sometimes missed the way things used to be? Just a little?

She returned her attention to the computer, and tried to skim through articles on *amygdala hyperactivity* and *stereotypical self-injurious behavior*. It was confusing reading to put it mildly, and not just because the technical vocabulary was way above her level.

Peter Demant was a productive guy, but a controversial psychiatrist. On the one hand successful with high-profile research projects in treating schizophrenia and borderline personality disorder. On the other hand accused of being in the pocket of private business interests and maligned in several Facebook groups for having prescribed the wrong medication or overmedicating patients. But there's a long way from utilizing questionable treatment methods to torturing and murdering. *Just because he prescribes too many pills, doesn't mean he kills,* she thought, smiling tiredly at her own rhyme.

The baby whined, and Anette started rocking the cradle again, humming absentmindedly until she settled down. She clicked on the story about a patient of Peter Demant's who had committed suicide. It was written as a blog post by the dead boy's aunt and brimmed with a rancor and rage that made it hard to read. Four years ago Charlie, the young boy, had suffered from depression and gone to Demant who had prescribed Cipralex, or unhappy pills, as his aunt called them. The way she told it, Charlie became addicted to the medicine and started deteriorating rapidly. One morning he packed his backpack for school and rode off on his bike as usual. But instead of going to school, he rode out to the highway bridge by Skallebølle, parked his bike along the railing, and jumped off the bridge. He was sixteen. The family demanded that Demant be held accountable for what they called malpractice.

Demant did not officially respond to the family's accusations, but on his own home page he had written a general piece on Cipralex treatment in pediatric patients, which explained and justified his methods.

In other words, Pernille Ramsgaard's parents weren't alone in their criticism of Demant. *But,* Anette thought, *that type of culpability is notoriously hard to pin down.*

She attached the relevant articles and links to an email, which she sent to Jeppe with the subject line: *Yeah, yeah, I know.*

Could Demant's alleged malpractice be related to the murders of the three employees? But if so, then what reason would Demant have had to kill Rita Wilkins, who had apparently supported him?

Anette rubbed her eyes. It didn't make any sense.

Svend carefully opened the door.

"Still not sleeping?" he whispered.

Anette peeked into the crib. Their daughter was sound asleep, looking like Tanja Kruse's pretty little doll baby, just in a warm, living version.

"Time got away from me, I guess. She's asleep." Anette shut the computer.

Maybe they could still enjoy a little grown-up time together before going to bed. A nice, uncomplicated break where they could be tender and loving like they used to. They needed that.

"Have you been on the computer while you were tucking her in?" His tone wasn't exactly accusatory, but still. "It's pretty important to establish a good bedtime routine early on, so she feels a sense of closeness and security before falling asleep."

Anette's desire for grown-up time instantly drained out of her. Aching all over she got up from the bed, pulled the blanket gently over her daughter in the cradle, and brushed past Svend out of the bedroom.

"I'm turning in — on the sofa. And I'm bringing my computer so that I can feel a sense of closeness and security before I fall asleep. Good night."

Copenhagen has a love affair with the sea. When you're by the shore, you can really feel how the city has been built to unfold toward its water, make use of it, and love it. The water softens the city's hard edges and gives them life, washes the filth away.

Jeppe lit a cigarette and pulled his collar tight against the cold. The undulating wooden boardwalk, aptly named the Kalvebod Wave, floated out over the water around him in different heights of viewpoints, benches, and play areas. An insufficient bandage to cover the eyesore inflicted on the Copenhagen waterfront by the criminally ugly and overbuilt Kalvebod Quay. Small groups of young tourists from the big youth hostel on H. C. Andersens Boulevard hung out under umbrellas along the water, laughing together in English and Italian.

When Jeppe had switched off the light in his office ten minutes earlier, it had suddenly hit him that he didn't know where to go. He would have given anything for a quiet evening at home on the sofa, but unfortunately his home had been sold and his sofa was in a storage unit on Gammel Køge Landevej.

There were two women in his life — Sara Saidani and his mother — but right now he didn't really want to deal with either of them.

Sara hadn't suggested they spend the night together, and Jeppe didn't know if he minded. Was he even ready to meet her daughters? Was he ever going to be? On top of that his mother kept calling and calling, instigating both annoyance and guilt.

In other words he had nowhere to go. Thus, here he was sitting by the water, smoking in the rain, next to Langebro bridge.

Bo Ramsgaard refused to cooperate; so far questioning him had been in vain. He didn't let himself be manipulated into a confession, on the contrary, he was now claiming that his wife lied about him not being home, and said she was trying to discredit him because she wanted custody of their daughter. They couldn't prove that he hadn't been home, could they?

They couldn't. For now he would remain in custody overnight, charged with *obstructing police work* and *violence against an on-*

duty officer. Then they would just have to see if they could get him to lower his guard tomorrow.

The streets were wet and deserted in the evening gloom; people were already heading inside for the winter, getting comfortable in front of their TV screens, wrapped up in sweets and woolen blankets. Copenhagen quietly folded in on itself, preparing to hibernate. Even Kalvebod Quay thorough-fare, which usually echoed with heavy traf-fic, was uncharacteristically quiet.

Jeppe's phone buzzed to life in his pocket. It was Monica Kirkskov. *Just what I needed,* he thought, and answered the call.

"Good evening, Monica."

"Good evening, Jeppe."

"What can I do for you?" Jeppe's pants were soaking up rain and starting to stick to his legs. Being wet actually wasn't so awful once you got used to it.

"It is I who can do something for you. Hopefully, at least. Do you remember me mentioning that I knew Peter Demant in medical school? Well, now I understand from the news that he's missing, and wanted in connection with the murder investigation . . . ?"

Jeppe hummed noncommittally.

"Well, it happened ten years ago, so it may

not be relevant, but back then there were rumors that he was stealing medicine." She paused for a moment and it sounded like she took a sip of something, probably wine. "He wasn't the only one there were rumors about. Theft is a pretty widespread phenomenon in med school."

"So, you think he was taking drugs?"

"I'm not sure. About the same time I decided to switch to history and philosophy, and I didn't run into him anymore. I don't know how things ended up."

She breathed and held the air in for a moment.

"At any rate, there were rumors."

Jeppe thanked Monica Kirkskov and wrapped up the call before it had a chance to get personal. He looked out over the water, letting his mind wander. Looked beyond the city lights reflecting on the surface of the water and into the depths, down into the dark layers, where truth lay hidden in the sediment of lies.

The whole thing began and ended with Peter Demant.

■ ■ ■ ■

FRIDAY,
OCTOBER 13

■ ■ ■ ■

CHAPTER 21

For Esther de Laurenti one of the great pleasures of life as a retiree was sleeping as long as she wanted, not getting up until her dogs wouldn't wait anymore. But on Friday, October 13, she woke up at six thirty in the morning unable to stay in bed even a second longer. The very idea of having allowed not only her home but her body to be invaded by a con artist was so awful that she felt sick. In the bathroom she took her temperature, which was completely normal, and washed down two aspirin with water from the tap. Not until after a long, hot bath did she feel well enough to take Dóxa and Epistéme for a walk. And even then, she went down the kitchen stairs.

The dogs were eagerly sniffing the lakeshore, darting to and fro on their little legs, and Esther let herself be pulled along without paying attention to the joggers, swans, or falling chestnut leaves. She couldn't handle the thought of Alain living downstairs from her. Could she get him evicted? Should she move? But then what about Gregers?

Her mind reeling, Esther didn't realize where she had gone until she was standing on Nørrebrogade in front of that fast food place Gregers sometimes brought dinner home from. She hesitated, but now that her feet had chosen to walk this way, she might as well take a peek inside. She tied the dogs up out front and prayed that no dog-nappers would come by. That was the last thing she needed.

The restaurant's sandwich board sign stood in the middle of the floor and the lights were off. The place clearly wasn't open yet. But when Esther gave the door a little push, it opened, and she stepped into the empty shop. The walls were covered with neon-colored cardboard displays featuring pictures of pita dishes at favorable prices, and sun-faded posters with Arabic text hung over the counter. The smell of frying hung heavily in the air, threatening to settle in her hair and clothes.

"We're not open yet, not until eleven!" a young man called. He had black hair, was clad in denim from top to toe, and was carrying a milk crate in his arms. He walked past her into the back room and returned without the crate.

"We're closed, lady. I can't help you until after eleven."

He paused by the front door and gestured for her to walk through it.

"Is this your place? Your . . . restaurant?" Esther asked, not moving.

"My family's. Why?"

"I'm looking for someone who works here. Or used to work here." Strictly speaking, she wasn't looking for Alain, because he lived downstairs from her, but this seemed like the easiest way to explain it.

The young man seemed to size her up. Apparently his curiosity won out.

"What's his name?"

"He calls himself Alain Jacolbe, but I don't know if that's his real name. He's tall and in his fifties, French guy?"

She could tell that rang a bell. He crossed his arms over his chest and gave a little nod.

"Why are you looking for him?" he asked.

There wasn't much choice other than to tell the truth, or at least some of it.

"He conned me."

The young man nodded a couple of times. Then he went behind the counter.

"Do you want a cup of mint tea with sugar? It's really good." He poured tea into two little glasses and handed her one.

Esther drank.

"Thank you. This *is* really good."

"I told you so," he teased with a friendly wink. "I know him well, Allan, gray-haired Frenchy-type dude. My uncle hired him as a cook last year."

"So he's a trained chef?"

"Oh, you don't need to be a trained chef to cook burgers. I don't know anything about his past or his private life or any of that. He was a nice enough guy in the beginning, but we ended up firing him."

"Why?"

"There was an episode." He drank his tea and didn't seem inclined to expand on that.

"And when you say episode, you mean . . . ?"

He shook his head a little from side to side.

"I'm sorry to be pestering you about this. But if he's the same guy I'm looking for, he stole from me. I just want to know if . . . well, if Allan stole from you guys, too."

"I don't know. It could have to do with money, but I'm not sure. I've never seen my uncle so angry. He fired him right here in the kitchen one Friday night."

Esther looked down at the floor. Alain's downfall from passionate concert pianist to common crook was so steep that she felt dizzy.

The young man chuckled to himself.

"Man, it was sick. Allan took that small fryer over there — the little one that lifts up — and threw it at my uncle. The oil is so hot it melts your skin. Luckily he missed, but he had to hightail it out of here to keep from getting his teeth kicked in. He ran with his apron still on and everything."

"You must have his information, identification number and that kind of thing?" She smiled hopefully.

"No information."

"Were the police called?"

He smiled smugly to indicate just how preposterous he found her question.

Esther set her tea cup down on the counter. Her hands were shaking slightly.

"Well, thank you very much for your time. I have to finish walking my dogs."

"No problem."

He chivalrously opened the door out onto Nørrebrogade for her.

"Hey, if I were you," he said, "I'd steer well clear of Allan. He's bad news."

Esther nodded and let the door close behind her, untied the dogs' leashes, and walked back to the Lakes. After having been numb for so long, the shifting emotions she was experiencing now were so intense they made her see double. From infatuation to humiliation, suspicion, and dread, all of it within twenty-four hours. The dogs tugged impatiently, wanting to go back to the water and the birds. She let herself be pulled along like a rag doll, temporarily knocked off-kilter.

The fear tasted like battery acid in her mouth.

"What have you been saying about me?"

The old man looked at her in confusion, as if he didn't understand what she meant.

"To the other nurses, what have you been saying?" Trine Bremen clarified, folding her arms over her chest.

He still didn't answer, just blinked, disoriented.

"Because if you have something to complain about, it would be better to just say it to my face."

"No," he protested. "Wait a minute . . ."

"I'm tired of your bellyaching! I come in to work every day ready to do my best. We don't have enough beds, people are lying in the hallways, and we're still working ourselves half to death trying to provide them with safe, high-quality medical care."

Her words hung uncommented in the

quiet between them. The old man averted his gaze. Just as she had experienced it so many times before, people couldn't handle it when problems were brought out into the open, when backstabbing was revealed and expressed out loud. They always clammed up, embarrassed.

"Next time you have something to say about my job performance, you just let me know. Thank you."

Trine spun around and left the room, her heart pounding, a familiar lump of nausea climbing in her throat. She stomped down the hallway to the staff room, found her bag, and dug out her pill box. The benzodiazepines were round and white in their blister pack. She had taken her morning pill and wasn't supposed to take another for a while, but the mere sight of them was soothing. She knew she was losing it, but she had no way of stopping herself. There was just no way to manage it all.

After she had been to his place yesterday Peter Demant had disappeared. Trine squeezed the pill box. He had started confronting her, had looked at her so angrily with his night-black eyes, that she had almost been afraid of him. She put the pills away and zipped her bag.

The police were looking for him. For

them. She prayed silently that he didn't turn up again for a while.

"Trine, haven't you done the medication rounds yet?"

Jette stood in the staff room doorway, an innocent look on her face.

Trine visualized the walls slowly tipping in over Jette, toppling and burying her in dust and rubble. Layer upon layer of lies and betrayal dissolved into white clouds that filled the air making it impossible to breathe. For a moment the vision overwhelmed her: Jette, obliterated forever.

"Are you okay?" Jette asked, her head cocked to the side. No collapsed walls, no dust.

Trine didn't respond. She wasn't about to play along with this two-faced concern, that look, the fake smile between the hamster cheeks. She squeezed past her coworker and out into the hallway. Jette's eyes burned into her back, fanning her smoldering rage.

At Copenhagen Police Headquarters, the day began with a confession. Bo Ramsgaard, who had spent the night on a cot in the lockup, woke up aching in both body and conscience and immediately summoned a guard, who got hold of the lead detective. Jeppe arranged a new interrogation right

416

away and hurried to headquarters, where he met Falck in interrogation room six and started a video recording with fingers that were trembling with excitement.

Unfortunately the confession Bo was burning to share with them was not the one they needed. Guilty and tearful, he choked down his humble pie and admitted that he had left his sleeping daughter Tuesday night and hadn't returned again until Wednesday morning before school. He had exited via the patio door at the back of the house and jumped over the fence into the neighbor's yard, the neighbor he occasionally slept with.

Bo realized that it was indefensible to leave his sleeping child, but he was kind of having an affair with a married woman. It was absolutely a secret and had obviously only started as a side effect of the looming divorce. He hadn't told the police about the visit, because he was afraid that Lisbeth would use it against him in their upcoming custody dispute.

Which she would be a fool not to, Jeppe thought, switching off the recording equipment with a disappointment he couldn't hide. Bo Ramsgaard's so-called confession hadn't done anything to help clear up or close the murder case. On the contrary, it had provided him with an alibi.

A call to his neighbor neatly confirmed that Bo was not guilty of anything other than getting a little action on the side, which in the context of a triple homicide case was relatively small potatoes.

They had to release him.

Jeppe returned to his office. In the hallway, he passed Sara. They were completely alone. Still, she merely nodded distantly to him as if he were some random coworker.

Fine, Jeppe thought.

In his office he removed Bo Ramsgaard's name from the bulletin board and moved the other suspects in closer together:

Peter Demant
Isak Brügger
Marie Birch

What if they were in cahoots? They knew each other from Butterfly House and could be linked in ways the police didn't know, doctor/patient, friends, even lovers?

Jeppe pushed the thought aside. His imagination was running wild. Not that there was anything wrong with contemplating different scenarios, but right now he was so anxious to solve this case that he was getting fanciful. It would fit so beautifully if the suspects, after disappearing simultaneously, were sitting on a beach in Venezuela holding hands or something. But there was no indication that Demant had much of any relationship with either Isak Brügger or Marie Birch, and the thought of some sort of joint crusade was rather absurd.

"Can I have a moment?" Larsen asked from the doorway, holding a thick stack of papers under his arm. Without waiting for an answer, he sat down in the chair on Anette's side of the desk. "I have exciting news. My girlfriend is in finance, so I asked her for advice," Larsen said with a wry smile, "without revealing any details from the case, of course."

Jeppe nodded reluctantly, the superintendent's threat to hand the case over to Larsen echoing in his ears.

"Can you make it snappy? I'm busy."

Unfazed, Larsen explained, "The Butterfly House books were cooked, seriously. To be very clear, it appears that they generated a large profit, which was channeled into a company owned by Robert, Rita's husband at the time."

"Is that illegal?"

"Not per se. The illegal part is that they made up fake expenses — wages, maintenance, medications, outings — that never existed. These all appear as entries in the books, but there are basically no receipts or supporting documentation. The financial result listed in their official account is far too low compared to their actual profit." Larsen tucked a lock of hair behind his ear with a satisfied grin. "In other words, ladies and gentlemen, a scam."

"How much are we talking about?" Jeppe asked, nodding skeptically.

"It could turn out to be quite a lot." Larsen flipped through his paperwork. "The Danish health-care system reimburses psychiatric treatment centers in the Zealand region with up to 1.8 million kroner per pediatric resident per year. With four residents at Butterfly House, that adds up to a pretty penny. I've only looked over the accounts for 2015 and 2014 so far, but I'd be surprised if this doesn't extend back even further than that."

"Good stuff, Larsen. Well done." Jeppe got up. "Keep digging, and let me know what you find. And have a talk with Robert Wilkins! I'm sure you've already thought of that."

Jeppe waited until the young detective had left his office and gone down the other end of the hall before closing the door. Tomorrow their roles might be reversed, him having to report to Larsen.

Jeppe massaged his temples. He was running out of space in his head for any more ill-fitting pieces of random facts. He had a feeling there was something he had not properly followed up on, but in this confusing flow of information it was hard to put his finger on what.

Maybe there was something to what Sara had said. Marie Birch, former resident of Butterfly House and friends with Isak Brügger. Homeless, a misfit, only nineteen. Victim, involved, missing, possibly guilty? According to Anette she didn't seem violent, but she could easily be. Or she could get help from someone who was. They had to make a new push to find her. And Isak Brügger.

Isak.

The missing piece fell into place with a gentle sigh.

Isak had supposedly stolen his case manager's keys out of his pocket, but how? What if the case manager with the guilty conscience had helped Isak escape?

Jeppe found the phone number for Ward U8 and called them. A woman picked up right away.

"Ward U-Eight, this is Ursula."

"Hi, this is Jeppe Kørner with the Copenhagen Police. I'm calling to talk to Simon Hartvig."

"One moment, please." The woman put her hand over the receiver and said something to someone in the background. "Do you know, I can see that he's working the night shift tonight and won't be in until later."

"Could you give me his home number, please?" Jeppe said after a moment's hesitation. "I have a couple of routine questions for him."

"Okay." She made some fumbling sounds. "Do you have something to write with?"

Jeppe wrote down the number, thanked Ursula, and called Simon Hartvig.

He didn't answer.

As he hung up, the superintendent opened the door to Jeppe's office.

"Anything new?" She stood there holding a coffee mug with the word *Grandma* printed on it, looking like a sweet, elderly lady who might have you over for tea. Jeppe knew better.

"Bo Ramsgaard has a rock-solid alibi. It wasn't him. We had to drop the charge and release him."

If there had been a glint of hope in her eyes, it faded fast.

"And?"

"And we're still searching high and low for Isak Brügger and Peter Demant. And trying to locate the cook from Butterfly House. We're questioning one of the two nurses from the place, Trine Bremen. There's an APB out for Marie Birch." Jeppe tried to keep the defensiveness out of his voice. "But unfortunately we don't have anything concrete yet."

She stared at him blankly.

"Luckily," Jeppe continued, "none of them have shown up in a fountain, and I guess we have to consider that a plus." He gave her a faint, tentative smile, which did not have the desired effect.

"You have until this afternoon, Kørner."

The superintendent shut the door with a small, hard bang.

Simon Hartvig looked out over the water in Erdkehlgraven at the bizarre assortment of boats and shacks that comprised the so-called Fredens Havn, and sighed, resigned. He was no Sherlock Holmes, and right now he was feeling both tired and discouraged, but he had to do what he could to find Isak.

Fredens Havn, Holmen.

It had to be somewhere around here. He walked down Refshalevej with the water to one side and the colorful DIY houses on

423

the other. Crooked and unconventional, but mostly well maintained and cozy. And with an unobstructed view of Fredens Havn and Holmen. About a hundred feet down the road a smaller house stood out, not as nice as the others. The facade's only window was boarded up with plywood, and weeds were growing unimpeded around the front door. He walked cautiously around the little house, peeking in the cracks where he could. It must be abandoned. No furniture, just dust and dried leaves on the floors. He tried the door, which to his surprise opened right up, creaking and complaining.

It smelled damp inside, like rotten wood. He walked carefully across the tender floorboards past heaps of trash. Two roll-up mattresses, sleeping bags, and a backpack full of clothes showed that someone had camped here for a while. In a corner an empty gas cartridge that looked shiny and new, and clearly hadn't been lying on the floor for long. Simon picked items up off the floor with his thumb and forefinger: food packaging, tin cans, and trash.

Under a cellophane bag that had contained dried seaweed snacks, he found a folder with a rubber band around it. It read *MARIE BIRCH* in all caps on the front.

Simon took off the rubber band and

opened the folder, moved over into a strip of light between the sill and the plywood in one of the windows, and read.

Word by word his heart stopped, slowly but surely. Shock blurred his vision, and yet the message beamed crystal clear.

CHAPTER 22

She was of two minds. Marie Birch literally changed her mind from one minute to the next, unable to decide what was the right thing to do. She had felt stable and functioning for a long time, but now Isak's presence threatened to change her own mental state. Insecurity spread like a heat flash. She had believed she could be the grown-up and handle the situation, be the safe figure that Isak needed when he had to go without his medication.

But Isak was in bad shape. Really, really bad shape.

Neither of them had slept much last night. Isak had woken up and seen bugs swarming until the walls were black with insects. He yelled for help and tried to kill them — even the ones that were crawling into Marie's ears, and explaining to him that he was hallucinating didn't help. At dawn she had managed to pull him out of the house to sit in the wet grass by the water and let the open sky soften his fear.

Her own experience of going off the meds had been so unproblematic. When Butterfly House closed, and Marie decided she would never again be dependent on anyone or anything, she had gone through a quick withdrawal period, cold turkey. Instinctively she had known that it was the way forward. And she had been right.

Now she was able to regulate her mood swings by sticking to a healthy, nutritious diet and avoiding alcohol and other triggers. She slept at least eight hours a night and spoke up when other people tried to overstep her boundaries. Marie had cured herself and become, if not healthy, then at least strong enough to manage on her own. She had hoped to be able to help Isak in the same way. But they didn't have the same condition. And Marie had no idea how to deal with a paranoid schizophrenic.

Now he was her responsibility, and she didn't even dare leave him long enough to go buy them anything to eat or drink. Isak was sitting on a tree stump a few yards from her looking out over the ramparts. Every now and then his head turned in an involuntary muscular tick. He was trembling.

When they were still living at Butterfly

House, Isak's antipsychotics had been injected once a week in a slow-release formula. She had hoped that was still the case, because that would have given them a few days to prepare together before the symptoms began. Unfortunately it didn't seem to be the case.

How was she going to take care of him?

Could she seek help from the Count, would that get them through the week and win a little time?

"Marie?" Isak didn't turn his head from the water. "I know I can do this. I'm strong enough and I want to!" He spoke in bursts in between his rapid breaths. "But can it wait? It's not because I won't do it. I just really want to wait."

Marie walked over to the stump and squatted beside him.

"It'll pass, Isak. I promise. It's bad now, but it'll get better soon. I'll get us to safety, to a nice place."

"Marie?" His head jerked up to the side in a prolonged spasm. "I'm scared. . . ."

She spontaneously wrapped her arms around his body, feeling him recoil from her touch.

"Marie, you don't understand. I'm afraid I'll hurt you."

She rested her forehead against the side of

his body and cried. Though she knew she was supposed to be the strong one, right now she felt small and scared and just wanted someone's mother to come and help them.

It started raining. She raised her head and felt the drops falling heavily on her forehead and eyes. She didn't even have any rain gear for him. She couldn't help him on her own.

The drops ran down her cheeks in a little rivulet and dripped from her chin. She stood up and reached out her hand to him.

"Come on! We're leaving."

"You're not taking me back to the home are you?" He looked at her in bewilderment.

She smiled and pulled him to his feet, so he towered over her.

"Never! We're never going back there again. But we do need to leave. Come on, this way."

She dragged him along, in under the trees along the ramparts, relatively sheltered from the rain until they reached Langebro bridge. It seemed to calm Isak to be moving, side by side without talking to each other. On the bridge she took his hand. He let her hold it the whole way across to the other side.

As they stood on Otto Mønsteds Gade looking at police headquarters, she let go.

"Isak, go over there, ring the bell, and ask for Anette Werner. She'll help you."

"Aren't you coming with me?" He twitched restlessly.

"I can't, Isak. I can't go over there. But don't be afraid. You're not going back; I'll keep an eye on you."

He stood at the curb, looking at a loss.

"Isak, it's going to be okay. I promise. Ask for Anette Werner, and tell her the whole thing! Anette Werner, remember that name! Let me see you walk over there and ring the bell!"

Isak took a step out onto the street and turned to look back. She smiled reassuringly at him. Then he took another step and another, until he was across the street by the door. He raised his hand and rang the doorbell, looked back at her and waved.

When the door opened and he disappeared into the building, she stuck her hands into her pockets. Her hunting knife was gone.

"Kim was the most wonderful human being I've ever known. I miss him every day."

The woman across from Anette sat quietly looking at her hands while she spoke. She wove and unwove her fingers, rubbed her palms together, and then lay them on the table in a fluid, unconscious choreography.

She was a mature woman, must have been a good ten years older than Kim Sejersen, whom she had dated until his death in the summer of 2014. Her name was Inge Felius, her features aristocratic with a high forehead, narrow face, and a slim nose. She wore her gray-streaked hair in a loose bun fastened by a decorative silver clip. She reminded Anette of a greyhound.

"I'm sorry for your loss."

Anette held her elbows awkwardly close to her body. She had already tipped over the sugar bowl and was doing her best not to bump into anything else. The low-ceilinged little town house on Fiskervejen in the village of Veddelev was crammed full of stuff, as if its owner had decided early in life to collect everything she came across and hang on to it.

There were books, vases, and lamps, but also bulletin boards with dusty photos and newspaper clippings from the 1980s, shelves full of porcelain figurines and music boxes, cracked leather jackets hanging on hooks, and baskets of magazines and cat toys. It was actually quite comfy in an artistic grandmotherly sort of way, but surrounded by all these trinkets, Anette felt twice as big and clumsy as normal, and that was saying

431

something.

"Thank you for agreeing to see me on such short notice."

"I'm just glad to finally get to talk to someone about Kim. The police closed the case right after his death, declaring it an accident. To be completely honest, I've been waiting for three years for someone to get in touch with me. Tea?" She poured the steaming liquid into two rustic cups and pushed one over to Anette. "It's been hard to process that night."

"How do you mean hard to process?"

"Well, witnessing it."

Anette swallowed her tea wrong and knocked over a stack of books on the floor while coughing.

"You were there?" she exclaimed.

"The party was for staff members with partners. I went. And even though Gundsømagle is only a fifteen-minute drive from here, Kim and I decided to spend the night at Butterfly House so we could both drink."

"You were there! You attended that party, the one where Kim drowned?!"

For a moment Inge Felius seemed to consider whether Anette was firing on all engines.

"Well, I'm sorry. . . . But did you witness the actual accident?" Anette wiped up the tea she had spilled with her elbow.

"The accident." Inge weighed the word in her mouth. "I had gone to bed, long before it happened. I was tired, Kim was drunk. The next morning he was dead. Rita knocked on my door at seven in the morning, yelling that she had called the police. I woke up and Kim was gone."

Her voice broke a little on that last sentence and she drank from her cup with distant eyes.

"Why don't you believe it was an accident?"

There was a scratching sound from the window facing the yard. A striped cat on the sill wanted in; Inge got up and opened the window. As thanks the cat allowed her to pet it a couple of times before it jumped down to the floor and disappeared around the corner.

"Intoxicated or not, why would he go out in a muddy pond in the middle of the night? Kim was a mature, sensible man even on those rare occasions when he got drunk. This idea of it being an accident is ridiculous, simply ridiculous! But the police were confident."

"So, what do you think happened?"

The elegant woman looked up at Anette with a defiant glint in her eyes.

"Is there any other explanation possible than the one: that he was murdered?"

"By whom? One of the patients?"

"The residents adored Kim." Inge brushed aside the question with an irritated gesture. "He didn't see them as patients, but as equals, as young people with a future. He worked with them, listened to them. They loved him."

"Well, then who?"

"That I don't know." Inge shook her head defeatedly.

"Which other staff members were present that night?"

"Yes . . . um, let's see. Tanja brought her girlfriend, Ursula, and Bettina Holte came with Michael. Rita's husband, Robert, was there of course, the co-owner. Nicola came alone, I think. Several of the temps were there, too. . . . A bunch of them were still sitting in the yard when I went to bed."

She brought the teacup to her lips, but set it down again with a hard clink.

"They were a pack of wusses, all of them, let Kim defend his criticisms of the place alone, even when they knew he was right. The next day, when the police came, they all claimed that Kim had been the last one to go to bed. But why would he stay up on his own and then wade out into the pond and drown?"

Anette accidentally brushed against a bouquet of dried flowers with her elbow and heard a couple of them crumble and fall to the floor. She pretended that nothing had happened.

"Something went wrong that night," Inge said. "I talked to Tanja and Ursula about it afterward and they agree."

Anette watched Kim Sejersen's girlfriend with a sudden empathy that took her by surprise. Maybe it wasn't so much empathy as a universal appreciation of loss that struck her. You can lose the one you love. Love does not make you invincible. She shook off the feeling.

"Do you remember Ursula's last name? I've already spoken with Tanja, but maybe I should hear what Ursula has to say as well."

"Yeah, we're still in touch. Her name is Ursula Wichmann. She's a nurse, too."

"A nurse, you say?" Anette scrunched up her eyes. "Do you know where she works?"

"Yeah, I even visited her there," Inge said with a smile. "One day when I was in town for a painting class, watercolors. She works at Bispebjerg Hospital in their pediatric psychiatry center. Actually that's where she and Tanja met, maybe five or six years ago . . ."

But Anette wasn't listening anymore. Her ears were filled with a rushing sound and the horizon line was tipping dangerously. She thanked Inge abruptly, and let herself be walked out of the crowded home without knocking anything else onto the floor.

In the car, Anette's heart threatened to leap out of her chest. Isak Brügger's ward, Tanja Kruse's girlfriend, Butterfly House, the accident — her thoughts swirled like confetti that's been shot out of a paper tube. Now what?

She checked the time. Svend had taken the baby to see his mother and had brought formula along so that Anette could sleep while they were gone. She still had a couple of hours to play with. Maybe she could just fit in a visit to Bispebjerg Hospital.

She wrote Svend a text but deleted it without sending. Lies tend to settle over the heart like plastic wrap, making it hard for the love to breathe.

Back in her apartment, Esther tried to clear her head with a pot of strong coffee. She ought to eat something, but once again her appetite was completely gone. Uninterrupted images of Alain kept flashing through her head: Alain sitting in a restaurant with a pretty, thirty-year-old blonde treating her to oysters with Esther's money, impressing her with his knowledge of opera and his French accent. Telling the blonde that she was too good for him and kissing her palms.

The thought was nauseating and sent the rage coursing through her like seething lava. That bastard! But along with her anger, an increasing sense of fear was growing. Why would a person con people like that? He had to be sick in the head.

Her newly replaced lock gave her a certain sense of security along with the hotel chain that she had had installed on her front door. Even so, she still had to go through every room to make sure she and the dogs were alone before she dared to sit down at her computer.

The owners' association regularly sent out news emails that Esther consistently didn't read. As long as the stairwell was kept nice and clean, she generally didn't care what was going on in the building. Now she opened up the most recent emails and read them. She quickly found what she was looking for: The unit on the second floor on the left had been sold as of October 15 and the owners' association wished Hugo and Ida Rasmussen a warm welcome to Peblinge Dossering.

Rasmussen?

She got up and tentatively walked down one flight of stairs clutching her phone in her hand. Even though she knew it was nuts, she punched 112 into her phone so all she had to do was press the "call" button to connect to the dispatcher. Then at least someone would hear it if he started chopping her into pieces. Irrational as it was, it was still marginally comforting.

With trembling fingers, she pushed the doorbell. From inside the apartment voices and footsteps could be heard. Then the door opened and a man stood there, smiling at her. He was about the same height as Esther herself and at least as old, had quite a paunch under his durable blue work shirt, the buttons of which struggled to hold the fabric together, and a white stubble on his round cheeks. In one hand he held a battery-powered drill. Esther stared at him, speechless, unable to behave like a normal person.

"Are we making too much noise?" he asked.

He opened the door wide, allowing her to see past him to the bare walls and moving boxes. A woman of about the same age waved from over by a wall where she was holding a shelf ready to be screwed into place. His question was such a reflection of her and Alain's first exchange that Esther's mind reeled at the thought.

"We're not the most crafty people, but the shelves need to go up," the man said. He moved the drill to his left hand and held out his right. "Hugo Rasmussen. Yeah, just like the bass player, only I'm completely tone deaf." He chuckled warmly. "That's my wife, Ida, with the shelf over there. I assume you live in the building?"

"I'm your upstairs neighbor Esther de Laurenti," she said, shaking his hand. "I . . . I'm sorry. I'm a bit confused. I thought an Alain Jacolbe lived here? Tall, gray hair . . ." She was about to say *concert pianist,* but managed to stop herself in time. How pathetically we cling to the lie instead of accepting a truth that hurts us.

"You mean the mover, Adam?"

"I don't know. He was here yesterday . . ."

"That must be our mover."

"So, he doesn't live here?" Esther asked. She was trying to understand, she really was.

"We live here," Hugo said, looking at her puzzled. "Ida and I. Well, we will once we've moved in anyway. The previous owners let us move our things in a couple of days early, so nice of them."

"Good. Well, I'm glad that's cleared up." Esther forced herself to smile. "Welcome!

439

This is a great place to live. You're gonna love it. We have fun here." She turned around mechanically and walked back up the stairs.

Hugo raised the drill in a jovial farewell salute and shut his door.

The concert pianist Alain was the same as the fast-food restaurant worker Allan, who was the same as the mover Adam, who didn't live in the building but stole and conned money out of people. It was insane. She had to tell her new downstairs neighbors to make sure nothing was missing from their moving boxes and change their locks.

Esther took a sip of strong coffee and let it burn in her empty stomach. Fraud is the worst crime, she thought, because it takes way more than whatever is stolen. It robs the victims of their self-respect.

She found her phone and called Jeppe Kørner. He sounded short-tempered.

"Is this a bad time, Jeppe?"

"These days there aren't any good times," he admitted with a sigh. "I'm at headquarters. What can I do for you?"

Esther focused her shattered thoughts. In actuality, it was very simple.

"Do you know anything about a con man who claims to be a concert pianist or a cook?"

"What?" Jeppe sounded like he really didn't understand.

"I met a . . ." Her stomach tied itself in knots. "I was conned. Out of money. How do I report a con man?"

There was silence. Then after ten seconds, Jeppe sighed.

"This isn't just about your feeling bored, is it, Esther?"

"What do you mean?"

"Well, I'm sorry, but I'm relatively busy at the moment, so if this is about you not having enough going on right now . . ."

"Now you listen to what I'm saying, Jeppe!" Esther exclaimed, gripping her phone tighter. "The day before yesterday there was a man who pretended he was my new downstairs neighbor and he stole money from me. How do I report that?"

Jeppe's tone softened.

"You can do it online. Go to politi.dk and file a report. It's not hard to do. Are you okay?"

She resisted the urge to unload on him. He had his hands full with the murder case and didn't need to be burdened with her petty problems.

"I'm fine, thanks."

"And Gregers?"

"He's okay, too. He's actually doing quite well."

"Good, Esther. Take care of yourself."

She hung up. A crying jag threatened to come over her, but she stopped it and walked to the window to look out at the dark green water, biting back her tears and shame. He was not going to get away with this.

A mild pandemonium broke out when missing person Isak Brügger rang the doorbell at police headquarters asking for Anette Werner. He looked a little worse for wear and was seated in the cafeteria wrapped in a blanket. Jeppe contacted the U8 Ward at Bispebjerg Hospital, where the charge nurse was relieved to hear that Isak had been found, apparently in good shape. When she asked when the police would bring him back, he evaded answering.

Three people had been murdered. They needed to question Isak. Because he was only seventeen, not to mention an inpatient in a locked ward, they were legally required to have an advocate from the city present. Initially Jeppe was going to flout that legal requirement. He brought Thomas Larsen to the cafeteria with him, put a cup of hot chocolate in front of the boy, and hoped that that would set an informal tone.

"Are you feeling better, Isak?"

"I want to talk to Anette Werner. Marie said I should ask for Anette Werner." His eyes darted anxiously back and forth between the investigators.

"I understand that, but Anette is at home with her new baby. She's not working these days. But she's my partner and a good friend of mine, and I promise that you can trust me as much as you would her. Tell me, Isak: Where have you been for the last day and a half?"

"Anette Werner. Marie said . . ."

"I understand, but Anette is not coming. So you were with Marie Birch? Your good friend?" Jeppe tried to maintain eye contact with Isak but he kept looking away.

"Marie is a good friend. I've always known that one day she would come and help me."

"Help you how?"

He seemed confused by that question, as if the answer was obvious.

"Help free me."

"Can you explain what you mean by that?"

Isak looked morosely down at his feet. "Wouldn't you agree that if you're committed in a hospital against your will and not allowed to leave, then you're trapped?"

Suddenly Jeppe understood. In those

443

instants when Isak was actually himself, he was sharp and clear.

"I would think being involuntarily committed is mostly about getting the help you need. . . ." Jeppe let his thought trail off.

Isak studied his feet for a long time before answering.

"People get up in the morning and put their pajamas in the laundry, take a shower, make breakfast, and bring their kids to school. They go to work and eat cake on Friday and make dinner and go on vacation. What is my life? I'm seventeen and locked up in a nursing home masquerading as a hospital. I have no privacy, no private life, no education, no future. I'm just in storage. Hospitals are for people who can be cured. I'm in jail."

Jeppe looked down, unsettled by the young man's pessimism. What could he say to that?

Sara cleared her throat discreetly right next to him and said, "Kørner, can I borrow you for a minute?"

Jeppe got up and left the cafeteria with a certain relief. His encounter with Isak Brügger's hopelessness left him feeling dismayed.

"Yes, Saidani, what is it?"

"Do you remember how we talked about where you could buy a scarificator? I've looked into it, and actually there aren't many places that sell that kind of thing." Sara held up a piece of paper. "Long story short, I contacted various online sellers and came across something interesting on antiquescientifica.com. Look at this!"

She pointed to a line that had been circled in red. Jeppe read it.

. . . thus I can hereby confirm the purchase of one antique brass scarificator on May 5 by Danish customer Mr. Bo Ramsgaard, shipped to the following address . . .

"It was sent to a PO box in Østerbro and paid for using a PayPal account, which I haven't been able to track so far. . . ."

"In other words, it could be a wild-goose chase," Jeppe said. "I see . . . But it's definitely interesting."

"I'm trying to see if I can trace that payment to a name and, if so, if the name is the same. You'd better get back to your interview." Sara walked off down the hall with the sheet of paper fluttering behind her like a kite. Jeppe watched her go. Then he returned to the cafeteria.

The somberness still hung heavy and low. Isak was sitting upright staring blankly into space.

Jeppe took a deep breath and tried hitting a cheerful tone.

"So how did you manage to escape from the hospital?"

"I just unlocked the window and jumped out." Isak sounded almost proud.

"Where did you get the key from? Did someone give it to you?"

Isak looked down.

"Was Wednesday night the first time you ran away from the hospital?"

He still didn't respond. Jeppe watched his tight-knit face closely, looking for twitches, side glances, anything that might give him away.

"Have you previously stolen keys and climbed out the window at night? Gone back to your room before anyone noticed?"

"I don't think so," Isak said, and then seemed to reconsider. "Why would I do that?"

"Maybe you had errands to run in the city?"

Isak wiped his forehead with his sleeve. "I was just going to meet Marie on Wednesday."

"The staff from Butterfly House, did you hear what happened to some of them this week . . ." Jeppe exchanged a glance with Larsen, to make sure that he was ready to intervene if Isak should react. "What do you know about them?"

"Marie said that I should talk to Anette Werner."

"Three people have been killed, three people you know. Do you have any information about that?"

"Only Anette Werner. I'll only talk to her." Isak put his hands on his neck, as if to protect himself.

Jeppe realized that though Isak might be psychotic and probably off his meds, he was also afraid of someone or something specific. If they were to get him to talk, Jeppe had to find a way to bring in Anette.

"Okay, Isak. Here's what we'll do. We'll go back to the hospital so you can get some clean clothes and rest for a bit. Medicine if you need it. Then I'll get Anette Werner to come and meet us there."

The movement came fiercely out of the blue and almost knocked Jeppe backward. Isak threw his hot chocolate right at his face and jumped out of his chair with astonishing speed. In a flash he was by the door. Larsen lunged at him and pinned his arms down.

Isak yelled and kicked.

Jeppe helped Larsen hold him. "Don't

hurt him! Hold him tight, but do not hurt him!"

"Oh, damn it, Kørner! He has a knife in his pocket. We need to put him in a leg lock."

"No leg lock!" Jeppe tried to push his way through to the boy. "Isak, we're not going to hurt you. Everything will be all right, I promise. No one is trying to harm you. Do you hear me?"

But his words had no effect. Suddenly Sara was squatting over Isak trying to pacify his desperately swinging hands with a zip tie.

"It was Peter!" Isak yelled the words, his face mashed against the floor. Then he burst into tears.

"What was Peter? What do you mean? Peter Demant?" Jeppe asked again and again but the boy just sobbed. "What do you know, Isak? We can help you if you talk to us."

Isak slowly quieted down and lay unresponsive, his eyes closed.

"We need to get him back to the hospital," Sara said.

Sara held him under one armpit and Jeppe took the other so they could stand him up. Falck and Larsen joined in. Isak hung like dead weight, and they were forced to carry him between the four of them.

"Come on, let's move! Falck, get a car, and meet us down on the street!"

More officers joined in, alarmed by the scuffle, and they followed the detectives down to their car in a bizarre procession.

Adrenaline surging through his blood-stream, one sentence pumped repeatedly under Jeppe's temples.

It was Peter!

CHAPTER 23

At 4:00 p.m. it started raining again, so heavily that it sounded like someone vacuuming. The water sloshed over the sides of the eaves and backed up out of the storm drains, which couldn't keep up. Peter Demant looked out at the rain from his tenth-floor hotel room, listening as it hit the water by Kalvebod Quay. He tried to find a meditative state standing there, but truth be told, it bored him.

Wednesday night he had hurriedly packed his bag and walked through the dark, out the back door and along the water, until he was far away from prying eyes. Around midnight he had checked into the Tivoli Hotel with muddy shoes and a heart bursting with adventure. It was only fitting to stay here, a stone's throw from police headquarters. Beautiful in all its irony. Peter had ordered the most expensive bottle of Bourgogne on the room service menu and drunk it in the hotel bed in front of the TV.

But adventure had quickly given way to reality: Peter was on the run. He was no longer safe, and those two dorks the Copenhagen Police had assigned to his surveillance team were no help whatsoever. The problem with going underground was that he had to keep himself in check, and he had neither the time nor the inclination to do that. He had an assignment that was waiting, a job to finish.

Peter watched the water, feeling more and more trapped by his own decision. A man who runs away is a mouse, but he was no mouse and absolutely refused to play that role. Time was slipping through his fingers while he stood here watching the world roll by. Yesterday had been yet another definite three, and today showed no signs of improvement. What was he going to do with himself in this twenty-five-square-foot luxury dungeon cell?

It is your fault! It's all your fault!

Trine had sneered this at him as she beat her empty pill box against his chest. But whether she was talking about herself or the murders wasn't quite clear to him. Obviously he had made mistakes. Anyone who works a lot messes up now and then. But his mission at least was to help, to cure.

Peter was in his raincoat before he even realized he was going out. She had summoned him, and now he was coming.

The coat hung on him like a shield, a suit of armor, and he felt his energy start to bubble. It was risky, moving around out in the world, but then he had always been a gambler. As far as he knew they weren't even looking for him. Besides, he would die a slow, lingering death if he had to stay here.

While waiting for the elevator, fury slowly rose in him. Society has a responsibility to protect its citizens against those who can't take care of themselves. Those who can't tell right from wrong because they're sick or have been damaged by childhood trauma, bad parents, or an inhibited family.

No matter how much people desperately want to believe that sickness can be treated and madness controlled, those who work with the seriously mental ill know that that's not always the case. In some cases, recovery is not an option, and then who should be protected? The person who is sick or those around him?

The elevator doors opened with a little ding. Peter walked into the boxlike space.

He was sick of permissiveness and misunderstood humanism. In the elevator's mirror he caught his own dark gaze; the intelligent, probing eyes in that stupid round face. He was done feeling guilty.

Peter pushed the button and went down.

When Anette parked in front of Bispebjerg Hospital, it was raining so hard that she considered staying in her car until it let up. She knew that it was audacious of her to even come here; that she might not get home before Svend and that he would be mad at her. Plus her breasts were so full she was having trouble ignoring it.

Hundred-year-old Bispebjerg Hospital had an expansive campus with well over forty hospital buildings and extensive gardens and park space. Anette was not entirely sure where Ward U8 was, so she just darted through the rain to the buildings that looked most plausible. That turned out to be a bad strategy. By the time she finally found the right place, she was soaked. She shook water from her hair and walked dripping and cursing to a receptionist desk, where a lady with green eyeglasses and a friendly smile looked up at her.

"Wow, you look like you got caught in it!"

"Boy, did I. Sorry if I'm dripping all over your floor. I had trouble finding my way." Anette tried to wipe her hands on her wet pants.

"Most people do. How can I help you?"

"I'd like to talk to one of your nurses, Ursula Wichmann. Is she working today?"

"One moment. I'll call in and ask. Who may I say is here?"

"Anette Werner. I'm a . . . uh, a friend of Inge Felius."

The woman adjusted her glasses and placed the call. She had a brief conversation, which Anette pretended not to eavesdrop on, and then hung up.

"She's not in the ward just at the moment, but she is working today so she'll probably be back soon. I don't know if you have time to wait?"

Anette didn't know if she had time to wait, either. She stood for a moment, trying to decide. It would be a while before she would again be able to defend spending several hours at a stretch away from her baby. At least not according to Svend.

"I'll just take a little stroll in the fresh air. Then maybe in the meantime she'll come back."

Anette ignored the woman's look of surprise and walked back out into the pouring rain. Since she was soaked anyway, she might as well go see the fountain where Nicola Ambrosio's body had been found.

She sloshed off, head hunched over, down

the hospital's muddy gravel paths and quickly got lost again among the old, confusingly laid out hospital buildings. At a crossroads, past a modern addition with a glass facade, she took a short cut onto a tree-lined avenue and wound up at a construction site. This shouldn't be that hard, damn it! The fountain was in the middle of the hospital grounds. She found her way back to the red stone building and was walking along a facade she recognized as being close to Ward U8 when an enormous flash of lightning tore the sky right above her.

"Oh, fuck!" Anette was not afraid of thunderstorms, but that one was really close. She felt the phone vibrate in her pocket and looked for shelter so she could answer it. A few yards ahead a short flight of stairs led down to a basement door. She ran down the steps to the door, found it unlocked, and hurried in out of the rain. The fluorescent tubes overhead were on, lighting up a long, high-ceilinged hallway. The linoleum floor and metal shelves were evidence that the basement at some point had been modernized and used, but it didn't look like people came by that much anymore. Dust was everywhere, and the air was damp and clammy. But at least it wasn't raining down here.

Anette pulled the phone out of her inside pocket. It had stopped ringing, but she could see that it was Jeppe, trying to reach her. Her fingers were too wet to open the phone, her clothes too drenched to dry her hands on. She looked around for some cloth or paper, but the shelves were empty. A little way down the hall a door was open. Anette walked down to it and looked in.

She was almost blinded. White tiles from floor to ceiling gleamed under bright fluorescent lights. The tiles were old and cracked, but appeared clean, like those at an indoor swimming pool. She was struck by a powerful smell of chlorine and soap. There wasn't anything to dry her hands on in here, either. And . . . her phone was now completely dead, drowned by the rain. Anette swore vigorously.

The ceiling curved overhead in two beautiful arches, and on one wall an old operating sink was mounted. Anette remembered a brochure she had seen from a spa in Eastern Europe; this place had the same dilapidated beauty. She walked to the sink and turned the old handle for the cold-water faucet. It stuck and groaned, but a thin stream of rust-colored water ran down into the sink, forming a red puddle. Anette stepped sideways to avoid being splashed and bumped into a gurney. It looked modern, with a stainless-steel frame and washable cover. She slid her finger over the gurney's cold metal and hit a leather strap. The leather felt stiff to the touch. As if it had been soaked with something. Blood, maybe.

"Welcome!"

Anette was so startled by the voice that her heart plunged to her knees, only to then rush all the way up her throat. She looked over to the door.

"You must surely be from the police. I assume you've come to find me?"

Even though they had never seen each other before, she had not even a lick of doubt about who was standing before her.

By the time the police car pulled onto Bispebjerg Hospital's Psykiatrivej, Isak had calmed down completely. Not in the sense that he was relaxed, but more that he had accepted his fate, and he sat with his cheek against the car window like an animal headed for slaughter, just waiting for the inescapable. A delegation from the pediatric psychiatry center stood at the ready under umbrellas, waiting to receive him. Falck turned off the engine.

Jeppe put his phone away — Anette wasn't

answering — and clicked the firearm holster off his belt and locked it in the glove compartment. No weapons in a psych ward.

They got out of the car and greeted the charge nurse.

"He started feeling bad and acting out at police headquarters. Unfortunately we had to cuff him. I'm sorry about that."

The charge nurse came up to the car with her umbrella and said, "Hi, Isak. Are you okay?"

Isak let her help him out of the car with downcast eyes. He didn't respond to her question or to being back at the hospital, just seemed withdrawn and listless. Passively, he let himself be guided to the entrance. Jeppe and Falck followed.

Could it really be true that there were young people in Denmark who didn't have a future? Was there nothing to be done for them?

It wasn't a thought that Jeppe was prepared to accept. When you're seventeen, the world should be like a buffet of options. Life should be one big, throbbing, vibrant future, not an endless loop of well-meaning but insufficient care workers and days spent alone.

When they reached Isak's room, Falck clipped the plastic tie off his wrists and Isak lay down on his bed, turning his back on the team of grown-ups.

The charge nurse gestured to Jeppe and said, "We're just going to give Isak something to help him sleep, so he can get some rest. If you'd like to wait outside?"

Jeppe and Falck stepped out into the hallway and let the team of social workers and nurses attend to Isak in peace. They waited in silence; Falck with his fingers interlaced comfortably over his gut, Jeppe deep in his own sad thoughts. After ten minutes the door opened, and the charge nurse snuck out into the hallway.

"He's asleep."

"That's good to hear." Jeppe nodded somberly. "But as I'm sure you can understand, we need to question Isak as soon as possible. We still don't know if he was involved in the murders. How should we approach it?"

"I don't really know," the charge nurse answered with a nervous smile. "Isak has just spent a day and a half off his meds and away from his usual sources of security. It's hard to say how strongly he'll react to that. Couldn't we decide on this tomorrow morning when we know how he's doing?"

"I guess we may have to." Jeppe pointed to the door of Isak's room. "Is there staff enough in the ward tonight to keep an eye on him?"

"We'll keep his door ajar and peek in on him at regular intervals," the nurse said with a nod.

"Good. We'll station two officers outside his window. Until we know more about Isak's connection to the murder case, we need to be here around the clock. I assume that's all right?"

The charge nurse held up her hand in protest.

"It seems really unlikely that Isak could have anything to do with those murders. It's inconceivable, actually —"

"We agree on that," Jeppe cut her short. "But we still need to question him."

A woman with green eyeglasses strode energetically past them, stopped abruptly, and grasped the charge nurse's arm.

"Did she find you?"

The charge nurse looked at her uncomprehending.

"A woman stopped by a few minutes ago. Anette Werner. She asked for you specifically, Ursula Wichmann. Said she would wait outside."

"Anette Werner?" Jeppe repeated, stiffening. "Are you sure that's what her name was?"

460

"Blond hair, strong, persuasive." The woman with the green glasses nodded eagerly.

That could only be Anette.

"Well, I haven't seen her." The charge nurse furrowed her brow.

"She probably gave up." The woman shrugged. "If it's important she'll come back."

Jeppe ignored Falck's questioning look.

"We'll call tomorrow morning and arrange the details for questioning Isak," he said. "Goodbye."

Jeppe pulled Falck along past charge nurse Ursula Wichmann.

They ran through the rain across the parking lot to their waiting police car. Jeppe scanned the parked cars, but didn't see Anette's anywhere. What the hell had she gotten herself into now? Was she continuing her rogue maternity-leave sleuthing?

Classic Anette Werner! And great timing, too. Now Jeppe was facing a humiliating forced handover of his case to Thomas Larsen, ten years his junior.

When they made it into the car, Jeppe took out his phone and called Anette again. Her phone was off. He left her a brief message.

"What's Werner doing here?" Falck turned

on the engine and switched on the windshield wipers.

"Who knows. But her car isn't here, so she must have left again. Let's get back to headquarters so the superintendent can clip the stars off my shoulders."

Falck fumbled with the gear shift and pulled out onto Tagensvej.

He closed the door and locked it in a quick motion, then pulled out an object from his raincoat, a knife with a wooden handle and a square blade.

"This is a meat cleaver. Back in the day these were used to amputate gangrenous limbs. Bought it online under Bo Ramsgaard's name, just like the scarificator. Antique, but sharp. Get up on the gurney."

Anette remained still for a second, watching the light glinting off the meat cleaver and in his eyes. She had no chance of overpowering him. Her only hope was to indulge him and try to gain more time. Or mercy. She sat down on the gurney.

With the cleaver at face height, he grabbed her right arm.

"Lie down, nice and slow. Hold on here, so I can buckle the strap."

Anette did as instructed, unable to spot any opportunity to get away from him, paralyzed like in those dreams where a train roars toward you but you can't get off the tracks.

He strapped her matter-of-factly to the gurney: first the one arm, then the other, then both ankles, and finally two extra straps that forced her fingers open. All the while holding the cleaver raised high, his hands not trembling in the slightest.

"I'm not part of your equation." Anette tried to speak neutrally, but her voice was shaking like a jackhammer, giving away her fear. Her mind raced, looking for options at rocket speed.

"I didn't come here to find you. You still have time to get away. This isn't necessary."

He set the cleaver on the floor and checked the straps.

"Unfortunately, it's the other way around. If I eliminate you, *I* don't need to run away. No one asked you to come snooping around. You brought this on yourself."

Anette hated knowing he was right. She could have just let it go and not gotten involved. But then that was a killer's logic. It could never be her fault that she was lying here.

He pulled a little brass box out of his pocket and held it up in front of Anette's face. With a solemn expression he pushed a

463

button and twelve little knife blades popped out with a metallic zing.

"This is a scarificator. Nice, huh? I would ask you to undo your pants, but of course you can't. Don't worry, I'm not planning on messing around down there. I just need to get to your femoral artery."

He tugged on the elastic waistband of her sweatpants until her left hip was exposed, then retracted the twelve little blades back into the box by turning a handle, positioned the box against her groin, and nodded apologetically.

"You know what happens now, right?"

He pushed the button and Anette heard the metallic zing again. The pain didn't come for another second. Then she screamed.

"Yeah, it hurts. And it only gets worse, I'm afraid, before it's over."

He pulled the blades back and set the scarificator on her left wrist.

The pain shot from Anette's groin, radiating throughout her entire body, sending her into a panic reminiscent of the childbirth she had just been through. This time, however, there was no light waiting at the end of the tunnel of pain. Or maybe there was.

Anette tried to clench her teeth and talk

through the pain.

"I have a little daughter. She's not even three months old."

"What are you doing here, then? Why aren't you taking care of your child?" He triggered the scarificator again. It felt like Anette's left hand was chopped off. He walked around to the other side of the gurney and retracted the blades, speaking over her moans.

"What happens now is that you're going to gradually bleed out. In about a half hour, you'll be dead. I'm genuinely sorry that it has to be this way."

He positioned the scarificator on her right wrist and released its blades again.

Anette howled.

"There's no one around to hear you, but for safety's sake . . ." He forced a soft rubber ball into her mouth. It was red.

"Now I'm going to exit through that door and lock it behind me. No one else has the key, so let go, and spend the last of your time preparing yourself for the other side."

Anette begged for her life.

The ball gag made her prayers inarticulate, but she begged for mercy anyway. She mumbled unintelligible sounds and blinked, trying to get through to him.

"According to the ancient Greeks, the soul

takes the form of a butterfly when it leaves the body. Isn't that a beautiful thought to die with?"

He closed the door.

Anette could hear him lock it from outside. She tried to scream, order him to come back and set her free, and wasted the last of her strength biting the ball and struggling against the straps. Half a minute after he left, the light turned off. The room became as dark as the grave it was.

Anette felt the life draining out of her. She closed her eyes, saw Svend, her beloved husband, her soul mate and friend. She saw all the years, the travels, the kisses, the dinners, the promises, and the nights. The dogs, the walks. She saw everything in fragments overlapping each other as the blood left her body.

And she saw her little daughter. That little searching mouth, those tiny fingers, the uncannily soft skin on her cheeks. She heard her breathing and finally felt, in the middle of the darkness and the loss, a rock-solid, transcendent love.

CHAPTER 24

They made it off the hospital campus and several blocks down the road before Jeppe remembered that thing he hadn't been able to recall. Falck was trying to raise Jeppe's spirits with a joke about a cannibal who had a magician in his stomach, and Jeppe had to shush him.

Guilt goes hand in hand with resentment at having felt pressured to do the thing one feels guilty about. A double-edged sword, which makes the bearer into both victim and executioner. Peter Demant's words as he sat, dark-eyed and determined, by the fire at the restaurant at Store Strandstræde.

"Turn the car around!" he blurted out. "Go back to the hospital, now!"

Falck did a U-turn and drove back up Tagensvej with surprising speed. Obviously he for once sensed that time was of the essence. As they pulled onto the hospital campus, Jeppe opened his window.

"Now slow down and drive past all the hospital buildings. Open your window and keep your eye out!"

"What are we looking for?"

"First and foremost: Werner's car. Drive!"

Falck let the car roll slowly down the narrow streets that ran through the campus of old brick and modern concrete buildings, parked cars, and grassy lawns. The air was dense, as in that moment when the conductor raises the baton and the whole orchestra inhales. Jeppe just didn't know what piece of music they were about to play.

"Stop!" Jeppe's shout made the car windows vibrate. He was out of the car before Falck had even pulled to a complete stop. Ran toward a bike rack, blinded by the rain.

Of course.

A cargo bike parked in the best hiding place in the world, right out in the open, in the bicycle parking on the sprawling hospital campus, surrounded by hundreds of other bikes. It sat among all the kids' bikes and other cargo bikes, just needing to be found in the jumble.

"Call for reinforcements!" Jeppe yelled through the rain to Falck, who was still in the car. "We need crime scene investigators out here, too."

"What's going on, Kørner?" Falck got out

of the car.

"He's here! The bike he used to transport the bodies is here somewhere. He's here in the area, I know it! Come, let's go that way." Jeppe pointed along the facade of one of the hospital buildings.

"But how do we know which way to go? What are we looking for?"

"A crime scene, Falck. We're looking for a crime scene." Jeppe marched off.

Falck reluctantly followed. Jeppe could sense his skepticism from behind. He knew it was crazy to just walk off into the rain, but they no longer had a choice.

"It has to be a secluded or disused wing nearby, where he has been able to work undisturbed. On the ground floor or in the basement, because he wouldn't be able to haul the bodies up and down stairs without risking being seen. Somewhere where he could leave the bike out front, and then haul the body away from the scene immediately afterward."

Jeppe let his instinct lead him like a bloodhound, breathing heavily as he explained, as much to himself as to Falck. He was not going to let this killer make them run around in circles anymore.

"What about this?"

Jeppe turned and saw Falck pointing

down a side road he himself had just walked right past. A black cargo bike was parked by a stairwell leading down to a cellar door.

"Let's check it out."

They walked down the short flight of exterior stairs to a door that was painted blue. It was unlocked and opened into a high-ceilinged basement hallway, dusty, clammy, and clearly not in use. On one side clerestory windows let in what remained of the daylight, on the other side lay a series of closed doors. Jeppe tried the first one. It opened, and bright overhead lights buzzed on. The room was empty, its original purpose hard to determine, maybe a storage room. The next room was pretty much identical. In the third room was an old gurney and some dismantled steel shelves. Otherwise it was empty.

"Kørner, what are we doing here? Shouldn't we go up and meet the reinforcements?"

Jeppe ignored Falck's reasonable questions and proceeded to the next door in the hallway. It was locked. He tried the door after that and found it open.

"Why is one of the doors locked? There's nothing of value down here and all the other ones are open."

Jeppe walked back to the locked door and

squatted down. The door handle was made of light-gray Bakelite, smooth and shiny as if it had been used regularly.

Jeppe leaned in closer. On the side of the handle, where your thumb would touch if you grabbed it, there was a dark red smudge.

"We're breaking down the door! Come on, Falck!"

Jeppe took two steps back and gave the door a well-aimed kick, just below the lock. The door shifted. So did his back. He kicked again. On the third kick, the frame around the handle splintered and the door flew open.

Fluorescent overhead lights turned on, reflecting sharply off the room's white tiled walls.

There was a gurney by the wall.

Anette Werner was strapped to it with a ball in her mouth and vacant eyes. The floor beneath her was awash in blood.

"For God's sake! Come on, you get the straps on that side. Hurry!"

Jeppe and Falck tried to undo the wide leather straps, but it was excruciatingly slow going. Jeppe knew he should feel her neck for a pulse, but couldn't make himself do it. They just had to get her free and up to the ER as quickly as possible.

Jeppe choked back bile as he lifted Anette's arm and saw the incisions. Twelve small, symmetrical cuts letting the life flow out of her.

He tore off his jacket and then his T-shirt, ripped it down the middle and tied strips around her wrists, tight, to stop the bleeding.

"Tie the jacket around her thigh, Falck! Tourniquet!"

He put his ear to her chest and listened. Come on, come on, come on!

A pause, nothing, silence.

Then the faintest thump imaginable. But it was there! And it was the best sound he had ever heard.

"She's alive!" Jeppe yanked the ball out of Anette's mouth. "We'll lift her up onto my shoulder and you steer us out, okay?"

"I'm afraid that won't be possible."

The voice came from the doorway.

Jeppe's heart froze.

Anette was dying in his arms two hundred yards from an emergency room. The world flickered like a dying lightbulb. Falck's fearful eyes. The blood. The killer, who had been right in front of his face the whole time. The meat cleaver in his hand.

Only two things were crystal clear:

His faithful Heckler & Koch service revolver was in the car.

And they were screwed.

"Have you heard of the butterfly effect, the chaos theory?"

The two policemen blinked, seemingly not understanding the question. For some reason the way they stared irritated him, as if he were some kind of a monster. But then, given their limited knowledge, he supposed he couldn't expect them to have a more nuanced view.

"According to Edward Lorenz's chaos theory from the 1960s, a butterfly flapping its wings on one side of the world can start a hurricane on the other side. In other words, there is a nonlinear dynamic between cause and effect. Sometimes an innocent little misstep can have catastrophic consequences. That's just life."

He struck the flat side of his cleaver against his palm, feeling its robust weight. Saw the policemen weighing their odds against him and it. They were unarmed, and the one in the suspenders, the one named Falck, was both old and overweight. Even though the meat cleaver was a close combat weapon and thus by definition more uncertain, he knew that they wouldn't be able to overpower him.

"That insignificant decision not to bring your guns with you seems to have proven lethal. Put your phones on the gurney. Falck, you go over there" — he nodded toward the sink on the wall — "and, Kørner, by the opposite wall. Sit down on the floor and put your hands on your head."

The moment the older detective took a hesitant step away from the gurney, he knew that he had won. Once there was distance between the two cops, they were defenseless. The old one would hardly be able to get off the floor without assistance. Kørner saw it, too. His regret was almost palpable as he walked to the wall opposite the sink and slid down into a sitting position without ever taking his eyes off the cleaver. Perhaps Kørner should have brought along a younger partner.

When the detectives were sitting on the floor against their respective walls, he walked over to the policewoman on the gurney.

"She's still alive, I see. Tough lady. Although I don't suppose she would survive losing an arm. If you move, we'll test that theory." He tossed their phones onto the floor and watched them shatter.

"We already called for backup," Kørner said, sounding haughty, self-confident. "The police will be all over this place in a second."

"Ah, but your colleagues have no idea where you are, and I can assure you that you won't be found, at least not alive."

"What are you going to do?"

"A magician never reveals his tricks."

"Why? All of this, all those people dead, why?"

"There was no other way, that's why," he said, shaking his head. "Unfortunately I don't have all the time in the world before I have to go, and I doubt that I could make you understand in brief terms."

"Try!" Kørner sounded commanding, as if he were the one making the decisions.

"If you're buying time, don't bother. But I'll give you a few of the headlines. Let's call it fulfilling your last wish."

Simon stood holding the cleaver over the dying policewoman. His arm muscles were burning, but the pain didn't matter. It was almost pleasant. The final spurt had begun.

"You can make good money off the sick. For Rita and Robert it was only ever about the money. They hired Peter Demant to give the whole thing a professional veneer, but no one else's qualifications mattered. As long as they were cheap."

Kørner moved, ever so slightly, but he caught it.

"Stay put, Kørner, until I say when . . ." Simon shook his head resignedly and rested the cleaver on the policewoman's chest. "Things went wrong at Butterfly House. Not from ill will, but from laziness, greed, arrogance . . . cowardice. And as we know, small acts of cowardice can trigger huge disasters. The victims were four young, innocent people, kids who couldn't protest, because no one believed them."

"Is that why the employees had to die?" Kørner asked. "Because they were lazy?"

There was an unpleasant taste in Simon's mouth and he swallowed to get rid of it.

"They failed their responsibility to vulnerable young people. Ruined their lives! After that they kept working in other health-care jobs as if nothing had happened. Do you get it? More children they could neglect, more children they could medicate."

"And you're their protector, is that it, protector of the sick and the savior of the weak?" Kørner asked from his spot by the wall, staring straight ahead. "I just want to understand why you made it your job to kill people."

"You're talking, Kørner, and time's running out." Simon pointed to a trapdoor in the floor, a few feet from where the detective was sitting. "That leads down to a crawl space. Not big, but big enough that two policemen can lie side by side until the oxygen runs out. Open it!"

Kørner crawled to the trapdoor and opened it with some difficulty. The lid was made of cast iron, and he struggled to lift it.

"Get in, feet first. It's not that deep. Come on! You have to lie down to make room for your head; then your colleague will come keep you company in a minute."

He watched Kørner swing his legs into the opening in the floor and lower himself in.

"If things go according to plan, you'll soon be accompanied by one high-profile psychiatrist as well. I just found documentation that shows he should have been the first one I got rid of. But better late than never."

Simon stepped closer to the hole.

"I'm sorry things have to end like this for you. In a hole in the ground. Think of it as a restraint, almost like a Utica crib. You know what that is, right? An escape-proof cage used for the most dangerously insane patients, even up until the late 1800s. So small you couldn't stretch out fully inside it. It wasn't used for punishment or to cure patients, just for storage."

Kørner ducked and disappeared into the hole, and Simon felt a ray of light shining on his face. Soon he would be able to look ahead again.

He nodded apologetically.

"Not a punishment, Kørner, just storage."

Jeppe saw the world disappear. The gleam of the tiles was replaced by the dark dankness from the raw walls around him. He lay down into the earthy smell and felt cool dirt underneath him. The crawl space was only about three feet deep, and his head and feet hit either end. Not much bigger than a grave.

Through the opening above him came light and air, but soon the lid would close and everything would turn dark. He and Falck would lie here like anchovies, stewing in their own juices, gasping for breath while Anette bled to death.

How fast would it be over? Jeppe couldn't remember how long it took to deplete the oxygen in a small, airtight space. There was probably an equation. Faster than their colleagues would find them, that much was certain. And that was the only equation that mattered.

All of that death caused by laziness and greed. A murderer driven by his sense of justice. A double-edged sword, which makes its bearer both victim and executioner, Peter Demant had said. He himself was next on the list. The only reason he was still free was presumably that he had managed to hide in time.

Did Jeppe have any regrets?

That he hadn't been nicer to his mother. That he hadn't solved this case fast enough. That Anette would never make it home to her baby.

He ran his hands over the walls, letting crumbling cement drizzle down over him. He could hear Simon Hartvig ordering Falck to stand up. Once he was lying in the hole, too, that was it. Then they would die here, side by side.

Jeppe hadn't exactly planned how he would exit this world, but buried alive next to Detective Falck was definitely not on the list of tolerable ways to die. He held his breath and scratched at the cement again. Heard Falck approaching.

A shadow fell over the hole, and Jeppe saw Falck's massive body kneel as he prepared to climb in. Saw Simon standing right behind Falck with the meat cleaver.

Jeppe caught Falck's eye. The old detective was fighting the effects of gravity and its years of wear and tear on his knees and back. His body was tired, his hunger for results not what it had once been. Those multicolored suspender straps simultaneously held him up and reduced him to one of those jokes he enjoyed telling. But he was still in there, Falck was, the young cop he had once been, that bulldozer of an investigator, the man with enough fighting spirit, stubbornness, and courage for a whole city. He was in there.

In one alert, crystal clear instant Jeppe saw him. That was all he needed. He clenched his hand around a fistful of cement powder and tensed his abdominal muscles.

"Now!"

Falck lunged to the side, nimble as a volleyball player. Jeppe raised his arm and in one smooth motion flung the cement dust at Simon's eyes. Simon covered his face with his hands and screamed in surprised outrage. The cleaver hit the floor.

Jeppe used the moment to try to lift himself up out of the hole, but he didn't get far. Simon moved his hands from his face and straight to Jeppe's neck. His grip was iron-hard and instantly blocked Jeppe's air supply. He couldn't get enough foothold to fight back.

Strangulation is a terrible way to die.

That sentence ran through Jeppe's head as he tried to grasp onto something with his hands and feet, his vision starting to fade.

Red behind the eyes, like when you turn your face to the midday sun, a smell of the wet dirt awaiting him. Static filled his ears, pressing painfully inward toward his brain. He hadn't been fast enough.

The sound of swishing metal cut through the static. Simon's grip loosened and oxygen flowed like heroin into Jeppe's brain, coursing through his bloodstream. He collapsed onto the floor, his lower body still down in the coal hole, and breathed greedily, black spots dancing in front of his eyes.

Then Jeppe raised his head.

Simon Hartvig lay unconscious on the floor, and behind him Detective Falck stood, broad like a giant and just as powerful, with the meat cleaver in his hand. He must have hit Simon with the blunt side, because there was no blood on the knife blade.

Falck raised his eyebrows questioningly. Jeppe pointed to Anette and tried to speak, but ended up coughing so much, his words were almost unintelligible.

"Run, Falck!"

CHAPTER 25

It wasn't until midnight that Jeppe reached Christianshavn in a taxi reeking so badly of stale cigarettes that he swore he would never smoke again. He decided to call his mother to let her know he was all right but then remembered that his phone had been smashed.

Sara opened the door, spread her arms, and pulled him into a hug so tight that he almost couldn't breathe.

"You're happy to see me."

"I'm happy to see you alive! Is Anette okay?"

Jeppe nodded, exhausted.

"In the trauma center at National Hospital with IVs in both arms. She had lost almost four liters of blood and was on the brink of death, but she's going to make it. Her condition isn't critical anymore."

"Oh, thank God." Sara kissed him again and again, holding him tight and pushing her face into the curve of his neck as if they both had to hurt a little before she dared believe he was okay.

He picked her up and carried her into the apartment, kissed her neck and shoulders, everywhere he could reach. In the bedroom they toppled onto the bed, Jeppe still in his raincoat and wet shoes.

She peeled the clothes off him, insistent, desire going hand in hand with the fear of death. Jeppe appreciated that this flash of lust, the kind of passion that burns without limit when you're a teenager, was a rare gift. He reached out and touched her soft breasts, kissed them. She pulled him down on top of her, and he ignored the gravel in his eyes and his sleep deficit. Surrendered to her.

Afterward, as they lay together, she didn't turn her back to him.

"Were you scared?"

The question was asked so innocently that Jeppe laughed.

"No, weirdly I wasn't. I'm more scared now than I was in that basement. . . ."

She looked at him questioningly.

Even in the dark he could see the little wrinkle she got on the bridge of her nose when she was skeptical, and suddenly felt such a tremendous rush of love for her that he had to turn and look up at the ceiling.

"Do you mind if I smoke?" Jeppe decided to postpone his smoking ban.

Sara flung the covers off with a laugh.

"You old nicotine junkie. Come, we'll go out on the back stairwell and open the window."

She hopped out of bed and pulled him up. Two minutes later he was installed in the stairwell with a blanket, a cold beer, and a postcoital cigarette that tasted better than anything else he could remember in his life.

Sara sat on the step below him and leaned against his knee.

"Where's Simon Hartvig?"

"In custody. If he's been released from the trauma center, that is. Falck gave him quite a whack on the old noggin, so I bet he's got a bit of a headache."

"Falck? Detective Falck?"

"The one and only. I wouldn't have picked him as the hero of the day, but if it weren't for him, I wouldn't be sitting here now. He's probably the one who's most surprised."

Jeppe blew his smoke upward and away from Sara. She didn't seem to mind.

"Simon Hartvig, protector of the weak." Jeppe wrapped the blanket around Sara, so she wouldn't be cold. "Wilkins, Holte, and Ambrosio were guilty in their patients' decline and suicide. In his head the murders were what it took to settle the score."

"Why do you think the victims agreed to meet him?"

"He must have threatened to reveal how their sins of omission were to blame for Pernille Ramsgaard's suicide if they didn't come."

"And then he waited for them with the meat cleaver?" Sara took the beer out of his hand and drank a swig.

"With the meat cleaver, the scarificator, and the gurney. And an account to settle. That basement room at Bispebjerg Hospital was ideal. It was a quiet, out of the way place to work and it had all the necessary appurtenances." The cigarette was starting to warm Jeppe's fingers. He inhaled and held the smoke in his lungs until it burned. "Simon could use his night shift for cover and sneak down to the basement claiming he was going on his break."

"Everything in one place," Sara said, wrinkling her forehead. "But why throw the bodies into fountains?"

"There was symbolism in that. A healing metaphor, a reference to Pernille Ramsgaard perhaps. Plus he had to create a geographic distance between the crime scene and where they were found."

Jeppe finished his beer and put the bottle on the stairs.

"Tuesday morning Isak wasn't feeling well and slept poorly. That was probably why Nicola Ambrosio was thrown in the hospital's fountain. There wasn't time to take him into town."

Sara pulled the blanket tighter around her bare legs and shivered.

"It doesn't make any sense. Who kills people they hardly know to protect the sick? He must be deranged."

"Let's see what the psychological profile says," Jeppe said with a shrug. "Maybe there's something we don't know, a missing piece to the puzzle."

"Yeah, maybe . . ." Sara rubbed her upper arms for warmth. "How is your friend's roommate, the old guy who had the heart attack?"

"Gregers? He's going to have an operation on Monday and should be on top of his game soon again." Jeppe stood up. "Come on, let's get you to bed. You're shivering. And I'm falling asleep."

"It's too late for you to drive home." Sara smiled up at him. "Spend the night."

Jeppe was too exhausted to argue. He would just have to sneak out before the kids woke. Right now the idea of sleeping next to the woman he loved outweighed the prospect of getting up early.

"You said you were more scared now than you were when you were being strangled." She stroked his cheek with a tender fingertip. "What did you mean by that?"

"Did I say that?" Jeppe was struggling to keep his eyes open and tried hard to focus on her. "I guess I was just babbling. Let's go to bed. It's finally over."

Marie Birch zigzagged across Sankt Annæ Square between flowerbeds, wet benches, and bicycles. The streetlamps cast their light on the asphalt making the parked cars look like overgrown LEGO blocks in metallic grays and blacks. At the front door she looked to both sides before she rang the discreet doorbell and was buzzed in. She had dressed for the occasion as best she could and looked, she hoped, more like a privileged, rebellious high school student than a homeless person.

The door to the clinic was locked, so she knocked, and he answered right away. She was expected. Still, his face tightened when he saw her standing in the doorway.

"I was starting to think you weren't coming."

"Yeah, you would have liked that. You're

not getting off that easily I'm afraid."

Peter Demant stepped aside and closed the door behind her after a long look into the empty stairwell. Marie strolled through the empty reception area into his office and hopped up onto his glossy desk, her legs dangling. He came in, his eyes like a panther circling its prey, dignified, intense, and cautious.

"Most people would have asked me long ago why I wanted to meet. But I guess you don't have to? You know why we're here, that there can only be one reason."

He stopped a few yards away from her. She could almost see his brain cells spinning. How much did she know?

Marie smiled at him assertively to show that the answer was *everything.*

"What do you want? Money?" He spoke through his teeth, his dark gaze still focused intently on her. Marie wasn't smiling anymore.

"Do I look like someone who's interested in money, Peter? All I want is justice, honesty, for things to come out into the open. That's the only chance Isak and I have of a future. You should just be happy that you still have a life to hold on to."

Peter took a couple of steps toward the window behind the desk, ending up diagonally behind Marie. She resisted the temptation to turn around, refusing to show that she was afraid of him.

"Regardless of who killed Rita and the others," he said, speaking slowly and tentatively, "the individual in question must be deeply disturbed."

"Yes, he must be sick in the head. Sad that he wasn't helped in time. Don't you agree with me? What is your professional evaluation?" She could sense his confusion as a mass of quivering energy he radiated without being aware of it.

"I'm sure the killer will be examined mentally by the police's expert psychologists and will probably turn out to be —"

"Oh yeah, right: *the murderer was a psychopath.* Like always. Then he should be medicated, right?" Marie calmly turned to face Peter, who was standing by the display cases with the dead butterflies. "Which medication would you give him?"

He stood frozen for several seconds. Then he shook his head.

"I don't understand what this conversation is about. And honestly I'm getting a little tired of it. . . ."

"Oh, really?" Marie smiled in fake empathy. "Well, let me try to explain: I'm here to ask why you used us, the four residents at

Butterfly House, for your medical experiment."

"Cut it out, Marie. I have never, ever —"

She stopped his protest with a look of disapproval that made it clear she wasn't taking any of his bullshit.

"Was it the money? What do you get for unofficially testing new antipsychotics that aren't approved yet? A million kroner? Two? Ten? Not ringing any bells yet?"

His face revealed nothing.

"The worst part is that you, of all people, understand what you've done. Gambled with the lives of four young people. You observed and cataloged our hallucinations and psychoses as if we were lab rats." Marie scrunched up her eyes. "Pernille couldn't take it. The medicine was what made her kill herself. You pushed her over the edge."

"You think I conducted *experiments* on you guys for some chump change? Do you have any idea how much money I make?"

"No, I'm sure you're right, the money wasn't the main appeal. You probably viewed it as a part of your research. If you want to be the psychiatrist who cracks the code and finds a drug to treat self-injurious behavior, then you would also have to find out what the negative consequences are, experiment with the side effects. Blow on the sick flame

490

that burns inside us, who aren't *normal.*"
She put the last word in air quotes. "Because
you really want to be the one who solves
the mystery, right? You want to be famous."

Peter held up both hands.

"You're clearly still blending imagination
and reality. I can only recommend, strongly,
that you get treatment as soon as possible."

Marie hopped down from the desk and
walked over to him.

"Do you want to hear something really
funny: for a long time I thought Isak was
the one who had gone too far that night at
Butterfly House. I was scared that he had
killed Kim."

She heard Peter inhale and hold his breath
in, not quite a gasp, but almost.

"Yes, it's shocking, I know. Luckily it's
also wrong. Isak didn't kill Kim." She raised
her hand and pointed her index finger
straight at him. "You did!"

His face didn't change, but she knew that
he never displayed anything he didn't want
to, never let down his guard.

"Isak knew it. He saw you guys argue that
night and heard Kim's threats about reporting you to the Patient Safety Authority and
ruining your reputation. He saw you holding Kim's head under until he wasn't
breathing anymore. But he knew that no

one would believe him."

Peter cocked his head to the side. He was making ready for the therapist talk.

"Marie, I'm genuinely sorry to see that you still suffer from delusions. The years on the streets have not been good for your sense of reality."

"Save me your crap, Peter," she said, rolling her eyes. "I know there's no way to prove it, but it's still true. We both know that. I only regret that the fountain killer didn't get to you before they arrested him."

"Isak would have made a great courtroom witness," Peter scoffed snidely.

"Luckily he doesn't have to."

The sharp light from the streetlight outside the window hit Peter diagonally from behind, making his dark eyes recede right into his skull.

"What do you mean?"

It was her turn to smile.

"Those digital journals, which your sweet receptionist put online for you so you can see them from home and do your research. So clever! The results of your tests, notes about adverse events and side effects. But, dear Peter, anything that's online can be hacked, no matter how password protected or encrypted it is. I have a good friend who lives underground, literally, and he accessed

492

the whole thing."

Peter's eyes glowed in the dark.

Marie turned her back on him and started to leave. In the doorway she turned around.

"The files were sent a few minutes ago as PDFs to the police, the Patient Safety Authority, and all the daily papers in the country. I suspect that there will be aspects of the treatment you gave Kenny, Isak, and me — and especially Pernille — that will be hard for you to explain. Maybe I can't get you thrown in the slammer for Kim's murder, but I might be able to put an end to your career, your precious career."

She held up her two middle fingers to the dark silhouette by the window.

"Nice butterflies, by the way."

Then she went back out into the rain.

SATURDAY, OCTOBER 14

CHAPTER 26

The ampoules lay in plastic boxes, next to disposable syringes, sterile wipes, and sharps containers. Analgesics, betablockers, and diuretics, all properly sealed in clear bags and cardboard boxes. Saturday morning at a little past seven, Trine Bremen stood in front of the unlocked medication cupboard in the cardiac arrhythmia ward, zoning out.

Her shift was supposed to have been over at 11:00 p.m., but someone had called in sick at the last minute and had forced her to work the whole night shift, too. She looked at her watch; she had been at work for almost sixteen hours now. Her feet were aching and her neck was stiff. Trine gathered up the ampoules she needed into the pocket of her white scrubs, yawned, and locked the cupboard behind her.

The head-scarfed cleaning lady pushed her cart down the hallway and Trine skirted around her with the medicine clenched in her sweaty hand hidden in her pocket. In the staff restroom she filled the disposable syringe, drawing three ampoules of ajmaline up, then flicking it to make sure there were no air bubbles. Not that it mattered. She unlocked the door with the syringe hidden in her pocket, full and ready.

In front of room eight she cast a discreet glance in both directions before pushing the door open and stepping into the darkness. She approached the bed, watching the old man, who was sleeping on his back with his mouth slightly open. Gray, wrinkled, and wizened, his body had long since served its purpose. Now it was just a vessel for a tired, troubled soul longing to be set free. Trine could see it in his eyes. She carefully lifted the syringe out of her pocket and connected it to the patient's central line.

He moved slightly, as if his sleeping conscience sensed her presence. Trine patted him tenderly on the hand. Then she pushed the plunger to the bottom.

She tucked the syringe into the waistband of her trousers while she curiously regarded the sleeping man. The seconds ticked away, she counted seven, and then finally something happened. The patient gasped for air and grabbed his chest, his forehead instantly beading over with sweat. His eyes were still closed, and he seemed to go straight from sleeping to unconscious. Trine watched him. After the first minute the survival rate dropped at a rate of about 7 to 100 percent per minute. She didn't want it to be too easy. Not until he showed the first bluish signs of cyanosis did she activate the code alarm.

When her colleagues pushed open the door to the room, Trine was already performing CPR on the patient, working hard, flushed and zealous.

"Cardiac arrest!" she yelled. "We need the defibrillator and the meds from the crash cart now!"

"Step away from the patient!" Dr. Dyring's normally friendly voice hit her like a whiplash. A second later she was shoved aside by Jette and two other coworkers who clustered around the bed in a flurry of activity.

"It's my alarm," Trine protested. "I found the patient. . . ."

An orderly grabbed her arm and pulled her out into the hallway. The door to the room closed, and Trine stood alone with the alarm ringing in her ears. She had been thrown out.

Her mind sprinted in an attempt to comprehend what had just happened. It couldn't be her skills they were questioning.

Trine quickly walked down the hall to the staff bathroom and locked herself in. She pulled the disposable syringe out of the waistband of her pants, wrapped it in toilet paper and tossed the bundle into the bottom of the trash can. Then she went back toward room eight.

The door was still closed.

She walked past it, forcing herself to count ten paces, and then turn around. Walked past it again, alternating between rage and fear.

Detached yells could be heard through the door. Trine stayed put.

The door to room eight opened, and a nurse came out. Her lips were drawn tight and she walked past Trine without seeing her.

"Is he okay?"

The question hung in the air, unanswered. Well, that crossed the line! Not even answering.

Dr. Dyring emerged from the room and stopped in front of Trine. He looked down at his hands, which he was rubbing with hand sanitizer.

"Trine, could you please join me in my office. Right away."

"Did he survive? Why won't anyone tell me what's going on?" The unfair treatment stuck in Trine's throat, making her voice tremble.

The doctor regarded her with the face of a disappointed teacher and started down the hall. Trine resisted the urge to smash something heavy into the back of his old, bald head and followed him to his cool, impersonal office.

"I think we'd better sit down."

The doctor looked like he might be coming down with something. The skin on his face resembled day-old sushi that had lost its color and shine. The situation was clearly extremely unpleasant to him.

"We lost the patient. He couldn't be saved."

Trine's chin fell to her chest and she sighed unhappily. Shook her head to show how difficult this bad news was to understand.

"You shouldn't have thrown me out. I could have saved him. Why did you throw me out?"

"We've been keeping a bit of an eye on you," he said, clearing his throat ominously. "There has been a noticeable uptick in these types of cardiac arrests while you've been on duty. Did you know that?"

"Is it Jette who's spreading rumors about me?"

"It's irrelevant who —"

"I knew that bitch was going around saying bad things behind my back. She has wanted to get rid of me from day one, but that she would stoop so low as to accuse me of . . ." Trine couldn't hold back the sob that crumpled up her face like a child's. "I'm taking this to the nurses' union! This is workplace harassment."

That made him waver; it was obvious. He was about to say something, but caught himself, weighing his words. Before he had a chance to speak, there was a knock on the door and Jette walked in.

"Got a hit, it was in the trash can in the bathroom." Jette tossed the disposable syringe and the empty ampoules onto Dr. Dyring's desk.

Trine instinctively reached for them, but Jette's gloved hand stopped her.

"Best not to touch."

Trine pulled back, folding her arms across her chest and looking sourly to the side as Jette peeled off her gloves.

"Ajmaline, fifty milligrams times three. The syringe is still wet. I suggest we call the police."

The doctor watched her without responding and a moment arose there in the office, a withheld breath, where time became elastic and hyperreal, like in the seconds before a diver hits the water. It occurred to Trine that this was a hole in reality, and that she could stand up and disappear before everything went back to normal, run down the hallway, light as a feather, flying, sailing over the worn linoleum, past beds and somber fates, out into the world, away. She almost managed to stand, preparing to set off, when the doctor spoke and the sand in the hourglass began to flow again.

"Do you know anything about these ampoules?"

"No!" Trine shook her head. "I have no idea where those are from."

"I hope you understand that we're going to have to suspend you. The police will need to decide what happens from here. Please remain seated here until they arrive. Jette, will you stay and keep Trine company until then?" Dr. Dyring stood up. "Unfortunately I need to go contact the next of kin."

He looked pained, eyeing Trine for a very long time, as if she was supposed to be able to help him.

Trine returned his gaze unblinking.

The sound of the key in the lock usually

brought Jeppe's mother to the door, but today she must have been practically waiting to pounce, because when he let himself into the apartment on Nørre Allé, she was standing right behind the door.

"Fuck!" Jeppe blurted out and then tried to get his heart back where it was supposed to be. "Sorry, Mom, you startled me. Why are you standing there?"

"Where have you been?"

Jeppe took off his raincoat and hung it on a hook. Were they really going to do this again?

"I'm coming from headquarters. We've been questioning the murderer who killed three people this week. We found him. The case is closed."

His mother pulled her bathrobe tighter around her neck, as if Jeppe had let in a draft.

"I mean last night, Jeppe. Where were you? Couldn't you have called?"

The morning's triumph began to wane. But for once Jeppe was fairly well rested. He spotted the dark circles under her eyes and was able to deduce that she, on the other hand, had not slept . . . because of him.

That thought made him ill at ease, and he shrugged defeatedly and went to the kitchen to hide it from her. She was equipped with a set of antennae that captured every mood change, and he hadn't had his breakfast yet — a bad combination that had proven fertile ground for conflict multiple times in the past.

Jeppe had left Sara's place early that morning and gone straight to work to question Simon Hartvig. That had been pretty horrible on its own. Simon confessed briefly, but refused to answer any questions and now stood accused of triple homicide plus attempted homicide. His confession was supported by the technical evidence and the autopsy results: The scarificator had his fingerprints on it and traces of several different blood types. There were rain gear and rain boots in his staff locker at Ward U8 that also tested positive in the crime scene investigators' blood tests. And in his apartment they found a large collection of antique medical devices. They had their guy.

Jeppe had been patted on the back by his colleagues and praised by the superintendent, who magnanimously urged him to go home and enjoy the weekend. Now his mother's attempts to make him feel guilty threatened to overshadow the rosy-fingered dawn.

"I need something to eat," Jeppe said, cutting himself a slice of bread. He filled the electric kettle and poured instant coffee into two cups. "Have a seat, Mom, please."

She sat down and graciously accepted the cup of coffee he placed in front of her.

"What's all this about?" he asked.

"I just think you could have —"

"Mom, I'm a grown man, who moved away from home more than twenty years ago." He placed his hand over hers. "You don't need to know where I'm sleeping, even if I'm borrowing your guest room at the moment. You call me eight times a day. . . ." Jeppe drank some coffee and worked to suppress the irritation that was growing with every word he said. "You know this doesn't work, Mom. What's wrong?"

Her eyes were on the table and for a long time she said nothing.

Jeppe studied his mother. She and his father had divorced when he was little and she had been single-handedly responsible for almost all of the childrearing — the school lunches, the PTA meetings, the early mornings, and the serious heart-to-heart talks and practical matters. At the same time she'd made a career at the university. She had been ambitious and conscientious about her job, and although Jeppe remembered how busy she had been, she had rarely complained about the challenges of combining their little family with her professional life.

In Jeppe's eyes, his mother had always been a fighter, a straightforward and principled woman who could accomplish anything in the world with her determination. Now, here she sat at the table, frail and sunken, and it hit him that she was getting old. He was overwhelmed by the need to stop her movement through time and keep her from dwindling until she was snatched away from him.

She lifted those blue eyes, which, over the years, had grown increasingly foggy and watery.

"I'm lonely."

Her words hit him like a punch to the kidneys. His strong, independent, fierce mother . . . lonely?

"What do you mean?"

"It's not that hard to understand, is it?" She smiled wistfully. "I live by myself. You're busy with your life. All my friends are in poor health or dead. I don't have a job anymore; nothing is expected of me. Plus, I'm starting to forget things . . . sometimes I feel so confused. I try to stay active and hold myself together, but . . . Maybe I had hoped that you and I could spend a little more time together while you were living here. You know, that it would maybe bring us closer. I miss you."

Jeppe's head fell. Damn it! Why do we insist on embracing our parents with sawblades on our arms? Did he really have to punish her for getting older?

"I'm sorry, Mom."

He went around the table and squatted down so he could put his arms around her. She leaned closer and tousled his hair, like when he was a kid.

"The coffee is probably cold."

"Should I heat more water?" Jeppe asked, standing back up with a smile.

She thought about it, and then shook her head.

"I can't drink any more, anyway."

"I slept at a woman's place last night," he admitted, sitting back down again.

"Yeah, I figured out that much. Is it serious?"

"I think maybe." Jeppe considered the question. "It feels more serious than anything else I've tried in my life. I don't really know where she stands on the matter, but . . . she's the one. Is it okay to say that when you've been married before?"

"It is!" His mother smiled warmly. "You

can say it as many times as you feel it. Who is she?"

"A coworker — yeah, I know, that's not optimal. Her name is Sara, and she has two kids, two girls. She's a little shy, has hazel eyes, is quick on the uptake, and —"

"And she really lights your fire?"

Jeppe held up his hand.

"Whoa, the two of us are not going there, Mom! But, yes, 'lights my fire' would probably cover it."

She laughed.

"Can I give you some good advice?"

One of those questions that is hard to say no to, even though very few of us ever really want good advice. Jeppe flung up his hands in a neutral gesture. His mother took that as a yes.

"Don't get boring, Jeppe."

"Boring?! What are you talking about?"

"Boring! Predictable. It happens to men so easily." His mother grasped his hand and squeezed it. "Women need variety. We always want to be loved in a new way. That tick-off-all-the-boxes tyranny that you seem to feel so comfortable with has the opposite effect on us."

Jeppe pulled his hand back, laughing.

"Are you seriously going to give me the *men are from Mars and women are from Ve-*

nus talk? Haven't times moved on from that interpretation of the sexes?"

"It's quite possible. But it is still true." She got up and started clearing the table. "It's about being true to yourself. Especially as a man, Jeppe." She took his plate with a slight smile, seeming pleased to have a glimmer of their old distribution of roles. "Just because you've inherited my sensitivity, that doesn't mean you're not strong. Some women misunderstand that kind of thing."

Jeppe smiled at his mother. For the first time in a long time, he did it without feeling annoyed or wanting to escape the conversation.

"What about her kids? Have you met them?"

"We want to make sure we're ready first." Jeppe felt his nose wrinkling skeptically.

"Did you not just tell me she was the one?"

"Yeah . . ."

"So what are you waiting for?" she asked, dishcloth in hand. "It is with love as it is with fish, Jeppe. You can't just buy the fillets: you have to take the whole carcass."

To begin with she just lay there, her eyes blurry, trying to orient herself as she drifted in and out of consciousness. The world was fuzzy and distant, in a way that she had never experienced before, like being wrapped in a cotton ball, isolated and grainy. Her lack of pain told her that she was either heavily sedated or dead.

"Anette, can you hear me?"

The voice was warm and firm and didn't sound particularly angelic. Anette forced her eyes open again and saw a smiling nurse standing next to the bed.

"Ah, you're coming back to us. That's wonderful! You've been through quite an ordeal. We've been really worried about you."

"Where's my family?"

"Your husband is taking a stroll with your daughter. She's a bit overtired. They're bound to be back in a second." The nurse hesitated. "It's been a hard night for your husband. He's . . . uh, quite upset."

Upset, of course he was upset. Nervous and worried, but probably also pretty angry. She would be, too, in his position.

The nurse took Anette's blood pressure and her temperature and stroked her forehead. She had survived. She had come through the darkness and the pain, had made it. She and Svend would grow old together like they had planned and she would see her daughter again, watch her grow up to become big and beautiful. Nothing else mattered at all.

"Are you okay?"

"Yeah, yeah, it's nothing. Just . . ." Anette sensed that she couldn't give words to her thoughts right now.

"I'll go find your husband and tell him you're awake. He'll be happy to hear it."

Anette smiled gratefully and closed her eyes again, exhausted from the brief conversation.

The sound of a baby crying made her look toward the door. Svend was on his way into the room, his eyes red-rimmed and glassy, the baby in his arms. *My family,* Anette thought, *my family is crying because of me.*

She reached up to Svend who placed their daughter tenderly into her arms. The baby smelled the milk and immediately started looking for Anette's breast.

"Are you sure it's okay to nurse her? You're on a lot of painkillers." He avoided making eye contact.

"I think it's fine. The amount that would come out in the milk would be negligible anyway." Anette opened up her hospital gown and put her daughter to her breast, watching her as she started nursing right away with her eyes closed and her little hands groping unconsciously. Anette's heart fluttered with relief.

Little human being, my beloved daughter.

"Your numbers look good, they say. With a little luck, you can come home tomorrow." Svend stood by the window with his hands in his pockets, looking out at the seagulls.

Anette sat up straighter in the bed.

"Can you manage until then, with the baby?"

He didn't answer.

"Maybe your mom could . . ." Anette stopped herself.

Svend didn't need help, he would be fine on his own. Maybe he didn't even need her anymore. Maybe she had crossed the line this time and pushed his patience too far. She looked down at the little girl in her arms. She had caused harm, irreparable harm, maybe. She had lied, and the lies had punched holes in their marriage. Anette felt her heart breaking in her chest, like a crystal glass dropped on the floor. She raised her arm and wiped her nose on her sleeve, carefully, without jostling the baby. Whispered to her daughter, "No matter what happens from now on, you can count on me, kiddo, no matter what."

"Did you say something?" Svend's voice was cool and distant, his back still turned.

Better get it over with. How hard could it

be to admit that she had screwed up?

"I'm sorry, honey. I know I've been a jerk. I'm really sorry." Actually, it wasn't that hard once she got going. Her voice started choking up. "It'll never happen again."

"What won't?" Svend turned around to look at her. He looked devastated.

"What won't ever happen again? You won't lie about where you're going? You won't run off on our baby? You won't risk your life for an investigation you're not even part of? I just need to understand what you're *not* planning on doing again, and what I may expect to be a recurring incident."

In their almost twenty-five years together Anette had never seen her husband like this. Resigned, as if he didn't love her anymore. He normally never got angry, and she could always coax a smile onto his face with a little teasing or a kiss. But not now.

"I can forgive a lot, Anette, but this isn't about me anymore. Or even about you for that matter. This is about her." He pointed to the baby. "We have a child. You're acting like it hasn't occurred to you what that means."

Anette didn't know what to say. And even if she had known, she wouldn't have been able to say a word, her throat was so constricted.

"What are your plans? I mean, for the future. Are you going to run out on her baptism because you're bored? Or on her first day of school? Is that the mother you want to be?"

The mother she wanted to be? Anette closed her eyes to avoid the look of defeat on Svend's face. How was she supposed to decide what kind of a mother to be when she didn't feel like a mother at all?

"You went after a murderer on your own and you were *this* close" — he demonstrated with his fingers just how close — "to dying! You are not at liberty to do that anymore, Anette. You have a kid now, who depends on you. You can't take chances like that anymore!"

She had to try to defend herself, to explain. She cleared her throat and spoke in an unsteady voice she hardly recognized as her own.

"I don't know who I am anymore."

"No one does, Anette." Svend squeezed his eyes shut. His words felt like a knife wound. "We've just been hit by a bomb. Do you think I know who I am anymore? I'm just putting one foot in front of the other."

"Yeah, but you seem so calm and happy."

"That's just because you forget to ask how

I'm doing, because you're so preoccupied with all the things you're missing out on! Of course I think it's hard right now. Everything in life that's worth anything is hard. But it won't always be like this. She'll learn to sleep and become more and more independent in time."

Anette knew he was right. He was also entitled to be angry.

"I just miss — Forgive me, Svend. You're right, about everything." She could tell from his shoulders that he relaxed a little.

"We'll get it all back again, Anette. You're not losing anything, not yourself, not your job. It's just right now, in the beginning, that everything is kind of chaotic, and we have to find our footing in all the new."

"Do you think other people find it this hard?" She tried to smile a little.

"What do I care what other people think?" He smiled back at her, still reserved.

Anette watched her husband and suddenly felt the love for him again, pulsating and alive.

"You know what?" she said. "Speaking up suits you."

That made him laugh.

"Ha! And apologizing suits you!"

The baby whimpered. Svend gently picked her up and kissed her before passing her back to Anette.

"She can't still be hungry, can she?" Anette carefully rocked her daughter, who settled down in her arms. She looked like a tiny little marzipan person who grunted and breathed, a perfect creature. Maybe this is just what parental love is, Anette thought. This moment, and then the next one, and then the one after that.

"I think you're right," she said, caressing the tiny, downy-soft head. "We'll name her Gudrun after my mom."

CHAPTER 27

Copenhagen is a dormant plant that lives off the scant sunlight falling on its leaves. The city can be all curled in on itself during the dark, wet, windy times that comprise most of a Scandinavian year. But when the sun's rays finally hit, the city unfurls in a blossoming that is every bit as sudden as it is breathtaking.

Today, Copenhageners sat on benches by the Lakes, their faces turned to the sky and their inner clocks on pause. Like an entire colony of lemmings with rechargeable batteries, they were sucking up the solar energy. It wasn't even particularly warm, just clear and sunny — apparently that was enough. Esther inhaled the mild air, letting it soothe her sorrow.

A pair of swans came into view by the water's edge, beautiful in all their monogamous self-sufficiency. She stopped to admire the white birds gliding through sunny patches on the surface of the water, felt in her pocket for her phone so she could take a picture, and realized she had forgotten it at home. When you've spent the first fifty-five years of your life without a portable telecom device, it's not always easy to keep track of where your cell phone might be.

Esther walked on along the lakeside, following the path under the embankment, and took a short cut through Fredens Park until she was standing in front of National Hospital. She had brought the newspaper and a bag of pastries for Gregers; if only she could bring him a little of the sunshine as well. But maybe he would be fit enough for a brief walk in the yard. The last few days he had seemed healthier than he had in years, almost as if the mere prospect of a balloon dilation had a curative effect.

Esther headed for entrance three and went up to the fourteenth floor. In a sliding glass door, she caught her own reflection, and was startled by how stern she looked. Bringing her bitterness up to Gregers wouldn't do any good; she would have to park her resentment for a bit. Afterward she might follow through on her plan to stop by the Netto supermarket on Korsgade, where the mover named Adam advertised his services according to her new downstairs neighbors.

Not that she knew what to do with his phone number if she found it, but it would be a start.

When Esther pushed open the door to Ward 3144, a nurse came right up to greet her. She nodded somberly.

"Good that you could come so quickly. I didn't even know they had managed to get in touch with you."

Esther froze.

"I haven't talked to anyone." She cursed her forgotten phone. "What's happened?"

In an instant, the nurse's eyes conveyed a series of emotions, going straight from compassion to resentment at being the one who had just drawn the short end of the stick.

"WHAT HAPPENED?" Esther dropped the bag she was holding and pastries rolled out, spreading crumbs and shards of icing across the floor.

"Oh, I'm so sorry . . ." The nurse grabbed hold of Esther's arm and guided her skillfully to the nearest chair. "It was an unexpected cardiac arrest this morning. I'm afraid he couldn't be saved."

Esther locked eyes with the nurse. This couldn't be true! Gregers couldn't be dead. He was just doing so well.

"But he was totally healthy when I visited

him yesterday. How could he suddenly die?"

Esther's chest imploded into a black hole, and she buried her face in her hands. Her protests were useless. Death always won in the end. Yet again she had lost a close friend without warning. As far as she was concerned, the floor could just open up and swallow her then and there.

She felt the nurse's hand on her shoulders and leg, trying to help her hold onto reality, calm her down somehow.

"I'm afraid I also need to inform you that the police have been called. We have reason to suspect that a crime may have been committed."

"The police, what do you mean?" Esther struggled to understand what she was hearing.

The nurse took her hands and squeezed them, preparing her for the awful news to come.

"We have reason to suspect that John was murdered."

"John?" Esther asked, furrowing her brow. And then, when the nurse didn't respond, she continued, "Who the *fuck* is John?"

In the awkward silence that followed, the nurse gaped at Esther, opening and closing her mouth like a goldfish.

Esther stood up.

"Tell me what's going on here! Is Gregers alive?"

"Are you Gregers Hermansen's next of kin?"

"Yes! I've been here every day since Tuesday. Is he okay?"

"I'm so sorry!" the nurse exclaimed, her hands flying up to her face. "I thought . . . they're both in room eight, so I . . . Oh my God, I'm really so, so sorry!"

The nurse pulled herself together and spoke rapidly.

"Gregers is alive and doing well, considering the circumstances. Of course he's upset about John's death, the other patient in his room, we all are. Gregers has been moved down to room four, where he's resting. I'm just so sorry about this!"

"Can I see him?" Esther had not a single second more to spare for this conversation. "I'll just go down there. Thanks."

Esther left the nurse — and the pastries on the floor — and walked to room four as quickly as her shaking knees could carry her.

Gregers was not dead.

Of course it was terrible that John, the friendly typographer in the other bed, had passed away, but Esther still allowed herself to feel relief.

She approached the bed by the window. Gregers was snoring in it, peacefully and soundly. Esther brought her face down to his and felt his soft cheeks, his breath, his life against her skin.

"For crying out loud, Gregers, you can't scare me like that," she whispered.

She sat for ten minutes watching her friend sleep. Then she got up and tiptoed back out into the hallway. Two uniformed police officers were standing outside room eight talking to a nurse with red hair in a pageboy cut. Esther approached them.

"Excuse me. I'm Gregers Hermansen's next of kin. He's the other patient who was in room eight with John. I understand a crime may have been committed . . . ?"

The officers exchanged glances.

"Okay, sure. You can't tell me anything, obviously. I'm really only interested to know if Gregers is safe here or if I should take him home today?"

The nurse sought confirmation from the officers before responding.

"I can guarantee you that your friend is absolutely safe here. The person who constituted the risk has been . . . removed."

"Thank you."

Esther walked past them out to the elevator and took it down to the exit. To hell and back in thirty minutes, and all on a completely average fall Saturday.

Gregers was alive. She wasn't alone. It would all work out.

She walked back to the Lakes on wobbly legs and headed home. Moving felt good and slowly reality returned. Home and listen to some music, cook some food, watch a movie, maybe open a bottle of red wine. She deserved it, needed a little self-indulgence at any rate. To feel alive. Around her everything was dying. The dry leaves of the chestnut trees hung dangling from the branches, nature was shutting down, preparing to hibernate. Esther wondered why she was so fond of this season when it actually ushered in the coming darkness and had a sadness as its core. They say that in heaven it's always fall. Beauty and transience dwell in the same chamber of the heart.

When she came out of the tunnel that ran under the Fredensbro bridge, she saw him. He was walking along the water next to the little island people referred to as Fish Island, loping along in the same direction as her with all the time in the world. She recognized him right away. The tall body with the broad shoulders, the hair trimmed short on the back of his neck that she had kissed as recently as three days ago.

Esther shorted out. He had some nerve walking here along the lake, as if everything was just hunky-dory, when he had in fact conned most of Nørrebro!

She sped up and gained on him without really knowing what to do when she caught up. Yell at him? Demand her money back? Give him the cold shoulder?

She wasn't sure what would pack the most punch, all she knew was that she meant business.

When she was only about five yards behind him, he suddenly cut across the path, heading for an empty bench by the water's edge.

Esther hesitated. Was he planning to sit down?

But Alain didn't sit. With a quick, practiced motion he lifted the lid of a trash can next to the bench and peered down into it.

Esther had seen that move many times before among the city's homeless population, looking for glass bottles to redeem for the deposit.

He was collecting bottles from the trash.

Esther noticed the worn webbing on his shoulder, suddenly saw his shabby shoes and his grubby jacket. Alain wasn't a cook or a mover, and he certainly wasn't a concert pianist. Alain was poor.

For the last three days she had been picturing him in all sorts of situations; usually something involving a beautiful young woman and the lavish spending of her money, perhaps at a casino or behind the wheel of a sports car. At no point had she even fleetingly entertained the idea that he might have conned her out of necessity.

He had fooled her. And yet he had also redeemed her and given her back her will to live.

Esther's thirst for revenge evaporated as if by magic. It simply disappeared, and all that was left behind was compassion and a modicum of the shame most of us feel when we come face-to-face with those who have less than we do. Maybe she had used him just as much as he had her.

She stood still, watching him tramp along the lakeshore, stopping at each trash can in turn. *You broke my heart,* she thought, but in that very moment, she knew it to be a lie. Her heart was bruised, but then it was also beating again. It was far from broken. In a little while she would be home in her lovely apartment, and he — whatever his name was — would still be walking around out here, collecting bottles.

And, Esther thought in an internal voice, which stemmed directly from her wounded pride, *Someday he will make a good story.*

The fountain in the middle of Tivoli was full of pumpkins. Scarecrows with jack-o'-lantern heads loomed atop hay bales surrounded by heaps of orange gourds, which Jeppe strangely enough remembered to be the largest berry in the world. He turned his back to the display. Regardless of what was in it, he had had enough fountains to last him for a while.

For the first time in weeks, the sun was out, and Tivoli was crawling with families, waiting in lines, eating ice cream, and taking pictures of the gardens and of each other. Between the classic amusement park rides were strings of slap-up wooden stalls selling Halloween-sweets shaped like eyeballs and severed fingers.

Two amusement park attendants walked by in their black and red uniforms. When they turned their heads, fiery red eyes stared out of pallid faces and Jeppe's heart skipped a beat before he realized that they were made up like monsters for Halloween. A weird twist on the cozy *hygge* that Denmark is renowned for, a sort of creepy-cozy un-*hygge*. After his experiences in Bispebjerg Hospital's basement the day before, Jeppe wasn't sure how he felt about it.

"Hi."

Jeppe turned to the mellow voice that he would recognize anywhere and looked into those dark brown eyes. They beamed, making him feel twelve years old.

"This is Amina and this is Meriem, as you know," Sara said, trying to drag her youngest daughter out from where she was hiding behind her legs. "She's a little shy."

Jeppe smiled down at Sara's two daughters, heart pounding in his chest. Could it really be that a nine-year-old and a six-year-old made him nervous, after he had just bagged a serial murderer?

"We've met before. I'm Jeppe."

The two girls peered nervously up at him with their mother's brown eyes.

"And I have a bit of a problem. I won two balloons from that balloon guy over there, but I have no idea what to do with them. Do you two happen to know anyone who likes balloons?"

"Me, me!" Amina, the older one grabbed his hand and immediately started pulling him toward the balloon seller.

"Sneaky trick!" Sara said with a grin and followed them, holding her younger daughter's hand.

"Hey, whatever works."

The girls each chose a balloon, which they

allowed Jeppe to hold for them, so they could concentrate on the lollipop he got them next and the ice cream that followed. Sara looked on with one eyebrow raised and a smile that suggested this sugarfest was a one-time event. They bought ride passes and agreed to push back lunch so the girls could go crazy on vintage car rides, carousels, and roller coasters.

Jeppe found himself in one of those parallel dimensions that occasionally opens up when reality becomes too surreal. Seventeen hours earlier he was being buried alive in a hole in the ground with Falck, while Anette bled to death across the room. Now he was roaming through Tivoli holding balloons for two children he didn't know, while looking for a chance to kiss their mother. *What a difference a day makes.*

"What did you say?" Sara asked.

"Nothing, I was just humming."

Jeppe realized that his ice cream was melting onto his hand and dutifully resumed eating it.

"The girls want to go to the playground."

Sara let her daughters run on ahead, took the balloons, and interlaced her fingers with his so they resembled all the other couples walking along the pond.

"Hey, did you hear that that nurse from

Butterfly House was arrested for murdering a patient?" Jeppe asked, throwing away what was left of his ice cream. "This morning. They think they caught her red-handed. And they're pretty sure it wasn't the first time."

"No way! Trine Bremen?" Sara stared at him, her mouth agape.

"Yeah, exactly. Peter Demant's patient. That type of murder is usually hard to prove, so let's hope she confesses. If she did anything, that is."

"The Butterfly House seems to have gathered up quite a crew of shady characters. Come, it's here." Sara led him up the wide steps to the playground, where the girls were already absorbed in a game that involved running around a tree trunk.

They sat down on a red-and-white-striped bench from which they had an unimpeded view. Jeppe noted, not without a certain irony, that the playground was shaped like a storm-tossed sea with capsizing ships and driftwood floating on rolling blue waves. There was just no escaping the water in Copenhagen.

Sara glanced at him and inhaled, preparing to speak.

"I need to tell you something. This morning I got my neighbor to watch the girls so I could go in to headquarters for a couple of hours. You had just left when I got there . . . but Lisbeth Ramsgaard stopped by."

"What in the world did she want?"

"I thought she had come to take out a restraining order against Bo. A man who's been violent in the past doesn't just stop all of a sudden. At any rate, Lisbeth told me a little about their marriage. The last few years haven't been fun. You remember that there was a conflict between Bo and the son, right?"

"After Pernille's death, right?"

"Exactly. Well, it was violent. Bo broke his son's nose. It was a terrible time for the whole family. And it's not over yet. . . . When Lisbeth signed the visitation papers, she used her maiden name. She's gone back to that because of the divorce." There was a slight twitch in the corner of Sara's mouth. "Lisbeth Hartvig."

"Hartvig?" Jeppe repeated, trying to understand. "As in . . ."

"She came in to see her son. Simon Hartvig is Bo and Lisbeth Ramsgaard's son, Pernille's older brother."

Jeppe tried to let those words sink in. A suicide, a shattered family, a big brother's act of revenge.

"He was avenging his sister's death?"

"Yes," Sara sighed. "He was avenging Pernille on the people who should have helped her, but instead let her down. Because they were too busy making money or just didn't care."

Jeppe leaned his head back and rested it against the playhouse behind the bench. Let the sunlight warm his eyelids. The butterfly effect. The minor indifference that leads to the end of the world.

Amina and Meriem came running over to the bench, rosy-cheeked and laughing.

"Mom, Mom, can we get ice cream?"

"You mean *another* ice cream? Definitely not. If you're hungry, you can have an apple." Sara looked self-conscious, like she just remembered that she was trying to project the image of an easygoing supermom. "Too much sugar makes them nuts and then they don't sleep well at night. That's why I'm a little strict."

She pulled two apples out of her bag. The girls took them without much enthusiasm. The little one eyed Jeppe skeptically.

"Mom, is that man from work coming home with us later?"

"Yes, he is," Sara said without hesitance. "And he's not some *man from work*. His name is Jeppe, and he's my boyfriend."

"Oh yeah, well then, kiss him!"

"Go play, you rascals!" she said, waving them away. "We're leaving in ten minutes, so hurry up and do whatever last things you want to do."

The girls ran off with happy shrieks, back to the capsizing boat structure, and started a new game.

"I have no idea what I'm doing, you know." Jeppe looked at his girlfriend. "I've never brushed anyone's teeth besides my own."

"Don't worry." She took his hands and held them. "You'll learn."

ACKNOWLEDGMENTS

Thank you!

This book was written with the deepest respect and gratitude to all the nurses, doctors, social workers, and teachers, who — under conditions that are not always optimal — tend to our sick, especially the children and teenagers, who have tough lives. You're truly society's heroes!

From the bottom of my heart, my most profound thanks to my readers, who spend time and money on my books. It's a privilege I will never take for granted. To the many who have written to share their criticism, praise, and thoughts with me — I cannot express how much that means. Thank you!

Former Copenhagen Police detective Sebastian Richelsen helped me with the policework, and professor Hans Petter Hougen at the University of Copenhagen's Department of Forensic Medicine assisted me with details about bleeding to death and autopsies.

Thank you to curator Adam Bencard at the Medical Museion for his inspiration on the murder weapon and general knowledge of the humoral body.

Thank you to Henrik Stender for the tip about the arches by Vesterport Station.

Warm thanks to Dr. Helle Skovmand Bosselmann and nurse Lis Krahn for your help in depicting everyday life in the cardiology department.

To Signe Wegmann Düring, MD, PhD, psychiatry consultant, for being an excellent sparring partner on mental illness and psychopharmacology.

And to Mette Juul Rasmussen, charge nurse in the Pediatric Psychiatry Clinic at Roskilde Hospital, who was a huge help in the genesis of this book. Thank you for the thorough information and inspiration you gave me. It's reassuring to know that competent experts like you take care of our kids.

Two people read this book long before it was done and provided invaluable feedback and support. My gratitude to Timm Vladimir and Sara Dybris McQuaid for taking the time when it mattered most. Thanks as well to Sysse Engberg and Anne Mette

Hancock for their support and encouragement.

To the amazing Salomonsson Agency, for their diligent efforts to disseminate my writing. Special thanks to my agent, Federico Ambrosini, also for letting me "borrow" his name.

To my Danish editor, Birgitte Franch, whose sharp eyes and tough-but-gentle give-and-take is indispensable to my books. A deepfelt thanks to everyone at Scout Press for receiving me with such enthusiasm and making me feel absolutely at home — Jen Bergstrom and Jackie Cantor in particular for your trust in me and for all your hard work.

To Cassius and Timm for being the light and color in my life. I love you.

ABOUT THE AUTHOR

A former dancer and choreographer with a background in television and theater, **Katrine Engberg** launched a groundbreaking career as a novelist with the publication of her fiction debut, *The Tenant.* She is now one of the most widely read and beloved crime authors in Denmark, and her work has been sold in over twenty-five countries. She lives with her family in Copenhagen.

The employees of Thorndike Press hope you have enjoyed this Large Print book. All our Thorndike, Wheeler, and Kennebec Large Print titles are designed for easy reading, and all our books are made to last. Other Thorndike Press Large Print books are available at your library, through selected bookstores, or directly from us.

For information about titles, please call:
(800) 223-1244

or visit our website at:
gale.com/thorndike

To share your comments, please write:
Publisher
Thorndike Press
10 Water St., Suite 310
Waterville, ME 04901